NIGHT
PLAGUE

NIGHT PLAGUE

GRAHAM MASTERTON

THE NIGHT WARRIORS 3

HEAD *of* ZEUS

An Aries Book

First published in the UK in 1991 by Severn House Publishers Ltd

This edition first published in the UK in 2023 by Head of Zeus,
part of Bloomsbury Publishing Plc.

9 7 5 3 1 2 4 6 8

A catalogue record for this book is available from the British Library.

ISBN (PB): 9781035904037
ISBN (E): 9781035904068

Cover design: Matt Bray / Head of Zeus

Typeset by Siliconchips Services Ltd UK

Printed and bound in Great Britain by
CPI Group (UK) Ltd, Croydon CRO 4YY

Head of Zeus
First Floor East
5–8 Hardwick Street
London EC1R 4RG

WWW.HEADOFZEUS.COM

"Here," said Madeleine Springer, and beckoned Stanley to follow her across the room. "Stand quite still—here, that's right—and *relax*. I know it's difficult. I know you're fighting the Night Plague. But you can do it, if you try. You can beat the plague and you can beat Isabel Gowdie. And you can beat Satan, too. He's out there, Stanley, he's out there now, tonight, while everybody's dreaming, and he's determined that this time, *this time*, he's going to have us all."

She laid her hand on his shoulder, and he felt that same prickling electricity. "It's the end of the world if we don't beat him now. You can forget about ozone layers and cutting down the rain forests. He'll take our morals, he'll take our families—he'll take everything, including our immortal souls. This is *it*. This is Armageddon. This is the pestilence that we were promised."

Top U.S. Fiddler Flies In

Master U.S. violinist Stanley Eisner, 44, arrived in London today to join the Kensington Chamber Orchestra for eleven months. Eisner, the star of the San Francisco Baroque Ensemble, will give master classes to especially talented young musicians, and play first violin in a series of new recordings of Bach suites and inventions. His place in San Francisco is being taken by John Bright, the Kensington orchestra's 41-year-old first violin.

—*Evening Standard*, November 25, 1989

I was that man—in a dream
And each world's night in vain
I patient wait on sleep to unveil
Those vivid hills again.

—Walter de la Mare

Chapter One

Knitted Hood

He had never felt rattled in London before. In New York, yes; and once in Haiti, in Port-au-Prince, when his car had been stopped and searched by the *Tontons Macoute* Ray-Bans and machine guns. Never in good old down-at-heel London.

But when he came down the steps of his apartment building at eight o'clock that frostbit morning, whistling the rondo from Mozart's *Posthorn Serenade*, the man in the gray knitted hood was already waiting for him on the opposite corner, just as he had been waiting on the opposite corner yesterday morning, and the morning before that, and the morning before that.

And Stanley, who had always considered London to be chummy and noisy and as safe as a city can be (as safe as Stockholm, anyway, or Bonn), stopped short, chin lifted, abruptly cautious, as it somebody had fingertip-slapped him, not too hard, but hard enough to irritate him, to shake his confidence. *Three straight mornings, and here he is again.* Stanley tasted salt and pewter in his mouth and that was the taste of authentic fear.

A radio played "… *great music for a great city …*" from somewhere not too far away.

Stanley in slo-mo closed the black-painted garden gate behind him, *squeak, clang*. Alert, frowning, breathing too deeply, he glanced around the streets of flat-fronted early Victorian terraces, yellow-ocher brick and freshly painted stucco. There was nobody else around, only the man in the gray knitted hood, and him, and a brindled cat with a live candy-pink fledgling in its mouth slinking low-bellied and guilty over the camber of the street. Less than fifty yards away the King's Road grumbled and thundered with the morning rush hour, but Langton Street was an abandoned world of its own.

"*Traffic update … with the Flying Eye …*"

All along the curb, bumper-to-bumper, the parked cars stood empty, unwashed Citroëns with dog-smeared windows and brand-new Rovers with dented fenders and overflowing ashtrays. In Fulham it was *infra dig* to treat your car with any reverence. The sky was low and cold and corroded-looking, as if it were soon going to snow.

Stanley stood still with his violin case in his hand and stared at the man in the knitted hood, willing him to turn around, but the man in the knitted hood didn't move or give any indication at all that he was aware that Stanley was staring at him. Underneath the knitted hood, the man wore a long gray gaberdine raincoat and oddly box-shaped shoes, like surgical boots or medieval clogs. He stood awkwardly, too, tilted to one side, as if he had been twisted by a spine injury.

Every day since his first appearance on Tuesday morning, the man in the knitted hood waited on the opposite corner of Langton Street until Stanley had started walking toward the King's Road; then he had promptly started off after him. He had remained twenty or thirty yards away, and whenever Stanley had slowed or stopped, he had slowed or stopped, too—not immediately, and not so obviously that Stanley could have been quite certain that he was being purposely or even *purposefully* followed.

While Stanley had waited for his bus, the man in the knitted hood had stayed well away from the bus stop, mooching this way and that, restless as a character in a Popeye cartoon, always keeping his head bowed and his face averted. When the bus had arrived, he had disappeared into the jostle of people. But somehow he had always managed to reappear on top of the bus, sitting six or seven rows behind Stanley, his face turned toward the window. By the time Stanley had reached his stop, however, and stood up, the man in the knitted hood had already vanished.

Now Knitted Hood was back for the fourth morning in succession, standing on the opposite corner by the postbox, slightly hunched, hands in pockets, not moving. The wind was as sharp as a lino-cutting knife. Stanley licked his lips in apprehension, then wiped them with his handkerchief so that they wouldn't get chapped. He wasn't sure what to do. The man obviously didn't intend to attack him, he always stayed so far away. He couldn't be panhandling, either, not unless he had the most abstruse technique of any beggar ever ... frightening his intended benefactors just by *being* there, just by silently lurking, until they approached him with money to leave them alone.

Irrationally (and this was *seriously* irrational), Stanley had even entertained the remote possibility that Knitted

Hood could have been a private investigator, acting for Eve, his wife. But Eve was back with her mother and father in Napa, California, in their neat expensive house with the mushroom-colored shagpile carpets, and Stanley couldn't really imagine Eve doing anything so quirky as hiring a private investigator from six thousand miles away—nor anything so expensive, either. For sure, Eve and he had wrangled for months over alimony for Leon, and Eve had accused him of arranging his exchange job in England to evade his paternal responsibilities and to conceal his true income (which was slightly true); but he couldn't imagine what good it would do her to send a clubfooted cripple in a gray knitted hood to follow him on to the bus every morning.

"Today's weather … cold and raw, with eight octaves of cloud and a strong north-east wind … temperatures in town down to—"

A more sensible proposition was that Knitted Hood was probably nothing more alarming than a down-and-out—one of those filthy but harmless fruit-loops who shuffle through London in their thousands. One of those aggrieved derelicts who live in abandoned cardboard boxes; or one of those gentle-manly eccentrics who play spoons in the street, or sit under bird-splattered statues of colonial heroes drinking Tennent's extra-strong lager and railing at the city as it thunderously ignores them on every side. It was even possible that Knitted Hood wasn't following Stanley at all, but just happened to catch the same bus—although if *that* were the case, why did he wait every morning until Stanley had started walking toward the King's Road before he himself set off, at almost exactly the same distance?

Stanley waited for two or three minutes, trying to make up his mind if he ought to cross the street and ask Knitted Hood what he wanted. He wasn't usually afraid to confront strangers. In New York, he had lived in the Village for eight and a half years, and he had been mugged twice; the second time unsuccessfully, because he had faced right up to the geeks and fought back. Three blacks with Mike Tyson necks, and eyes like rivets. They had hit him in the face with an adjustable wrench and broken his cheekbone, and then they had kicked him in the mouth. He had scarcely felt it. He had been high on vodkatinis and self-righteousness at the time, not to mention a recent viewing of Woody Allen's *September* and *Death Wish III*, but this morning he didn't feel so high.

There was something else, too. Something in Knitted Hood's appearance which invoked a feeling of disquiet that he had never experienced before. It was a quality which he could only think of as *medieval*. It reminded him of monks and lazars and some of those crippled creatures with gray-bandaged stumps in Breughel paintings.

Something *diseased*.

He hesitated for nearly half a minute; then tugged back his woollen glove and checked his watch: 8:17. His bus would be coming any minute, although the traffic looked thick this morning. It was the second day of the January sales.

"Hey!" he called across the street.

Knitted Hood remained where he was and gave no indication that he might have heard.

"Hey!" shouted Stanley, louder but higher.

Still Knitted Hood didn't respond. Stanley was tempted

to forget all about him and go; but it had taken quite a surge of adrenaline just to shout, and it seemed incredibly wimpish and defeatist just to walk off and leave Knitted Hood where he was—especially if Knitted Hood started following him again.

He stepped off the curb and started to cross the road. A single van passed him, a bright yellow British Telecom van, and for a moment he had to wait. But then the van was gone and there was nobody but him and Knitted Hood.

"I say, hey, excuse me!" he called, trying to sound English.

Knitted Hood remained motionless and silent.

"Excuse me!" he repeated, taking two or three steps nearer. "Excuse me, sir, but I have the distinct impression that you've been following me!"

He waited. Knitted Hood gave no indication that he might have heard. The wind curled up the tails of his gray gaberdine coat, exposing soiled striped trousers tied at the cuff with knotted parcel twine. *No private eye he*, thought Stanley. *Even the sleaziest shamus doesn't tie his pants up with string*.

Stanley circled around Knitted Hood, trying to see his face. But as he did so, Knitted Hood somehow managed to edge himself around so that he was still facing diagonally away from him.

For a whole minute there was silent impasse between them—a shortish American musician with thinning brown hair and a velvet-collared Harrod's overcoat; a tall lumpish English scare-crow in a gray knitted hood. Neither of them moved, neither of them spoke. Eventually, Stanley coughed into his hand and looked away, like a teacher trying to be patient, and then looked back again.

"Listen, friend, unless I get some kind of answer out of you. I'm going to miss my bus, okay? And if I miss my bus I'm going to get measurably mad. Okay?"

Still no response. Above their heads, a jet scratched invisibly through the clouds on its descent toward Heathrow, and even if Knitted Hood had said anything, Stanley wouldn't have been able to hear what it was. The street remained peculiarly empty. They could have been thousands of miles from anywhere, instead of fifty yards away from one of the busiest roads in London.

"All right," said Stanley, "if that's the way you want it, forget it. But let me tell you this. If you're standing here tomorrow morning, I'm going to call the police. Do you hear me? I see you here one more time, that's it."

Knitted Hood turned his back. Stanley had been about to walk away, but when Knitted Hood did that, he felt madder than he had for a long time, and he stopped and turned back. He felt madder than he had with Eve, in a way. At least he had understood what Eve was up to. Eve had been chiseling money and obstructing his visitation rights. Plain and simple. Eve had been chiseling money and obstructing his visitation rights. Plain and simple, Eve had wanted revenge. But what did Knitted Hood want? If it was money, he had a goddamned weird way of asking for it. But what else could he possibly want, except for money?

Conversation? Company? Who could tell? Maybe Knitted Hood had heard that Stanley was a well-known international violinist. Maybe he was some kind of brilliant but horribly disfigured musician who desperately wanted private lessons, but didn't dare go to the Kensington

Chamber Orchestra to ask for them. You know, like *The Phantom of the Opera*, something like that.

"Listen, friend," said Stanley, taking three or four paces closer. "If there's something you want, why don't you tell me what it is? I may not be able to help you, but I can listen. You know what they say. If you can share a problem, it's only half a problem."

He tried to skip between Knitted Hood and the postbox, so that he could see Knitted Hood's face. But the figure managed to swivel around at the last possible instant, so that all he glimpsed was the glossy-white tip of a nose.

"Listen!" Stanley repeated. "This is totally crazy! You've been following me practically every morning for the past week, now you won't even show me your face! For Christ's sake, if you want something, come down off the fucking ceiling and tell me what it is. If you don't, then stop showing up here, do you mind? Stop following me! Goddammit, there's a law against following people!" He wasn't at all sure that there *was* a law against it, but it sounded authoritative.

Knitted Hood remained silent, with his back turned. Stanley checked his watch. He had a choice now—either to manhandle Knitted Hood, to turn him around by force, or to forget the whole thing and go catch his bus.

He didn't relish touching that greasy gaberdine raincoat, and if he was honest, he didn't much relish seeing what Knitted Hood really looked like. But there was some kind of principle involved here. Stanley was willing to admit that it could be the kind of principle that only an American would be concerned about. Maybe English people followed other English people for no reason at all and nobody got upset about it. In less than three months, he had already begun to perceive that English people had a radically different concept about civil liberties. They were secretive and deflective; and they seemed to think that the sharing of information was almost as unhygienic as sharing the same toothbrush.

Stanley suddenly thought: *This is absurd. Walk away from it. This guy isn't going to tell me anything. He probably has nothing to tell. He's just a public nuisance, like traffic wardens or flag-day collectors or black plastic bags of trash in the street.*

He turned away. But, as he did so, Knitted Hood uttered an extraordinary sound, halfway between a whistle and a cough.

A slide whistle, *hooo-eee, oop* with a barking end to it.

Stanley said, "Oh, you've decided to explain yourself, have you?" and turned back.

His scalp prickled with shock. He found himself confronted by a face as white and as glossy as celluloid, a face that could have been a mask, neither man nor woman, but frighteningly beautiful. A saint's face; an angel's face.

Because it was so seraphic, it was ten times more terrifying than it would have been if it had been ugly. How could such a misshapen creature have been blessed with such ravishing looks?

Stanley stepped back, and he was deeply scared. The face was empty-eyed—black eyed, anyway. Night-black-eyed. Expressionless, sweet, glistening, a Mardi Gras martyr.

"What do you want?" Stanley demanded, his throat choked up with a hair-ball of fear.

9

Knitted Hood said nothing, but took one awkward step towards him. *Chip-shuffle.*

Stanley heard soft, harsh breathing. Breath against celluloid.

"What do you want?" he repeated. He felt pee in his trousers. He was ready to run.

Knitted Hood's perfect white forehead began to crinkle. His black eyes became distorted and small, and spread themselves further and further apart. The chin warped and dropped.

Stanley had the terrible feeling that he was witnessing somebody die; watching somebody's whole physical integrity collapse, right in front of his eyes. How could that happen? How could somebody simply fall apart, one piece from another?

There was a split second in which he could have run; could have escaped. But then—without warning—Knitted Hood snatched at his sleeve, swung him around, and half jumped, half collapsed on top of him.

"*Jesus!*" Stanley cried out. Knitted Hood's weight was enormous, like a five-hundred-pound sack of beets, and instantly Stanley's knees gave way. He fell into the gutter, twisting off one of his shoes, his brown tweed trousers torn. "*Gel off me! Jesus Christ, get off me!*"

But Knitted Hood seized the back of his neck with a hand like a claw and forced his face right down to the pavement. Stanley fell one of his front teeth break. His lower lip dragged against concrete, his forehead scraped. His wrists were pulled right up behind him in a full nelson, so fiercely and quickly that he heard cartilage crack. A pain as fierce as white-hot iron was poured into the crucibles of his shoulder sockets and brimmed over into his arm muscles. He tried to shout out but his lungs were empty and he couldn't snatch enough breath. *Dear God, don't let him dislocate my arms.*

Knitted Hood was not only oppressively heavy. His body was lumpy and awkward and wrapped up in all kinds of rags and scarves and metal-buckled belts and pieces of blanket. He stank of grease and sweat and some nostril-burning synthetic-violet odor, like air freshener for toilet bowls. Facedown on the pavement, Stanley gasped, "Get off, will you? For God's sake, you're breaking my arms, get off!"

Without a word, Knitted Hood grasped Stanley's hair and banged his head against the concrete, almost knocking him out. Stanley tasted blood and sicked-up coffee and floods of saliva. He could hardly believe what was happening to him. All he knew was that he wanted it to stop.

He heard traffic, radio music, people talking. Surely somebody could see what was happening to him.

But then he felt a relentless claw-nailed hand pulling at his coat and then his trousers. There was some fierce and prurient fumbling between his legs. The buckle was torn from his Gucci belt; then he felt corduroy tearing, cotton shorts tearing.

"*God! Get off me! What are you doing?*" he shrieked out, his voice as high as a woman's.

They crouched struggling on the pavement under Knitted Hood's raincoat, one on top of the other, like some grotesque gray camel. Stanley tried to crawl forward, pushing against the curb with his knees. He couldn't cry out any more. He was too frightened even to speak. He was too desperate to get away.

But then Knitted Hood's filthy clawed hand closed

around his bare genitals; not crushing them, but squeezing them just tightly enough for Stanley to gasp, and to stay where he was, shivering, his vision intermittently blocked out by the wind-blown tails of Knitted Hood's raincoat.

Knitted Hood's thumbnail found the opening of Stanley's penis and started gently and almost lovingly to scratch at it. Stanley's stomach tightened, his eyes filled with tears. *Oh, dear God, this can't be happening*. His testicles shrank; his whole soul shrank. *Riboyne Shel Olam*, protect me.

"Oh, God!" he managed to choke out. "I'm rich, look. I'll give you money!"

But all he heard from the creature pressing down on top of him was course, irregular breathing. And at the same time, that terrible scratching continued, until Stanley was sure that he must be bleeding.

"Can you speak?" he gasped. "Listen—can you understand what I'm saying?" He scarcely recognized his own voice.

Knitted Hood grunted and whooped in two different tones, almost like two people speaking at once. But he pressed his weight even harder on Stanley's back, and probed his fingernail even deeper into Stanley's penis; and then he mounted Stanley with all the unthinking forcefulness of one animal mounting another; the same way a bull heaves itself up on a cow. Stanley felt his buttocks clawed apart, skin ripped. Then something rubbery and greasy and uncompromisingly hard pushed up against him. Something as big as a baseball bat, pungent and obscenely hot, forcing itself into his anus.

It hurt him so much that he wept, bitterly wept, in a way that he hadn't wept since he was a child. He bit his lip with his broken tooth, and blood ran down the side of his mouth. But the pain wouldn't stop; and he couldn't stop it. It drove into his bottom and he felt that his back was cracking apart. It pushed and it pushed until he was screaming out loud (or silently, he couldn't tell). He felt the cold, heavy, regular swing of Knitted Hood's scrotum against his thigh. He heard breathing that sounded like leather bellows. Then he felt his bowels flooded with hotness and wetness, deep up inside him; and Knitted Hood immediately slithering out of him; and he vomited coffee and half-chewed crackers all over his hands.

His cheek was resting against a surface that was hard and flat and deadeningly cold. He wondered if he had been sleeping. He didn't like falling asleep during the day. There was always that feeling when you woke up that the world had irrevocably changed while you weren't looking; that muffle-footed scene-shifters had been rearranging your life.

He saw black patent high-heeled shoes, with bows on the front, very close to his eyes. Then he heard a girl coughing and a worried voice say, "'Ere, you ain't dead?"

He tried to shake his head. "No," he whispered. "I'm not dead."

"Well, you stay there. I'll call a namblunce."

"I just want to get up."

"What?"

"I just want to get up, get on to my feet."

There was a silence. Then the girl's voice said, "I wouldn't do that if I were you, mate. You wait there. I'll call a namblunce."

★

He felt that he was being jostled. He saw lighted windows going by. Faces that danced in front of his eyes like clouds of midges. He was surrounded by whiteness and coolness and the sliding whisper of sheets; and a strong smell of antiseptic. A warm voice with a foreign accent reverberated deep inside his brain, reassuring him that he was being taken care of, that he was in hospital, and that everything was going to be fine.

You're going to be fine, Mr. Eisner! Can you hear me? You're going to be fine! Fine. Fiyyynnee. Yiiiiine.

He felt the vinegary prick of a needle. He wanted to say, *I hate needles. I never have needles.* But then his consciousness fled backwards into empty darkness, and there was nobody to hear him.

He was back out on the street again. The clouds moved past the rooftops at a strange hurried speed. A cat slunk past him, carrying something in its mouth. He knew that it was something terrible but he didn't want to look.

He heard a whistle, high and hollow, with a whoop at the end of it. He turned in alarm, and on the other side of the street he saw Knitted Hood, waiting for him, taunting him.

Hooo-eeeee, oop.

Knitted Hood slowly began to turn his head. Stanley stared wide-eyed, expecting to see that white exquisite face. But then Knitted Hood's head turned around and around, rotating slowly at first, then faster, while his shoulders remained hunched in the same position. Stanley realized that the gray hood covered his head completely, without any hole for his face. It was more like a hangman's hood than a balaclava.

Heart beating, mouth dry, Stanley started to cross the street. Not walking, but sliding. He was less than halfway across, however, when he knew for a certain fact that he didn't have the nerve to continue. Knitted Hood would turn around and jump on top of him.

Stanley tried to stop himself, to turn around, to dig his heels into the road surface. But the gray tarmac rumpled up like a thick soft carpet, and he continued to slide towards Knitted Hood, quicker and quicker, and he couldn't scream; couldn't even speak.

Knitted Hood whirled around, faceless. As he whirled, he grew impossibly taller, up and up and up, until he blotted out the sky. He paused and swayed, his coattails softly thundering in the morning wind. *No*, thought Stanley. *No*. But then Knitted Hood collapsed on top of him like the sky falling in.

Stanley screamed. But he knew that nobody could hear him. The screaming was only inside his head.

He convulsed, rigid, his teeh clenched, still unable to scream, still unable to do anything but tighten his muscles until he felt as if they were going to burst out of his skin. Then he opened his eyes. He saw shifting, dancing whiteness, blurry figures.

"Pulse rate's up," said a young woman's voice.

"Otherwise stable?" asked a young man's voice, further away.

There was some shuffling, and somebody coughed. Then the young man's voice said, "Has Gordon Rutherford been in?"

"Dr. Patel told him to wait till later."

"What about the filth?"

"Oh, *they're* here. Detective Sergeant Brian Morris, waiting in reception."

"You've told him to wait?"

"Of course. But he didn't seem to mind much. He's brought a book."

Stanley slowly opened his eyes. His body felt as if it had been bruised all over, muscle and bone. Even the palms of his hands felt sensitive and sore. But it was the pain in his back that he couldn't bear. A bitter, cracking pain right in the lumbar region that made him feel like bursting into tears.

A broad young gingery-bearded face loomed in front of him, so close that it looked more like a freckled landscape than a face. Stanley breathed in the smell of cigarettes, masked with Trebor extra-strong mints. "Ah! We're awake, then!" The young doctor grinned at him.

Stanley nodded.

"Do you know where you are?" the young doctor demanded.

Stanley shook his head.

"St. Stephen's," the young doctor replied. "You've been— well, attacked, sort of."

"St. Stephen's where?" Stanley whispered.

The young doctor stared at him with eyes like blue glass marbles. Sea-blue sailors, they used to call marbles that looked like that.

"I've only been in London since November," Stanley explained, almost apologetically, as if it were his fault that he didn't know where St. Stephen's was.

"Fulham Road," the young doctor told him. "Just opposite the gas fire shop," as if that should make it any clearer.

Stanley cleared this throat. "What time is it?" he asked.

"Quarter to two. You've been sedated for most of the morning."

"I have a pain in my back."

"Only to be expected, I'm afraid, after what you've been through."

Stanley swallowed. He was silent for a long time. The young doctor watched him and smiled; but there was no genuine humor in his smile; and no genuine sympathy, either.

"Is there any … damage?" Stanley asked him.

"You mean physical trauma?"

"Sure. Physical trauma."

The young doctor looked at him steadily. "Grazing, bruising. Broken incisor. External lacerations of the buttocks. Some internal laceration of the lower rectum. Dr. Patel gave you seven internal stitches. Nothing too serious, though. Some bruising, of course. But give it a little time."

"How long will I have to stay here?"

"Depends. You're pretty fit, on the whole. A week, ten days. Not much longer."

"I have two major recording sessions scheduled for Monday and Tuesday."

"Not a hope, I'm afraid. You won't be able to walk for at least three days; and you won't find sitting down very comfortable, either."

Without warning, Stanley found that his eyes filled up

with tears. He wiped them away with the edge of his sheet, and then the young doctor offered him some tissues.

"I'm sorry," he said. "I don't know what the hell came over me."

There was a long silence. The young doctor continued to stare at him. "We'll be carrying out some tests," he said at last.

"What kind of tests?" Stanley asked him.

"Oh, the usual. Blood pressure, heart rate, liver function. Sexually-communicable diseases."

Stanley tightened his mouth with pain. "Sexually-communicable diseases?"

"Gonorrhea, that kind of thing."

"I don't have gonorrhea. I don't have any sexually-communicable diseases. For God's sake. I've been in London less than three months. I haven't done any sexual communicating."

"You did this morning," the young doctor told him, in a tone of almost threatening blandness. "Or, at least, somebody sexually communicated with you."

"Goddammit, he—" Stanley began; but then his body winced, and his brain winced, too. He felt the dark greasy flapping of Knitted Hood's raincoat, like the wing of some huge diseased bird. He heard the thick whistling of Knitted Hood's breath.

The young doctor stood up straight and sniffed. "You'll be tested for HIV, too."

"You means AIDS?"

"That's right. Mr. Eisner. AIDS. I'm sorry, but given the nature of what happened to you. Exchange of bodily fluids, and all that."

Stanley couldn't do anything but nod and tremble. When he had been hit in the face in New York, the pain had been very much worse. But this, in a different way, was almost unbearable. This was the most terrible thing that had ever happened to him. He felt as if his entire soul had been invaded; as if everything that made him a human being had been forfeited, his emotional buttons pulled off, the sword of his virility broken. His cottage in Los Angeles had been burgled two or three years ago, and the thieves had torn down the drapes and urinated on the bed. He had felt then that his privacy and his personal dignity had been threatened. But this was something else altogether. Right out in the street, for everybody to see, this had been the brutal denial that he had any freedom of choice, that his body was his own, and that he was anything more than a receptacle for another man's hideous urges.

"Listen," said the young doctor, suddenly more sympathetic, "just at the moment you probably feel as if it's the end of the world. You're still in shock. Also—well, it wasn't a very pleasant experience, was it, to say the least? A chap called Gordon Rutherford is coming to see you. He's very understanding about this kind of thing."

"Did they catch the guy who did it?" asked Stanley.

"I don't think so. The police are here, too, but you don't have to talk to them yet. Does them good to keep them waiting. Reminds them where they stand in the hierarchy. A shade below bus conductors and about two points above estate agents."

"What about the people I work for?" said Stanley. "I should put in a call to the orchestra."

"Don't worry," said the young woman's voice from

19

the door. "The bursar telephoned your orchestra as soon as you were brought in. Somebody's coming to see you later on."

Stanley raised the head a little and saw a blond-haired woman in red designer spectacles and a white doctor's coat, standing by the door. "Thanks," he told her.

"You should get some rest now," the blond woman told him. "Drink as much as you possibly can. I'm afraid you won't be able to touch solids for at least a week."

Stanley lay back on his pillow. He felt bruised and exhausted. The gingery-bearded young doctor told him, "Don't worry, Mr. Eisner. People do get over these things. You just have to give yourself a little time."

Later that afternoon, he propped himself up on his pillows and watched *Neighbours* and *The Young Doctors* and drank half a bottle of orange barley water. The day began to darken around four o'clock, and he looked across the air shaft at the lighted windows on the other side of the hospital. He was beginning to feel oddly detached and unreal, but the gingery-bearded young doctor had told him that it was only natural, after shock and concussion.

There was something else, though: a feeling inside him that he couldn't quite put his finger on. A kind of prickling in his blood, as if his arteries were filled with thistles. And no matter how much he drank, he always seemed to be thirsty.

At half past five, there was a knock at his door, and a tall, thin young man with brown wavy hair appeared. "Mr. Eisner?" he asked in a breathy, excited voice.

"That's right."

"I'm Gordon Rutherford. I'm sorry I've taken so long. I had to collect my cat."

He came into the room and dragged a blue plastic chair up to the side of the bed. He was very intense-looking, with a large bony nose constructed of complicated angles of bone and cartilage, and bright pink bow-shaped lips. He wore a large shapeless jacket of hairy green tweed, and he was so thin that he had punctured an extra hole in his leather belt, so that it would fit around his waist.

"Poor Roger," he said, opening his cheap W.H. Smith briefcase and taking out a clipboard.' "He was so resentful he wouldn't even *speak* to me afterwards."

"I'm sorry," said Stanley. "Who's Roger?"

"My cat. I had him neutered this morning. Well, he was causing such a disturbance. All that yowling and screaming in the middle of the night. The neighbors used to throw stones at him. He couldn't leave the lady cats alone for a minute."

Stanley said, "Are you a cop? A social worker? What?"

"Didn't they tell you? I'm from the Rape Crisis Center," Gordon explained.

Stanley frowned. "You deal with men as well as women?"

Gordon looked surprised that Stanley had even found it necessary to ask.

"Oh, yes. It doesn't matter what sex you are. If you've been raped, you're going to suffer the same problems. Sometimes *worse* problem if you're a man. Your average heterosexual male is completely psychologically unprepared for the experience of being sexually penetrated. Physiologically, too, of course."

Stanley started to speak, then found that he couldn't. His throat was constricted with self-pity. "I didn't—" he began.

Gordon reached out and squeezed his hand. "The first thing you're going to have to come to terms with is that it wasn't your fault; not in any way at all."

"He was just standing there," Stanley gasped. "I asked him what the hell he was doing—and then he fell right down on top of me."

He couldn't stop himself; he started to tremble again, and tears ran down his cheeks as freely as they had the day that his mother died. "He was so goddamned *heavy*, so goddamned *strong*. I struggled as much as I could, but he hit my face on the sidewalk and damn near knocked me cold. Then he just did it, and there wasn't a thing I could do to stop him."

Gordon listened and then nodded. "Do you really believe that?" he asked.

"Do I really believe what?"

"Do you really believe that there wasn't a thing you could have done to stop him? Do you really believe that you did everything within your power to prevent him from raping you?"

Stanley wiped his eyes with a wad of screwed-up tissue. "I don't know. I keep thinking I should have kicked him, or reached in back of me and tried to gouge his eyes. I keep thinking how stupid I was to try to challenge him at all. I mean you should have seen this guy. He had some kind of woollen hood on, and he was all hunched up like Quasimodo. *Nobody* would have challenged him; nobody streetwise, anyway, like I keep trying to make out I am."

He took a shallow, shuddering breath. "I must have been crazy. Or else I was asking for it."

Gordon pursed his lips. "What you're feeling is very common among rape victims. It doesn't matter what sex they are; or even what the circumstances were. I've talked to women who were held down by four men and raped by a fifth, and they *still* believe in the back of their minds that it was partly their own fault."

Stanley said, "I could kill him, you know? I could physically kill him with my bare hands. I never felt that way about anybody, ever before."

"That's not unusual, either. You feel guilty about what happened to you; and your subconscious mind is suggesting to you that one way to get rid of your guilt is to punish the person who made you feel that way."

Gordon paused, and then he added, "Sometimes, Mr. Eisner, rape victims feel so guilty that they try to punish the only person they can lay their hands on, which is themselves. I think you're probably intelligent enough for me to be able to tell you that, and for you to understand the symptoms, if and when you start to feel them. In other words, Mr. Eisner, when the initial shock has worn off, you're going to start feeling depressed; and your estimation of yourself is going to take a steep nose-dive."

"At that time, you're going to feel self-destructive."

"You mean I'm going to feel like killing myself?"

Gordon nodded. "It happened to me, too."

"But you survived?"

"I'm a survivor."

"Did they ever catch the guy who did it to you?"

"Guys plural, actually. I was hanging around Piccadilly,

trying to make myself enough money to cover my rent. I was picked up by four Turkish gentlemen in a Mercedes. They took me back to some woman's flat in Shepherd's Bush and did things to me that you wouldn't even Want to have *nightmares* about."

He patted Stanley's hand and smiled. "And, no, they never caught them. They never even tried. Diplomatic immunity, all that sort of thing. And who was I? Nothing but a spotty young rent boy, from Leeds. All I got from the police was, 'Piss off, you horrible little pooftah, before we break the other arm.'"

Stanley said, "They broke your arm?"

"They almost broke my soul, believe me. And I was gay to start with."

"I'm sorry."

"*You're* sorry? How do you think I felt? Actually, you know jolly well how I felt. Or you will, anyway, when you talk to the police. As far as most coppers are concerned, Mr. Eisner, male rape is one of those offenses which give rise to nothing but innuendo and ribald humor. They'll accuse you of being gay, too. I hope you're ready for that. They'll suggest that you egged this character on, whether he looked like Quasimodo or not. You're a musician, too, that doesn't help. Anything to do with the arts is limp-wristed, as far as your average British woodentop is concerned. *And* you're American; *and* you're Jewish."

"What I am doesn't alter the facts," Stanley insisted, trying to keep his reasoning straight, trying not to cry. "All I did was *talk* to the guy, for God's sake—ask him what he was doing there. Then he jumped on me. No warning, no come-on, nothing."

Gordon shrugged. "All the same, the police will certainly try to suggest otherwise. It makes life easier for them if you're guilty, too. It fits in with their pig-Freemason-racist view of the universe. Sod justice, my dear—*every*body's guilty, victims and perpetrators alike. In fact, as far as the police are concerned, the victims are usually more guilty than the perpetrators. Serves them right for getting in the way, do you know what I mean? Apart from that, if you're just as guilty as the guy who attacked you, the police won't feel that they're under so much of an obligation to find him."

"I always heard your British policemen were wonderful," said Stanley dryly.

"Oh, good gracious, that was in the days of Jayne Mansfield," Gordon replied. "But don't misunderstand me. I'm not a professional cynic. I'm a firm believer in flowers and balloons and lambs gamboling in the sunshine, not to mention the fortitude of the human spirit. I'm simply saying that you should gird your loins for the kind of questions that Detective Sergeant Brian Morris, God bless him, will be putting to you. Detective Sergeant Brian Morris is Anglican, white, thirty-three, and straight. He lives in Wandsworth with his wife, his Alsatian dog, his budgerigars, and two-point-four children. Detective Sergeant Brian Morris is also overworked, overpaid, nauseated by gays and druggies and football hooligans and people who park their cars on double yellow lines, and is very interested in getting an easy result."

Stanley swallowed. His mouth was feeling dry again. Without being asked, Gordon reached over and poured him another glass of orange barley water, which Stanley drank in two long drafts, without breathing.

"Let me tell you this," said Stanley. "If the police aren't interested in finding this character, then I will, and I'll kill him personally."

Gordon slowly and mechanically shook his head from side to side. "Believe me, Stanley—you don't mind if I call you Stanley?—taking the law into your own hands would be the very worst thing you could do. That would prove to the police beyond a shadow of a doubt that you and Quasimodo were nothing but a couple of quarreling ginger-beers; and you'd probably be banged up forever, amen."

"So what do you suggest I do?"

"I suggest you answer every question factually; and unemotionally; and as fully as you can. Try to imagine that what happened, happened to somebody else, not you, and you're simply a witness. Whatever Detective Sergeant Morris suggests to you, don't lose your temper. Don't theorize, don't speculate, stick to the facts."

Gordon hesitated, and then he added, "One more thing."

"What's that?"

"Whatever you do, don't allow yourself to burst into tears."

Dr. Patel came to visit Stanley before Detective Sergeant Morris was allowed in. He was slender and dark-eyed and sad-looking, like a disillusioned Indian ascetic, and his touch was infinitely gentle. Two young Chinese nurses manhandled Stanley on to his stomach, so that his face was pressed against the pillow, and waited with their arms folded and their eyes bright while Dr. Patel examined Stanley's stitches.

"You have been quite lucky," Dr. Patel remarked.

"If this is lucky, what's unlucky?" Stanley wanted to know.

Dr. Patel covered him up and signaled to the nurses to turn him back over.

"You were forcibly penetrated by an object that was nine or ten inches in length, with a diameter of two and a half inches," he replied in his soft, melancholy voice. "Unlucky would have been a perforated bowel, Mr. Eisner. Unlucky would have been dead."

Detective Sergeant Brian Morris was short and bull-shouldered, with a mustache that was clipped too small for his face and a complexion the color of Sainsbury's unsmoked bacon. His eyebrows were so fair they were almost invisible, and this gave him the appearance of being astonished at everything he came across, but not much.

He had a bent-back copy of Little *Gloria Happy at Last* in the pocket of his pale blue windcheater, which struck Stanley as incongruous enough to be threatening Right now, however, Stanley found almost everything threatening. He had never realized how vulnerable he actually was; how easily hurt; how quickly his dignity could be stripped away from him.

The room was very poorly lit. Detective Sergeant Morris didn't help matters by sitting in the far corner, in a black shadow the shape of a teacher's mortarboard, next to a faded color print of *The Wye at Symonds Yat*. He kept his head lowered over his notebook, so that all that Stanley could see of him was the meticulously accurate parting in his hair. He was the kind of man who used shoe trees, and resharpened his old razor blades, and bashed at his hair before he left for work with two hog's-bristle brushes.

"Dr. Patel was cooperative enough to retain a semen sample and to pass it on to us for pathological examination," he remarked in a flat accent which sounded to Stanley like cockney; but which Gordon Rutherford could have told him was South London, not a stone's frow from Streatham Bus Garridge.

Stanley didn't know what to say. The thought that his attacker had discharged semen into his body made the assault seem even more disgusting. There had been no passion in it, no reproductive purpose. Just brutal penetration and the ejaculation of fluid, for his attacker's own filthy and mindless satisfaction.

"Obviously, once your assailant is apprehended, the semen sample can be used for the purpose of genetic identification, and very useful, too," Detective Sergeant Morris continued. "But what we urgently require from you, Mr. Eesner, is some sort of physical description so that we can circulate our forces on the ground."

"Eisner," Stanley corrected him. "It's not Eesner, it's Eisner."

Detective Sergeant Morris looked up with a carefully-prepared expression of policemanly surprise. "Well, sir, you say 'eether' and I say 'either.' You say 'neether' and I say 'neither.'"

"He wore a gray knitted hood," said Stanley.

"Ah," said Detective Sergeant Morris.

Stanley watched him for a while. Then, "Aren't you going to write that down?"

"Not much point, is there, Mr. Eesner? Gray knitted hood, probably would've taken it off by now. Disposed of it."

"Well, sure, but somebody may know who he is. I mean, if he was in the *habit* of wearing a gray knitted hood—"

Detective Sergeant Morris reached into the pocket of his windbreaker, where three pens and two pencils were neatly fastened by nerd clips, and produced a ballpen. On the top line of his notebook, he wrote (softly mouthing the words as he did so) "*gray ... knitted ... hood.*"

"He was tall," said Stanley. "Six one, six two. And heavy. I never felt anyone so heavy."

"*Heavy,*" wrote Detective Sergeant Morris. Then he looked up. "See his face, sir?"

"Yes, I saw his face. It didn't fit his general appearance at all. It was very white, almost like a mask. Have you ever seen a Mardi Gras mask, or a saint's day mask?"

"No, Mr. Eesner, can't say that I have."

"Well, I can probably find a picture for you. But it was like that. White, and glossy, and very beautiful. I mean exquisitely beautiful."

Detective Sergeant Morris gave Stanley an odd small-eyed stare. "Not sure what you mean, sir."

"He wore a gray knitted hood, right? A really disgusting gray knitted hood. And a greasy old raincoat, and boots like—I don't know—coal miner's boots. He looked like a hobo, a tramp. But when he turned around and looked at me, his face was incredible."

"You mean beautiful, sir?"

"That's right. He had the most beautiful face that I've ever seen in my life."

Detective Sergeant Morris wrote this down, slowly and laboriously, with lots of loops in his writing. It was the writing of a small boy who is trying hard to impress his teacher.

"What time did you leave your flat, Mr. Eesner?" he asked at last.

"Eight-ten, dead on the nose."

"And when did you first see your assailant?"

"Immediately. He was waiting for me across the street."

Detective Sergeant Morris clenched his tongue tip between his teeth, writing and murmuring, "*He was ... waiting ... for me ...*"

Stanley said, "This was the fourth straight day. He's been waiting for me every day since Tuesday. He's been following me, all the way to the King's Road and on to the bus."

"Had you *asked* him to wait for you?"

"What do you mean? Of course not, I didn't even know the guy!"

"Then why was he waiting for you?"

"How should I know? You should ask him! I tried to find out, and look what the hell happened to me!"

Detective Sergeant Morris carefully wrote this down. Then he said, "If you didn't know this gentleman, sir, and he didn't know you, it seems very odd that he should be waiting for you every morning. Had you met him at all before, in any context whatsoever?"

"I told you, I didn't know him from Adam. I never met him before anywhere, ever."

"What you mean is, you hadn't seen him before he started waiting for you across the street—which was, ah, Tuesday?"

"That's correct."

"And to quote your own words, Mr. Eesner, he had the most beautiful face that you had ever seen in your life?" In the expressionless way that Detective Sergeant Morris intoned them, Stanley's words sounded absurd, like a line out of Monty Python. He could almost have added, "nudge, nudge, wink, wink."

Stanley tried to keep a tight rein on his irritation. *Answer every question factually and unemotionally*, Gordon Rutherford had warned him. "That's right," he agreed.

Detective Sergeant Morris remained silent for a moment, still writing. Then he said, "Who approached whom, sir?"

"I'm sorry?"

"What I'm trying to establish, sir, did you approach him or did he approach you?"

Stanley winced and frowned. "What the hell difference does that make? He attacked me!"

"I realize that, sir, but if we're thinking about prosecution, in the courts, we're going to have to come up in front of a judge, and twelve good men and true. And that judge, and those twelve good men and true, they're going to be asking themselves, was this beautiful young chap in the gray knitted hood approached by you; and, if he *was* approached by you, was it possible that he was justified in assuming that you were actively seeking the kind of sexual pleasures which he then proceeded to provide?"

Detective Sergeant Morris leafed back through his notebook and added, "In simple words, sir, were you essentially, as it were, asking for it?"

Stanley lifted himself up on his elbows, trembling with shock and anger. "He attacked me! What the hell are you trying to say here? He attacked me! He smashed my face against the sidewalk, he broke my tooth!"

Detective Sergeant Morris was undeterred. "There are some who like it a bit rough, sir."

"Rough? What are you, some kind of retard? He practically killed me! He hit my head against the sidewalk and then he sodomized me, can't you understand that? He raped me, against my will!"

Slowly, with more loops, Detective Sergeant Morris wrote, "*raped me ... against my ...*" When he finished, he added in that leaden tone, "And, believe me, Mr. Eesner, insults won't help us at all."

Stanley was juddering with tension. His heart banged dryly against his ribs, too much adrenaline, too much stress.

Detective Sergeant Morris said, "How was the rape actually effected, Mr. Eesner?"

"What?" asked Stanley.

Detective Sergeant Morris was obviously trying not to smirk. "Can you tell me how the rape was actually effected? I mean, without putting too fine a point on it, sir, there are practical difficulties. Quarts into pint pots, if you follow me."

"I don't understand, he raped me," Stanley replied.

"Yes, sir," Detective Sergeant Morris repeated patiently. "But what the judge and the jury will want to know is, how? Perhaps you remember *Last Tango in Paris*, sir? In that case the practical difficulties were overcome with butter."

"Butter?" Stanley repeated. "*Butter?*" and then, fatally, began to cry.

★

He had one more visitor that day—Frederick Orme, the director of the Kensington Chamber Orchestra, who arrived with a bunch of daffodils from the flower stall outside the hospital, and a copy of Jeffrey Archer's *Twist in the Tale*. Frederick Orme was tall and airy and vague, and sat back on his chair showing seven inches of white leg, his russet eyebrows rising up his forehead like flames.

"The evening papers seem to have been discreet about it," he remarked. "They say simply that you were mugged, rather than go into the grisly details of—well, what actually happened to you."

Stanley had the disturbing suspicion that Frederick Orme felt the same way as Detective Sergeant Morris— that even if he hadn't actually *encouraged* it, any man who had been anally raped must at least have accepted his attack submissively. ("Catch me letting anybody near *my* rear end!")

Frederick Orme reached over and picked one of Stanley's grapes. "The doctor told me that you were quite lucky."

"He seems to think so," said Stanley. "At least I'm still alive."

"But I gather you won't be playing with us for quite a while. Six weeks' convalescence at least, that's what the doctor suggested."

Stanley nodded.

"That's really quite a nuisance, you know," Frederick Orme told him, eating one grape and picking himself another. "We have Nils Planck coming over from Düsseldorf next week to finish recording the Adagio and Fugue in C Minor; and then we were hoping to arrange a concert at the Royal Festival Hall."

"I apologize for being attacked," Stanley told him flatly.

"My dear boy, it wasn't your fault. We all sympathize dreadfully. But it does make life rather difficult. I would have thought an American would be rather more, what do you call it? Roadworthy?"

"Streetwise," Stanley corrected him. His painkillers were beginning to wear off, and the aching in his back was almost intolerable. He watched Frederick Orme eat another grape, and then he said, "I'll ask Dr. Patel if I can come out sooner. I could play from a wheelchair, I guess."

Frederick Orme nodded. "Helpful if you could." He stood up quite abruptly and tugged down his brown tweed waistcoat. "Everybody sends their best, anyway. Fanny Lawrence said she'd pop in to see you tomorrow. And if there's anything you need …"

"A little rest, as a matter of fact," Stanley told him.

"Of course, dear boy. I must be off, in any case. Wonderful grapes. Are you allowed Guinness?"

He slept badly that night. Again and again, he woke up with a start, convinced that there was somebody in the room with him. But he was alone, and the room remained overheated and silent, except for the muffled grinding of London's traffic and the occasional whistling of a night porter.

He felt feverish and hot; and not completely real; and his blood prickled as it coursed around his body as if it were filled with fine hairlike fibers.

He tried to think of some soothing musical score, to calm himself down. *Eine Kleine Nachtmusik*, maybe. It usually worked: he had never gone past the andante without falling asleep. But all he could picture tonight was a stave without notes or notations, ribboning out of one side of his mind like an empty five-lane highway, and ribboning away out of the other. He felt as if he were musically illiterate; as if he had forgotten every crotchet that he had every played.

There was something wrong with him. It wasn't just shock. It wasn't just concussion and bruising and violently-torn tissues. There was something inside him; something was hiding inside his body that wasn't him, and wasn't his; something was hiding inside his mind.

You're sick, he told himself, dry-lipped, in the half-darkness of his hospital room. *You're badly, seriously sick*.

For the first time since he had left New York in November, he felt like talking to his father. He checked the time. He would be sleeping by now; but he promised himself that he would phone him during the day. He would have liked to be able to talk to Eve, too; and he would have called her right now, if he could. Two A.M. in London, six P.M. the previous day in Napa. She would probably just be starting supper. He wished now that they hadn't argued so bitterly over money. It had probably been the only way they knew how to punish each other. Ever since they had known each other, way back at Berkeley in the days of Leon Russell songs and flared jeans, he and Eve had always been able to discuss their problems and their anxieties together, even if they hadn't really loved each other enough to stay married. Stanley's old college pal Pete Chominski had always said that he and Eve should have stayed friends; and never tried to pretend that they could be man and wife.

He missed Leon, too; serious-faced Leon, who had been

named for Leon Russell; he missed him more than he could ever have imagined.

He lay back on his pillow with his eyes open. At the same time, he had the extraordinary feeling that at some time in the past few minutes he had fallen asleep—that he had passed from waking to dreaming without even noticing the transition. He wouldn't have believed that his mind could have arranged for him to pass so seamlessly from one state to another. Not even a blink; and London's traffic still thundering outside, exactly as it had been before.

Now, however, somebody was standing in the shadows, in the darkest corner of the room. A tall hunched figure, with its face concealed. A figure that must be a dream because the door hadn't opened and closed, and he heard no footsteps; no rustling of clothing.

A figure that must be a dream, because he felt no sense of terror, only a helpless curiosity.

"Who are you?" he whispered.

The figure said nothing, and remained buried in darkness.

"Who are you?" Stanley repeated. "What do you want?"

After a long pause, the figure slowly raised its head, and Stanley saw the cold beautiful face of the man in the knitted hood. Pristine, angelic, glistening.

"*I am the pestilence that was promised.*"

"You're what? What are you talking about?"

"*Don't you remember? If you were unwilling to obey, you were promised that the plague on you would be increased by seven times, according to your sins.*"

"You're crazy."

"*Am I? Who could be crazier than you, who disobeyed? Don't you remember what you were told—that when you*" *gathered together in your cities, pestilence would be sent among you, so that you should be delivered into the hands of your enemies.*"

"I'm dreaming," said Stanley.

The figure uttered a strange, soft, mocking sound; not so much like a laugh, more like a sack being slowly dragged across an unswept cement floor. "*Who dreams? Who's awake? Am I dreaming you, or are you dreaming me?*"

Stanley said, "You attacked me, you bastard. You could have killed me."

"*Ha! We are cutting a swathe through the world. You can hardly complain if you were chosen to be the first.*"

"I don't understand a word of this," said Stanley. "Dream or no dream. I'm going to call for the doctor." He heaved himself up on to one elbow.

"*It will serve no purpose,*" Knitted Hood told him. "*We are dreams, you and I, both of us. We are wraiths of each other's imagination, nothing more.*"

Stanley hesitated for a moment, then stripped off the surgical tape which held his dextrose drip in place, tugged out the tube, and swung his legs off the side of the bed. "All right, then, pal, if this is all a dream, and it's just me and you, then let's see what you're made of."

Again Knitted Hood uttered that gritty whispering noise. Then—while Stanley eased himself carefully and painfully off the edge of his bed—he moved to the window and drew aside the curtain with his gray-bandaged hand.

"*You doubt the truth of what I say?*" he asked Stanley, his eyes black, his face seraphic but utterly expressionless, "*Look out of the window, tell me what you see.*"

Stanley approached the window at a slow, geriatric

hobble. Blood slid from his wrist where he had pulled out his drip. Now that he was closer to Knitted Hood, he could smell that same sourish odor that he had smelled yesterday morning, when he was attacked; that same strong scent of lavender. His stomach knotted up, and the roof of his mouth felt as if it were coated with grease.

"*Look*," Knitted Hood insisted.

Stanley looked out of the hospital window and saw that the sky was beginning to lighten. The landscape was a hard, chilly gray, a winter's morning as cold as a witch's teat. But there was no traffic to be seen, no buildings, no streets and buses and backyards. All he could see were boggy, deserted fields, and disconsolate trees, and a small collection of huts and sheds and pigpens.

Fulham seemed to have vanished. In its place was nothing but marshy farmland and winding tracks of glistening black mud, as far as Stanley could see.

"I don't understand," he said hoarsely.

"*Perhaps it's a dream*," Knitted Hood suggested. "*Then again, perhaps it's a memory.*" He was silent for a moment, and then he added, "*Then again, perhaps it's real.*"

As Stanley watched, a woman in a bonnet and a shawl emerged from behind the huts, pushing a handcart. She was too far away for him to be able to see her clearly, but she didn't look older than twenty-one or twenty-two. She had greasy blond hair tied up in a scarf, and a blue-gray dress with a plain square neck and skirts that were heavy with mud. The handcart appeared to be heaped up with old rags.

"Is this a dream?" Stanley demanded.

Knitted Hood said nothing, but turned away from the

window and stood in the shadows, so that Stanley could barely see him.

"Is this a dream?" Stanley repeated. "Am I asleep, or what?"

"*Who can say what it is?*" Knitted Hood replied. "*It could be your past, it could be your future. Ha! It could be nothing more frightening than something you ate.*"

Stanley turned back to the window. The girl had managed to wrestle the handcart onto the muddy track, and for a moment she paused, looking in his direction. Although she was pale and her cheek was marked with mud, she was almost beautiful, in a starved kind of way, and strangely familiar.

Stanley raised his hand, compelled for some reason to wave to her. He felt that he wanted to call our her name, although he didn't know what her name was. Could she see him? Was he really here? Could she see the hospital even? How could a large red-brick Victorian hospital be standing in the middle of a boggy country farm?

We shall cut a swathe through the world, Knitted Hood had assured him; and now Stanley was beginning to feel frightened and chilled. He turned around quickly, terrified that Knitted Hood had suddenly come up close behind him; but Knitted Hood had folded himself so darkly in the shadows that Stanley wasn't sure that he was there at all.

He looked back at the girl with the handcart. She was struggling to push it over a rutted part of the path, close to the farmyard gate. One of the wheels became deeply enmired; and no matter how hard she pushed it, and jostled it backwards and forwards, the handcart refused to move any further.

The girl looked around, as if she needed help, but didn't know whom to call, as if there wasn't anybody she *could* call. She glanced towards the hospital, and Stanley pressed his hand against the window; but he couldn't decide whether she had seen him or not. *Who's dreaming whom? Maybe this farm girl is dreaming about me. Maybe Knitted Hood is dreaming about both of us. Maybe we're all dreams. Maybe we're all dead.*

The girl tried rocking the cart yet again, but the wheels sank even more inextricably into the mud. She was almost knee-deep in black ooze, and her dress trailed heavy and bedraggled in the puddles.

Each time she pushed, the rags on the handcart slipped further and further to one side, and suddenly Stanley saw something pale appearing from underneath them. Two more pushes, and he realized with horrible fascination that he was looking at a human arm. It lolled lifelessly from one side to another as the girl struggled to push the handcart out of the mud.

How can this conceivably be a dream? This is far too real to be a dream. All right, London has disappeared, I don't know how, and I'm out in the country someplace. But this girl is pushing a dead body on a handcart and I can see it as clear as if I'm awake.

He had to find his way outside. The girl desperately needed his help. Yet somehow he couldn't bring himself to leave the window. Supposing she vanished, and London came back? How could he possibly help her then?

The girl appeared to lose her temper, and she shook the handcart violently from side to side. As she did so, the rags dropped away, and a heap of greenish-white naked bodies slithered off the edge of it, like fish being emptied out of a basket, and into the mud.

Stanley stood at the window, panting with shock. *Oh, God. Oh, God.* A dead child, no more than two years old, had fallen facedown into a puddle. Close beside him, with her eyes wide open, lay a dead girl with dark bushy hair, her sticklike arms crossed over her chest, her ribs emaciated like a Belsen victim. She could have been anything from ten to fourteen years old. A little further away, curiously crouched up, lay a dead woman in her early thirties, gray-faced, wearing a gray linen cap. She had such an appalling expression of despair on her face that Stanley could almost have believed that she was still alive. A dead newly-born baby had been strapped tightly to her back with strips of torn bandage; a tiny purple doll with terrible black eyes; as if she were expected to carry it with her into death in a way that she had never been able to carry it in life. A punishment or a consolation? Stanley couldn't even begin to guess.

"*Your plague shall be increased seven times, and we shall cut a swathe through the world.*"

Behind him, the door of his room suddenly opened. Stanley turned around, still trembling, still gasping. He found himself face-to-face with one of his Chinese nurses.

"What are you *doing*, Mr. Eisner?" she demanded in astonishment. "You are under very strict orders to stay in bed till Dr. Patel says you can get up! And what have you done to your drip?"

Stanley swayed. The nurse caught him with matter-of-fact efficiency as he began to faint, and helped him back on to the bed.

"I saw something—" he began, but the nurse sharply, "Ssh! No more talking!"

Briskly, she reconnected his drip. Then she made sure that he was settled in bed and firmly tucked up. "You rest, Mr. Eisner! Don't you dare to move! In a minute we'll be bringing you some breakfast. I must call Dr. Patel, too, to make sure you haven't pulled any of your stitches."

Stanley lay on his side, tucked up as tightly as a small child, his face turned away from the window, while the morning gradually grew brighter. Outside, quite distinctly, he could hear the churning of early-morning traffic, the juddering of taxis, the sniffing and bellowing of buses. He thought once that he could hear a girl's voice crying out, plaintive and high, but with his cheek against the starched hospital sheet he had to admit to himself that it was probably nothing more than a dream.

Chapter Two

Nylon Stocking

He sat by the window of his flat for over an hour, watching Langton Street grow darker and darker. A mug of espresso coffee grew cold on the table beside him. He made no attempt to switch on the lights, or to change the record which circled silently and endlessly on the hi-fi on the opposite side of the room.

He was watching the corner where Knitted Hood had waited, on that hideous morning four and a half weeks ago. The pavement was deserted now; Langton Street remained empty.

At half past six he pushed back his chair and stood up. *It's no use thinking about it, Stanley. It happened, and all the thinking in the world isn't going to make it un-happen.* He picked up the coffee cup and took it through to the kitchen, and switched on the lights.

This was his first night back in his own flat since leaving hospital. The *Sun* newspaper had printed a front-page story, "Attack on Top U.S, Violinist 'Was Rape,'" complete with a photograph of Stanley shaking hands with Sir Georg Solti in Chicago; and for the sake of Stanley's "emotional convalescence" and the orchestra's "general equilibrium," Frederick Orme had decided it would be "generally preferred" if he didn't immediately return to the orchestra. The second bassoon, Nigel Bromhead-Jones, had given Stanley the use of his late mother's bungalow in Oxshott, in the Surrey commuter belt, and Stanley had spent over three weeks reading and going for walks and watching television.

In all that time he had spoken to hardly anybody, except the woman in the local post office, who believed that her migraines were caused by the depletion in the ozone layer, and the landlord of the Feathers, who was gruff and belligerent and thought that anybody who couldn't trace their English ancestry back at least three generations should be forcibly repatriated at their own expense, regardless of the fact that this would have emptied the cities of Bradford and Wolverhampton overnight.

Only one of Stanley's fellow musicians from the orchestra had come down from London to see him—Fanny Lawrence, a pale bespectacled girl with wild pre-Raphaelite hair and hems that dangled with fraying cotton threads. She worshiped Stanley. She had told him so several times. "You're my god, you know," she had announced when they were sitting in the pub eating chicken-in-the-basket. Stanley had taken her to the station afterwards and kissed her cold, plump cheek.

The days had passed gray and detailed and tedious, like the spokes of a bicycle wheel ticking around and around. Walking along the puddly roads, Stanley had almost forgotten who he was, or why he was here. He had found himself increasingly afflicted by a huge inertia.

Some afternoons he had sat for two or three hours at a time, listening to his heart beat, feeling that strange thistly prickling in his veins, thinking of nothing at all.

He could have stayed in Oxshott forever, gradually absorbed by English suburbia until he became a mirage, a reflective disturbance in the air, and nothing more.

Yesterday, however, he had caught sight of himself in a fish-eye security mirror in the local supermarket. He had stopped, stepped back towards the mirror, and stared at himself more closely. A tired Buster Keaton-looking man with a wire basket full of cheese and kitchen towels and shredded wheat. A voice inside him had asked urgently, *What the hell's happening to you, Stanley? Are you sick or something? Are you dying? You look like you're dying!*

Very carefully, he had walked back around the supermarket and replaced all his shopping on the shelves. Then he had walked back along the narrow pavement to the bungalow, turned off the gas and the power, and telephoned for a taxi to take him to London.

In the back of the taxi, staring at the passing suburbs, hairdressers, garages, mile after mile of 1930s semidetached houses, gray skies, pylons, he had admitted to himself that Knitted Hood's assault had taken something away from him that he might never be able to recapture. It had taken away his spirit, his joy in being alive; and that man he had seen in the Oxshott supermarket mirror had only just been managing to cling on to his identity by his fingernails. It had been more like peering through the spyhole of a padded cell and seeing a lunatic peering back at him.

*

Tonight he walked around his flat, tugging the brown velour drapes and switching on the lamps. He resisted the temptation to take one last look out into the street.

On the television screen, in a thick Northumbrian accent that Stanley could scarcely understand, the BBC weatherman was explaining that tomorrow would be bitterly cold. Somehow the BBC seemed to have convinced itself that weathermen with thick regional accents would be more believable, like shepherds or crofters.

Red sky at night, shepherd's delight. Red sky in the morning, shepherd's warning. Red sky in the afternoon, shepherd's house is on fire.

Stanley's flat was spacious and quite comfortable, in a stuffy London way. He had a large living room, with beige-papered walls and brown furnishings, and a beige tiled fireplace with a six-bar electric fire. Above the fireplace hung a huge reproduction of *Prince Baltasar Carlos with a Dwarf*, by Velázquez, bought from Boots the Chemists. Stanley found the portrait unsettling and strange. It showed two small creatures in elaborately-embroidered dresses—one of them pale and royal, and painted in an odd perspective, as if he were floating in the air, the other one stunted.

Stanley carried his cold coffee through to the kitchen, trying to hum Handel but sounding flat. The kitchen was modern, fitted in brown oak, with a large Zanussi refrigerator and a window that overlooked some dark small yard between the houses; a yard which intrigued Stanley because he had heard children playing there, but couldn't see how anybody could gain access to it.

Stanley tipped away his coffee and went to the refrigerator and took out a half-empty bottle of Pouilly-Fumé. Dr. Patel had advised him against drinking alcohol while he was still on medication, but the way he felt tonight, what the hell. He shook two capsules into the palm of his hand, clapped his hand against his mouth, and washed the capsules' down with cold wine.

He went back into the living room and sat down in front of the television. Channel 4 news was reporting on the day's debates in the House of Commons. The Conservative MP Mr. Robert Adley had called the Labour MP Mr. John Prescott "a freak." The Speaker of the House had decided that this remark was "not un-Parliamentary but certainly inelegant."

The longer he stayed in England, the quainter and more claustrophobic Stanley found it. It was like living in a novel by Charles Dickens, *Our Suffocating Friend*.

The news turned to the subject of the Channel Tunnel. Protestors in woolly hats were claiming that it would "cut a swathe of devastation through the sublime county of Kent."

A swathe, thought Stanley. *We shall cut a swathe through the world*.

He could still feel that prickling in his blood. He had told Dr. Patel about it while he was in hospital, but Dr. Patel had assured him there was nothing wrong. His blood samples had been sent back twice for re-analysis—once to the Hospital for Tropical Diseases—but now Dr. Patel was fairly sure that he hadn't caught anything nasty from his encounter with Knitted Hood. "You are a physically well man, Mr. Eisner. If you are feeling anything in your body, then it is your mind that it is creating that feeling."

Stanley leaned his head back in his armchair and closed his eyes. He had never felt so tired in his life, although he couldn't understand why. He had been resting for almost a month, after all. He hadn't even practiced his violin. It lay on the chair beside the window, its case closed. He had taken it down to Oxshott with him, but he had only taken it out once. He had played two quick, scraping, discordant notes, and then immediately put it back again. He didn't seem to have any music in him any more.

The clipped monotonous voice of the Channel 4 newscaster went on and on; humorless and English and peculiarly unintelligible. *And today clams were still being mabel that fortitude was passing wild recessions.* Stanley began to breathe more deeply and more regularly. His hand slid from the arm of his chair.

He wasn't quite asleep, but he could feel his consciousness slowly sinking, like a saucepan gradually filling up with water. He thought about the landlord of the Feathers. *Never in calming positions, but always in falling necessities.* He thought about the woman in the Oxshott post office. *Even today, when almost all tankards have interested trees.*

He slept. He thought he was asleep. But then he opened his eyes and the television news was still on, and the living room seemed exactly the same as before. He felt cold, however, uncomfortably cold. He sat up shivering and trembling; and as he did so he was conscious of that sharp prickling sensation in his veins.

He eased himself out of his chair and knelt down in front of the fireplace to switch on the electric fire. Why did he suddenly feel so cold? He felt as if all the skin had been stripped off him and his raw flesh had been exposed to the wind. He switched on all six bars of the electric fire and hunched down close to it while the bars gradually reddened.

As the fire warmed up, he held his hands close to it. *Why*

do I feel so terrible? Why do I feel so goddamned shivery and weak? He was beginning to wonder if his experience might not have brought out something worse, like chronic delayed shock, or even ME—myalgic encephalomyelitis. He had never felt so sensitive before.

He coughed. He coughed again; and this time his cough was thicker. His stomach felt queasy, as if he had been swallowing phlegm. He coughed again and again, thicker and thicker; and between each bout of coughing he found he had to fight for breath.

Oh, God, I feel so lousy. What the hell's the matter with me?

He coughed for almost a minute, pressing his handkerchief over his mouth. Then suddenly he felt something slippery in the back of his throat; and he retched loudly, a terrible ripping retch that made his stomach contract, and almost made him vomit. A large slimy gray lump, the size and shape of an oyster, slithered out of his mouth and into his handkerchief.

He stared at it, sweating and panting, his stomach still convulsing, his mouth flooded with foul-tasting saliva.

What is it? A lump of mucus? A lump of coughed-up lung? Perhaps he had cancer and Dr. Patel hadn't wanted to tell him. He felt weak with exhaustion and fear, and his head swam. He could smell the burned-dust smell of the electric fire, and it almost choked him.

Cautiously, he squeezed the gray lump in his handkerchief. At first, nothing happened, so he squeezed it again. It felt exactly like an oyster, or a soft cyst. He opened up his handkerchief again so that he could examine it more closely. He was still swallowing with nausea. He prodded it with his fingertip, and then took hold of one of its slippery tubules and tried to tug it apart.

Instantly, it tightened and convulsed, as if it were alive. Stanley cried out, "*Ah!*" and flung it away from him in disgust and fright, and it landed on the top bar of the electric fire. A sharp sizzling noise; a smell so repulsive that Stanley clamped his hand over his nose and mouth; and then the lump dropped into the fireplace, twitching furiously, rolling and unrolling, as if it were suffering hideous agony.

Stanley picked up the wine bottle and tried to crush the thing; but it felt just like a human tongue, and he couldn't stand the feeling of it, wriggling between the bottle and the tiled hearth, as if it were determined to stay alive, no matter what pain it had to endure, no matter how hard Stanley tried to kill it.

He grasped the arm of his chair and heaved himself upright. He retched again and almost vomited. *God Almighty, what was happening to him?*

He turned, half expecting to see what he saw.

There—in the shadow of the curtains—close beside the chair where his violin case lay, stood Knitted Hood. White-faced, silent, shining, as beautiful as sin.

Stanley stood shivering, saying nothing. This was a dream now, he knew it. It had to be a dream. The only terrifying part about it was that he didn't know how to wake up.

"*It could be your past,*" Knitted Hood whispered. "*It could be your future. It could be nothing more frightening than something you ate.*"

"Leave me alone." Stanley swallowed, wiping his mouth with his hand.

"*We have something in common now, you and me,*"

Knitted Hood told him. "*What was mine has now passed to you; and what is now yours will pass to the rest of the world; one to another; and together we shall cut a swathe through all mankind.*"

"Wake up!" Stanley shouted to himself.

"*Perhaps you're awake already,*" whispered Knitted Hood, and his voice was chillingly benign.

Stanley swung his arm and slapped himself hard across the face. "Wake up! Wake up, you stupid *putz*! Wake up!"

He shut his eyes tightly and slapped himself again and again.

"Wake—*up*!—wake—*up*!—wake—*UP*!—wake—*UP*!"

He was suddenly aware that something was different; that the atmosphere in the living room had subtly altered. Slowly, his cheeks stinging, he opened his eyes.

The Channel 4 newscaster was saying, "... and that's all for this evening ... and a very good evening to you."

Stanley looked around the room, sniffing and trembling. Behind the curtains there was nothing but shadow; and in the hearth there was nothing but broken glass, and a steadily-widening pool of white wine, in which the scarlet bars of the electric fire were reflected.

"God protect me," he said out loud.

He went through to the kitchen to find a mopping-up cloth. On the scribble board next to the telephone he had written Gordon Rutherford's number. He stared at it for a while, undecided, then he picked up the telephone and mechanically punched it out.

The phone rang for almost a minute. Then a cautious voice answered, "Ye-e-es?"

"Gordon?" said Stanley with a catch in his throat.

"Ye-e-es?" Quite archly, this time.

"Gordon, it's Stanley Eisner. Listen, Gordon, I have to see you."

"Are you all *right*, Stanley? You sound positively—I don't know—discombobulated."

"Can I see you? Please? It's very important," Stanley paused. Then he said, "To be frank with you, Gordon, I don't have anyone else."

The next morning the weather was brighter and warmer, almost like spring. For all of his burr, the BBC shepherd had been dramatically wrong. Stanley took the bus to St. Stephen's to keep a last appointment with Dr. Patel. It was little more than a formality. Dr. Patel had already told him that his internal injuries had healed well, and that he had suffered no brain damage from hitting his head on the pavement.

"But somehow you don't seem convinced that you *are* well," Dr. Patel remarked as he shuffled Stanley's notes and closed the folder.

Stanley tried to sound calm. "I keep having dreams that I'm sick ... that I'm coughing lumps of terrible stuff. I look out of the window and all I can see is people lying dead."

Dr. Patel looked melancholy and steepled his long, slender fingers. "Your mind is simply trying to find a way of dealing with what has happened to you, Mr. Eisner. Let me put it this way: your subconscious is seeking an explanation for something which is still inexplicable. Why did this fellow attack me? He hasn't yet been caught; he didn't explain himself in any way. So your mind is trying to construct an explanation—based on your religious upbringing, perhaps, and also on your quite-natural fear of contagious disease."

Dr. Patel took out a blindingly clean handkerchief and wiped his sad, watery eyes. "There is some element in your blood sample which has caused us some mystification, but as you already know, you are HIV-negative, and as far as we can say, you have no trace of any communicable infection of which modern pathology is aware."

Stanley swallowed tightly. "Thank you."

"I could recommend a psychiatrist, if you feel you have the need," Dr. Patel suggested.

Stanley shrugged. "I need something, but I don't know what. Revenge, maybe. I don't know. I didn't do anything, you know? Some goddamned revolting creature knocked me down on the sidewalk and raped me. I fought back. I mean, I really fought back. But he was so goddamned strong. And what did he weigh? Three hundred fifty, four hundred pounds. A gorilla."

"Yes, a gorilla," Dr. Patel replied, as if he had been thinking about something else altogether. Then he stood up and extended his hand. "Your body is healed, Mr. Eisner. You are free from infection. Any other difficulties you are experiencing are unfortunately outside my field of expertise. But do speak to my secretary if you wish to know the name of a psychiatrist. Whatever happens, I wish you all the best."

He hesitated and smiled faintly, and then he added, "You may be interested to know that I am quite a fan of yours, you know. I have all of your quintets on CD."

★

Gordon sat on the concrete embankment swinging his scuffed suede shoes. Beside him, he had almost ritualistically laid out his Carlsberg Special Brew and his packet of Silk Cut cigarettes and his Zippo-style lighter with a picture of Cliff Richard on it. Only a few yards away, trains echoed and rattled across a light-green-painted latticework bridge, on their way to Richmond, south of the Thames; and the narrow riverside path outside the Bull's Head pub was crowded with drinking and laughing weekenders; but Gordon lifted his beaklike nose to the unseasonably warm sunshine as if he were sitting alone, out in the countryside.

"Do you know something?" he remarked. "You could get quite a respectable tan if you sat here long, enough."

"Sure, but who wants to sit here for a year?" Stanley replied. He was leaning on the railings, looking out at the broad wind-ruffled surface of the Thames. The tide had turned about a half hour ago, and already a small dinghy moored by the steps was beginning to bob and spin in the rising current. Ducks paddled around, snatching at cheese-and-onion potato chips that a ginger-headed Duchess of York look-alike was tossing into the water.

"You're not beginning to feel homesick, are you?" Gordon asked him, basking, his eyes closed.

"Not yet. I guess I'm just disoriented, that's all. A stranger in a strange land."

"Any news when you might be invited to play again?"

Stanley shook his head. "In the opinion of the great and omnipotent Frederick Orme, it would be wiser for me to make completely certain of my recovery before I rejoin the orchestra."

"Did he say that before or after that report in the *Sun* that you'd been you-know-whatted?" Gordon wasn't usually shy of the word "rape" but the embankment outside the pub was very crowded and he didn't particularly want anyone to overhear. Stanley had suffered enough.

"After, of course," Stanley replied. "What do you think?"

"I think that the sooner you get back to normal, the better."

Stanley sipped his Guinness and shrugged. "I don't know. Frederick has some kind of a point. The way I'm feeling at the moment, I couldn't play anything worth shit."

"Have you *tried* playing? Or practicing, even? Even shit's better than nothing."

Stanley kept his eyes on the squabbling ducks. "I haven't even opened my violin case since I was attacked. Well, once, but I put it straight back again."

"Any particular reason?" asked Gordon. "I thought that music was therapeutic. They play Andy Williams records to people in comas. It's practically infallible. Nine out of ten times the patients wake up, shouting 'No more, no more! I'll wake up, please, but no more!'"

Stanley smiled. He liked the way Gordon refused to allow him to take himself too seriously. "I don't know. All the music seems to have drained out of me. I used to be able to think in staves, night and day. I used to be able to write music in my head. Now my whole brain seems to be filled up with guys in gray knitted hoods, and peculiar nightmares, and how crappy I feel."

"I still think that getting back to the orchestra would do you good. You know, get you cranked up again."

"That all depends on Frederick. My contract says that I'm obliged to play whenever the musical director asks me to play; but it doesn't give me any kind of guarantee that he *will* ask me to play. If he wants to pay me for sitting on my hands, there's nothing I Can do about it."

"Have you spoken to him about it?"

"Not lately."

"Perhaps you should. Perhaps you *need* to play."

"I don't know. I'll think about it."

"You're not embarrassed, are you? You know, by what's happened to you?"

"I don't know," said Stanley. "I suppose that's part of it. Embarrassed; maybe a little humiliated, too."

"What on earth do you have to be humiliated about?" Gordon asked him.

Stanley sipped his Guinness. It was strange stuff, black and earthy and gloomy, more like molasses than beer, but he was growing to like it. It had a bitterness that seemed appropriate. "Frederick seems to believe that what happened to me was entirely my own fault, that I actually left home that morning with the *intention* of getting myself assaulted."

Gordon, his eyes still closed, slowly nodded. "Tell me the old, old story," he said.

"What do you mean?"

"I mean, my dear Stanley, that you've come up against the English perception of sex. Sex, in England, is bracketed with road accidents; it's always considered to be somebody's *fault*, and more often than not it's the fault of the victim. The raped rather than the raper, the buggered rather than the bugger."

Stanley said, "I didn't think that this was going to be so hard to deal with."

"I told you it wouldn't be easy."

Stanley swilled the last of his Guinness around in his glass, and drained it. Watching him, Gordon suggested, "You could always go back home to New York."

"Not yet," said Stanley. "I need to face up to what's happened to me. I need to understand it. If I go back to the States, I might forget about it superficially, you know, but it's always going to be there, right in the back of my head, and I'm always going to be thinking *why*? Why did it happen to me? Why did I cross that street? Why did that guy attack me? Why couldn't I stop him? Why *didn't* I stop him?"

He paused, and then he looked around and added, "Besides, I feel that I haven't finished up here yet. There's something I have to do. Something I'm kind of caught up in."

"Such as?" asked Gordon.

"I don't know. It's just a feeling."

"Do you want another drink?" Gordon asked him.

"Sure, I'll pay for it."

"No, no. Have this one on Desert Orchid," said Gordon. When Stanley looked blank, he smiled, "It's a horse. It won."

He climbed to his feet and smacked the dust from the seat of his jeans.

Stanley said, "Do *you* think that it was my fault? Maybe just *partly* my fault? I mean, was there something inside of me, something subconscious, that actually encouraged that guy to jump on me?"

"Let me tell you something," Gordon replied. "I deal with six or seven rape victims every single month. Some of them are men—remand prisoners, or army cadets, or young male prostitutes. Most of them are women, from all kinds of backgrounds. You couldn't meet a more varied collection of people anywhere. But they all have to come to terms with the same feeling of self-doubt, and they all have to come to terms with the change in the way that people treat them after it's happened."

"Nine times out of ten, a rape victim will find that her friends and colleagues treat her radically differently from the way they did before she was assaulted. Her women friends will find excuses not to be quite so close any more, almost as if she's caught some terrible disease. And the men in her life will ostracize her, too, because she didn't play the game. A chap's entitled to a bit of fun, after all, and if she got knocked about a bit, well, sorry and all that, but that's sex for you. No need to whine about it."

Stanley said very softly, "How do they cope with it? These other victims you deal with? How the hell do they come to terms with it?"

Gordon took his empty glass. "The way that you're having to come to terms with it: by learning to ignore the monstrous prejudices of the world at large ... at least for as long as it takes you to convince yourself in your heart that what happened to you was a violent and totally unpreventable act for which you weren't at all to blame."

"Coming to terms with it, my dear Stanley, starts here, inside your own head. Treat yourself first; worry about the rest of the world later. Now, do you want some crisps?"

"Crisps, sure. Worcester sauce flavor, if they have them."

"Yuck. You're becoming too bloody Anglicized for your own good. Apart from the fact that it's pronounced *Wooster*, not *Whirr-sess-ter*."

"'Wooster,' got you."

★

Stanley watched the river traffic passing as he waited for Gordon to come back with their drinks; and listened to the ferocious rapid-fire sniping of weekend conversation.

"Dennis stripped the dado, and then we rag-rolled the walls in apricot," a young woman in a horsey headscarf was explaining.

"Well, I don't know, I've gone orf rag-rolling," another woman replied, her Butler & Wilson costume earrings swinging in the February sunlight. "It looks so desperately Habitat."

Behind Stanley, a meaty-shouldered young man in a houndstooth jacket was booming with satisfaction, "—beautiful job on it, tweaked the carbs, stiffened the rear suspension, goes like an absolute bomb."

A sight-seeing boat puttered slowly past, and everybody on deck waved at the shore, although nobody outside the Bull's Head waved back, or even looked at them. Stanley found himself wondering why they had waved. To show that they were having fun, even if they weren't? To try to reassure themselves that they were real? They wouldn't have waved if they had been simply walking past. In fact, they would have turned their faces away.

He wished he would stop having thoughts like that. But there was something about England that brought it on. Something not quite right, as if everybody were in a play.

He was still Watching the sight-seeing boat when he glimpsed somebody standing on the opposite bank of the river, over a quarter of a mile away. The trees were dark on the opposite bank, tall and melancholy poplars, their leaves glittering occasionally in the wind. The kind of trees that reminded Stanley of cemeteries, or municipal buildings.

He wasn't sure what it was that first attracted him to look at the figure. Maybe it was the way that it was just standing there, close to some broken-down railings and a boat shed, not moving. It was too far away for him to be able to see it clearly, but when he narrowed his eyes, he managed to distinguish that it was wearing a gray coat and some kind of gray hat.

A terrible cold feeling poured down him. He couldn't tell for sure, but supposing it was Knitted Hood? It *looked* like Knitted Hood, the way it was standing there, not moving. Its face was white—white as a distant handkerchief—but Stanley couldn't distinguish any more than that.

Should he call the police, even if he wasn't one hundred percent sure that it *was* Knitted Hood? Jesus—supposing Knitted Hood was watching him? Supposing Knitted Hood was out to get him again?

He looked urgently around for Gordon, but the pub was crowded to the doors, and Gordon was probably still waiting to be served.

It was then that he saw a pigskin binocular case that somebody had left on one of the outdoor tables. He pushed his way over to it and picked it up. "Pardon me!" he called out, holding them over his head. "Who do these belong to?"

The young man in the houndstooth jacket replied, "Me, as a matter of fact, and you can jolly well put them down. They're Zeiss."

"Would you mind if I borrowed them for just a couple of minutes?"

"Actually, I make it a rule not to lend anything, old man. Even my girlfriends."

His friends hooted with laughter.

"Listen, how about drinks all round?" Stanley suggested. He glanced quickly back across the river. The figure was still there, unmoving.

"Come on, Alex, that's a fair deal," one of the young men called out.

"Yes, come on, Alex, what about the special relationship?"

"Well, all right," said Alex. "But for God's sake don't drop them."

Stanley took out the binoculars and elbowed his way back to the railings. His place had already been taken by a tall girl with straight blond hair and a cigarette, and she was very reluctant to give him any room.

"Would you mind?" he asked her.

She looked at him down her nose and moved at least an eighth of an inch.

Stanley lifted the binoculars and focused them on the opposite bank of the river. He found the boat shed, the broken-down railings. He inched the binoculars a little to the left, where the figure had been standing, but the figure had vanished. Immediately, he swung the binoculars to the right, but there was no sign of the figure in that direction, either. He lowered the binoculars and peered across the river with his hand shielding his eyes against the sunlight.

He was still trying to see where the figure had disappeared to when Gordon came back with their drinks.

"What are you doing, bird watching?" he asked.

Stanley was almost about to tell him, when it suddenly occurred to him that he had probably been mistaken, and that the likelihood of the figure across the river being Knitted Hood was not only remote but ridiculous. It had probably been nothing more sinister than some old man taking his dog for a walk. If he told Gordon what he thought he had seen, Gordon would either call the police, with all the humiliation and embarrassment *that* would cause, or else he would begin to think that Stanley was becoming obsessive.

"I was watching the boats, is all," Stanley explained sheepishly. "That young fellow was kind enough to lend them to me."

"At a price!" called out one of Alex's friends loudly. "At a price!"

"That's right, mine's a large Bells and American," put in a leggy dark-haired girl with a profile like a thoroughbred horse.

"Holsten Pils for me," Alex declared.

Gordon asked Stanley, "What *have* you got yourself into, my dear? The Chiswick Mafia?"

"Give me a minute, I promised to buy them a round," Stanley told him.

Inside the Bull's Head it was smoky and noisy and jam-packed with drinkers. Stanley managed to force his way up to the oak-beamed bar, where he had to stand for nearly five minutes pressed between an old rheumy-eyed man with a hand-rolled cigarette smoldering between his lips and a potbellied young Australian with a bellowing laugh.

At last he was able to catch the attention of the young black man serving behind the bar; but while he was waiting for the drinks to be poured out, he felt somebody tapping him on the shoulder. He turned around and found himself face-to-face with a petite girl of eighteen or nineteen, her blond-streaked hair pulled up into a ribbon on top of her head so that she looked like a firework. Her blue eyes were heavily made up with glittery purple eye shadow, and her lips were almost white. She wore a black leather jacket and the shortest black miniskirt that Stanley had ever seen, exposing three inches of bare thigh, black nylon stocking tops, and black garters. In Napa she would have caused a serious public disturbance.

"Wotcha!" she shouted above the noise of laughter and conversation.

"Hi." Stanley smiled.

She looked him right in the eyes, smiling mischievously. "You don't know 'oo I am, do you?" she demanded.

"Have we met?" he asked her.

"Once," she told him. "That day you was attacked. I was the one what called a namblunce."

"Oh," said Stanley, nodding furiously. "In that case I owe you one."

"Are you all right now?" the girl wanted to know. "I read about it in the paper."

"I think the entire universe read about it in the paper," Stanley replied. "But, sure, I'm fine now, thanks. I'm still waiting to have my tooth fixed. You know, capped. Apart from that, though, I guess I'm pretty much fully recovered."

"That was really awful," the girl told him. She was watching his eyes with a sort of innocent relentlessness, to see how he was going to react.

"Yeah, it was—really awful," Stanley agreed. He couldn't stop himself from flinching, turning away.

"Did they ever catch the bloke?"

Stanley shook his head. "Doubt if they ever will. I don't know whether you saw it, but he was wearing some kind of mask. Not to mention that hood."

"'E was so bloody 'orrible, don't you think? Ugh. All dirty and greasy. Know what I mean? Are you all right now, then?"

"I'm fine, believe me. Can I buy you a drink?"

"I'm supposed to be with my boyfriend."

"Will your boyfriend mind if I buy you a drink?"

"Not so long as you buy 'im one, too."

Stanley asked for a pint of Fosters for the boyfriend and a gin-and-orange for the girl. The whole round cost him nearly twenty-two pounds. While he was rummaging through his coat pocket for change, the girl said, "My name's Angie, by the way. Angie Dunning."

Stanley shook her hand. "Pleased to know you. Do you live around here?"

"Just across the road, 'erbert Gardens. Got a flat there—well, there's five of us sharing. Lived 'ere for ages, ever since I come to London. The only reason I was in Fulham that day you was attacked was that I was coming 'ome from a party."

"Well, listen," said Stanley, "maybe there's something I can give you ... you know, something to say thank you. A record, maybe. What kind of music do you like?"

"Oh, I dunno. Roachford, Bros, Kylie Minogue."

Stanley smiled. "Not quite what I'm into, I'm afraid."

"What do you play, then? Classical? Like James Last and stuff?"

"Something like that."

A tall young man with cropped fair hair and

scarlet-erupting cheeks came pushing his way over from the adjacent bar.

"'Oo's this, then?" he asked Angie.

"Stanley Eisner," said Stanley, holding out his hand.

"'E's the violinist bloke what got attacked and I was the witness," Angie explained.

"Oh, yeah?" demanded the young man belligerently.

"This is Paul," said Angie, as if that explained everything.

"I, uh, bought you a drink, Paul," said Stanley.

"Oh, yeah?" said Paul.

Stanley went back outside and rejoined Gordon, who was checking his watch and looking tetchy.

"Your Whirrsesster crisps are getting stale," said Gordon rather tartly.

"I'm sorry," Stanley told him. "I just met the girl who called the ambulance when I was attacked. I wanted to say thank you."

Gordon looked at his watch again. "I'm going to have to leave you in a minute. My brother and his family are coming up from Maidenhead."

"Listen," said Stanley, "I haven't thanked you yet for everything you've been doing for me. I want you to know that I appreciate it. I don't know how I would have kept my sanity if it hadn't been for you,"

Gordon pursed his lips, then smiled and nodded. "I'm not sure that sanity is worth keeping, but you're quite welcome."

Stanley opened up his bag of crisps and leaned back against the railings. The river was so high now that waves were beginning to slop over the embankment, and the ducks could swim right up beside their feet. "Do you know much about dreams?" he asked Gordon.

"In what way?" said Gordon. "You mean Freud, symbolism, that kind of thing? Carrot equals penis, grotto equals vagina?"

"I'm not sure," Stanley told him. "I had a dream when I was still in hospital, about the guy in the knitted hood, and it wasn't like a dream at all. It was like it was really happening. I mean, I wasn't at all aware that I'd fallen asleep. Then I had another dream last night. It was just the same ... I went straight into the dream without any real sensation of going to sleep. I was sick, I puked up this lump like a clam or an oyster, and it was alive. And Knitted Hood was there, too."

Gordon swallowed beer and said nothing.

"Do you think I'm going crazy?" Stanley asked him.

"Maybe," said Gordon. "Sometimes I think that being crazy is the only thing that keeps me sane."

"I mean seriously."

"Did you mention these dreams to Dr. Patel?"

"He thinks my subconscious is trying to come to terms with my being raped. He said I should go see a shrink if it got too bad."

"I used to dream about my Aunt Millie's knickers once," said Gordon. "I think that was what finally decided me to go gay"

"I thought I saw him just now," said Stanley.

"Who?" Gordon asked him, squinting against the sunlight.

"Knitted Hood. I thought I saw him across the river."

Gordon frowned across the Thames, towards the tall dark trees. Then he looked back at Stanley. "Is that what you were doing with those binoculars?"

Stanley said, "I didn't want to tell you directly. I didn't want you to do anything—I don't know, *official*, like calling the cops. It could have been a hallucination. It could have been somebody else altogether—somebody who looked like Knitted Hood, but wasn't. It's a good half mile off."

"I wouldn't have called the police, you know," Gordon replied. "Not unless you'd wanted me to. As far as I'm concerned, the most important thing is for you to get your head back together again. Catching this Knitted Hood character comes a pretty long way behind that."

He finished his beer. "I'd better go now, Bryan and Margie will kill me. But if there's anything you want, you can always call the center, anytime you like. You've got a long way to go, you know. Inside your head, you haven't even started to accept what's happened to you. So, take it easy, *comprende*?"

He gave Stanley a ride in his unwashed Austin Montego as far as Kew Bridge, On the back seat were stacks of old Sunday newspapers and a stuffed otter that had seen better days. Around his feet as he drove were tides of crumpled red Topic wrappers. "I never get time to eat lunch. A Topic's a meal in itself, don't you think?"

Stanley had intended to catch a bus or a taxi back home; but after Gordon dropped him off, he realized that he was only three or four minutes' walk from the Royal Botanic Gardens. He crossed the river, half deafened by passing buses and trucks, and then walked along Kew Green, bordered on both sides by elegant eighteenth-century town houses. As he passed St. Ann's Church, bells began to toll, slowly, funereally, and a breeze scurried across the bright green grass like frightened cats. Stanley wished he had brought his Burberry. The sun was glaring, but out in the wind the day was still chilly.

He entered the gates of Kew Gardens and walked alone along the wide, open pathway. On either side, trees nodded in the wind, nondescript to Stanley, who knew nothing about trees, but each with a label announcing that it was rare or special. The trees were still leafless, most of them, but already budding, and in the middle distance Stanley could see crowds of daffodils, almost too yellow to be real. He walked for almost five minutes, hearing nothing but the wind, and his own breathing, and the crunch of his shoes, and seeing scarcely anybody at all, just a few raincoated figures moving on other diagonal paths between the trees, their faces blurred in the shadows.

He passed a bench where a very old man sat in a plaid scarf and a barathea coat and a beautifully-brushed homburg. The very old man was patiently eating an ice-cream cone with two chocolate flake bars stuck in it like rabbit's ears. He passed another bench where a worried-looking black woman sat, endlessly rocking a baby buggy. A small coffee-colored half-caste boy with curly blond hair sat in the buggy, fast asleep.

A swathe through the world, thought Stanley.

At last he emerged beside a wide slate-black lake, where swans circled. Overlooking the lake was a vast Victorian glasshouse, two or three stories high. Its windows were steamed up, but through the misted glass panes, Stanley could make out the shapes of huge tropical palms and creepers, and iron catwalks that allowed visitors to view them from high above.

It was like something out of a dream; or *The Lost World*, by Arthur Conan Doyle, a vision of pterodactyls in Victorian London. Although he couldn't put his finger on the reason why, Stanley began to feel stressed and disturbed, and his mouth felt dry.

He looked around. A toddler was lying on the ground, kicking his legs, refusing to walk any further. His mother called, "Stay there, then! See if I care!" The wind was blowing even more penetratingly, and although he felt unsettled, there was no doubt that the Palm House looked warm. Stanley circled around to the end of it, opened the white-painted door, and stepped inside. Immediately he started to cough. It wasn't just warm inside, it was tropical, and the humidity was overwhelming. Stanley had to stay by the door for a moment, taking deep breaths to acclimatize himself.

With every breath, he took in the dank smell of equatorial vegetation. An old woman in yellow-tinted spectacles was standing not far away, watching him oddly, almost as if she recognized him. He tried to smile at her, and gasped, "Good morning."

After a while, however, the woman abruptly disappeared, and he caught his breath. He waited for a moment or two, and then he ventured further inside, making his way through huge feathery palms and twisted trunks. He saw two or three other visitors, at the far end of the glasshouse, but apart from them he appeared to be alone. He wiped his forehead with the back of his hand. The humidity was so high that perspiration was beginning to trickle down his back.

He walked to the very center of the Palm House, craning his neck so that he could see the tallest trees. He had almost decided that he was warm enough now—*too* warm, in fact—when he glimpsed somebody high on one of the iron catwalks above him, half hidden by the dark silhouetted leaves.

He shivered. There was something about the way the figure was standing—leaning, not moving—that reminded him too much of Knitted Hood. He cautiously circled the pathway around the palms, glancing upwards from time to time to make sure that the figure hadn't vanished. But it remained where it was, motionless. Who went to visit a Palm House and just *stood* there?

Stanley came around the iron pillars, keeping well back among the palm fronds so that the figure wouldn't be able to see him. He parted the fronds with his fingers and peered up at the catwalk. The figure had somehow contrived to keep its back to him, but there was no doubt about it. That soiled gray raincoat, that gray knitted hood; that hunched and peculiarly distorted posture.

Stanley looked around. No bobbies in sight. Never were, when you really needed one. So what was he going to do? Climb up to the catwalk and challenge Knitted Hood to a face-to-face fistfight? Run for the nearest telephone booth and risk Knitted Hood escaping?

He bit his lip. He was still feeling a whole lot less than one hundred percent physically, and he had already experienced enough of Knitted Hood's strength and weight to know that he wouldn't stand a chance, not without a baseball bat or a .44 Magnum. He was a classical violinist, for God's sake. His fingers were strong, he played a mean game of squash, but his pectorals could hardly be described as Ramboesque. Quite apart from sheer physical strength, he would need something else to deal with Knitted Hood, and that was will. Right now he wasn't sure how much of that particular commodity he possessed.

Supposing he went for the cops? There didn't seem to be much future in that, either. Knitted Hood had obviously been following him, and would see him straightaway, and guess what he was doing. He would have to be a retard to be still waiting here when Stanley returned with the boys in blue.

No, thought Stanley. *What I'm going to do is. I'm going to turn the tables on you, my friend. I'm going to follow you.*

He shuffled back into the palm fronds, just far enough to make it more difficult for Knitted Hood to see where he was; but not too far to restrict his own reasonably clear view of both ends of the Palm House. There was no chance now that Knitted Hood would be able to leave the building without Stanley spotting him.

Then Stanley waited, quietly perspiring, his hands clasped in front of him like a saint, or a tailor's dummy, trying to remain calm, trying to remain still.

Several people passed him by and stared at him curiously. Two young girls said, "Excuse me, are you Tarzan?" and burst into fits of hysterical giggles. All Stanley could do was smile, and hope that Knitted Hood hadn't heard them. He glanced surreptitiously sideways now and again. Each time he looked, the grayish figure was still standing there, hunched over the white-painted railings of the catwalk.

Waiting for Knitted Hood was both tedious and

frightening. Although it seemed highly probable, he didn't know for sure that Knitted Hood had been following him. There was still the possibility that Knitted Hood didn't even realize that Stanley was around; and that his appearance here was nothing but a hideous coincidence. Maybe he was waiting for somebody else. Maybe he was watching somebody else. Maybe he had come here to look at the palms, and to warm himself up, just like Stanley had done.

Almost twenty minutes went past. Outside the misted-up windows, the sun abruptly swirled itself behind the clouds, like a temperamental opera singer flouncing off the stage, and without warning the afternoon turned photographic and hard. Inside the Palm House, it was suddenly so gloomy that Stanley could scarcely see from one end to the other.

He looked up at the catwalk. Knitted Hood had turned into a fretted shadow; but as far as Stanley could make out, he was still there, still motionless, still waiting. Stanley tugged his handkerchief out of his pocket and wiped the perspiration from his face. His shirt was clinging to his back, and his handmade Alan McAfee shoes felt as if they were totally sodden.

Another five minutes went by. Then Stanley heard the door of the Palm House open, and close again. A woman in a long black silky-finished coat came rustling through the palms. Stanley couldn't distinguish her face very well in the shadows, but her hair gleamed thin and fine and very long, so blond that it was almost silver. Her shoes tip-tapped softly on the wet flagged pathways between the plants.

She came directly to the center of the Palm House, around the pillars, and suddenly stopped, only four or five feet away from Stanley's hiding place, although she didn't look at him. She appeared to be young middle-aged, late thirties or early forties, with the kind of high-cheekboned Zsa Zsa Gabor looks that had been popular in Hollywood in the 1960s. Stanley caught the scent of Giorgio perfume, Beverly Hills' best.

The woman hesitated, and looked around, and then up at the towering palms.

"You're interested in palms, Mr. Eisner?" the woman asked him, still without looking at him. She emphasized the word "interested."

Stanley stared at her. "You know me?" he asked her, keeping his voice to a hoarse whisper.

She turned and smiled. Her eyes were the palest amber, the color of agates.

"Of course I know you. Why are you so surprised? You are a musician of international standing. There is a photograph of you in the *Encyclopedia of Music*."

Stanley shrugged. "I don't know. I'm sorry. To me that seems like some kind of exceptional talent, you know? To be able to walk right into a tropical greenhouse in London and recognize a musician from San Francisco without even taking a breath. I mean, I'm a classical violinist, not a pop star."

"You have other qualities, Mr. Eisner."

Stanley quickly glanced up at the catwalk to see if Knitted Hood was still there. The Palm House was so shadowy now that it was impossible to tell for sure. But he hadn't heard Knitted Hood's cloglike feet on the iron staircases that led down from the catwalks, and he hadn't heard either of the doors opening, so it was pretty safe to assume that Knitted Hood was still here.

"Listen," he said softly, making a patting gesture in the air with his hand. "I'm very flattered that you recognized me, ma'am. But I'm a little preoccupied right now. I'm sort of waiting for someone."

The woman made no attempt to move on. "Palms are worth studying, you know," she told him. "We get raffia from palms, we get oil from palms, we get sago from palms. They are all so different, yet so alike. Look at this huge tree here, *Lodoicea*, the coco-de-mer. It has a nut which weighs several kilograms. Yet it belongs to the same family as this long thin rattan, of the genus *Calamus*, which can grow to a length of one hundred and fifty meters, occasionally more."

"That's very interesting, ma'am, very nice," Stanley told her. "The only trouble is—I really have to wait for this person—and if I miss them—"

"He has already left," the woman replied.

Stanley coughed. "I beg—I beg your pardon? What?"

"The person for whom you are waiting. He has already left."

Stanley gingerly parted the palm fronds with his hand. Then he stepped out and peered directly up at the catwalk. The woman was right: Knitted Hood was no longer there.

"Son of a bitch," Stanley muttered under his breath.

The woman watched him calmly and without comment as he hurried across to the spiral staircase and clanged noisily up to the place where Knitted Hood had been standing. It was unnervingly high up here, overlooking the tops of the palms, like an aerial view of the jungle. Sparrows twittered all around him, rushing from one perch to another in noisy flocks. He looked from one end of the Palm House to the other, but there was no sign of Knitted Hood anywhere.

No movement, no shadow. Only the darkly-steaming palm leaves, and the trailing creepers, and the first flicker of lightning in the far distance, toward the southwest.

"Did you see him go?" Stanley demanded, his voice echoing.

The woman shook her head. "He decided to leave, that's all; and so he left."

"I don't understand."

"There is much that you don't understand; but you will."

"What, are you a friend of his or something?"

"Of course not. But come down here, and I will tell you."

Stanley took one last look around the upper galleries of the Palm House; then slowly he descended the iron stairs. The woman was waiting for him when he came down.

"I think you owe me some kind of an explanation," he told her. His voice was trembling.

The woman smiled; and Stanley saw then that there was more to her personality than her appearance had led him to think. She may have looked like Zsa Zsa Gabor, but she knew who he was; and she knew her botany; and she knew where Knitted Hood had gone, too; and even the fact that Stanley had been looking for him.

"Mr. Eisner," the woman told him, "I owe you nothing at all. On the contrary, it is *you* who owe something to me; or, at least, you owe something to those whom I represent."

She held out her hand. Her fingernails were very long and painted Hawaiian pink. She wore five or six diamond rings on one hand alone; peculiarly ostentatious for a woman whose words were so subtle and oblique. Stanley noticed one thing: the skin on the back of her hands was very taut and smooth, suggesting that she was much younger than she had first appeared. Eve had sat in front of the dressing-table mirror every evening, pinching the skin on the back of her hands. The time it took for the pinch of skin to return to normal was an infallible giveaway to a person's genuine age. "You can tighten your face, you can lift up your boobs, but you can never change your hands." That was Eve's theory, anyway; and whenever Stanley was introduced to women these days, he found himself discreetly checking the backs of their hands.

Stanley said, "I don't even know who you are. How can I owe you anything?"

"Come for a walk," the woman suggested. "I will show you where you can find the person you have been looking for; and I will also tell you why I have come to meet you."

"Now, wait up a goddamn minute, will you?" Stanley objected. "I don't even know who you are. I mean, for all I know, you could be this guy's friend—accomplice, or whatever."

"If you come with me, I will try my best to explain everything," the woman told him. Stanley found it impossible to place her accent. It certainly wasn't British; and it wasn't French; but it was flatter and more precise than any American regional variations that he had ever heard; an unidentifiable mixture of gentrified Charleston and privately-educated Swiss. Posh, but somehow lacking in poshness because it boasted no recognized background.

Stanley wiped his forehead with the back of his hand. "Okay," he agreed at last. There didn't seem to be anything else that he could do.

They left the Palm House and walked around the lake. Behind them, the sky was as black as Bibles, and there were spatters of rain in the wind. The swans had left the water and were strutting inelegantly across the pathway. The woman's coat flapped and rustled as she walked. She said, "You don't have to hurry, he's not going very far."

"Do you know who he is?" Stanley asked her.

"I know *what* he is."

"All right, then, what is he?"

"He's what we call a Carrier. There are ten or eleven of them at least, perhaps more."

"A Carrier? You mean like a truck driver?"

"No, Mr. Eisner. Not like a truck driver. He carries a virus, of sorts. A kind of disease."

Stanley swallowed. "A disease? He has a *disease*? Is it catching?"

"That depends."

Stanley stopped, and the woman stopped, too, just outside the garden turnstiles. "Listen," he said, "don't think I'm being deliberately offensive here, but do you mind telling me who the hell you are? You didn't come here by accident, did you? How come you know so much about this Knitted Hood guy, this Carrier? How come you know so much about *me?*"

"You've been having dreams, haven't you?" the woman asked him. The wind blew her fine blond hair across her face.

Stanley gave her an almost imperceptible nod, which he tried to turn into a shake of denial, but too late.

"Dreams of sickness? Dreams of plague?"

"Yes," Stanley told her. He felt disturbed, panicky. Dr. Patel had told him he was clear of any infection, but he hadn't been feeling particularly well, and the dreams had unsettled him even during the day. He didn't even have to close his eyes to recall the way those corpses had come sliding off the pushcart, like a load of dead fish. The mother's face, agonized. The smudged black eyes of the baby.

The woman said, "You feel anxious, am I correct? Your blood feels as if it's full of tiny prickly particles? You feel giddy and disoriented, as if you're jet-lagged?"

"What is it?" Stanley insisted, "Does it get worse? How serious is it?"

The woman glanced toward the turnstiles. "We'd better be moving on, we don't want to miss him."

"You know what happened to me, don't you?" said Stanley, breathless, keeping close beside her. "You know why I'm following this son of a bitch?"

"Yes, I know," the woman replied. "I knew about it almost as soon as it happened. That was how you contracted your infection."

"But what the hell is it? Is it some kind of blood disease, what?"

"It's a form of immune deficiency."

Stanley's lips felt numb, as if his mouth had been anesthetized. "You mean I have AIDS?"

"You have an infection. It has parallels with AIDS in some respects. It's passed on by sexual intercourse, particularly by anal intercourse, but also by biting and by sharing of hypodermic needles."

"It's similar to AIDS but it's not AIDS, is that it?"

"That's right."

"Is it as serious as AIDS?"

They had left the gardens now and were waiting by

the curb to cross the main road outside. Buses and trucks bellowed past them, blowing up showers of fine grit.

The woman said, "I would be deceiving you, Mr. Eisner, if I pretended that it wasn't."

"Does it have a name?"

"In the seventeenth century they called it the Bard's Disease, because Shakespeare was supposed to have died of it. It has also been called the Haitian Pox. There is no question at all that Mozart was infected."

"I never heard of it. Believe me, I never even heard of it."

"It's been lying dormant for a long time, Mr. Eisner. There haven't been any major outbreaks recorded since the late 1600s. One or two isolated cases, yes; some of them well recorded; but nothing widespread."

Stanley swallowed again. He felt as if he were suddenly going mad. "Is it, uh …? This—what—Bard's Disease? Is it terminal? I mean, is there any chance of recovery? Any kind of treatment?"

"That will depend on you; and those who are chosen to help you."

"I don't understand."

"You will, Mr. Eisner, if you trust me."

"Trust you? I don't even *know* you!"

The woman, unexpectedly, smiled at him. "You're *sure* you don't know me?"

"Why should I know you? Are you a doctor? A reporter? This doesn't make any kind of sense to me at all!"

"Please, Mr. Eisner, don't get angry. I'm here to help you, if I can; as well as to ask for *your* help, in return."

"Help? You want *my* help? You're telling me I've contracted some fatal disease that Shakespeare died of, I mean what kind of crap is that? *Shakespeare?* And then you want me to help you?"

A tour coach had parked across the street, *"Glückliche Fahrt, Düsseldorf,"* and as they disembarked, a group of German teenagers turned to stare at them as if they were a local tourist attraction: Stanley's sudden anger, the woman's dated beauty.

"Mr. Eisner—" the woman cautioned him. "Please, don't get upset."

"Don't get upset? What are you trying to do to me here?"

"Mr. Eisner, the Carrier didn't attack you at random. He knew who you were. He was waiting for you."

"He purposely wanted to infect a violinist, is that it?"

"Aaron, you're much, much more than just a violinist." Stanley stared at her. "What did you call me?"

"Aaron. It's your name, isn't it?"

"Sure, yes, but how did *you* know?" Stanley retorted. "The only living people who know that my name is Aaron are my mother and my sister. That's it, nobody else."

"Please, Mr. Eisner, I'm sorry," the woman soothed him. "You were named Aaron, but everybody called you Stanley when you were little because you had such a squeaky voice and your hair stuck up like Stan Laurel's, and you just— well, you just *looked* like Stan Laurel."

"How the *hell* did you know that?" Stanley raged at her.

"Will you stop being angry and let me explain?"

"I don't think I want to stop being angry."

"Mr. Eisner—Stanley … listen, let's just carry on walking. Walk, listen. Don't be angry. The truth is, you've become involved in something that you can't really deal with, not on your own, and not as yourself."

"Not as myself? What's that supposed to mean?"

The woman took his arm; the gesture was sisterly and peculiarly comforting. They were walking up a side street now, between dull big Victorian houses and rows of blistered plane trees.

"My name is Madeleine Springer," the woman explained.

"You're not British, are you?" Stanley asked her.

"Not exactly. But not exactly American, either. But that really doesn't matter so much. What matters is who *you* are; and who your ancestors were."

"Why should that matter?"

Madeleine Springer smiled at him. "To most people, Stanley, it isn't important who their ancestors were. Miners, weavers, farmers, what does it matter? Their skills and their failings died when they died, and they were never remembered. But some ancestors had a special duty and accepted special obligations—not only on their own behalf but on behalf of all of their descendants, forever."

Stanley had a sudden urge to escape, to pull himself free from Madeleine Springer's arm and walk briskly away. In most respects, however, she appeared to be sane; and more than anything else it was this penetrating sanity that kept him from leaving. He found the obscurity of her conversation infuriating. He was a man who was used to saying what he had to say, in the simplest words he could think of. Her patronizing attitude annoyed him, too. Yet she was calm and beautiful, and she had already convinced him that what she had to tell him was important; life-and-death important.

He just wished that she would come out with it direct. His mind was in enough of a turmoil, holding on to his sense of reality, holding on to his musical talent, trying to deal with Eve and Leon and all the physical and emotional consequences of Knitted Hood's attack; and there would be even more for him to cope with if Madeleine Springer was telling the truth and Knitted Hood had infected him with some AIDS-like disease.

He said sharply, "You're talking about *my* ancestors, or what?"

"Of course."

"My ancestors had some special duty, and they passed that duty on to me?"

"Yes, in a word."

Stanley stopped beside a low brick garden wall and a privet hedge clogged with discarded ice-lolly wrappers. "Listen, Ms. Springer, I don't even know who my ancestors were. My family goes back as far as Hamburg, Germany, in 1880 something. We were emigrants. That's all I know."

"Your ancestors, Stanley, go back much further; to 1620 at least; and to London. Thirteen generations ago, Jacob Eisner was a ragpicker in Whitechapel."

Stanley lifted both hands in mock surrender. "Ms. Springer, this is really very entertaining, but I think that you've mistaken me for somebody else. I'm a Jewish American, my grandfather came from Hamburg, my family have no connection with Britain whatsoever. I'm here on a professional exchange scheme, that's all. A British musician went to San Francisco, I came here."

"How did I find you?" Madeleine Springer challenged him. "How did I know your name was Aaron?"

"I don't know, Ms. Springer; and I don't really think that I care. Maybe you read the *Sun* newspaper and have a perverted interest in men who have been assaulted by other men. I don't know. But I think I'm going to leave now, and go back to my apartment, and pour myself a very large drink."

Madeleine Springer suddenly switched her gaze to look over Stanley's shoulder. "There he is," she said, her voice quiet but very clear.

Stanley immediately turned around. On the opposite corner of the street stood a large brindled-brick house, with broken guttering and a sadly-neglected garden. But Stanley had turned just a split second too late to see anyone entering it. All he saw was the weather-faded front door slamming shut, its knocker barking once. The lights switched on, then lights switched off.

"That was him?" Stanley demanded.

"Tall, with a gray raincoat and a gray woollen balaclava?" Madeleine Springer asked him.

"That's it, kind of a hood."

"Yes, that was him. He was the one who attacked you, wasn't he?"

"Does he *live* there?" said Stanley.

Madeleine smiled faintly at the brindled-brick house. A sign on the half-collapsed front gate announced that somebody had once named it "Tennyson." "Nobody *lives* there, Mr. Eisner. Not in the sense that you think of anybody living there."

"What is it—a what-do-you-call-it—a squat? I mean, if that's his permanent address—if he comes back every night—"

Madeleine said, "It's no use calling the police, Mr. Eisner. The police couldn't find him, not in there, and neither could you. I can't stop him. The police can't stop him. *You* can't stop him, not as you are. You could search that house until doomsday; and he simply wouldn't be there."

"You told me he just went in through the door."

"That's right, he did. And you were waiting for him in the Palm House."

Stanley thrust his hands into his pockets. "Ms. Springer, I think I've had it up to here with this game. I don't know who you are, or why you're here, but enough is enough."

Almost immediately a black taxi came around the corner with its For Hire light on. Stanley raised his arm and gave the cabbie his special Broadway-after-the-theater whistle; the one that was guaranteed to stop a Doberman pinscher in its tracks. The taxi pulled into the curb, and Stanley opened the door.

At the last moment, however, he relented a little. He turned to Madeleine Springer, opened his wallet, and took out one of his cards. "Look, listen—if you want to call me sometime … provided you want to tell me something that makes some kind of sense …"

Madeleine Springer smiled and shook her head. "Don't worry, Aaron, I know where to find you."

He frowned at her. "You're not upset, are you?"

"Of course not," she replied.

"You knew that I was going to lose my temper, didn't you?"

"I would have lost my temper, too, if I had been you."

"Then what happens next?" he asked her.

"What happens next is that you go home, and you think about what I have told you. Then, when you are ready, we will talk some more."

"You know that I don't want to believe you."

"Of course you don't."

Without saying anything further, Stanley climbed into the taxi and slammed the door. "Langton Street," he told the driver.

They drove away. Stanley turned and looked out of the taxi's rear window. Madeleine Springer remained where she was on the sidewalk, not smiling, her hair lifted by the wind. For a flicker of a moment, Stanley thought, *Yes, you're right, I do know you. I've met you before.* But then the feeling vanished, and the cabbie was saying, "Langton Street, that's just past the World's End, innit, mate?" and all that Stanley could do was sit back in his seat and think about Knitted Hood, the Carrier; and the real or imagined infection known as the Bard's Disease.

Chapter Three

Violin Song

Back at Stanley's apartment, a letter was waiting for him, hand-delivered. He didn't open it immediately, but tossed it on to the table in the dining area and left it there while he drew the curtains and switched on the fire. In the left-hand corner, the envelope carried an embossed treble clef and the name "Kensington Chamber Orchestra." Whatever Frederick Orme had to say, Stanley didn't want to know what it was; not yet.

He went to the kitchen, chipped three or four ice cubes out of the freezer with a dinner knife, and poured himself a jumbo-sized glass of Wodka Wyborowa. Then he went back into the living room and put on a CD of Handel's *Messiah*.

He had the strangest feeling that ever since Knitted Hood had attacked him, he had lost control of his own destiny—that it didn't matter where he went or what he did, he was playing out a part in a carefully-arranged plan. Why had he gone to Kew Gardens, for instance, when he could have gone anywhere, from Richmond Park to Hampstead Heath?

Or perhaps Knitted Hood would have been waiting for him on Hampstead Heath, too, with Madeleine Springer not far behind.

He sat down in his armchair and took a large mouthful of vodka. Tomorrow he would go back to Kew, he decided, and take a look at the house in which Knitted Hood was supposed to live—or *not* live, however Madeleine Springer's words could be interpreted.

Hallelujah! sang the Handel chorus, *Hallelujah! Hallelujah!*

Stanley drank more vodka and loosened his necktie. He felt slightly feverish, and although he had been trying to persuade himself all afternoon that the prickling sensation in his blood was less uncomfortable than it had been before, it was still noticeable, and if it was anything at all, it was slightly worse.

Hallelujah! screamed the chorus. *Hallelujah!*

Although he couldn't understand why, he found the singing irritating. What the hell did they think they were doing, screeching out their adoration like that, to some completely illusory God? They sounded worse than orangutans screeching in the trees, and just as mindless.

Hallelujah! Hallelujah! Halle-loo-oo-jah!

Stanley stood up again. He went to the sideboard and unscrewed the top of the vodka bottle and poured himself another large drink. He was confused and irritated, and the bottle rattled against the side of the glass. He had always adored the *Messiah* in the past. Why did it grate on him so much now? Yet the longer it went on, the more it annoyed him, almost as if the chorus were insulting him personally by praising the Lord.

He crossed the room and opened the curtains a little

way, so that he could see outside. Maybe Knitted Hood was prowling around again. Maybe that was what was causing his blood to prickle and his nerves to scrape like a badly-tuned violin. But outside in the sodium-orange street, there was nobody. Only parked cars, and a cat that fled across the intersection like a drop of mercury pouring across an orange carpet.

I am the pestilence that was *promised*, Knitted Hood had warned him.

He stood staring at the empty street for minute after minute, his teeth clenched together, while the chorus sang *Hallelujah* and his hand gripped the curtain so tightly that he heard the metal curtain hooks tearing one by one out of the fabric binding.

King of kings! Hallelujah! Hallelujah!

He couldn't stand it. It was worse than listening to a thousand knives scraped across a thousand plates. It wasn't just cacophonous, either. It was insulting; and it was *painful*. It made his blood feel like barbed wire, racing viciously furiously through his arteries, snagging and tearing at his veins, all the way down his legs and his arms, around his shoulders, into his neck, ripping at the membranes of his brain, catching and snagging at his heart muscles.

He tried to control himself. He squeezed his eyes tight shut and bit the flesh inside his mouth until blood-streaked saliva began to creep down his chin. He uttered an extraordinary noise; halfway between a groan and a deep hum. Then everything burst.

He stormed across the room, heaved up the hi-fi, and smashed it down on the table. The CD gave a single warped shriek and stopped. Stanley tore out all of the hi-fi's wire, lifted it over his head, and threw it across the room, so that it hit the doorjamb with a deafening crash and tumbled over and over into the kitchen.

He stood in the middle of the room, panting and shivering. *I am the pestilence that was promised!* He felt as if he had been running hard for six or seven blocks, his mouth parched, his breathing harsh, his heart pounding. Very slowly, rubbing his upper arms like a man trying to reassure himself that he was still real, he sank to his knees, and remained on his knees.

What's happening to me? I used to adore Handel. The Messiah used to bring tears to my eyes. Now it sounds lewd and discordant, an outpouring of smutty absurdity, set to music. King of kings, what kind of shit was that?

After a long time, he grasped the arm of the sofa and levered himself up into a standing position again. He turned and went back to the window. He had tugged the curtain so violently that half of it was hanging down and could no longer be drawn all the way across. He tried, feeling irritated and petulant, but all he succeeded in doing was tearing more of it down.

Langton Street remained orange-lit and deserted. "What's happening to you?" Stanley asked himself, out loud this time, as if he were somebody else. *Am I really sick, or is this nothing more than delayed shock? Dr. Patel explained that people in shock can suffer strange changes in personality. They can become strangers to themselves, as well as to other people.*

He swallowed the rest of his vodka and retched loudly, bringing some of it back up into his mouth, awash with half-digested shepherd's pie, from the lunch he had eaten at the Bull's Head. Strangely, it tasted good. Sour and thick, a soup of alcohol and potato and grainy fragments of ground lamb, which Gordon had called "mince." He swallowed it back slowly, relishing it. *That's better. Who cares what doctors think? Dr. Patel can go screw himself. Madeleine Springer can go screw herself. The whole screwing world can go screw itself.*

He went back to the sideboard to refill his glass, his tongue still probing fragments of sour mince from the side of his mouth. As he unscrewed the cap of the Wyborowa bottle, he looked down and saw the letter from Frederick Orme. He turned it this way and that as he poured out more vodka; then he ripped the envelope open with his teeth and shook the letter out one-handed.

"Dear Stanley: We have arranged a magnificent charity concert at the Albert Hall on March 8, comprising all of Mozart's six string quintets. The concert will benefit the National Society for the Prevention of Cruelty to Children, and we are hoping that at least one member of the Royal Family will agree to attend. This concert would be a most auspicious and fitting occasion for your return to the orchestra, and I am hoping—"

Slowly, Stanley crumpled up the letter and tossed it across the living room. Who the hell did Frederick Orme think he was? When Stanley had been hurt and degraded, Frederick Orme had given him nothing. Nothing but a bunch of five forced daffodils and a cretinous book of short stories. But it was different now. Now that his rape had been forgotten by the daily press, Frederick Orme wanted him back. *A most auspicious and fitting occasion*, bullshit.

He took a large mouthful of vodka, swilling it around his

mouth before he swallowed it. The whole world was crowded with liars and idiots and sycophants. There was no future in it, everybody knew that. We were all wallowing in our own shit and our own self-righteousness. How could anybody sing "Hallelujah!" when we were up to our necks in our own sewage, and even the air we took into our lungs to praise this so-called Lord of Creation was unfit for human consumption?

The world was a joke. A ridiculous maniacal joke. And if Knitted Hood had infected him, and he passed on that same infection to somebody else; and if that somebody else passed on the same infection to two somebody elses; and those two somebody elses passed it on to eight somebody elses; and so on; forever; until the whole damned world was infected and damned; then what of it?

He went angrily back to the window, tore down the curtain completely, and swirled it across the room like a heavy brown cloak.

When he turned back to the window, however, he stopped absolutely still. A cold prickling feeling brushed down the back of his neck. His hyperventilated breathing abruptly quietened; so much so that his lungs felt starved of oxygen, and he started to pant.

Langton Street was still orange-lit and lined with parked cars. But down the center of the street, very slowly, with all the determination of great disgust and inconsolable grief, a girl was pushing a handcart heaped high with lolling bodies. The corpses were so silvery-white that they were almost fluorescent, like the skin of decaying mackerel. Their eyes were dark with the anger of dying. A tousle-bearded man, his head hanging so that it shook from side to side with every jolt of the pushcart, a silent but endlessly-repeated denial of his own extinction. A young girl, not more than fourteen years old, her arms crossed over her chest like sticks, her hair wild and dark and matted with grease. A woman, her face contorted in desperation, one leg twisted beneath her in a posture that would have been impossible for anyone living. Babies—who knew how many babies?— their fat white limbs heaped together like a plateful of slippery cod's roes.

The girl who was pushing the handcart was dressed in a long brown skirt, so heavy with damp and dirt that it dragged along the road surface. Her face was half shadowed by a brown linen headscarf, but she was startlingly beautiful, in a tragic hollow-cheeked way; the kind of girl you could sit and watch and wonder about for hours. Her expression was extraordinary. In the whole of his life, Stanley had never seen anybody look like that before. Exhausted but uplifted. Nauseated but strong. She pushed her grisly load with such terrible calmness that Stanley felt ashamed of himself for having insulted God and for having believed that the world He had created was such a cruel joke.

He remained where he was; quite still; trembling; with tears running down his cheeks. Already, he could faintly distinguish the grinding of the pushcart's wheels; and he had never heard anything so terrible. Grind, grind, grind. Metal rims on tarmacadam. And the lifeless jiggling of all of those bodies, as if they were jostling and pushing each other in rage and humiliation, because they were dead.

Stanley was still staring out of the window when his doorbell rang. His mouth flooded with saliva. He turned around. He wasn't expecting anybody. He thought for one

terrifying moment that it was the girl with the pushcart—
that she had somehow managed to enter his house and
climb the stairs with her ghastly burden of bodies. He
turned back to the window. She had gone; and the grinding
of her pushcart's wheels had died away.

The doorbell rang again, longer this time. Stanley said,
"Coming." Then, when it rang again, "I'm coming, for
God's sake!"

He opened the door. The landing was so dark that at first
he couldn't see who it was. A shadowy figure with a pale
face. He didn't speak, couldn't speak. His whole being felt
clenched up like a fist. Then she leaned forward a little and
asked him, "Is it awkward? I only come to see you on the
off chance, like."

"It's you," he said in a watery voice.

She peered into his apartment. "Can I come in? I was
supposed to be going to a party with Glenys but she's got
ever such a stinker."

"A stinker?" Stanley asked her in disbelief.

"You know, a cold. So I thought to meself, why not see
'ow poor old wossname's getting on? Stanley."

"Come in," Stanley invited her. He had been so sure
that she was the girl with the pushcart that he still hadn't
stopped shivering. But when she stepped into the hallway,
she was so clearly Angie Dunning that he felt immediately
calmer, almost himself again. He closed the door and asked
her, "How about a drink?"

"I'll 'ave a glass of wine if you've got one. If not, cup of
tea'll do."

"I've got some Pouilly-Fumé."

"Pooey Foomay? Not sure I like the sound of *that*."

"It's dry white wine, French."

"All right, then."

She was obviously dressed for a party. She took off her black ankle-length coat and threw it over the arm of the sofa. Underneath she was wearing a short tight dress of red ribbed wool, and red panty hose, and red shoes with heels like Lucrezia Borgia's daggers. Her wrists jangled with cheap chunky chromium-plated bracelets.

Stanley went into the kitchen. The smashed hi-fi lay on its side in the middle of the floor. He heaved it aside with his foot and opened the icebox. Angie stood in the doorway and said, "What 'appened to your record player? You drop it?"

Stanley took out the chilled bottle of wine and filled a large Boda goblet with it. "I threw it," he told her. He might just as well tell her the truth.

"What, didn't it work or nothing?"

"It worked fine. I didn't like the record it was playing, that's all."

Angie took her wine and gave him an exaggeratedly taken-aback look. "Bit drastic, wasn't it?" she asked him.

He guided her back into the living room again. "I've been having what you might call moods."

"What, since that bloke attacked you?"

Stanley nodded. He poured himself another vodka and sat down next to the fire. Angie perched herself on the edge of the sofa, hitching her dress up dangerously high. "Paul has moods," she remarked.

"Your boyfriend?"

"I've been going out with 'im ever since I left school. I think he thinks we're going to get married or something."

"And are you?"

"Not likely. A stupid wally like 'im? Anyway, I want to 'ave a bit of fun before I get married. I met one of my best friends from school just before Christmas, and she 'ad two kids already, and a pushchair, and she looked like she'd been pulled through an 'edge backwards. And she used to be ever so fashionable."

"You don't have to get married at all, you know," Stanley told her. "It's not obligatory."

"Are you married?"

"I was. I'm divorced now."

"Got any kids?"

"One son."

Angie crossed and uncrossed her slippery red-sheathed legs and laughed. "Is that your way of telling me that you're old enough to be my father?"

"Maybe. But that doesn't mean that I don't wish I was twenty years younger."

"'Ow old would you be if you was twenty years younger?" Stanley swallowed vodka. Angie really amused him. "Twenty-four."

"Still too old," she told him.

Stanley laughed. "God almighty." And then thought, *God Almighty, am I really that old? This girl makes me feel like I'm ready to be laid out.*

She stood up, pranced over to the window, and looked out. "What 'appened to the curtain?" she wanted to know. "Did you 'ave another mood? Didn't like the way it was drawn or something?"

Stanley gave her a sloping smile. "Something like that."

He watched her over the rim of his vodka glass as

she continued to poke around the living room, picking up ornaments, picking up his gray fedora hat. In hatless London, Stanley hadn't yet had the nerve to wear his fedora, but Angie put it on top of her own blond firework of a hairstyle, and he had to admit that she looked good in it. In fact, he had to admit that she looked good, period. He found his yes straying around the curves of her hips; at the way her dress clung to the tops of her thighs. Her legs were so slender that there was an inverted triangle of clear space in between her thighs, wide enough to accommodate a man's hand, without it touching the sides. That had always turned him on, and it turned him on now.

"I always fancied a titfer," she said. She stood in front of the mirror, pouting her lips and tilting his hat this way and that. When she raised her arms, Stanley could see how large her breasts were—large and high and almost impossibly firm. Eve's were small and droopy and slanted, with olive-dark nipples. He had never liked Eve's breasts. In fact, he had mentioned it to her, in a letter about Leon's support money. *P.S. Even your tits were dull.* He wished now that he hadn't written it, but he supposed that a certain amount of craziness was always permissible during divorce, on both sides. Eve had probably thought that his ass was dull, too, although she had never said so.

Angie had turned around and was giving him a questioning look. "You look like you're thinking about something," she told him.

"I am. I'm wondering whether my ex-wife thought my ass was boring."

Angie turned back to the mirror. "You've gone bonkers, if you ask me."

"Yes, maybe I have." He was watching the way the hem of her dress lifted a fraction of an inch over the rounded cheeks of her bottom, whenever she raised her arms. He had never felt this way before. Girls had aroused him, for sure. Girls on the beach, girls who asked for his autograph, and when he was twenty-seven he had fallen so furiously for a lady cellist from the Limoges Baroque Ensemble (bobbed chestnut hair that swung when she played, classic nose, lips like pink satin cushions) that he had followed her home and played his violin for her outside her front door. After ten minutes her scruffy husband had come out with a Gitanes between his lips and told him to **** off, you *catiche*.

But the way that Angie was stimulating him was different. He felt lustful, even violent. He could imagine himself seizing hold of her, forcing her facedown over the sofa, and pulling up her dress. He could imagine twisting her arms behind her back and hurting her. He could imagine forcing her thighs apart and pushing his fist inside her. Damp curls, slippery knuckles, gasps of pain.

"Do you know what the time is?" she asked him.

His eyes refocused. He glanced at the clock above the fireplace. It had stopped. He looked down at his wristwatch. That had stopped, too. He held it up to his ear and shook it. "I guess it's a little after eight."

"Do you fancy going for a drink?" Angie asked him.

"I don't know. I think I've drunk too much already."

"'Ave you 'ad any tea yet?"

Stanley had learned enough about the English working class to know that "tea" meant a full-cooked early-evening meal, sausages and chips or fish fingers and chips or steakburger and chips.

"I haven't eaten since lunchtime," he told Angie. He kept shaking his watch, but it remained obstinately silent. A Jaeger-le-Coultre, too. It had stopped at the same time as the clock, 7:01.

He looked up. "What do you say we go get something to eat?" he suggested. "Do you like Thai?"

"Never 'ad it. But I'll eat anything. Paul calls me gannet-face."

They left Stanley's apartment and walked to the Busabong Restaurant in Fulham Road, only five minutes away. The night was clear but piercingly cold. Angie unselfconsciously held Stanley's hand as they crossed Limerston Street, as if she were his daughter, or even his girlfriend. He could feel that her nails were bitten down, and for some reason that made her all the more appealing. It was something to do with girlish innocence, he supposed. The child-woman.

In the restaurant, among the usual ethnic-restaurant paraphernalia of mock palm roofs and copper pots and tapestries, they sat on cushions on the floor in the *khan toke* style and ate the sour prawn soup called *tom yam kung* and the chili beef called *nua pad prik* and the chicken in peanut and coconut sauce called *kai penang*. Two Thai waiters changed into satin boxing shorts and gave a demonstration of kick boxing, perilously close to where they were sitting.

Angie liked the boxing (she clapped and cheered out loud) but she wasn't sure about the food. "It's ever so 'ot, some of it," she said. "Not 'ot 'ot, like, but peppery 'ot. And I don't like this green stuff," which was fresh coriander. "Tastes like the inside of old ladies' 'andbags."

It was well past eleven by the time they left. They stood

on the pavement outside the restaurant in the freezing wind, and Stanley said. "How about a nightcap?"

"No, thanks, Stanley," Angie told him with considerable kindness. She reached up and pecked him on the cheek. "I've got to get up early tomorrer. Thanks for the nosh, though."

"That's all right," Stanley replied. "Maybe you can cook me some tea sometime. Egg and chips?"

He whistled for a taxi; too loud the first time, because the cabbie gave him two fingers and drove past without stopping.

"Tell you what, Stanley." said Angie as he opened the door of a second taxi for her. "You come round next week and we'll 'ave bangers and mash."

Bangers and mash. That sounded exciting; like fireworks. Angie herself was a firework. He stood on the pavement waving to her as the taxi took her back to Chiswick. Pronounced *Chizzick*, thought Stanley. For the first time since he had arrived in London, he began to feel like a native, or at least an honorary native.

Perhaps he was growing acclimatized. Perhaps, on the other hand, London had worked its baleful influence on him, like an old gray grandmother who takes in orphaned children from all over the world, but then refuses to let them go.

He was sitting up in bed at two-twenty A.M. reading *Our Mutual Friend* when he thought he heard the street door open and close. He lowered his book, took off his reading glasses, and listened. Nothing. Only that low, endless muttering of traffic.

He was too tired to sleep; too tired and too distressed. He had tried switching off his bedside lamp and closing his eyes, but every time he did so, his blood seemed to prickle furiously, so that he felt as if he could scratch his flesh to ribbons, and all he could think about was Madeleine Springer in her rustling black coat, and Knitted Hood, perching up on the catwalk of Kew Gardens' Palm House like some hideous worm-ridden bird of prey.

He kept picturing that house of brindled brick, with its shabby and derelict front garden. He kept hearing the grinding of metal-bound wheels.

Once tonight he had climbed out of bed and walked through to the kitchen, just to stare at the smashed-up hi-fi lying on the floor. Had he really thrown it himself? Had he really torn down the drapes? Maybe Angie was right. Maybe he was going bonkers.

Or maybe Madeleine Springer was right, and he was infected.

He picked up his book again. *"So deeply engaged had the living-dead man been, in thus communing with himself, that he had regarded neither the wind nor the way, and had resisted the former as instinctively as he had pursued the latter."*

He heard footsteps, somewhere in the house. The creaking of early-Victorian floorboards. By American standards, this house was old when *Our Mutual Friend* was written. Charles Dickens himself might well have passed it, glanced up at Stanley's window, and never known that a hundred years in the future Stanley would be sitting up in bed with his book on his knees, listening for footsteps, listening for doors that opened and closed.

He heard the front door of his apartment open. The chain slide in its socket. The chain swing free.

How could the chain swing free?

He closed the book and laid it on the right-hand nightstand, next to his alarm clock and his empty vodka glass and his leather-framed photograph of Leon. Eve had always said that Leon looked just like him, "poor boy." The bedroom, like the living room, was decorated in dull expensive browns. Brown hessian walls, brown curtains, and a beige shag-pile carpet that was so matted that it looked like the coat of an Old English sheepdog. Dull brown lithographs all around.

He heard somebody walking along the hallway.

"Who's there?" he called out.

There was no reply.

"Who's there? Is anyone there?"

Still there was no reply.

He looked around, half panicking, for some kind of weapon. On the other side of the bed, on the left-hand nightstand, was a heavy ashtray of brown and white onyx. He leaned across the bed, straining his chest muscles as he did so, and hefted it up in his hand.

"All right!" he shouted, feeling bolder now. "Who's there?"

His bedroom door, which had been two or three inches ajar, was pushed open a little wider. Stanley knelt up in the center of the bed and eased the ashtray back in his hand like a baseball pitcher. He used to be terrific at baseball, in high school. Anybody who walked into the room right now was going to get the hardest-hitting surprise of their whole goddamned life. Solid ashtray, with the mustard on it.

A face peeked around the door. It was Angie, firework hairstyle and spiky black eyelashes and everything.

Stanley, surprised, relieved, lowered the ashtray and sat back. "Angie? What the hell are you doing here? I thought the goddamn door was locked."

"It was." She grinned. Then she came prancing right into the middle of the room, and she was wearing nothing but her shiny red panty hose and her skyscraper-heeled shoes.

Stanley stared at her. His mouth changed shape, ready to say something, ready to protest, ready to ask her what the hell she thought she was doing, but words didn't seem like enough. All he could do was to watch her in fascinated perplexity as she came right up to the end of the bed and bowed to him.

Her skin was pale and soft; so pale that it gleamed. Her breasts had looked large beneath her tight red woollen dress; but bare they looked even larger, with wide magnolia-pink are-olas, and the faintest tracery of bluish veins, and a way of counter-swinging against the way that she moved that reminded Stanley of the French cellist's counter-swinging hair.

Her panty hose had the hard shine of scarlet nail varnish, giving the curves of her thighs and her bottom a gleaming emphasis that Stanley found startlingly erotic. Her pubic hair was trapped beneath the nylon in a fine fan-shape.

She betrayed no trace of shyness whatsoever. On the contrary, she seemed to be deliberately displaying herself. She giggled and swung her hips, and her breasts swung, too.

"Angie?" asked Stanley in disbelief.

"I thought you'd like me to play for you." Angie smiled.

"You know, the gypsy violinist. Sorry I couldn't find a rose to grip between me choppers. All the shops was shut."

Like a conjuring trick, Angie produced from behind her back Stanley's Vuillaume violin. "'Ere we are! What would you like me to play? 'Ow about "Oo's Talking You 'Ome Tonight, 'Oo's the Lucky Gel?'"

Stanley lifted a cautioning hand. "Angie ... come on now, no playing around. That violin is worth more than fifteen thousand dollars. It was custom-made, okay? And that's a Tourte bow, worth more than the goddamned violin."

"Oh, come on, Stanl-ee, don't be a spoilsport!" Angie teased him. She lifted the violin and nestled it under her chin.

"Angie, please—that violin is so damned delicate!"

Stanley hop-vaulted across the bed in his pale blue Saks pajamas. But Angie stepped back, so that he couldn't reach her, and immediately began to play. Not "Who's Taking You Home Tonight?" or any other cockney ballad, but the *Allegro molto appassionato* from Mendelssohn's violin concerto in E minor; and played as exquisitely as Stanley had ever heard it, even better than Anne-Sophie Mutter had played it with Herbert von Karajan.

He stood up and watched Angie playing, transfixed. She kept smiling and winking at him as she played, as if she had been playing like this for years, as if it were all a huge joke. He took another step towards her, but she took another step back. He couldn't try to snatch the violin away from her; it was far too fragile for that. His insurance company would go apeshit if they found out that he had let anybody else breathe in the same room as his violin, let alone *play* it.

Yet her playing was incredible. She made the strings weep

with emotion. He had heard the allegro a thousand times; he had rehearsed and played it himself. But he had never heard anything like this. It soared; it shrilled. It filled him with grief and it filled him with delight. He fell to his knees in front of her, staring at her. She brought the allegro up to its climax and smiled down at him tartly. Why hadn't she told him before that she could play like this? Why had she spent the whole of their evening together talking about Paul and his secondhand Ford Granada, and her friend what had the cold, and why she wouldn't never go to an 'oliday camp for her 'olidays, never again. "Bloody knocking-shops, those 'oliday camps, that's all they are."

And yet she could play like this, without hesitation, without rehearsal, on an unfamiliar, untuned violin!

He reached up and grasped her hips. The nylon of her panty hose felt harsh and glossy and cheap. He dug his fingertips in between her soft skin and the elasticized waistband, and rolled the waistband down, over her hips, down her thighs, until her legs were completely bared. He could feel the warmth radiating from her skin against his face. He disentangled her feet from the rolled-down nylon. She kept playing, her elbow vigorously sawing, her breasts swaying, her entire body tense with passion.

Stanley cupped her right buttock in his upraised hand, drew her towards him. He kissed her soft, flat stomach. He slid the tip of his tongue through her pubic hair and into the liquid warmth of her vulva. She shuddered; she smiled; but she continued to play.

He licked her, persistently and quickly. All of a sudden she stopped playing and lowered the violin. The silence fell around them like a cloak.

He closed his eyes. Her liquids coursed down his chin. Her thighs were tensed. One bitten finger tapped and scratched at the strings of his Vuillaume, off-key, irritating, but peculiarly arousing, too.

And we are cutting a swathe ... tra la la, tra la la ... through the world ... tra la la, tra la la ...

She opened wider and wider like a soft, sweet-tasting oyster. The muscles in her thighs were so taut that they trembled. Then she whispered something that sounded like "*Oh, deus,*" and dropped quaking to her knees, her cheek against the carpet, her arms outstretched, panting, her pale white bottom lifted.

Now Stanley rose to his feet, stripped back his pajama top, pulled open the fly of his pajama pants. Brandishing his raging crimson-headed penis, he forced himself violently into her, so harshly that she cried out. But all that Stanley could hear was the thundering of blood against his eardrums, like tropical rain cascading against a tarpaulin, and somewhere beyond this thundering, the Mendelssohn violin concerto scraping its elegant and painful way across his consciousness.

He clawed the firm white cheeks of her bottom as far apart as he could. He was confronted by a flower as small and as reticent as a hothouse pink. He pressed his fingertip against it, as if to protect it, while all the time he slogged himself in and out of her, his thick slippery shaft between her swollen slippery lips, setting up a rhythm that was insistent and crude and yet cheerful, too, like a crowd clapping loose-wristed at a Mardi Gras carnival.

She said nothing, but kept her cheek pressed against the carpet and her bottom dutifully uplifted. The bird-dog position, his college pal Meanie Collins had called that. He slogged in and out, gasping.

And, yea, we are cutting ...

... a swathe through the world ...

At the final instant, he took himself out, and his sperm surged all over her. It stuck to everything in hot strings and globules. He fell to the carpet beside her, gasping, pleased, exhausted. He hadn't had sex like that for years. Crude and brutal and completely demanding. No foreplay, no whispered promises. Just shoving and panting and gasping, and a climax like an automobile accident.

Her face was turned away from him. All he could see was the disorganized firework of her hair. He reached across the carpet and stroked it, and twisted it around his fingers.

"You're brilliant," he whispered. "Do you know that? You're brilliant. I never met anyone like you."

Angie said nothing, but her rib cage rose and fell as she slowly got her breath back.

"Are you going to play for me?" asked Stanley. "Why didn't you tell me you could play like that? You're amazing."

Still Angie said nothing, but continued to pant.

Stanley lifted himself up on One elbow. "Listen, what do you say we take a shower together, then have a drink? Or help ourselves to a drink first and take a shower afterwards?"

No response, only the rising and falling of those thin ribs.

Stanley said, "You know something ... what you've done for me tonight—I haven't felt this way for years. You can play music like an angel, you make love like a devil."

He reached across and cupped her heavy bare breast in his hand. Her nipple tightened and crinkled. But she continued to pant, almost like an animal now; a dog left dehydrated in a sun-baked station wagon. Stanley began to have the smallest inclination that something was wrong; that he might have hurt her somehow; maybe not physically but emotionally. He had been rough, after all. He had dragged down her panty hose and forced himself into her. Maybe she wasn't used to that kind of treatment. Maybe she had hated it, even, but hadn't had the courage to tell him or the strength to resist him. *Oh, hell.* She spoke in a brash cockney accent, for sure—or what Stanley assumed was a brash cockney accent—and her behavior had seemed fairground-brazen, but she had played violin with stunning virtuosity. The kind of virtuosity that made tears spring into your eyes; the way that tears had sprung into Stanley's father's eyes, on his deathbed, when Stanley played him Al Jolson favorites, "Mammy" and "Wonder Bar." He could have read her all wrong. Maybe her nudity had been meant to be artistic, rather than erotic.

"Angie, listen to me, are you okay?"

She stirred. She growled, "I'm all right." Her voice sounded off-key, as if she were talking into a chloroformed handkerchief.

"Angie?"

"*I'm all right, you bastard, how many more times?*" she roared at him, and twisted her head around; and he wasn't looking at a young snub-nosed punk from Herbert Gardens, Chiswick, but the glacial celluloid face of Knitted Hood, with its perfect nose and its perfect cheeks and its perfect bow-shaped mouth, and its eyes as black as railroad tunnels rushing toward him.

Oh, God, I'm—

Oh, God, I'm—aaahhh!!

Intense shriveling terror wriggled through every nerve in his body. He rolled over, his arms flailing. His head struck the side of the bureau. He clambered to his feet, gasping, thrashing around for balance.

It took a moment or two before he realized that he was quite alone; that his bedroom was empty; that all he could hear was traffic and the sound of pop music from a room upstairs. Rick Astley, "Hold Me in Your Arms." A song so banal that Stanley couldn't distinguish it from rattling plumbing.

Angie was gone; his violin was gone. He looked down at himself. He was naked, with something wet and sticky drying on his thighs. *Oh, God. I've been dreaming. That was all a dream. I must be so goddamned frustrated—*

He bent over, feeling old, and picked up his pajamas. He tried to drag his pajama pants on to his right foot, but stepped on the fabric and almost toppled over. In the end he had to sit on the end of the bed and dress himself. He could smell the pungent briny aroma of semen. He felt ashamed and shocked and frightened all at once. It was almost impossible to believe that his ferocious lovemaking with Angie had been nothing more than a fleeting erotic dream. How could a dream talk like that, play music like that? How could a dream *feel* like that, so fleshy and substantial?

Quaking, he stood up, steadied himself, and walked across the bedroom to the half-open door. He waited and listened. "Angie?" he called out. His voice cracked, and he had to cough to clear it. "Angie?"

There was no reply. Only the tinny *thump-thumpity-thump* of Rick Astley. He was tempted to call Angie again, but then he decided against it. If there was somebody else in his apartment, he didn't want to advertise where he was. It might be a burglar. It might be Knitted Hood.

He eased open the bedroom door and went along the corridor to the living room. The brown furnishings were harshly lit by sodium light. As far as he could see, there was nobody there. He hesitated a moment longer; then made his way around the back of the sofa to the chair where his violin case lay. He stood staring at it for a while; then he flicked open the catches and eased back the lid.

At first he couldn't understand what he was looking at. His violin seemed to have turned pale, a ghost of itself. Yet it was *alive*, too. It moved and shifted, as if he were looking at it through rippling hot air, or underwater. He frowned and leaned forward. It was only then that he understood that it was a powdery outline of a violin, a dust-covered shell, almost completely devoured by writhing woodworm.

He let the lid drop. Dusty varnish puffed silently out of it like talcum powder, "*Gevalt!*" he whispered. His sanity felt like a balancing rock in a Road Runner cartoon. Was this a dream, too? Or had dreams and waking become so inextricably tangled up together that he would never know whether he was awake or asleep? It would have been different back home. He could have gone to the drugstore on the corner of Lexington and Fifty-ninth and asked Mo behind the lunch counter if he was real; and Mo would have told him yes or no. Mo could tell kosher franks from nonkosher franks, just by the way they squeaked. He could tell a *gontser macher* from a *lump*. But here in London, who could Stanley rely on? Mr. Rasool, in the mini-market? Fanny Lawrence, from the orchestra? Frederick Orme?

Maybe he should try phoning Eve, and asking her if she Was dreaming or awake?

His throat was parched and his breath stank of stale alcohol. He felt as if he were even sweating alcohol. He went through to the kitchen and poured himself a pint of water in a glass tankard that he had liberated from the World's End pub, and drank it straight down, so that it poured out of the sides of his mouth. He closed his eyes. He didn't feel as if *this* were a dream. It was too mundane; too believable. Yet he had walked straight out of the living room where he had seen his violin riddled by grubs, and into here, without any perception of having woken up.

Perhaps an inability to distinguish between sleeping and waking was a characteristic of Bard's Disease. Perhaps, in the end, Shakespeare had been unable to decide which was real, his life or his plays. And Mozart? Hadn't Madeleine Springer said that Mozart died of the same infection? How could anybody bear to live their lives not knowing for sure if they were asleep or awake? How could you continue to write music if you knew that you might open your eyes at any moment, and it would all be gone, as if it had never existed?

He opened his telephone book, the small maroon morocco-bound volume that Leon had given him for his last birthday, with his own name and address entered in it already, Leon Eisner, Atlas Peak Road, Napa, California. *Just in case you forget, when you go away.* Dear God, children could say the most innocent words, and yet they resounded down the days. *Just in case you forget, when you go away.* As if he ever could.

He punched out Gordon Rutherford's number in Putney.

The phone rang and rang and rang, and Stanley was about to put it down when a tired, effeminate voice said, "Y-e-es?"

"Gordon?"

A tight sniff. "Who wants him?"

"Stanley, Stanley Eisner."

"He's asleep. He's had a difficult night."

Stanley cleared his throat. "I'd really appreciate it if you woke him up."

"I'm really—I'm *terribly* sorry. But Gordon's had such a grotty time of it."

"Please." Stanley begged him. "It's really critical. I wouldn't ask you to wake him if it weren't."

A very long, unsociable pause. Then the voice said, "Who shall I say wants to talk to him?"

"Stanley Eisner. I'm a violinist, with the Kensington Chamber Orchestra. Well, temporarily anyhow."

"A violinist, *hmmmmmmm*? I think you've got the wrong man. Gordon isn't interested in anything classical. His favorite record is 'Relax,' You know, *relax, don't do it, when you want to commmee*."

Stanley took a deep breath. "Listen, my friend, I'm sorry, but I think you have the wrong idea about this."

"Oh, yes? Don't you know what time it is?"

"I'm sorry, no. Around midnight, I guess."

"It's just gone *two*, my old china!"

Stanley glanced at the digital clock on his New World oven. For some reason, he couldn't focus on it; it didn't seem to make any sense. "I'm sorry. But do you think I could speak to Gordon ... just for a couple of minutes? I wouldn't ask if it wasn't really urgent."

Long pause. Undecided breathing. Then the receiver was put down, sharply, on a table or a shelf. Voices in the background. Somebody arguing? Then the sound of footsteps, and a sleep-clogged voice saying, "Stanley? What's the matter? It's the middle of the night."

"Gordon, I need you to meet me."

Another long pause; a sniff. "What's the matter, Stanley? Tell me."

Stanley unexpectedly found himself very close to breaking down. "Gordon, I need you to meet me, that's all."

"You don't mean now?"

"How about an hour?"

"Stanley, I had a really long day at Shepherd's Bush Green police station, then I had a meeting in Hammersmith. I didn't get to bed until one. I'm exhausted. I'm naked."

"Go on, tell the world," said the fussy, effeminate voice in the background.

Stanley asked Gordon, unbalanced and unsteady, "Gordon, do I sound *real?*"

"*Real?* What do you mean by *real?*"

"Are you awake?"

"Of course I'm awake! I wouldn't be talking to you if I wasn't awake!"

"Does it sound like *I'm* awake?"

Guardedly, Gordon asked him, "Stanley ... what's the matter? I want you to tell me."

Stanley covered his eyes with his hand. "I don't know what's happening, Gordon ... I keep seeing things and feeling things and talking to people, and I don't know whether I'm sleeping or awake or what. I feel like I'm going out of my head."

"Do you want me to come around to your place?" asked Gordon.

"Oh, God!" said the voice in the background. "To the bat-poles, we haven't a moment to lose!"

Stanley said, "I'll meet you at Kew. Do you know that café called the Original Maids of Honor?"

"You want to meet me at the Original Maids of Honor at three o'clock in the morning?"

Stanley said, dry-mouthed, "Yes."

"I hope you'll be there, that's all."

"Oh, yes, I'll be there. Because if I'm not, you can forget that I ever existed."

"Stanley—"

"If I'm not there, Gordon, it will be because this phone call is a dream, and you're a dream, and I never really asked you to meet me anywhere."

"All right then, three o'clock," Gordon assured him.

He went back to the living room and opened his violin case. His polished Vuillaume violin nestled in its purple velour bed, uneaten by worms, shining, unplayed, intact. He looked at it for a very long time, then he lifted it out and plucked each of the strings in turn, and tightened them, just to make sure that they were in tune. Then he lifted his bow and played a short improvised melody in the style known as *ondeggiando*, or undulating.

He lowered the violin, his face composed and serious, and then returned it to its case and snapped down the catches. He was beginning to believe that the woodworms he had seen had not wriggled out of his own imagination, or out of his dreams, but that they were real, in an inexplicable way; that they existed outside of his own shock; outside of his own dreams, outside of his own hallucinations. Perhaps they had been left for him to find as a clue. Perhaps they had been intended to frighten him. Perhaps they were simply *there*, as blind and uncomplaining as any mass of creatures, humans included. Perhaps that was the point.

Even great music was bound to decay in the end; because the men who could play it were bound to decay; and their instruments would corrode and collapse into dust.

He went back to the bedroom and dressed in fawn corduroy pants and a white Scottish sweater. He knew that it would probably be impossible to find a taxi on the streets at this time of night, so he called the Carib Cab Company. A strong West Indian accent told him that the cab would be "wit' you in a quahtah of an owah, man; and it's dobble fayuh aftah mid-*night*."

He poured himself a vodka. For courage, for luck. If he was dreaming, he might just as well be drunk. If you got drunk in a dream, did you wake up with a hangover? He stood by the window waiting for the minicab to arrive. There was no traffic, no passersby. The view was so static that it could have been an orange-tinted photograph.

Only five minutes had passed when his doorbell rang. It startled him, and he stood rigid for a moment wondering whether he ought to answer it or not. If it was the cabdriver, he had arrived here incredibly quickly. He leaned close to the window and peered down into the street. No sign of a car. The doorbell rang again, then again, then again.

Knitted Hood, he thought, his stomach shrinking. But

then he heard hammering on the door and a voice calling, "Stanley! Stanley! It's me!"

He put down his glass and went to open the door. It was Angie. She hurried past him into the hallway, directly into the living room, and went straight to the chair where his violin case was lying. She started to wrestle with the catches.

"What?" Stanley demanded. "What?"

She turned to stare at him and her eyes were wide and glistening and smeared with black mascara. "I 'ad a dream," she said. "I was round my friend's place but I thought I was 'ere. But it wasn't like a normal dream. I really couldn't work out whether I was really 'ere or whether I wasn't."

Stanley glanced sideways at the violin case. "You had a very clear ... very realistic dream that you were here?"

Angie shrugged. She suddenly realized how ridiculous it sounded.

"Okay," said Stanley, trying to stay calm. "What were you doing in the dream?"

She laughed, although her laugh was more hysterical than humorous. "It's stupid, really. I was playing your violin. I mean not just scraping it or nothing, but playing it brilliant. I woke up and I couldn't work out whether it was real or not. I just 'ad to come round and find out whether I could. You know ... play it," she concluded rather lamely.

Stanley felt as if the wing of death had brushed across him. "Do you know what time it is?" he asked her, his mouth dry.

She nodded. She remained straight-backed, wide-eyed, small fists clenched. Defiant, fearful; but no more fearful than Stanley.

Stanley said, "It's two o'clock in the morning. And you came back here just to find out if you could play the violin?"

"It wasn't just that," she admitted. "I mean it wasn't just the violin."

Stanley said nothing. He waited for Angie to find her own words. She lowered her head, then lifted it again and said, "I had a dream about you and me. We was ... well, you know. We was 'aving it away."

"You dreamed that you and I had sex together," said Stanley.

Angie nodded.

"God," said Stanley, turning away from her.

"Stanley?" she asked him. "You never 'ad the same dream?"

"Yes. I had the same dream."

"You never!"

"It's true, Angie. You came into my bedroom wearing nothing but your red panty hose and you played my violin You played Mendelssohn. You played Mendelssohn better than I ever heard anybody play Mendelssohn before, ever, in the whole of my life. Then we made love."

Angie approached Stanley slowly and touched his sleeve. "Oh, Stanley."

Stanley let out a quaking breath. "Angie, I don't know what's happening to me. I don't know whether I'm dreaming or awake."

"You're awake, of course, silly. Do you want me to pinch you?"

"But when you came into my room ... when you started playing my violin like that ... I wasn't even aware that I'd fallen asleep. I was even getting all ticked off and mad at you, because I didn't want you to touch it."

"I know," said Angie.

Stanley pressed his hands against his face, as if he were breathing into an oxygen mask. "It's impossible," he said. "Two people can't have exactly the same dream."

Angie continued to hold his sleeve, as if she didn't want to let him go. "I read in the *Readers' Digest* once that identical twins can 'ave the same sort of dream."

"The same *sort* of dream, for sure. And they're identical twins. But you and me, we're total strangers, and our dream was *exactly* the same."

Angie hesitated for a moment, and then she said, "Well, we're not *total* strangers, are we? I mean, not any more."

Stanley stared at her. "You don't think I—? Come on, that was only a dream, right, whatever we did?"

"Just because it was a dream, that's not to say that I didn't enjoy it."

"Angie—I'm forty-four years old."

"I know. Old enough to be my dad. But don't tell me *you* didn't enjoy it, either."

Stanley swallowed, shrugged, looked around. "I don't know. I'm not sure that *enjoy* is quite the right word."

"Well, you didn't actually 'ate it, did you? It was better than a poke in the eye with a dirty stick?"

"Yes," Stanley admitted, and couldn't help smiling. "But I don't know … I've gotten myself involved in something weird. Something I don't fully understand. I don't want you to get involved in it, too."

Too late, a voice inside him whispered. *You've dreamed your dream about her; and she's involved already. You've passed your infection on. And why should you worry, anyway? Why not use her while you have the chance?*

She's young, she has a beautiful body. She's impressed by what you are and the way you look. Have her, have a good time. There won't be many more good times left for anyone now.

"I don't mind being involved," said Angie. "I've always liked fortune-telling, that kind of thing. And 'orror stories, you know. Dennis Wheatley and that. Paul's always saying I'm weird. I don't think you're going to make me any weirder."

Angie's going to dream of Paul; and Paul's going to dream of all the other girls he goes out with. Two times two makes four, four times four makes sixteen, sixteen times sixteen makes two hundred fifty-six. An unstoppable equation of unstoppable infection.

Stanley said, "Maybe, you ought to try the violin."

"Beg your pardon?"

"Maybe you ought to try the violin … see if you can really play it."

"Well, that's what I come 'ere for. But now that I'm 'ere …"

"Go on, give it a try. Just so long as you don't drop it."

Stanley lifted the Vuillaume out of its case and handed it to her. He demonstrated how she should hold it, how to adjust the chin rest; then he gave her the bow. As he stood beside her, showing her how to draw the bow across the strings, she turned and looked at him in such intense close-up that he could feel the breath from her nostrils on his cheek.

"What's that after-shave you've got on?" she asked him.

He stared back at her. Their eyes were so near that they could hardly focus. "Grey Flannel," he told her.

"Did your ex-wife buy it for you?"

He shook his head. "I bought it myself. At Harrod's."

"It's nice. It's like lavender."

Stanley said, "Would you like to try playing now?"

She looked away. He could see the soft curve of her cheek. The fine curly hair at the back of her neck tickled his ear. "I was wet," she whispered.

"What?"

"After that dream, I was wet. It was just like we'd actually done it."

Stanley took a shallow breath. "You mean …"

She turned back. "Spunk, that's what I mean. We 'ad it away in a dream only we really did it."

He stepped away from her, lifting both hands defensively. "Angie … I told you this was weird. I think it would be a whole lot better if you and I just kind of parted company, you know? Just forgot about it. Forgot about each other."

"But what if I don't *want* to forget about it?"

"Angie, this is for your own good. Ever since that guy attacked me—well. I'm not normal any more. I have some kind of illness. I don't think that you and I should see each other again."

"Supposing we dream about each other again, what then?"

"Dreams are dreams, Angie. That's all. They're just shadow theater. Figments of stressful imaginations."

"I was full of spunk, Stanley," retorted Angie. "It was real and I liked it."

"It wasn't mine," Stanley told her. "There is no possible way in the world that it could have been mine. Maybe you were tired and Paul made love to you and you forgot."

"Paul wasn't there. It was you."

"Angie, for God's sake! It was a dream! If it wasn't a dream, I'm going out of my mind!"

"Oh, yeah?" Angie demanded, and lifted the violin, and without hesitation played a dazzling flourish from Mendelssohn's violin concerto. "I suppose *that's* a dream, too?"

Stanley stared at her. Angie stared back. Slowly, she lowered the violin, her face white, her lips quivering. First she looked at the bow; then she looked at the violin.

"I can't play the violin," she whispered.

"What?"

"I can't play the violin. I never, ever, in my whole life, even *touched* a violin."

Stanley stepped forward and gently took the instrument away from her and replaced it in its case. He kissed her forehead, and she pressed herself close to his chest.

"Something really weird is going down here," Stanley told her. "I want you to keep well away from it."

"I want to stay with you," Angie appealed. "Please, Stanley. We made love in that dream together. I played the violin and I can't even play the violin. I have to stay. I have a right to."

"A *right*?"

"I'm not leaving, Stanley. Can I call you Stan?"

Stanley heard a car door slam outside; then a few moments later the street doorbell rang. "Okay," he told her. "But don't say I didn't warn you."

Chapter Four

Empty House

West London was deserted as Stanley and Angie were driven at high speed over the Hammersmith flyover toward Chiswick and Kew. The flyover passed within feet of a block of Victorian flats, and Stanley could see a man and a woman furiously talking to each other through an uncurtained window. The digital clock on the RCA building reminded them that it was 3:02, and that the temperature was two degrees Celsius. The orange glare from the streetlights was reflected on the low, slowly-moving clouds.

Stanley felt exhausted; but much more real. He was reasonably sure now that he wasn't dreaming. Perhaps tiredness alone had restored his sense or wakefulness and sleep. He held Angie's hand on the back seat of the car and watched the rooftops of Hammersmith revolve around them. Off to the left, the Thames gleamed like a steel door key.

They had been collected at Stanley's door by a tall spidery Rasta in a huge woollen tom. His silver Granada had stood by the curb, throbbing with reggae music like a cartoon car from *Roger Rabbit*. Stanley had asked him to turn the music down a little as they drove to Kew. "I like it, okay, but I'm a little tired."

The driver had turned his radio off completely. "There is no comprom-eyes with the real music, man. There is no way that you can listen to it kwai-hut."

"You're right," Stanley had agreed. "You can't listen to Mozart quiet, either."

They were driven across the river, through Kew Green, and past the dark brick walls of the Royal Botanic Gardens. "Left, left here," said Stanley. "Just by the Original Maids of Honor."

The Rasta dropped them off next to the old-fashioned tearooms, and Stanley gave him ten pounds for the double fare and a five-pound tip. The Rasta called him back and dropped three pound coins into his hand. "That was too much, man."

"Excuse me?" Stanley couldn't believe what he was hearing.

"Five-pon' tip on a ten-pon' fare is too much, man. I wouldn't give it to *you;* I don' expect you to give it to *me*."

"I think I just witnessed a miracle," Stanley told Angie as he returned to the Original Maids of Honor.

Angie clung to his arm and pressed her head against his shoulder. "Bloody taters out 'ere," she told him.

Stanley was taken aback. "Bloody taters? I never heard that one before."

"Taters, you know, cold. Potaters in the mold, cold."

"Oscar Wilde was right," Stanley remarked.

"I don't like jazz much," said Angie.

"Jazz? What the hell does jazz have to do with it?"

"Oscar Wilde. 'E played piano, didn't 'e?"

"I think you're thinking about Oscar Peterson. Oscar

Wilde was a poet and a dramatist. The reason I mentioned him was that he said Britain and America were separated by a common language."

"Oh."

They waited, Angie clinging close. Stanley said, "You probably want to know what we're doing here."

"Well, waiting for your mate, aren't we?"

"Sure, but we're here for a reason. That guy who attacked me ... the guy in the knitted hood. He lives just around the corner."

Angie stared up at him. "So what you going to do?" she asked him. "You're not going to do 'im over or nothing, are you? You and your mate?"

"I don't know. I don't think it's going to be as simple as that."

Angie twisted her head around. "Well, 'ow d'you know 'e lives 'ere? 'Ow d'you find that out, then?"

"It's a long story, but I met this woman in Kew Gardens, in the Palm House ... and *she* showed me."

"Oh," said Angie, apparently satisfied. Stanley was amazed at the way in which some topics aroused intense curiosity in her, while she would accept others without blinking an eye—particularly anything concerned with authority or grown-ups. He supposed it was something to do with the British education system. "This woman" had sounded authoritative—as authoritative as Mrs. Thatcher—and therefore Angie had accepted the truth of what she had said without question.

After ten minutes of shuffling around in the cold, Gordon's Austin appeared from the direction of Kew Green and drew in beside the curb. Gordon leaned over the passenger seat and wound down the window. "I hope this is bloody well worth it," he said. He was wearing a maroon sweater, with a collar folded over it that looked suspiciously like the collar of a pair of pajamas.

"Take the first left, then park," Stanley told him.

Gordon parked his car in Kew Gardens Road and switched off the lights. "Jeremy was furious," he said as he locked the door.

"Oh, yes. You told me about him. Jeremy the Jealous."

Angie nudged Stanley and raised her eyebrows. "He's not a gay, is 'e?"

Stanley pressed his finger to his lips, but Gordon said loudly, "Gay as the day is long, *ma petite*."

"I don't reckon gays," Angie retorted in a challenging voice.

"Oh, no?" Gordon replied. "I don't suppose many gays would reckon you much, either, darling."

"For God's sake," said Stanley. "Do you know what happened to Angie and me tonight? We both experienced the identical dream."

"Oh, yes?" said Gordon. In the lamplight he looked haggard and scruffy. "And for that you got me out of bed?"

"Gordon, we both dreamed the identical dream. Just like we'd lived it. Don't you understand how *extraordinary* that is? What are the chances of that happening?"

Gordon raked his fingers through his hair, trying to comb it straight. "All right, that's very unusual. But it's hardly a crisis, is it? And why the hell did I have to drive all the way *here* to discuss it?"

Stanley told him how he had encountered Knitted Hood in the Palm House; and how Madeleine Springer had brought him here. He explained about the Carriers, and Bard's

Disease, and what had happened to him after he had returned to Langton Street.

Gordon took out his Silk Cut cigarettes and lit one, blowing smoke across the street. His eyes remained foxy and uncommunicative. He waited until Stanley finished, and then he said, without any preamble, "You should take Dr. Patel's advice. Go and see a psychiatrist."

"Gordon—I don't need a psychiatrist! If I need a psychiatrist, then Angie needs a psychiatrist, too, and she's not crazy! Goddammit, Gordon, I'm telling you the truth!"

Gordon pursed his lips. "Did this Madeleine Springer leave you a number where you could contact her?"

"Unh-hunh."

"Do you think you might have imagined her?"

"What do you mean?"

"Well, Stanley, my dear fellow, you don't know whether you're asleep or awake. Isn't it possible that after I left you on Kew Bridge, you took a taxi back home and went to sleep, and simply *dreamed* that all of this happened? Isn't it possible that you dreamed you saw Knitted Hood in the Palm House? That there *is* no Madeleine Springer?"

Stanley was defensive. "I guess it's possible. But that's not what happened."

"Stanley," Gordon persisted, "are you actually awake now? There is a chance, you know, that you're suffering from some incredibly convincing form of somnambulism. Do you understand what I'm suggesting? Your mind won't accept the world the way it is, not while you're awake, so most of the time you're technically sleepwalking."

"What, are you crazy?" Stanley shouted. "Sleepwalking, what is this? Are *you* awake?"

"What?"

"Are *you* awake?"

"Well, I don't know," Gordon replied. "I may appear to *you* to be awake. On the other hand, you might be dreaming that I'm telling you that I'm awake. For all you know, I might be home in bed with Jeremy, absolutely fasters."

Without any hesitation, Stanley slapped Gordon across the face; so hard that Gordon staggered two or three steps back across the narrow grass verge, and trod in some dog's muck.

"Jesus!" he exclaimed, holding the cheek. "What the hell did you do that for?"

"Are you awake now?" Stanley shouted at him. "Or am I just dreaming that you're awake?"

"I'm awake, for Christ's sake. I'm awake! Look at the state of my bloody slipper!"

"Oo-ah, 'e's got 'is Marks & Spencer's slippers on." Angie giggled.

"Jesus," said Gordon, scraping his slipper against the pavement.

Stanley clasped Angie's arm. "I'm going to take a look at Knitted Hood's house," he told Gordon. "You don't have to come if you don't want to. I just thought you were the kind of guy who was prepared to go out on a limb."

Gordon stopped wiping his slipper and stared at Stanley resentfully. "Who the hell helped you to recover after you were raped? Felix the Cat?"

"No," Stanley replied emotionally. "*You* did; and you'll never in your whole life understand how much you helped me. But what happened to me was something different than anything you've ever had to handle before—totally different. It was a rape, sure, on the surface of it. But it wasn't just a physical rape. It was like my whole soul was raped. Knitted Hood didn't just take away my physical dignity. He didn't simply traumatize my conscious mind. He took something else, too. My dreams ... the way I feel about the world ... he raped everything I believed about right and wrong."

"Stanley," said Gordon, like a parent talking to a small child, "I don't think I understand a single word you're saying."

"You want it straight?" Stanley retorted. "He's *infected* me."

Gordon made a conspicuous effort to hold his ground; not to back away. "Not with AIDS?"

"For God's sake. Of course not with AIDS." Stanley jabbed a finger at his right temple. "He's infected me right inside my mind. Inside of my head."

"Inside your *head*?"

"I keep thinking things that I don't want to think. I can't work out if I'm dreaming or awake."

"So what are we doing in Kew?" Gordon demanded. "If you believe that you've been infected, in your head or anywhere else, you'd be better off back at St. Stephen's, instead of here, in the middle of the night, slapping people and making them step in dog's dirt."

"Because the *answer* is here," Stanley insisted.

"What answer? The answer to what?"

"The answer to who these guys are, these Carriers, and what they're carrying, and why I was attacked, and what the hell is happening to me."

"Stanley," said Gordon very soberly, "I don't think anything is happening to you, except stress and delayed shock. People think you can get over shock in days, or weeks, but you can't. I think you need to talk to somebody who can help you."

"You're damn right! And that's why we're here! You see that house? That's where the guy with the knitted hood lives. We're going to go directly to the front door and we're going to confront him. Him and his fellow Carriers, if they're at home, too."

Gordon looked dubious. "Do you think that's a good idea?"

"What else can I do? Wait until I've gone completely crazy?"

"I don't know. You could call dear old Detective Sergeant Morris."

"Are you serious? He didn't believe a word of what I said when he interviewed me in hospital. You don't think he's going to believe me how?"

"I'm not too sure that *I* believe you now."

"It's true, Gordon. All of it. It's disgusting and it's weird, but it's true."

"So you want to beard Knitted Hood in his den, so to speak? And what do you think *that* will achieve?"

"At least I might find out what he's done to me."

Gordon glanced at Angie. "And what do *you* think about all of this?"

Angie shrugged, "We 'ad the same dream, didn't we? Both at the same time. Something must 'ave 'appened."

"God, I wish I was back in bed," said Gordon.

That may not have been a statement of unqualified enthusiasm for knocking at Knitted Hood's door; but Stanley took it at the very least as reluctant cooperation. He took hold of Angie's hand, and together they crossed Kew Gardens Road to Knitted Hood's house and went right up to the dilapidated front gate. They looked around. The night was bone-cold; the distant traffic echoed like a roaming herd of mournful buffalo. They waited while Gordon caught up with them. Stanley squeezed Angie's fingers. They had both experienced the same dream. Perhaps, in some peculiar sideways dimension, they had actually made love for real. She had pressed her face against the carpet, in the dream; in a gesture of complete submission. She had whispered words that he still failed to understand. He and Angie had nothing in common, only fate. But maybe fate was more than enough. Maybe the greatest of historical events were assembled from coincidence, accidents, two people meeting by chance.

He wondered how much of a chance it was that he had been attacked by Knitted Hood.

Gordon stopped in the middle of the deserted street to chafe his slipper against the tarmac. "Is this it? *Tennyson?* 'Do we indeed desire the dead should still be near us at our side? Is there no baseness we would hide? No inner vileness that we dread?'"

"What's that?" asked Stanley.

"Tennyson," said Gordon. "Alfred Lord, 1809, 1892."

Tennyson was typical of the large suburban dwellings that had been built in southwest London in the years before the Great War, in the years before zeppelins and Passchendaele Ridge and "Pack Up Your Troubles in Your Old Kit Bag." The house was unfashionably but handsomely constructed of hard red brick, with tile-patterned pathways and stained-glass decoration in the downstairs windows. Around Kew and Barnes, most of the larger family houses had been subdivided into flats and were occupied now by lonely building-society clerks and promiscuous British Airways stewardesses and fat Australian girls who had found nothing in Brisbane, no husband, no love, and wouldn't find anything here, either.

Angie said, "What you going to do, knock once and ask for Mr. 'Ood?"

"Why not?" asked Stanley. "You know what they say: the best way to deal with your fears is to face them head-on."

"'Oo said that?" Angie wanted to know.

"I don't know. My mother, I think." Stanley forced open the gate. The front garden was small and clotted with rubbish and stank sourly of dereliction and bad drains and cat's pee. The bottom of the gate scraped against the tiled pathway with a sharp squeaking sound. Something black and alive fled into the grass: a rat probably, London was still alive with rats.

"But s'posin' 'e answers?" Angie wanted to know.

"If he answers. I'll know for sure that meeting Madeleine Springer wasn't a dream, and that I'm not dreaming now, I've got Gordon here as a witness."

Gordon said, "Madeleine Springer? That name rings a bell. Was she your mysterious lady?"

Stanley nodded.

"Well," said Gordon, "even if Knitted Hood *does* answer, that's no absolute guarantee that you're not dreaming, is it? I mean—the way I feel—I'm probably at home, even as I speak, and fast asleep in bed."

Stanley gripped Gordon's fingers and almost crushed them. "You're here, right? You're awake. I need you."

"Ow! Shit! All right," Gordon protested, blowing on his hand.

Stanley stood halfway up Tennyson's path and looked

up to the second floor. Unlike every other house in the street—even those houses which remained unlit—Tennyson appeared to be empty. More than empty—derelict. A house in which unhappy lives had been lived out; lives that were gone now; ways that were parted. Stanley had often wondered whether houses could be witnesses to the pain of the people who lived in them. He thought of his own house, the house that he had shared with Eve and Leon on Dolores, in San Francisco. If somebody moved into that house in a hundred years' time, would they still pick up the echoes of all of those rows that he and Eve had been through, all of those screaming matches?

Was it still there, somehow, the moment when he and Eve had faced each other across the living room, their faces like masks, and known without even vocalizing it that this was the moment, this was the end? *Thus far, and no further. And we shall cut a swathe through the world.*

Gordon said, a shade petulantly, "Are you going to knock, dear, or not? Because if not, my beddeth calleth."

"You aint 'alf gay," Angie scolded him.

"Listen to it," Gordon complained. "She's more like Samantha Fox than Samantha Fox."

"For God's sake," Stanley said, shushing them. He approached the front porch. It was generously deep, and plunged in shadow. Seven or eight empty milk bottles were arranged in a soldierly line along one side of it, half filled with green murky rainwater. What Stanley couldn't have known was that they were all of a style of tall thin milk bottle that had been changed more than twenty years ago.

He reached out for the front door. The paint felt weather-dulled and dry, and cracked in places into razor-sharp blisters. He couldn't see very much, but he ran his hands over leaded windows, scarred putty, a corroded brass letter box. Then gradually he raised both hands up the center of the door and felt something bronze and heavy and gnarled. Something metallic, something which had always possessed its own cold-hearted independence, as some metallic things do, even if they have been made by men. Horseshoes, and hammers, and hooks.

"Gordon," he whispered. "Pass me your lighter."

"My what?" asked Gordon in a stridently normal voice.

"Your lighter, you idiot! And keep it down!"

Gordon passed over his Zippo. "Who are you calling an idiot? I came down here, didn't I?"

"*A shanim donk in pupik*," Stanley retorted.

"I don't even know what that *means*," Gordon hissed back furiously. "I'm not the United Nations, for Christ's sake!"

"It means, much appreciated thanks in your belly button. In other words, thanks for nothing." He flicked the Zippo's metal-grated wheel with the ball of his thumb, and the wick immediately flared up, smoky and orange and pungent.

"This thing stinks," Stanley told him.

Gordon nodded, as if Stanley had paid him a compliment. "I fill it with eighty-five percent petrol, five percent methylated spirits, five percent olive oil, and five percent Brylcreem body splash. Works a treat, doesn't it?"

Stanley held the flickering cigarette lighter up to the door. When its guttering flames eventually illuminated the knocker, however, he involuntarily took two steps back.

"God Almighty," he breathed.

The door knocker was the head of a woman, with a

blindfold wrapped tightly around her eyes. Her mouth was stretched wide open, and three fat tongues protruded from it. A coronet of spikes encircled her hair—spikes which, on closer examination, turned out to be twisted nails.

Something else became apparent as Stanley scrutinized the door knocker more closely. Her three tongues were not tongues but toads, warty and swollen, forcing their way out from between her lips, as if they were determined to choke her.

For some reason that he couldn't understand, Stanley felt a splintering sensation of alarm—but of excitement, too, as if after years of searching he had come face-to-face with something whose existence he had suspected ever since he was a boy.

It seemed absurd, but he felt for an instant that this horrifying woman's face was the key to his whole existence—as if he had been born under its influence, as if he had been schooled for the sole purpose of finding it, as if he had been bar mitzvahed in order to acquire the ethical and moral courage to face up to it.

The woman's face was terrible because she was being tortured. But what made it doubly terrible was the look of triumph which the artist had somehow managed to convey; as if she were proud of her debasement.

"Dear me," said Gordon, leaning forward to look at the door knocker more closely. "I'm surprised nobody's nicked it before now." He stepped back again and looked around the front of the house. "I mean the whole place looks completely empty, doesn't it?"

"I definitely saw him come here," said Stanley. "Maybe he's let things slide."

"Understatement of the year," Gordon replied. He rubbed the heel of his hand against the stained-glass windows in the front door. "Look at the state of these windows."

Stanley lifted the cigarette lighter higher. The stained glass was grimy, and some of the panes were chipped and cracked. But as he strained his eyes against the swiveling flame, he gradually made out the pictures which had been formed out of triangles and curves of colored glass. Unlike most Edwardian houses, which displayed stylized arts-and-crafts flowers or Elizabethan galleons under full sail, these windows showed a ghastly parade of human death. Heaps of naked white bodies were being carted through narrow streets, in the shadow of tilted buildings. Skeletons walked with skeletal dogs at their heels, elegant and terrible, with scythes over their shoulders and hourglasses in their bony hands. Fat men were lashed to posts, their bellies slashed open with huge double-headed axes, so that their bowels gushed over the feet of their executioners. Women were paraded around high in the air, impaled on tall poles, holding their arms out wide so that they wouldn't lose their balance and have even more horrifying damage inflicted on their insides.

The lower quarter of the windows was taken up by the depiction of an open mass grave, into which hundreds of bodies had already been tipped, like shoals of herring.

Just as the expression on the face of the door knocker suggested a kind of masochistic triumph, this stained-glass charivari of agony and death was made all the more grisly because of the glee on the faces of both torturers and tortured; as if pain were something to be celebrated; as if death were a huge delight.

"Jesus," Gordon whispered.

Angie came and looked at the windows, too, openmouthed, standing very close to Stanley and exuding warm wafts of Lou-lou perfume. "Bloody 'ell," she said at last. "It's 'orrible. 'Oo on earf would want a bloody 'orrible winder like that?"

"I'm having a nightmare," said Stanley, with no confidence whatsoever. "I'm still asleep and I'm having a nightmare. *No*-body has stained-glass windows like that, not in London."

"You ain't asleep, Stan, love," Angie told him, taking hold of his hand. "I promise you. I can see it, too."

Stanley kept the cigarette lighter lifted. Normally, he was repelled by pornography, and particularly by sadistic pornography. A friend in the San Francisco orchestra had once shown him a Dutch magazine with pictures of women tied up and tortured. The brightly-colored images had remained in his mind for weeks afterwards, lurid and inexplicable. What kind of woman would want to pose for a magazine like that? What kind of person would want to take pictures of her? Who could possibly derive any erotic pleasure from looking at them?

Yet tonight he found himself fascinated by the parade of torture and mutilation that flickered in the light of Gordon's Zippo. Repelled, and yet aroused. Almost as if— He extinguished that thought like extinguishing a candle flame with wet fingers.

Almost as if you'd relish such torture yourself?

"Are you going to knock, then?" asked Gordon. "I don't really feel like standing here for the rest of the night."

"What do you think?" asked Stanley dubiously.

"I think you should do what you came to do, especially

since you've dragged Angie and me along, too. To be quite honest with you, I shouldn't think there's anybody at home, Knitted Hood or not, and if there is, he certainly isn't Mr. Tasteful Home of the Year, is he?"

"These windows ..." whispered Stanley, running his fingertips across the grimy images. He held the lighter flame really close, so that he could distinguish the colors of the glass. They were drab ambers and sickly grays and diseased-looking greens.

"Certainly not things of beauty and a joy forever, are they?" Gordon remarked.

"Are you going to knock, then?" asked Angie. Even she was growing impatient.

Stanley reached out gingerly for the huge, frightening door knocker. As he did so, however, Gordon said, "There's a bell here."

Stanley pressed the brass button. They heard the faint trilling of the bell somewhere in the back of the house, where (in hinter times) the servants would have heard it.

"Bet you five quid there's nobody in," said Gordon with a confident sniff.

"You ain't 'alf pessimistic," Angie told him.

"That's me," Gordon retorted. "The gay pessimist."

But it appeared as if Gordon was right: the arcane door remained closed, and they heard no noises or footsteps inside the house. Stanley, with some reluctance, hefted up the door knocker and gave it a timid bang, but again there was no response.

"Well ... I'm sorry, it looks like I've dragged you out of bed for nothing," Stanley admitted.

"Oh, come on, give it one more shot," said Gordon, and

gave the knocker three tremendous slams against the door. A dog started barking across the road, and in the house opposite, a bedroom light was switched on, and then a curtain was drawn back.

"You didn't have to wake the whole damned neighborhood," Stanley hissed. "You were right, okay? There's nobody home."

As he said that, however, the front door squeaked very quietly on its hinges and opened a little way, no more than two or three inches. Stanley and Gordon collided with each other as they both stepped hastily away from it, expecting to see Knitted Hood confronting them, or worse.

Angie said, "You're not *scared*, are you?"

Stanley kept his eyes on the slightly-open door. It was completely dark inside, and as far as he could make out there was nobody there, although he thought he could detect the faintest pattering noise, and he thought that he could smell cold and damp. Rotten carpets, dry rot, disused store cupboards with unnamable fungus growing in them.

"Hello?" he called, his voice strangulated. "Hello?"

Gordon gave the door a cautious push. It swung open even wider, revealing a shadowy hallway, with stairs rising on the right-hand side. At the very end of the hallway, another door stood ajar; and through that door they could dimly make out another stained-glass window, a very pallid and yellowy stained-glass window, on which was depicted yet again the face of the blindfolded woman. This time, however, she wore no coronet of twisted nails, and her mouth was tightly closed.

"Hello?" Gordon ventured. "Is there anybody home?"

"Coo-ee!" called Angie.

Gordon turned to stare at her. "'Coo-ee'? That's no way to call on a diseased maniac rapist, for God's sake."

Angie flushed and looked embarrassed, until she realized that Gordon was ribbing her. In fact, Gordon had woken up sufficiently to have regained his waspish sense of mischief; and even if they weren't going to have a real adventure, at least they could have some laughs.

"I vote we go inside and take a look," he suggested. "I mean, just look at the state of this place, nobody lives here. Then if you see your lady again, your Madeleine Stringer or whatever her name is, you can tell her that she's talking through the back of her head."

"Actually, she said that he *didn't* live here," said Stanley thoughtfully, remembering Madeleine Springer's words.

Gordon planted his hands on his lips. "She said he *didn't* live here? Then what on earth are we doing here at all? I thought you said that—"

"No, no," Stanley interrupted him. "She didn't mean in the sense that he didn't live here ... more like he didn't *live* here."

"I fail to see the distinction," said Gordon.

"To tell you the truth, I didn't totally understand myself what she meant. But the more I think about it, the more it seems like she was trying to say that he's here, but he's not alive—I mean not in the sense that you're alive and I'm alive."

Gordon gave an exasperated little sigh. "Oh, *very* clear."

"You mean 'e's dead?" asked Angie.

"I don't know. Maybe he's neither."

"Are we going inside or not?" Gordon wanted to know.

Stanley turned back towards the shadowy doorway. He could still hear that faint pattering noise ... still smell that terminal sourness. It was like the sourness of death, corpses washed in vinegar.

—*swathe through the*—, somebody whispered.

He stepped into the hallway without another word. If he had spoken, he may not have had the courage to go in. He had always thought that people in horror movies who deliberately go to investigate strange noises in the night (*always* in the dark, *always* alone) were acting completely at odds with human nature. With *his* nature, anyway. He didn't mind facing up to real-life threats, he wasn't scared of bullies or blowhards, but when it came to noises in the night he was an advocate of the famous bury-your-head-under-the-blankets-and-wait-until-it-goes-away technique.

Gordon hesitated for a moment, then followed him inside, holding out his hand for Angie. Angie hesitated, too, looking dubiously at Gordon's hand.

"Homosexuality isn't *catching*, you know," Gordon told her.

They stood together in the darkness. Inside the hallway, the smell of decay was almost overwhelming; partly sweet, partly fishy, partly acidic.

"Smells like a mortuary," Gordon remarked.

Angie said, "Ssh! Can you 'ear anything?"

Again, that light pattering sound; steady and insistent. Gordon looked at Stanley, and Stanley looked at Gordon. "Sounds like dripping water," said Stanley at length. "Maybe a pipe's burst. That could account for the smell, too."

"Only one way to find out," said Gordon. He flicked his cigarette lighter and held it up in front of him. Its dripping flame made shadows come alive on the walls, leaping and froghopping all around them. The walls were papered in a pattern of huge faded roses. So much of the color had soaked out of them that they looked more like decaying cabbages. There were no pictures on the walls, although grimy rectangular outlines marked the places where pictures had once hung. At the far side of the hallway was suspended an old barometer, its veneered case corrugated by years of damp. Its face was thick with dust; its needle was stuck at *Rain*.

Gordon ventured further along the hallway, and Stanley followed him. Angie came close behind, clinging on to Stanley's sleeve. Ahead of them, the stained-glass window of the blindfolded woman gleamed and stirred in the light of Gordon's Zippo, almost as if it had suddenly awakened. Now that they were closer to it, Stanley could see that the background to the woman's head was made up of dozens of hooded figures, facing left and right, their outlines interlocking like one of the illusory drawings of M. C. Escher.

"What do you make of that window?" Stanley asked Gordon. But he was interrupted by Angie exclaiming, "Urggh!" and suddenly lifting up her left foot. "This carpet's bloody *soaking*!"

In her strappy little shoes, she had noticed the sodden carpet first. Gordon lowered the lighter, and Stanley could see that the crimson-patterned Axminster was swollen with water, and that every time he put his foot down, he squeezed out a large wet footprint.

"Burst pipe, no doubt about it," said Gordon.

They had reached what Stanley presumed to the the door to the main downstairs living room. They paused; and now they could hear the water much more clearly. Gordon placed his hand against the door and said, "Soaked through, absolutely soaked through."

That pattering sound, thought Stanley. *That doesn't sound like a burst pipe. That sounds like—*

"Can we go now?" Angie fretted. "I'm going to ruin me shoes."

"Let's just take a shufti in here," said Gordon, and turned the door handle. But the door wouldn't budge. He turned the green key and announced, "It's not locked. The frame must have swollen in the wet. How about putting our shoulders to it?"

Angie held the cigarette lighter while Stanley and Gordon thumped their shoulders against the door panels. "Come on," she jeered. "You two couldn't fight your way out of a paper bag."

Gordon gave the door a petulant kick.

"We have to do it together," Stanley told him. "It's no good us bouncing backwards and forwards alternately. It's like music, okay? Timing!"

"All right, then," Gordon agreed. "One, two, three, Geronimo!"

Together they walloped their shoulders against the door; and this time they jarred it inwards a quarter of an inch, wet wood protesting against wet wood. "Again!" shouted Stanley, and this time they almost managed to open it. "One more!"

The door hurtled open and juddered a quarter of the way back again. Angie let out a sarcastic "Hoo-ray!" but she swallowed it almost as soon as she said it. Inside the living room, it was gloomy and cold, and a persistent wind blew. The walls snaked with running water, the carpeted floor was awash. In the middle of the room a three-piece suite of heavy brown 1930s design stood miserably dripping. The tiled hearth overflowed; on the sideboard water trickled out of the brimming fruit bowl, in which three or four swollen apples still bobbed, blotchy and brown, like human kidneys in a specimen jar.

Inside the living room, there were no burst pipes. *Inside the living room, it was raining*.

Stanley held out his hand. It was rain, there was no mistaking it. He stared up at the ceiling but there was nothing to be seen there except water-stained plaster. The rain was falling out of the ceiling as if the ceiling simply weren't there; as if it were open sky. Yet he could see the ceiling clearly. He could see its damp-blurred acanthus-leaf moldings and the ugly brown glass lampshade that was suspended from the center of it.

He took one step into the room, then another. The wind was the same as the rain—it blew keenly through the room as if the walls simply didn't exist. Yet the walls *did* exist; he could see that they existed, he could feel them, and even though the rain was falling from nowhere at all, it was making the walls wet.

Stanley touched the sofa. It was upholstered with soggy brocade. He lifted an antimacassar from one of its cushions and held it up for a moment. It dripped, he dropped it. It was real, he could *feel* it was real. But this whole room was very much more than it appeared. It wasn't just a dowdy wet living room in southwest London; it was somewhere else, too. In defiance of all the laws of matter, in defiance of any kind of logic or sense, this room was two places at the same time.

Stanley turned back to Gordon, who was standing in the doorway, with an odd expression on his face, as if somebody had just tried to explain the theory of relativity to him and failed.

"Am I dreaming?" Stanley asked.

Gordon stared at him. "It's *raining*. How can it be raining?"

"Am I asleep or am I awake?" Stanley demanded.

Gordon stepped into the room, too, and lifted his face to the ceiling, and to the falling rain. "You're awake, Stanley. And I'm awake, too. What about you, Angie? Come on in!"

"No fear," said Angie. "It's bad enough getting me shoes wet wivout getting me hair wet, too."

Stanley walked around the room in a slow, measured circle. The rain plastered his hair against his forehead and darkened the shoulders of his coat. It was extraordinary. It felt exactly the same as if they were standing outside, and yet here they were, in somebody's living room. He drew back the brown brocade curtains, heavy with water, and through the murky, misted-up window he could see the orange sodium lights of Kew Gardens Road.

"Maybe this is what Madeleine Springer meant by not living here," Stanley suggested. "Maybe this is two places at once … two different places kind of overlapping each other. So you could be here and not here, both at the same time."

"It's rain," Gordon repeated. "That's what I can't get over. It's actual rain."

He went to the wall beside the fireplace and laid his hands flat against the wallpaper. "I can feel the wind on my hands, but I can feel the wall, too. It's incredible. It's the most incredible thing I've ever seen."

Angie, who was still patiently holding up Gordon's cigarette lighter, asked, "Can we go now? I'm ever so cold."

"Do you see this, Angie? It's rain," Stanley explained.

There was a look in Angie's eyes which told Stanley that she didn't want to talk about it; that it was all too frightening for her. She didn't even want to marvel at it. She just wanted to leave, as quickly as she could.

"Okay," he told her, "let's go. Maybe you'd all like to come back to my place for breakfast."

"Don't you think we ought to take a look upstairs?" said Gordon.

"Upstairs?"

Gordon nodded toward the ceiling. "I'd be interested to know if it's raining upstairs, that's all. I mean—is the rain coming through the ceiling from the room above, or is it in this room only?"

Stanley turned his face toward the wind. It was pungent, the wind. It smelled of river. "I don't know," he told Gordon. "I really don't know. I'm not so sure that I care any more."

"You came here to face down this Knitted Hood character, didn't you? You came here to find out what he was all about?"

"I don't know. I'm confused. How the hell can it be *raining* in here?"

"My dearest Stanley, I haven't a clue. But let's try to find out, shall we?"

Stanley felt an unexpected surge of hatred for Gordon. He couldn't think why he had invited him to come here to Kew in the first place. It was raining, the wind was blowing, what more did Gordon want? Sometimes things happened because they happened, and you didn't question them. Why did Gordon want to interfere?

Gordon came out of the living room and shook his

wet hair like a dog. He came up close to Stanley so that Stanley could smell the wet leather of his jacket and the strong undertone of Cerruti after-shave. "I'm converted," he announced. "Just like Saul, on the road to Damascus, I done seen the light. You, my dear, have got yourself involved with something really"—he searched for the word—"*outré.*"

"I just want to know whether I'm asleep or awake," Stanley replied stiffly. His whole being felt as if it were rigid with panic, like a jammed-up ten-lever dead-lock.

Gordon looked at him for quite a long time. "You really don't know?"

Stanley shook his head.

"He's done something serious to you, hasn't he?" Gordon asked. "Even if he hasn't actually infected you ... he's had an effect on your mind. He's altered your whole perception of things."

"What the hell is it to you?" roared Stanley. "What the hell difference—!"

"Hey now, shush, come on now," said Gordon. "You're under a strain, right? You're still trying to make sense of what happened to you. That's why you came here today. But let me tell you this ... you're awake and I'm awake, okay? You can see that rain and feel that wind, but so can I. It's all *real*, my love. So if we're going to find out what your problem is, we're going to have to understand what's happening in this house. Yes?"

Angie said, "Can we go now? My plates are freezing."

Stanley was instantly enraged, almost as if he were drunk. "Will you shut up?" he screamed at her. And then, angrily, at Gordon, "I'm sorry! All right? I'm very, very, very sorry! I'm sorry I dragged you out of bed, I'm sorry I brought you here. I'm sorry I came here myself! You were right the first time! It's a burst pipe! It's nothing! It's a waste of time! So we're going, all right? *Vamos!* Forget it!"

Gordon folded his arms and leaned obstinately back against the door frame. "I'm still going upstairs, Stanley. You don't witness the greatest miracle since the loaves and the fishes, and turn your back on it and go back home for Gold Blend coffee and a bowl of Rice Krispies."

"Gordon, this is *my* life and *my* problem," Stanley replied, trying his best to be patient, his voice wet-sand-slushy with badly-contained rage.

"Exactly," Gordon replied. "And that's why I'm going to go on helping you, whether you want me to help you or not."

"God preserve me," said Stanley.

"He will." Gordon smiled. "And so will I."

Gordon took the hot flickering lighter from Angie and squelched back along the wet-carpeted hallway to the foot of the stairs. He mounted one stair, then another, then another, while Stanley stayed where he was, with his back against the faded rose wallpaper, watching him, and Angie shivered like a young child lost at Coney Island. After a sixth or seventh stair, Gordon leaned over the banister rail, the lighter flame held close to his face, so that it looked like an illuminated clown's mask suspended in the air, and asked, "Coming, are we? Or are we scared?"

"Do we 'ave to?" Angie asked Stanley.

"I'll go," Stanley told her. "You wait outside. We won't be long."

"I'm not waiting outside by myself."

"Well, in that case, come on upstairs with us. I doubt if there's anything up there."

They walked to the foot of the stairs, and Stanley went up first, turning to Angie and saying, "It's okay. There's nothing to be frightened of. It's just some kind of weird natural phenomenon. You know, like St. Elmo's Fire, or mirages in the desert."

"All right," Angie agreed, although she didn't sound very happy about it.

Gordon climbed on ahead, taking three and four stairs at a time. He turned a bend in the stairs, and for a moment all they could see of him was his huge hunchbacked shadow. "Sounds like it's raining upstairs, too!" he called back.

"Bloody 'ell," Angie muttered. "Right 'ow's-your-father this is."

"Come on," Stanley encouraged her. Gordon's insouciance had given him new courage. "It's only rain, after all."

They joined Gordon on the upstairs landing. There were five doors off it, four bedrooms, probably, and a bathroom. On the walls hung dozens of dark and diminutive paintings and prints, so small that they were almost miniatures, of the same blindfolded woman whose likeness appeared on the door knocker, and in the stained-glass window at the end of the hallway. Stanley peered closely at the pictures and discovered that each of them varied slightly. In one, the woman had a coronet of what looked like fishhooks piercing the skin of her forehead. In another, her mouth was crammed full to choking with a green herb that looked like parsley or coriander. In a third, the head of a dead martlet protruded from her lips.

"What the hell do you think these pictures are all about?" he asked Gordon.

Gordon, leaning over his shoulder, slowly shook his head.

"I haven't the faintest idea. Perhaps they're all symbolic. They remind me of tarot cards a bit. Rather *medieval*, if you know what I mean."

When Stanley examined the paintings even more closely, he could see that their backgrounds varied, too. In some, there were gloomy forested landscapes or the battlements of broken-down Teutonic castles. In others, there were deserted beaches, or overgrown gardens, or long empty corridors with harlequin-patterned tiles. All that every one of the paintings seemed to carry in common was the blindfolded girl and a small hooded figure in the distance—a figure that was always looking away or hurrying off in the opposite direction.

Stanley stopped in front of a painting in which the blindfolded girl was depicted in front of a landscape of boggy, deserted fields, and a ramshackle collection of huts and lean-tos and pigpens. In this picture, thick whitish fluid was pouring from the sides of her mouth, and Stanley could only guess what it was supposed to be.

"I recognize that landscape," he whispered to Gordon.

"You *recognize* it?"

"I saw it when I was in hospital … in a dream or some kind of hallucination. It's the same landscape, I swear it."

Angie shivered. "D'you mind if we 'urry up, please?"

They all looked around the landing and listened. The same sound of rain pattering on to wet carpets was just as apparent up here as it had been downstairs in the hallway. "Let's try some of these doors," Stanley suggested. "This room looks like it's directly on top of the living room, right?"

They opened it up but it was nothing more than a linen cupboard, still filled with neat stacks of pillowcases and towels and yellowing sheets. Gordon said, "I get the feeling that whoever lived here left in rather a hurry, don't you? I mean, who's going to leave all their best linen behind?"

"P'raps they died," said Angie.

"Yes, well, perhaps they did," Gordon agreed. "But I'm beginning to think that Stanley could be right, and that Knitted Hood *does* live here. Or *not* live here, whichever way you want to put it."

"You're actually beginning to sound like you believe me," said Stanley.

"Well, yes," Gordon admitted with a complicated little smile. "It's not every day you see it raining inside somebody's living room, is it? And—listen—if you're right about that landscape—if it's really the identical landscape you saw when you were in hospital—then there must be some connection between whoever lives here and what happened to you when you were attacked."

"You should've been a lawyer," Stanley complimented him.

"I nearly was," said Gordon. "Unfortunately, you know … I was always a little bit too flamboyant." He turned to Angie. "Too much of a raging gay, in other words, my little buttercup."

"Are we going or what?" Angie wanted to know. Her teeth were chattering, and she was obviously far too frightened to be riled by Gordon's bantering. Stanley thought that it was remarkable that Gordon was able to remain so lighthearted. He might be effeminate and over-sensitive, but now that he had decided that he was going to find out what was happening in this extraordinary house, he seemed to be nerveless, completely lacking in fear.

He remembered his father telling him about a transvestite

sergeant in the Japanese-American 442nd, in Italy during the war, who had taken a German dugout by galloping towards them in an electric-blue ball gown, screeching a soprano battle cry, and firing his machine gun from the hip. The Germans had been too stunned by his appearance to fire back.

"There are brave *timtums* and coward *timtums* just like normal people," his father had told him, and anybody else who was prepared to listen to his war memoirs. But Stanley knew that he would have been mortally grieved if Stanley had turned out to be homosexual. He was almost pleased that his father hadn't lived to witness the breakup of his marriage to Eve.

"All right, what do we next?" asked Gordon.

"Let's try this one," Stanley suggested, taking hold of the handle of the door to the left of the linen closet. The handle was duller and more corroded than any of the others. The wood felt damp.

The door was easier to open than the living room door downstairs, although Gordon had to give it a sharp kick to free it from its frame. Inside, it was raining hard; but it was much lighter than the living room, because the streetlamp directly opposite Tennyson was able to shine into the window. The floor was covered with linoleum, scattered with sodden rugs. The only furniture appeared to be an iron-framed bed, heaped with blankets, and a small battered bureau, which somebody had once painted medicine-pink and covered with My Little Pony stickers.

Gordon and Stanley walked into the room and looked around. Stanley raised his collar against the persistent rain. It seemed to fall right out of the ceiling and right through the floor, into the living room below. If anything, it was even heavier up here; and the wind was certainly keener.

"Maybe it's some kind of microclimate," Stanley volunteered. "Some kind of electrical disturbance."

"Maybe it's raining in somebody's bedroom," Gordon replied. "No more, no less. One of those things you have to accept."

He walked across the window and looked out. Then he crossed to the fireplace. It was small and arched; a typical Edwardian bedroom fireplace, in olive-green tiles, with stylized lilies curving around it.

"These fireplaces are worth a bit, these days," said Gordon, "Everybody ripped them out when they put in central heating, so they're getting quite rare. Burglars don't take stereos and televisions any more, they dismantle your Victorian staircases and tear out your period fireplaces. Sign of the times, hmh? I used to hate these fireplaces when I was a kid. They remind me of my grannie; and toast-and-dripping, because that's all she could afford to feed me."

They were just about to leave when they heard a high, shuddering sigh. Stanley stared at Gordon in alarm, his wet neck tingling. "What was that?" he whispered. "Did you hear that?"

"Yes, I don't know," said Gordon. "It sounded like it came from the bed."

Angie, from the landing, pleaded, "Can't we go now? Please? This is 'orrible."

"Just a minute," Stanley begged her. He circled around the end of the bed and frowned at the filthy ragged blankets that were heaped up on it.

"Is anybody there?" he asked, as sharply as he dared.

"It looks like nothing but a heap of bedding to me," Gordon remarked.

Stanley leaned closer. "You want to lift some of it up and find out?"

"No. Do you?"

"No. Me neither."

They waited, and listened, while the rain continued to patter against the carpet, and water continued to drip down the walls. For no logical reason, Stanley began to feel an immense sense of fear; a sense of fear unequaled to anything he had ever experienced. It was even worse than that light-airplane tour of the Napa Valley wine country that Eve had given him three years ago for a birthday present. He hated to fly at the best of times: but the Cessna's engine had cut out just as they were climbing toward Lake Berryessa, and the mountains had relentlessly swollen larger and larger like a panful of milk boiling over, and he had bent his head forward and squeezed his eyes tight shut and prayed that dying wouldn't hurt too much.

Now he felt a sensation that was deeper and more gut-wrenching than anything he had ever known; as if his actual *soul* were being swayed from side to side; as if the world he walked on wasn't safe.

We shall cut a swathe, the voice whispered in his ear. *It could be your past, it could be your future.*

In his dream, the girl's handcart had been heaped up with old rags. Just like these rags that were heaped on the bed. Filthy, soft, and swaying.

They're bodies, he thought, and froze rigid.

"Stan?" queried Gordon. "Stanley?"

They're bodies, he repeated, although he wasn't sure that he had spoken out loud.

"Stanley, what's the matter?"

On the bed. They're bodies.

He swiveled his head around slowly and looked toward Angie standing in the doorway. For a split shuddering second he could have believed that Angie was blindfolded; but then she opened her eyes and she was staring at him in terror. Her mouth opened and closed, and the words reached him through the rain, like somebody talking on a radio through thick electric static. *Stanley I'm scared Stanley I want to go now please Stanley please.*

He turned back to Gordon, and Gordon was reaching his hand out towards the heap of rags and so much fear collided in his mind that he couldn't even find the air in his lungs to shout out *Don't!*

All he could think of was the girl pushing the handcart up that muddy road, and the bodies nodding as she pushed them, nod, nod, nod, in the obscene helplessness of death, almost as if they were taunting him because they were nothing but meat now and their movements were controlled not by muscle and not by consciousness, but by inertia and by gravity.

"Don't," he said; and this time he heard his own voice, clear and quiet.

Gordon had already lifted one of the blankets. "They're blankets," he said, although the look on his face made it clear that he understood what Stanley had been thinking. "Stanley? They're blankets."

He stripped them off the bed, one by one. They were rancid, and heavily stained, and clotted with rainwater, but they were only blankets, after all.

Stanley wiped rain from his forehead with the back of his hand. "I'm sorry. I didn't realize."

"What else did you see in that dream?" Gordon asked him.

Stanley lowered his head. He felt unexpectedly emotional. "Dead people," he said. "Like the plague, you know? When they came around to collect dead bodies on handcarts. Or like the Holocaust maybe, Belsen or Auschwitz. I've seen it two or three times since then. A girl, a young woman, pushing a handcart heaped up with bodies."

Gordon smeared rain from his face with his hand. Stanley had never seen him look so serious. At least he was convinced that Stanley wasn't traumatized or mad. How could he not be convinced, in a house full of blindfolded faces, a house where it rained indoors?

"I think before we go any further we'd better find somebody who understands this kind of thing," Gordon said. "I'm a counselor, not an exorcist."

"Maybe a priest might know," Stanley suggested.

"I don't know. Either a priest or a meteorologist."

Gordon dropped the blanket he was holding, and they turned to leave.

"Are we going?" asked Angie in shivering relief.

They had almost reached the door when they heard a scratching, tumbling noise in the fireplace. Stanley hesitated, and frowned at it. "Did you hear that?"

"Sounded like a starling, falling down the chimney. They do that sometimes."

They stood in the chilly, persistent rain, listening. Another scratch; and then a quick, furtive dragging sound, and a sharp *pitter-patter* that sounded like a dog's claws on parquet flooring.

"There's definitely something there," said Stanley.

"If it isn't a bird, then it's probably a rat," Gordon told him. "I wouldn't go too close. They're infected with just about every disgusting disease you can think of, and a few more you wouldn't even *want* to think of."

But Stanley shielded his eyes against the rain and peered intently at the small arched Edwardian fireplace, and he could see brownish soot showering softly down inside it, into the narrow rusted grate, and hear scratching and scuffling and *whispering*, he was sure of it, somebody was *whispering*.

"Hello?" he called unsteadily.

Gordon said, "For goodness' sake, Stanley, there can't be anybody stuck in the chimney. It simply isn't big enough. You're saying hello to a rat."

"Gordon, I can hear whispering."

Gordon listened. "It's the rain, that's all."

"Can we please go now?" Angie called, even more plaintively than before. "It's absolutely brass monkeys in 'ere."

Gordon ignored her and knelt down in front of the fireplace. He listened again, and this time he nodded. "I'm sorry, Stanley, you're right. I *can* hear somebody whispering. Maybe it's somebody in the house next door; or somebody's radio."

"Can you hear what they're saying?" asked Stanley.

Gordon shook his head. "Sounds like they're laughing, or *growling*, I don't know. It's very odd."

Stanley said, "It's almost three-thirty. Maybe we'd better leave. It doesn't look like we're going to find Knitted Hood."

"Just a minute," said Gordon, angling his head so that

he could see up the chimney. "There's something here. An opening."

Cautiously, he reached his hand into the fireplace and felt up inside the canopy. "There's an opening here, definitely. I can feel the draft coming through. It feels as if somebody's knocked the bricks out of the back of the flue."

He withdrew his hand and looked up the chimney again. "Damn soot keeps dropping in my eyes. I'm going to look like Al Jolson after this."

He stared up into the darkness for almost a minute. Stanley, with his hand resting on the rain-spotted tiles of the mantel, began to feel impatient. Outside on the landing, Angie was pacing nervously and irritably backwards and forwards, and letting out louder and louder sighs of annoyance.

Stanley was about to suggest that they call it a night when—without any warning at all—Gordon jerked away from the fireplace and fell back against the bed, knocking his shoulder against the iron upright.

"What?" Stanley demanded. "What?"

Gordon looked up at him in astonishment. "There's a boy in there."

"A what? What are you talking about?"

"There's a boy up the chimney! I saw his face."

"For God's sake, Gordon. How can there be a boy up the chimney?"

"How the hell should I know? I was trying to make out where that opening was, and all of a sudden I saw this white round face, with black eyes, and this sort of bristly hair, and it was staring right back at me."

Stanley swallowed dryly. He dropped down on to one

knee himself, and slightly lowered his head, and looked up inside the chimney canopy.

"I don't see anything."

"I saw him, I swear it."

Stanley waited for a moment and then called, "Hey! Up in the chimney! Anybody there?"

A flurry of scratching; another soft shower of soot; but no reply.

Gordon came closer. "Hello? Hello, can you hear me? Are you stuck up there?"

Still nothing; so Gordon said, "We're friends, we can help you! If you're stuck, we can call the fire brigade. Are you stuck up there, or did you just climb up there?"

A short, harsh noise, but still no reply.

Stanley called, "Why don't you tell us your name? Did you come here alone, or did you have friends with you? You won't get into any trouble, I promise. But if you're stuck, we sure can't leave you up there, can we?"

Angie came into the room, her collar turned up against the rain. She hunkered down close behind Stanley and laid her hand on his shoulder.

"'Oo you talking to?" she wanted to know.

"Gordon says he saw a boy up the chimney."

"You what?"

"Gordon says that when he looked up the chimney, he saw a boy's face. White, with bristly hair."

"P'raps it's a reflection. But if it's got bristly 'air, p'raps it's an old sweep's brush, aye?"

"There's a boy there," Gordon insisted. "I saw his face quite clearly."

"'E ain't answering back, though, is 'e?"

"Maybe he's in shock," said Stanley. "Maybe his chest is wedged so tightly in the chimney that he can't draw enough breath to speak."

"He doesn't *sound* as if he's tightly wedged. He sounds as though he's almost—I don't know—running around up there."

"Maybe the opening goes through from the chimney into another room, and he's just poking his head out."

Gordon shuffled himself right up against the fireplace. "Boy!" he called. "Hey, you up there! Boy! We're going to call the fire brigade, do you understand me? We're going to call the fire brigade and get you out!"

There was a moment's pause, and then Gordon suddenly said, "There! He's looking at me! I can see his face! Hey, you up there! Can you nod or blink? How about one blink for yes, two for no?"

"Let me take a look," said Stanley, and crouched down beside Gordon's left shoulder.

He couldn't see anything at first, the inside of the chimney was so dark compared with the dim orange light in the bedroom. But then gradually he distinguished a pale round face, with dark and rather protuberant eyes, and short bristling hair. The face was looking at him from just above the breast of the flue. Looking at him, without any expression at all, so that Stanley couldn't even be certain that the boy could see him. Maybe it just appeared that he was looking at him. Maybe he was blind.

Maybe—and this was the most chilling thought of all—*maybe he was dead. Maybe he was wedged tight upside down in this chimney, within four feet of the open fireplace, and that's where he had suffocated, or starved. A lonely, agonizing, long-drawn-out death. He had heard of Victorian boy chimney sweeps dying that way. Maybe it had happened by accident to this boy, too.*

Yet, if he were dead, who had been doing all that scratching and shuffling?

Rats, maybe, gnawing his flesh? Or crows. Crows picked at dead flesh, too.

Stanley glanced back at Gordon. "Do you think he's still alive?"

"I don't know," Gordon replied. "He could be comatose, from lack of oxygen."

"I think we ought to call a namblunce," said Angie. "And the fire brigade. *And* the Old Bill."

"Yes, you're right, we ought to," Gordon agreed. "Perhaps I should try to reach him … I should be able to feel if he's breathing or not, or if he's still warm."

"Well, for God's sake be careful," Stanley cautioned him.

Gordon sat in the tiled hearth tailor-fashion with his legs crossed, and tugged up the sleeve of his coat. Then he rested his cheek against the curved iron canopy over the hearth and reached as far up the chimney as he could.

"Can you reach him?" asked Stanley.

"Unh-hunh, not quite yet. He's just—"

He shuffled himself a little closer to the hearth and grimaced as he reached even further up the flue.

"You should be able to feel 'is breaf on yer fingers," said Angie. "That's if 'e's breaving."

"I can't feel anything." Gordon winced. "Not so far, anyway."

"Oh, God, he's dead," said Stanley. Although another voice said, *Serve him right, the stupid dumb bastard kid. Serve him right if he suffered and choked. I hope he panicked. I hope he cried. I hope he understood what death was going to be, before he died.*

He saw Angie looking at him suspiciously; her face rain-streaked, her mascara smudged, her hair bedraggled, not bright, but child-pretty, and sharp as a knife; far too knowing and erotic for a girl of nineteen. He suddenly realized how insanely he was smiling and tried to reassure her by smiling more naturally. It didn't seem to work. He seemed to have lost control of his face. All he could think about was the way (in his dream) that she had played his Vuillaume violin, her bitten fingernails skip-dancing up and down the fingerboard. All he could think about was the curves of her naked bottom and his own ejaculation. It was like watching a pornographic video set to the most exquisite sound track.

"I can feel him," said Gordon. "I can feel his forehead. He feels *cold* … I can't feel any breathing."

"That's it, he's dead," Stanley heard himself saying.

Gordon said, "Hold on, wait … I thought his eyelashes flickered. Perhaps he's—

"*Aaaahhhhhh!*" Gordon screamed, his voice so high-pitched and penetrating that Stanley's brain didn't register at first that his ears had heard anything at all—only that the air in the room had been somehow condensed into an expression of concentrated pain.

"*Aaaah, my hand! Oh, Christ, my hand!*"

Stanley threw himself down on his knees beside him and gripped the shoulder of his coat. "Gordon? *Gordon?*"

Gordon stared at him wildly, his face emptied of color.

He blurted out something, but it sounded like a foreign language, the dialect of unremitting agony.

"What?" Stanley demanded. "What's happened? For God's sake, Gordon, what's happened?"

"My ha—" Gordon began. But his survival instinct must have decided that rescuing himself from further pain was far more important than talking, because he twisted his head away, his teeth gritted, the tendons in his neck as tight as violin strings, and wrenched his arm downwards, out of the chimney, in a shower of soot and a bursting splatter of rusty-colored blood.

But something else flopped heavily out of the chimney, into the hearth, and thrashed furiously from side to side on the end of Gordon's bloodied arm. Angie screamed and tripped backwards against the wall. Stanley grabbed the end of the bed and pulled himself on to his feet—terrified, incredulous, his mind exploding like a fission bomb.

This cannot be! This simply cannot be! And yet it must be, because I'm here now, watching it, and it's jerking and tussling around in front of me.

Clinging ferociously to Gordon's hand was a boy's head; a white-faced, bristly-haired boy's head, with protuberant eyes and a snubbish nose. His teeth were sunk deeply into the meaty flesh just above Gordon's thumb, and already Gordon's thumb was waggling dangerously sideways as if the boy's teeth were an eighth of an inch away from ripping it off altogether. Gordon's hand was smothered in blood; and the boy's face looked as if it had been toothbrush-sprayed in carmine red.

But it wasn't the blood or the savagery of the boy's attack

that caused Stanley to stumble away so quickly. It was the boy himself. He had the head of a boy, but the short brutish body of a dog. He looked like a pit bull with a human head. Four paws, a deep-barreled chest, brindled fur, and a tail. And although his face was handsome, in a bulgy-eyed Donald Sutherland kind of way, his teeth were curved and bloody, and he snapped and snarled with all the ferocity of a dog.

Gordon heaved himself sideways, hitting the boy-dog loudly and wetly against the floor. He was screaming all the time, out of rage, out of pain, but mostly out of absolute terror. Angie screamed, too, and the rain lashed down from the ceiling, and for a moment Stanley didn't know whether he was in London or in hell.

What brought him back to stark reality was the sight of the boy-dog's teeth tearing the rumpled skin from the back of Gordon's hand, and then—with a sharp crackling sound—the raw scarlet flesh of the lumbrical muscles, the palmar muscles, and even the interosseous muscles between the fingerbones. It was like watching a bloody glove being wrenched off; because then the arteries fountained, the deep palmar arch and the princeps pollicis, which feeds the thumb.

Angie shrieked, "Stan-*leeee!*"

Stanley didn't really know what to do. But he dragged one of the sodden blankets from the bed, swung it around like Dracula's cloak, and hurled it over the boy-dog's back. It landed with a thick, felty slap. The boy-dog snarled and whiplashed, but Stanley took hold of its body and tried to heft it away from Gordon's hand. He could scarcely hold it. It was solid bunched-up muscle from head to toe, writhing and fighting and wriggling. He couldn't believe how much it *weighed*. Its claws lashed his knuckles, then his wrists. He gripped it as tightly as he could; but then the blanket slipped away from its head and it twisted around and snarled at him and *God Almighty! It was the face of a boy!* and his fingers locked and he let it drop to the floor.

It retreated across the bedroom floor, growling softly, with the bloody rags that it had torn from Gordon's hand dripping from its mouth. Rusty-red splashes, instantly diluted with rainwater.

Stanley gave Gordon one quick sickened sideways glance. Gordon was lying on his side, too shocked to whimper, his right hand reduced to red-stripped bones, his left thumb pressed on to his wrist to stop the blond pumping straight out of his ulnar artery all over the floor. He looked as if he had borrowed his eyes from Peter Falk: black, glassy, not quite focusing.

Angie said, in an off-key voice, "It's not real, is it?"

"I don't know," Stanley replied, picking up the wet-heavy blanket and holding it up in front of the pit-bull boy like a cautious matador. "Maybe we're dreaming, maybe we're not. Do you think you could make it to the door? Call an ambulance?"

"God, I'll try," Angie told him.

"Gordon?" asked Stanley. "Gordon, are you okay?"

Gordon stared back at him, desperate to speak, but shuddering too violently to say anything coherent.

The boy-dog gagged down the rest of the flesh that he had torn from Gordon's hand with two sickening twists of his neck. As he chewed it, he watched Stanley with bulbous, suspicious eyes. Stanley lifted the blanket and shook it, trying to be threatening. The boy-dog took two or three paces back, his claws clicking on the floor, but he didn't look frightened. He was obviously more interested in finishing his meal than in attacking Stanley's blanket.

Shakily, Stanley challenged him. "What are you? Hunh? Are you a boy, or a dog, or what?"

The boy-dog watched him and continually licked his lips and said nothing.

"Am I dreaming about you?" Stanley asked him. "Are you a dream? Come on, let's have some honesty here. Dogs with boy's heads? No such creature! *A nechtiger tog!*"

The boy-dog swallowed, and snarled a blood-bubbly snarl.

"Angie?" asked Stanley without turning around. "Did you call that ambulance yet?"

"Stanley," Angie called him. Not loudly; a shade above a stage whisper. The rain still sifted down between them.

Stanley flicked his eyes sideways once; twice. And then he saw what was worrying her. Two more boy-dogs were standing in the doorway, blocking Angie's escape, one white and one greasy-brown, with human heads, their tails slapping noisily against their haunches. A boy who looked almost angelic, with bright blue eyes; and a darker boy, with freckles and a mad serious look, as if he could happily tear out Angie's throat.

"Stanley ..." moaned Angie. "Stanley ..."

Stanley backed away from the fireplace, still holding up the blanket, with the intention of circling around Angie and protecting her from the two boy-dogs in the doorway. But as soon as he took one step back, the boy-dog by the hearth took two or three steps towards Gordon.

"Stanley, for Christ's sake," Gordon croaked, his hand all bones and blood. "Stanley, he's going to kill me."

The boy-dog snarled and barked, although it sounded more like a sharp high-pitched human shout than a dog barking. The other two boy-dogs growled, too, and came into the rain-drenched room with their teeth bared and their eyes bulging. Strings of saliva swung from their chins, and the boy-dog with the bright blue eyes began to foam around the mouth. Their claws *chip-chip-chipped* at the linoleum flooring.

Angie retreated until she and Stanley were standing back-to-back. She reached behind her and clung on to Stanley's rain-soaked coat. "Stanley, I'm so bloody scared. Is it a dream, Stanley? Can't you wake me up?"

"Just take it easy," Stanley told her. He could feel her shivering. "So long as we don't make any sudden moves … upset them, or anything."

"Upset them? Bloody 'ell, Stanley, they want to kill us, that's all!"

Stanley was numb with cold and soaking wet and his arms were already aching from holding up the heavy wet blanket for so long. The boy-dogs edged closer still, never taking their eyes off them. It occurred to Stanley in a detached way that Angie was right, and the boy-dogs were quite determined to tear them to pieces, and that there was no hope at all of any of them leaving Tennyson alive.

Chapter Five

Braided Whip

The two boy-dogs stretched back their lips and bared their teeth, and started to advance on them with quick little steps, their tails stiffened and their ears flat back against the sides of their heads. Angie gasped and gripped Stanley even more tightly. On the floor, weak from shock and loss of blood, Gordon abruptly dropped back and lay helplessly panting, while the first boy-dog ventured close enough to sniff at his shoe.

Stanley was sure now that the boy-dogs couldn't be reasoned with. They might have human heads, but they were totally animalistic and blindly ferocious. All the same, it was difficult to look down at the freckled face of the boy who was sniffing at Gordon's ankle and not believe that he was capable of human speech; or at least of human thought. All the time that he was stalking Gordon, his eyes remained fixed on Stanley, as if he were daring Stanley to stop him.

Go on, then, stop me. Try to stop me. You don't dare, do you, Stanley? You just don't dare.

Stanley leaned his head back towards Angie. Out of the corner of his mouth, he murmured, "It's no use staying here.

We won't stand a chance. We're going to have to try to rush our way out. If we wrap this blanket around ourselves, it should stop them from biting at our legs."

"What about Gordon?" asked Angie, her teeth chattering.

"I don't know. Gordon?"

Gordon opened his eyes, but his face was gray, and he didn't seem to have heard.

"Gordon, it's Stanley! Gordon? Can you hear me?"

The boy-dogs hesitated and listened. *Supposing they can't speak, but can understand what we're saying?*

"Gordon, we have to get out of here!"

Gordon coughed and slowly lolled his head from side to side. "Can't be done, dear. Can't even feel my feet."

"Gordon, if you stay here they're going to tear you apart."

Gordon half smiled, and coughed again. The rain was falling directly into his face. "Jeremy always said I looked like a dog's dinner."

"*Gordon!*" Angie screamed. "*Gordon, you've got to!*"

Her scream instantly triggered off one of the boy-dogs, who leapt at her, caught his teeth in her sleeve, and swung from her arm snarling and scrabbling his legs. Stanley twisted around and grabbed hold of the boy-dog in his blanket and tore it off Angie. For a second, he thought that he had managed to get a grip on its throat, but it lashed so wildly from side to side that he had to drop it back on to the floor.

Angie was gasping, and shaking, and sobbing. "Oh, Stanley, I've wet meself. Oh God, Stanley, what are we going to do?"

The boy-dogs didn't hesitate. Now that their blood was roused, they came snapping back at Stanley's and Angie's ankles. The fair-haired creature ripped at Stanley's trouser leg and snagged the skin of his calf. He felt blood stream down his leg. Swearing, he kicked the boy-dog away, but it rolled over and came snarling back at him, its blue eyes swollen with fury.

Angie screamed again. The other boy-dog had jumped on her shoulders and was trying to bite at the back of her neck. Stanley kicked the fair-haired boy-dog away a second time and punched the boy-dog on Angie's shoulders in the side of the head. It yipped and clawed at him, but he punched it again, straight between the eyes, and it dropped backwards on to the floor with a thump.

Gordon cried out: a terrible whining cry of pain and despair. The first boy-dog was tearing at his thigh, ripping a long scarlet string of flesh and skin away from him. Stanley could actually *hear* it: like calico being ripped apart.

"Gordon!" Stanley shouted, but the fair-haired boy-dog jumped up at his face and raked his cheek with three hard claws.

At that moment, however, over the snapping and the snarling of the boy-dogs, and the ceaseless trickling of the rain, they heard another sound. A sharp, explosive crack, and then another, and then another. At first Stanley thought that somebody had started shooting; but then he turned towards the door and saw Madeleine Springer standing there, in black leather thigh-length boots and an impossible outfit like a black leather corselette, with a long black leather cape thrown around her shoulders. Her hair was still blond but dramatically upswept. Her face was alight with commanding righteousness. In her left hand she was holding a bullwhip, a heavy braided black leather whip with a long silver-knobbed handle, the kind used by South African stockbreeders.

She cracked her whip at the fair-haired boy-dog, caught it around his forepaw, and sent him swinging against the wall. He tumbled over, snarled; but Madeleine Springer whipped him again, lashing his cheek open. Then again, splitting the tight wiry fur across his back. Then again, across his shoulder. Bleeding, limping, uttering a low curlike whining, the boy-dog limped toward her, with foam crackling thickly out of his mouth. Madeleine Springer whipped him once more, *kkkrakkkkk!* and then again *kkkrakkkk!* and his blue eyes burst. He rolled over on to his back, his legs thrashing, blinded, shrieking, twisting his spine from side to side.

Madeleine Springer lashed his exposed belly. The tip of her whip cut through the skin like squid being sliced. Intestines bulged from every slice; then bile; then blood. The boy-dog lay quivering on his back, one paw scratching at thin air; then died.

The other two boy-dogs backed cautiously away. But Madeleine Springer wasn't going to allow them to escape. She whipped one, then the other, so that they gradually retreated towards the hearth, whining and cringing. Angie clung to Stanley clockspring-tight; in hysteria and fear and elation. "Who is she? Who is she? What's she *doing*?" she screamed; but she didn't really want to know. She was too frightened and excited by the sight of Madeleine Springer's whip lashing and cutting at the boy-dogs, laying open fur and flesh and cheeks and muscle.

Madeleine Springer cornered the boy-dog who had torn at Gordon's hand, and snapped her whip three times around his neck. Then, with a stormlike shake of her wrist, she heaved him clear of the floor and flung him violently against the side of the cast-iron hearth. They heard his bones smash inside his body like a china jug smashing inside a sack.

Stanley tried to stop forward to help Gordon, who had passed out. The arteries in his mutilated wrist were jetting blood in Jackson Pollock squiggles all over the floor, and his trouser leg was darkly strained, too. But Madeleine Springer said, "Wait!" and lashed the last of the boy-dogs until it lay trembling in the hearth in the throes of imminent death.

Only then did she kneel down beside Gordon and lift his spurting wrist.

"Shall I go and get that amblunce now?" asked Angie in a quaking voice.

Madeleine Springer glanced up at her. "No. Stay. I should have known this was going to happen."

"But he's bleeding to death!" Stanley protested. "We *have* to call an ambulance!"

Without saying a word, Madeleine Springer touched Gordon's bloodied hand with the tips of her fingers. "*Ashapola, help me*," she whispered, and closed her eyes. Stanley frowned at Angie and then back at Gordon's hand. Almost immediately, in front of his eyes, the bleeding dribbled and stopped, and the torn skin folded in on itself, like the petals of a flower closing up at twilight. In less than a minute, Gordon was left with a stump of a wrist that was still crimson-sore, but which was almost completely healed.

"Is he okay?" Stanley asked Madeleine Springer in astonishment.

"He'll survive. But we must get him at once to a place of safety."

She felt around on the floor and picked up the bones

and tendons of Gordon's dismembered hand, as deftly as if she were scooping up tiles in mah-jongg. She carried a large black silk purse around her waist, and she dropped the bones into it and tugged the drawstring tight.

"It can't possibly be put back together, can it?" asked Stanley with a pit-of-the-stomach feeling of disgust.

Madeleine Springer shook her head. "There is a saying that the man without a hand can never say farewell. Besides, we should leave no evidence that we were here."

Already the rain was streaking and diluting the blood that Gordon had pumped all over the floor, and it was swirling away through the cracks in the floorboards Presumably, in the room below, it would rain blood for a while.

Between them, Stanley and Madeleine Springer heaved Gordon on to his feet. He was still semiconscious, and his feet dragged on the floor. For somebody so slim, Stanley wouldn't; have believed how heavy he was.

"Where are we going?" he asked Madeleine Springer, wiping the rain from his face with the sleeve of Gordon's coat.

"I have a car outside," she told him. "I'll take you to my place. You'll be safe there. Safer than Langton Street, anyway."

It took them three or four awkward, jostling minutes to half carry, half shoulder Gordon down to the hallway and out into the street. It was still dark. The sun wouldn't rise for another three and a half hours, and in any case it was probably going to be a gloomy, overcast day. A friend of Stanley's had once described winter Sundays in London as the nearest simulation to the end of the world that anybody could imagine. (That was before he spent a winter Sunday in Wolverhampton, in the north of England.)

Angie opened the front door for them, and they helped Gordon along the path and out of the front gate. The cold wind was beginning to revive him, and he kept letting out grunts and moans, like a man experiencing a nightmare.

Madeleine Springer's car was parked across the street, half-way around the corner, hidden from anybody who might have been watching out of the house. It was a large gray British car from the mid-1960s; Stanley couldn't remember having seen one like it before. He and Angie supported Gordon while Madeleine Springer unlocked the door. Then, between them, they gently lifted Gordon on to the back seat.

"I'll sit with 'im," Angie volunteered.

"Thought you were down on gays," said Stanley, although he wasn't seriously mocking her.

"I can change me mind, can't I?"

Stanley climbed into the front passenger seat beside Madeleine Springer. The interior smelled of leather and old carpets and engine oil. The engine started with an irregular blaring noise, and when she pulled away from the curb, Stanley heard a nasty nasal whine in the transmission. It sounded more like a truck than a car.

"How long have you had this?" he asked her.

She glanced at him. "Ever since it was new. It's a Humber Super Snipe. They used to be plutocratic, once upon a time."

"Where are you taking us?"

"Richmond. It isn't very far away. We have rooms there."

"Those … dog-creatures," Stanley began.

"You want to know what they were?"

"Did they really have human heads, or did they just look that way?"

Madeleine Springer turned left at Kew Road and headed south. The wide road that ran beside the black brick wall of the Royal Botanic Gardens was completely deserted; not even a police car.

"They weren't human in the sense that you might understand them to be human. It depends how much humiliation you're prepared to suffer in order to stay alive."

"Are there many more of them?"

"It's impossible to say for sure. This latest outbreak of the Night Plague has only been with us for two or three years. Historically, though, it looks like the worst by far."

"The Night Plague?"

"Bard's Disease, Mozart's Syndrome, call it what you like."

Stanley was silent for a moment. Then he said, "I think I'm going to need to know a whole lot more about this."

"I intend to tell you," Madeleine Springer promised him. She drove oddly, a little too fast for Stanley's liking, with mechanical, exaggerated movements, as if she had only recently learned. He supposed that it couldn't be easy driving in high-heeled black leather thigh boots. He caught himself looking at the smooth whiteness of her bare thigh, in between the top of her boot and the black satin frills around the legs of her corselette. *I wonder what it would like to plunge my hand now between those warm white thighs, while she's driving and unable to stop me.*

"How have you been feeling?" Madeleine Springer asked him, as if she had read his thought as clearly as the motto in a Christmas cracker. They had reached the traffic lights at Lower Mortlake Road. The large roundabout, usually teeming with cars and buses, was silent and deserted. Stanley could easily have believed that they were the only people left alive.

"I've—uh … I've been experiencing a little confusion from time to time."

"What kind of confusion?"

"'E don't know whether 'e's kipping or whether 'e's awake," Angie put in, trying to be helpful.

"Not only that," said Stanley. "But this mixed-up feeling that I can only call *moral* confusion."

"Oh, yes? And how does that manifest itself?"

"In all kinds of different ways. I keep having waves of anger and disgust against God, and music, and other people. Even people I like. Even people I *love*."

The lights changed to green and Madeleine Springer changed gear. "You have waves of violence, too, right? And sexual lust?"

He looked at her acutely. She smiled, although she didn't look back at him. "I know how strong your urge was to thrust your hands in between my legs, Mr. Eisner. 'She's driving, she won't be able to stop me.' And it's warm there, and smells of leather and woman and some perfume that you can't even identify."

"I reckon Gordon's coming around," called Angie, who obviously hadn't heard what Madeleine Springer was saying.

Stanley stared at Madeleine Springer hard. "How do you know all that? Are you a mind reader, or what?"

"I'm a very good psychic, that's all," she replied. "You saw what I did to Gordon's wrist, back at the house. That was nothing more than faith healing, as it's usually called; although it was very much more effective faith healing than most psychics are capable of."

"You're not kidding," Stanley told her.

Madeleine Springer said, "There are natural powers in the universe of really devastating magnitude. I know how to call on them; and to direct them; and there's nothing more mystical to it than that. These days, nobody would think of gasping in astonishment when they switch on an electric light bulb; yet what I do is no more remarkable than that, and in some ways a great deal simpler. The natural powers have certainly been around a whole lot longer."

They were turning toward Richmond Hill when two police officers stepped out into the road and lifted their hands. "Damn it," said Madeleine, and slowed the Humber down to a whinnying walking pace, and then to a stop. One of the police officers approached Stanley's window and rapped on it gently with his knuckles. Stanley wound it down.

"Morning," the policeman greeted him. His breath steamed in the cold, and his nose was pinched red, and he looked what Angie would have called "right cheesed off." His companion had steel-rimmed shatterproof spectacles and kept sniffing and wiping his nose with his glove.

"Can I help you, Officer?" Stanley asked him.

The policeman peered inside the car. Then he said, "Just interested to know where you're going at a quarter to four in the morning."

Stanley turned to Madeleine, his lips already forming the shape *W* to ask "Where are we going, Ms. Springer?" when he saw that she wasn't there. There was no steering wheel, no brake or accelerator pedals, no gearshift. All of those controls had mysteriously moved across the car and materialized in front of him, as if he were driving.

He twisted quickly around. The back seat was empty, too. He was sitting in the car alone.

It had been a dream. Tennyson, the boy-dogs, everything. It had all been a dream. But what was he doing in this strange car, in the middle of the night?

"American, aren't we?" the police officer asked him.

"Well, *I* am," Stanley replied.

Unamused, the police officer inspected the tax disc on the windshield. "This your vehicle, is it?" The policeman with the eyeglasses was walking slowly around the other side of the Humber, inspecting the tires and the lights.

"Well, ah ..." Stanley began, but then out of the corner of his eye he saw the shimmering transparent whiteness of Madeleine Springer's upper thigh, almost completely invisible, like the reflection of a thigh glimpsed in a dark window. He spread his fingers across the steering wheel in front of him, too, and realized with an involuntary shiver that it had no actual substance, it was the *illusion* of a steering wheel and nothing more. He just hoped that the police officer hadn't seen his hands pass right through it.

If Madeleine Springer had gone to all the trouble of rendering herself invisible—and Angie and Gordon, too— then she must very badly want to conceal the fact of her presence here tonight—perhaps her very existence.

"Yes, it's ... my car," he concluded.

"Do you mind telling me what the license number is?"

"Sure, it's—" *NLT 683*, said Madeleine Springer's voice,

right inside of his head, as clearly as if she had spoken out loud in his ear.

"That's right, sir." The policeman produced a black leather pad and began to write. "You've got a faulty offside indicator light, sir. Flashing too slowly. Can you make sure you get it seen to?"

"Oh, sure, yes, I'm sorry. I didn't realize."

The policeman tore off the ticket he had been writing. "And if you'd care to produce your driving license and MoT certificate and insurance documents within the next seven days, sir, at the police station of your choice?"

"Yes," said Stanley. He was aware of a huge charge of static inside the car, like passing his hand in front of a television screen, and his hair prickled on the back of his neck.

The police officers returned to their car, swinging their arms and clapping their hands together to warm themselves up. The Humber's engine started up again, and the elderly car began to pull away. As he passed the police car, Stanley pretended that he was holding the steering wheel, even though he could feel no substance whatsoever, only the soft crackling of psychically-focused electricity.

It was only when they had reached the top of Richmond Hill that Madeleine Springer gradually reappeared, grainily at first, like the picture on a poorly-tuned television; then completely.

"Blimey, that was totally weird, that was!" Angie blurted out. She held her hand in front of her face to make sure that she was still there. "'Ow d'you do that?"

"It's a little bit of conjuring with refractive light, that's all," Madeleine Springer told her. Stanley turned around in his seat, and for Angie's benefit pulled a face that showed how impressed he was.

"Can you imagine being able to do that all the time?" he asked her. "You could sit right next to people and listen to what they're saying about you, and they wouldn't even know."

"I'm afraid it takes too much natural energy for anybody to sustain invisibility for very long," said Madeleine Springer. They passed an old-fashioned pub called the Lass of Richmond Hill where Stanley was disappointed to notice that they were offering New Orleans-style barbecue. When he first arrived in England, he had expected it to be crowded with fish-and-chips shops and eel-and-pie stalls and Dickensian chophouses. Instead it had exactly the same fast-food franchises as downtown Napa, all Burger King and McDonald's and Kentucky Fried Chicken.

They had reached the very crest of Richmond Hill, high above a wide curve of the Thames. The terraced gardens that led steeply down to the river were buried this morning in a deep foggy shadow, but the river itself shone dully through the trees as it flowed between Petersham Meadows on its eastern bank and Marble Hill Gardens on its west. A haunted, melancholy view, one of the most romantic in southern England. To think that Henry Tudor had seen the same view; that Elizabeth I had passed this way in her carriage. Sometimes London's sense of history made Stanley feel elated; sometimes it made him feel oppressed.

The suspension of Madeleine Springer's twenty-five-year-old car clonked noisily as she turned it into a narrow private slip road. She parked, switched off the engine, and announced, "We're here. I'll help you carry Gordon inside."

They climbed out of the car. They were parked beside a stately terrace of cream-painted four-story houses, which had now been divided into apartments. Madeleine Springer led them through the front door and into the hallway. It smelled of new Axminster carpets and stifling central heating. An arrangement of dried flowers stood on a small table in front of a mirror, and Madeleine Springer went across while they waited for the elevator to arrive, and refurbished her lipstick.

Gordon had recovered sufficiently to be able to walk, although Stanley insisted that he lean on his shoulder. "Quite a place," he whispered in a gray voice.

"It's wonderful in the summer," said Madeleine Springer. "The view over the Terrace Gardens is absolutely beautiful." She looked at Gordon in the mirror and smiled. "You're just the way I imagined you would be," she told him.

They rose in the quietly-humming elevator to the top floor, and then Madeleine Springer ushered them along the corridor to her apartment. She opened the door, and they stepped inside, and at last Stanley felt that they were safe.

Madeleine Springer had furnished her apartment ascetically, to say the least. Their footsteps echoed on a bare oak-parquet floor, absolutely immaculate, so highly polished that they looked as if they were walking across the surface of a lake. The walls were painted the faintest shade of yellow. The only furniture in the living area was three Chippendale armchairs with faded pink satin seats, a yucca plant in a basketwork planter, and a curious hybrid sofa, part French Provincial, part Chinese, with an elaborately-carved back. There were no paintings on the walls, no drapes, no net curtains. The night filled the windows, black and uncompromising.

They helped Gordon to sit on to the sofa. He was still deathly pale, but he was almost cheerful. Madeleine Springer went through to another room and returned with a white gauzy scarf, which she wound around the stump of his left hand, and then ripped, so that she could tie it in a bow.

"You saved my life," said Gordon as he watched her.

"You would have survived in any case," Madeleine Springer told him. "It was always your destiny to survive; for the time being, at least; just as it was always your destiny to lose your left hand."

"I don't understand," Gordon told her.

"Of course you don't, not yet. But what I am trying to tell you is that you would have lost your hand somehow, sometime soon; and that nothing you could have done would have prevented it."

"I don't believe in fate," said Gordon.

"Not believing in it doesn't stop it happening."

"I could use a drink," said Stanley.

"There's vodka in the kitchen," said Madeleine Springer. "You'll find some glasses there, too."

"Can I use the toilet?" asked Angie.

Stanley switched on the fluorescent lights in the kitchen. They flickered, jolted, and then stayed on. It was an expensive, modern kitchen, a real cook's kitchen, with white cupboards and a polished brass rail around the counters. But Stanley swung open one wall cupboard after another and found them all empty. The entire kitchen was innocent of food, or any suggestion that anybody ever intended to prepare any food here.

"Looks like you're fresh out of vodka," he called to Madeleine Springer. "In fact, it looks like you're fresh out of everything."

He opened one of the drawers and found a cutlery tray containing two very ancient and corroded knives, with hair twined around their handles, and a corroded iron talisman on a leather thong. It was a Celtic cross, with a blindfold of rotten linen tied tightly around it.

Stanley picked the talisman out of the drawer and held it up. It swung from side to side, and spun around and around. As it turned around, he saw that there was a face on the obverse side. He caught it in the palm of his hand and examined it more closely. There was no question about it. It was the same face that he had seen again and again at the house called Tennyson.

The blindfold woman, with the coronet of twisted nails.

Stanley was suddenly aware that Madeleine Springer was standing in the doorway watching him, with a faint smile on her face.

"Can't you find the vodka?" she asked him. She crossed the kitchen and slid out a tall narrow drinks drawer. She took out a full bottle of Finnish vodka and unscrewed the cap.

Stanley turned to her while she knocked ice out of the ice tray, still holding up the talisman. "What is this?" he asked her. "I saw it everywhere back in that house at Kew. The door knocker, the stained-glass window. Then dozens of paintings and etchings, all around the upstairs landing. Now I open a drawer looking for vodka, and here it is again."

Madeleine Springer handed him his drink. It was clear and cold and aromatic, in a tastefully-designed Boda glass.

"I would prefer to begin at the beginning," she said. "But I can tell you who the face is supposed to represent. The name by which she is most commonly known is Isabel Gowdie."

"That doesn't strike any chords at all."

"There's no reason why it should."

"But when I first saw her, on the door knocker, I had the feeling that she was kind of familiar."

"It's possible that you've seen her picture before. You could even have met her. She's lived as many lives under as many different names as—"

Stanley swallowed vodka. "As a cat?" he suggested.

"I'm sorry?"

"Cats have nine lives, don't they?"

"Oh, I see what you mean," said Madeleine Springer. "But no, Isabel Gowdie has lived far more lives than any cat. Every one of those paintings and prints of her on the first-floor landing at Tennyson showed a different Isabel Gowdie, in a different life."

"What about the rain? And the boy-dogs?"

"They were both manifestations of Isabel Gowdie's influence."

Stanley said, "I think you'd better begin at the beginning."

Madeleine Springer nodded. "All three of you are more than ready."

Stanley clinked the ice in his drink. "Before we start, I think I'd better thank you for saving us back there. I don't know how you knew we were there; or how you managed to show up just when we really needed you. But you did, and I'm grateful."

"Well ... I shouldn't really have been there," Madeleine

Springer told him. "But there are times when even fate requires a little assistance."

She led him back to the living room, where Angie and Gordon were sitting together on the strange French-Oriental sofa. She dragged over one of the Chippendale chairs for Stanley, but remained standing herself. As she talked, she paced slowly backwards and forwards, and her long black leather cape hissed softly on the polished oak floor.

"There are dire warnings in the Old Testament time and time again about the punishment that God has in store for those who disobey Him. The punishment is plague. *'The Lord will smite you with consumption and with fever and with inflammation. The Lord will smite you with madness and blindness and bewilderment of the heart. The Lord will smite you with the boils of Egypt and with tumors and with the scab and with the itch, from which you cannot be healed.'"*

"Charming," said Gordon weakly. But considering his hand had been violently torn from his arm less than an hour ago, his composure was extraordinary. It was Gordon's recovery more than anything else that convinced Stanley that he ought to listen to what Madeleine Springer had to say. The disappearing trick in the car was one thing. But he had seen Gordon bleeding to death in front of his eyes; and now he was ridiculously well.

Madeleine Springer smiled. "Whether God really *does* punish anybody who disobeys him by striking them down with the plague ... well, that's a matter for theological argument. Paracelsus believed that syphilis was a punishment invented by God for those who were guilty of 'general licentiousness,' and there are plenty of people today who are quite willing to believe that AIDS is God's punishment for homosexuality.

"They ignore the simple truth that an illness is an illness, however it happens to be transmitted; and not a metaphor for divine judgment."

"All the same," Stanley interrupted, "Knitted Hood gave me a very direct warning. He said, 'I am the pestilence that was promised, if you disobeyed.'"

"Did he specifically mention God?"

"I don't really remember too clearly. I don't think so."

"He wouldn't have. The Carriers loathe to utter the name of God, in any of its forms. If he did he was lying and trying to confuse you. The Night Plague isn't a divine punishment any more than AIDS is. The Night Plague is what you might call an infection of the soul. It's the moral virus which Satan himself uses to spread his influence through human society."

Angie glanced worriedly at Stanley. Madeleine Springer may have rescued them from Tennyson, but already she was beginning to sound as if she wasn't teeing off with a full set of clubs.

Stanley said, "Can we wait up a minute? On the one hand, you're telling us that plagues aren't a punishment handed out by God. But on the other hand, you're telling us that they're a punishment handed out by Satan."

"I don't even *believe* in Satan," put in Angie. "I mean, not with 'orns and a tail and a toasting fork."

Madeleine Springer continued to smile. "Out of all the epidemic diseases, only the Night Plague is spread by Satan. And he certainly doesn't spread it as a punishment. He spreads it as a way of turning the hearts of men and women away from the principles that have always denied him dominion over the world. Trust, faith, self-control, truthfulness, and loving other people as you love yourself.

"It's a particularly vicious joke that he uses the sexual act, the act of love, as a means of spreading his disease."

"So you reckon 'e's real?" asked Angie.

"With horns and a tail and a toasting fork? Not quite. But the entity which people call Satan *does* exist; and although I call him 'he,' as if he were nothing more than a black-hearted man, he is much more understandable as an 'it.' A huge intense concentration of horror."

"Where does 'e live, then?" Angie wanted to know. "'Ave you ever seen 'im? Or it, or whatever?"

Madeleine Springer was completely undisturbed by Angie's skepticism. She swirled her soft whispering cloak around her, and her heels tapped on the hardwood floor. "He occupies the furthest recesses of human awareness; that unlit lake of shared consciousness that Jung described as the collective mind. There are times when you can sense his actual presence in the back of your head. Something very cold, something very dark, sliding past you like a giant stingray sliding over an underwater shoal, but *inside* your mind, inside your own imagination."

"Can he be summoned into the physical world?" asked Stanley. "I mean, all that stuff about Black Sabbats, raising the devil ... is there any substance in that?"

Madeleine Springer nodded. "He can be called; and of course a few people *do* call him. The Sumerians were aware of the feeling of evil in the backs of their minds, and there are several recorded instances of Sumerian priests raising out of a particular well in the desert some terrible black creature that fed on masses of children and goats. The

Egyptians raised him, too, believing that they could use him to overcome the mystic power of the Israelites; and that was how the biblical plague was first spread through Egypt.

"In a sense, the outbreak in Egypt was a punishment for disobeying God; although more accurately it was the pathological consequence of trying to enlist the power of evil against the principles of good."

"So how is this Night Plague communicated?" asked Stanley. "What does it actually do?"

"You've probably heard how witches are supposed to copulate with Satan during the Black Sabbat," said Madeleine Springer." That's not just an incidental part of the Sabbat, it's the entire point and purpose of the Sabbat.

"Satan infects the witches with his virus by violent intercourse which tears the internal tissues of the witch's body and opens a wound through which her blood can be infected.

"The witch retains the Night Plague virus in her body for the rest of her life. She has intercourse herself with seven men. Each of them is chosen because he is terminally ill with some ordinary physical disease, such as leprosy or cancer or AIDS. In return for becoming Carriers, the witch grants them extended life. Their task is to pass on the Night Plague virus to as many innocent people as they possibly can, especially people who are imaginative and creative and who have a strong influence on society. That was why Shakespeare was infected. He was visited by an apparition who looked to him like a Dark Lady. That was why Mozart found a horrific gray stranger knocking at his door. Something happened to Mozart that night, nobody quite knows what, but his health and his music never recovered from it."

"I think I'll 'ave a drink now, if you don't mind," said Angie.

"Gin-and-orange, isn't it?" asked Madeleine Springer. "You'll find everything you want in the kitchen."

Angie said, "'Ow …?" but Stanley lifted his finger to his lips to shush her.

Madeleine Springer went on: "Once the Night Plague virus has entered the bloodstream of an innocent person, it enters the brain and invades the hypothalamus. Here, it gradually alters; and it begins to exert an insidious effect on the sufferer's mind. It begins to change his morality. It causes him to have spasms of petty hatred, and spitefulness, and irrational violence. It loosens his perception of reality, so that he never quite knows whether he's dreaming or awake. It creates grotesque symptoms of physical sickness, such as vomiting worms or molluscs or great choking balls of animal hair, or urinating streams of blood. All of these symptoms serve to heighten the sufferer's sense of degradation and self-disgust."

Stanley said nothing. He knew exactly what Madeleine Springer was talking about. Even now, he could feel himself growing impatient with her and feeling an irrational urge to slap her and twist her hair.

She turned to look at him. She must have been able to sense what he was thinking. She kept her eyes on him steadily as she spoke.

"Gradually, the symptoms of Night Plague become increasingly severe. The sufferer becomes depressed and irascible, and there will be a noticeable coarsening of his personality. He will start using foul language, drinking more, making crude remarks. Usually, he becomes much more sexually active, sometimes frantically so, even though he will find it more and more difficult to achieve a physical climax. He will often become sadistic, too.

"By this stage, the Night Plague has transmuted itself into an infection of the spirit; a disease of the unconscious mind. And it is spread from one person to another through dreams—dreams of sexual intercourse or rape. It is remarkably similar in its pathology to recent strains of syphilis ... except that it infects the soul rather than the body."

Stanley swallowed vodka. "This is all very well, Ms. Springer ... but what's the *point* of it? Assuming that Satan does exist ... assuming that this Night Plague is exactly what you say it is ... why does Satan want to spread it in the first place?"

Madeleine Springer replied softly and sadly. "Because a soul infected by the Night Plague is a soul which cannot be admitted to heaven, that is why. The Night Plague can be passed on from one soul to another even after death. So any soul who is infected must be denied entry to the Kingdom of Light. Satan has already contaminated the temporal world; we cannot allow him to contaminate the hereafter, too.

"The Night Plague is Satan's way of garnering souls, Mr. Eisner. And this time, he seems determined that he shall infect not just the Caribbean and a third of Europe, as he did in the days when Columbus and his crew brought it back from Haiti; nor most of England, as he did in the days of the Black Death. This time, he seems determined to infect the whole global population; to make *all* of us his, forever."

Gordon was beginning to shudder, although Stanley

wasn't sure if he was shuddering from the shock of losing his hand or in dread of what Madeleine Springer was telling them. Because—to his own surprise—he *did* have a feeling of dread. He had seen enough of Knitted Hood and the horrors of the house called Tennyson to believe that Madeleine Springer was telling them the truth, or at least the truth as far as she understood it.

He had also felt the symptoms of the Night Plague for himself; and he was fighting against them now.

"Is there any cure?" he asked Madeleine Springer.

"There is only one antidote," she told him. "You must find the witch who originally infected the Carrier who infected you. In your case, it was Isabel Gowdie, the blindfolded woman whose likeness appears all over Tennyson. You must find her and have relations with her, to pass back the virus in the same way that it was transmitted. As soon as you have done that, *while* you are doing that, you must kill her, so that she cannot pass it back again."

"Relations?" Stanley demanded. "What kind of relations? You mean *sex?*"

Madeleine Springer nodded. "It's the only way."

"But supposing she doesn't want to have sex? Supposing *I* don't want to have sex? Supposing I can't even find her to have sex with?"

"You will have to find her. You will have to have sex with her; or your immortal soul will be forfeit forever."

"You're not putting me on?"

"I wish in the name of Ashapola that I were."

"Well, do you have any idea where this Isabel Gowdie is?"

"None at all. She was eventually captured and imprisoned

by Night Warriors, but it is a strict rule that Night Warriors never reveal to anybody where a witch or a demon has been imprisoned. In that way, nobody can ever be tempted to release them. And, believe me, the temptation can be great. Satan and his agents can offer you almost anything that you have ever desired."

"Don't you even have an inkling of where she might be?"

"No. The last known official record was that Isabel Gowdie was sentenced to be burned at the stake on May 13, 1662, after she confessed to the Scottish court that she was a special domestic servant of the Devil, and that she had conjured up storms all round England's coastline by slapping a rock with a wet rag, and that those storms had drowned scores of fishermen."

"Then she's dead?" asked Stanley."

Madeleine Springer shook her head. "Somehow she managed to escape. Whatever was burned at the stake, it wasn't her. In fact, one eyewitness said that it looked more like the ashes of a Great Dane.

"She *must* be alive, and even if she hasn't broken free from her imprisonment, she must at least have broken free from the bonds which the Night Warriors used to seal her mind. Her Carriers are roaming abroad and spreading her infection, and they cannot do that unless she is conscious and capable of giving them strength and mobility. Without her, they are nothing, literally, but corpses. She is dreaming, too. Powerful, vivid dreams of the way things were when she was locked away. That is why the house called Tennyson is full of her pictures, and why it rains there, just as it rained in the same spot in 1666, when Isabel Gowdie was still free. Her influence is very strong; she was said to have placed one hand on her head and one hand on her foot, and renounced everything in between her two hands to Satan.

"Satan dearly favors her. That is why he awarded her such powers. Your hallucinations of plague-ridden landscapes are the result of *her* influence in your infection. Her psychic DNA is inside you now, inside your mind. When Isabel Gowdie sleeps, her dreams are just as real to you as they are to her."

There was a long silence. Angie came back with her gin-and-orange and sat close to Stanley, resting one hand on his knee.

Madeleine Springer said, "You haven't yet asked me what *I* have to do with all of this."

"I had the feeling you were going to tell us, anyway," Stanley replied.

"In actual fact," said Madeleine Springer, "what *you* have to do with it is much more important than what *I* have to do with it."

"I don't follow you."

"You don't think that you were infected at random, do you?"

"What are you saying? That Knitted Hood picked me out specially?"

"Of course he did, because you're the direct descendant of a Night Warrior. Not just any Night Warrior, either—one of the Night Warriors whom Isabel Gowdie killed before she was finally captured."

"Now you've really lost me," Stanley complained.

Madeleine Springer walked across to him and touched his shoulder with her fingertips. Stanley felt a tingling sensation, as if he had touched a live electric wire. But it was something more than electricity: it had a resonance, too, like thunderous silent music.

"You feel that?" she asked him. "You're the direct descendant of Jacob Eisner, the ragpicker from Whitechapel. Jacob was a Night Warrior, and that means that *you* are a Night Warrior, too. That was why you were followed and assaulted by Knitted Hood. He wanted to make sure that Isabel Gowdie's infection got to you before *you* got to Isabel Gowdie."

"I came to London to play the violin. I didn't come here to look for some witch."

"In time, I would have called on you and required you to do it."

"*Required* me?"

"You're a Night Warrior, Mr. Eisner. You have no choice."

"I don't understand any of this," Stanley told her, trying to be patient. "Do you mind explaining exactly what you mean by a Night Warrior?" The feeling that she was playing a gigantic hoax on them began to resurface; and apart from that his head had started to throb with a vicious migraine. He hadn't had a migraine in ten or eleven years, but there was no mistaking it.

Madeleine Springer said, "There was a time when the earth was infested with demons and devils, like vermin. In those days, the Night Warriors were both necessary and numerous. They were a holy army, if you like, who were charged with the task of hunting down evil creatures in the landscape of the human unconscious ... in dreams, where demons and devils had previously been able to conceal themselves and remain unscathed and undetected.

"In human dreams, you see, demons could escape being

exorcised. The priests simply couldn't reach them. Dreams were a sanctuary for some of the most horrific of all the medieval creatures. People who didn't believe in demons in waking life were quite prepared to believe in the demons they encountered in dreams; and demons thrive on those who believe in them, just as they are weakened by those who don't.

"But, over the centuries, the Night Warriors entered the dreams of thousands of people, and tracked the demons down, and destroyed them; and those whom they didn't destroy they imprisoned forever with sanctified locks and holy seals. They imprisoned witches, too, and all of those agents and familiars of Satan that they could find.

"The Great Fire of London in 1666 was started not by a careless baker, but by one of the greatest dream battles of all history. Five Night Warriors entered the dream of a ratcatcher who lived close to Pudding Lane. They laid an ambush for thirteen of Satan's most favored witches, who had agreed to meet there. '*When shall we thirteen meet again?*' They were laying their plans to spread the Black Death even more widely.

"The witches were caught by surprise, and most of them were destroyed within the first few minutes. But one of them—who was probably Isabel Gowdie—caused the ratcatcher's brain to explode and catch fire. She escaped from the dream, but all five Night Warriors were killed, and the ratcatcher's house caught alight. As you know, most of London was burned to the ground."

Madeleine Springer's eyes remained fastened on Stanley. They were the strangest eyes that he had ever seen. Faint kaleidoscopic colors seemed to flicker through them, and in some extraordinary way they seemed to be focused *inwards* rather than *outwards*, as if all that she needed to see, she could see inside her own mind.

"Jacob Eisner was one of the Night Warriors who died that night," she explained. "The other Night Warriors were *your* great-grandmother many times removed, Miss Dunning, and *your* great-grandfather many times removed, Mr. Rutherford, and one other, the ancestor of an American professor called Henry Watkins. So you can see now that destiny truly brought you all together."

"That's only four Night Warriors," Stanley interrupted. "You said there were five."

"That's right. Jacob Eisner's older son Joshua was a trainee Night Warrior. He died, too."

"Well, that's too bad," said Stanley. "But what does it have to do with us? We're not Night Warriors."

Madeleine Springer unfastened her cloak and let it slide to the floor. "The oaths that were taken by your ancestors bind you, too. They always have. You are beholden to fight this plague, just as much as your ancestors would have been."

"This is a joke," Stanley retorted irritably.

"No joke," Madeleine Springer replied. "And what's more, it's your only hope of finding Isabel Gowdie and ridding yourself of the Night Plague."

"Listen, who the hell *are* you?" Stanley barked at her. "You've been sounding off for ten minutes now, all this ridiculous baloney about Night Warriors and witches and plagues and God knows what."

Madeleine Springer smiled calmly. "Not *God* knows what, Mr. Eisner; Ashapola knows what."

"Ashapola? What are you talking about? What's Ashapola?"

"Ashapola, if you like, is the god of all gods. When anybody on this planet speaks of their god, no matter how they happen to imagine Him, they are referring to Ashapola. It is Ashapola who created the world. He is what the Freemasons call the Great Architect of the Universe. It is Ashapola who takes care of you. If you are threatened by the forces of darkness, it is Ashapola who dispatches *me* and those like me to warn you, and to marshal your forces. He cannot directly intervene in the destiny of the world. If He were to do that, then the world as you know it would cease to exist; because a human society that is not required to face the consequences of its own actions is a paradox.

"But there is nothing paradoxical about a Creator caring for his creation, and sending somebody like me to warn you of overwhelming danger."

"You mean you're an angel?" said Angie.

Madeleine Springer glanced at her. "You're a bright girl. I *am* an angel, if an angel is a messenger sent by a divine being. But I am less of a messenger than a message. The body in which you see me is a borrowed memory. You remember the little holographic image of Princess Leia which R2-D2 carried in *Star Wars*? I am much more like that, a picture, an illusion."

As she looked at Stanley, he thought he could see her face and her body subtly altering. Her wide, feline face began to narrow, as if he were seeing negatives of two different faces, one on top of the other. Her voice, which had been quite gentle and mellifluous as she had told them about the Night Plague, began to sound choppier and gruffer. Stanley could almost have sworn that she was changing into a thin-faced young man, right in front of his eyes.

"And you expect us to believe all of this cock-and-bull story?" he demanded, clearing his throat.

"I expect nothing, except that you will do your sworn duty."

"I don't have to do squat, and neither do my friends here."

Madeleine Springer came forward and stood very close to him. The remarkable thing about her was that she didn't have any smell, none whatsoever. No perfume, no leather, no skin smell, nothing. Without asking him, she reached out her hand and laid it on top of his head.

"Hey, what—!"

She smiled. "You have a sick headache," she said. "Quite often, when the Night Plague takes hold of you, you start to suffer from all the illnesses you've ever had, all over again. Colds, chickenpox, measles, flu. It's raging immune deficiency, with a vengeance."

She paused. Then she nodded and said, "It's gone now, yes?" and it was true, his migraine had vanished, just like the tiny glowing spot in the center of a switched-off television tube.

"How did you do that?" he asked warily. Madeleine Springer was looking more like a man than ever. Her blond hair seemed to be shorter; her jaw was much sharper, and he could see flaying gingery hairs under her arms. *Am I awake, or am I asleep? Is this really happening or not?*

"You're awake," Madeleine Springer told him. "And, as I've told you. I'm a message more than a messenger; and a message can take many different shapes and forms."

Stanley slowly rubbed his forehead with his fingertips. He turned to look at Angie, who sat close beside him, still trembling a little, peaky and distressed; and at Gordon, who had closed his eyes now, and appeared to be asleep, his mouth open, his scarf-wrapped stump lying in his lap. If he were awake, and all this were real, if he were actually *here*, in this apartment, then he knew that he had no alternatives.

"Tell me about the Night Warriors," he asked Madeleine Springer.

"Your ancestor Jacob Eisner was one of the most powerful and respected of the Night Warriors," Madeleine Springer told Stanley. "His name was Mol Besa, and he was what in the seventeenth century they used to call a Mathematick Grenadier. These days, we call them Equation Warriors. He was able to make the mathematical calculations that would change energy into matter, matter into heat, heat into speed, speed into time—and apply them to his immediate surroundings. For instance, he could work out that if a horde of horse-demons were riding towards him at twenty miles an hour, the kinetic heat that they were producing as they rode was sufficient to raise a wall of bricks in front of them which would stop them dead. He couldn't create bricks out of nothing. Einstein and Newton still apply, even in dreams. But he could convert their own energy into something which would stop them. Mol Besa was the master of what you might call mental judo ... using your enemy's own strength to bring him down.

"Here," said Madeleine Springer, and beckoned Stanley to follow her across the room. "Stand quite still—here, that's right—and *relax*. I know it's difficult. I know you're fighting the Night Plague. But you can do it, if you try. You can beat the plague and you can beat Isabel Gowdie and you can beat Satan, too, because he's out there, Stanley, he's out there now, tonight, while everybody's dreaming, and he's determined that this time, *this time*, he's going to have us all."

She laid her hand on his shoulder, and he felt that same prickling electricity. "It's the end of the world, Stanley, if we don't beat him now. You can forget about ozone layers and cutting down the rain forests. He'll take our morals, he'll take our families, he'll take everything, including our immortal souls. This is *it*, this is Armageddon. This is the pestilence that we were promised."

Stanley looked towards Angie; but Angie was too tired to do anything but shrug. Gordon was fast asleep now, his head resting on the cushion of the sofa.

"Watch the window," said Madeleine Springer.

Stanley faced the window. He could see himself reflected sharply against the night, and Madeleine Springer, too. They seemed to be standing outside in the darkness, three stories up, like Peter Pan beseeching admission to the nursery window, or Victorian levitationists.

As he watched, a gleaming outline began to form itself around Stanley's head and shoulders: the outline of a spherical helmet, like an old-fashioned diver's helmet, but made of thick glass instead of brass, and surrounded by a cage of metal circlets, which appeared to be constantly contra-rotating.

His shoulders were armored with upswept fins, which reminded him of the air inlets of a Ferrari Testarossa. On his chest he carried a huge bank of instruments and switches and computers, including a holographic astrolabe and the most complicated mathematical calculator that he had ever seen in his life. The visual displays winked at him in sapphire blue and infrared.

Around his waist he wore a heavy-duty telephone-linesman's-type belt, from which swung a huge pistol-grip instrument, the size of an Uzi submachine gun, and a whole variety of cylindrical nickel-plated containers that looked like cartridges.

"This is incredible," said Stanley, staring at his reflection in the window, and then looking down at himself to make sure that it wasn't just a trick of the light. "But it's almost—I don't know, transparent. I can't see it too well."

"That's because you're still awake," Madeleine Springer explained. "I'm creating an illusion of your armor for you out of my own memory, to show you what it looks like. When you're asleep, and dreaming, this will all take on its own reality."

"But I don't know how to *use* all of this stuff."

"You will, once you start dreaming. You have inherited Jacob Eisner's mathematical skills, as well as his duties. Those circlets around your helmet will enable you to pinpoint your psycho-geographical location within the sleeper's imagined landscape. And you'll be able to use those calculators and computers to convert latent energy into heat, heat into matter, matter into time, time into water, whatever you wish.

"Once you've made your calculations, all you have to do is insert one of those empty equation cartridges into the side of the computer and load the program into it. Then you slide the equation cartridge into the gun—like this—and you fire it. Your program arrives where you've fired it;

and pure math is instantaneously detonated into pure action."

"I hate to disillusion you, but I flunked math," Stanley admitted. "I couldn't even remember my times tables. I'm not sure I could even recite them *now*."

"This is something different," said Madeleine Springer. "This is mathematics with a mission."

She stepped away from him, and gradually his suit of armor crackled and faded. Stanley felt depleted somehow—as if the armor had given him courage, and strength, and a new sense of purpose. He hadn't felt that kind of determination since he had first played with a professional orchestra. In those days (God Almighty, in those days, twenty years ago) it had seemed like the whole world was his.

Maybe, some day soon, he could claim it back.

"What about me?" asked Angie, who had been watching Stanley's transformation wide-eyed.

Madeleine Springer walked over to the sofa, took Angie's hand, and led her back to the center of the room. "Your ancestor was called Elisabeth Pardoe, and she was the wife of a fisherman in Dover. Not a very faithful wife, I'm sorry to say, but not many fisherwives were. Not many of the prettier fisherwives, anyway. I think you can excuse her. She was married on her twelfth birthday to a man nearly twenty years older than she was; and the fishing fleet was usually away for days, or weeks if the weather was rough. She was very alluring, too; as you are."

Angie blushed. Madeleine Springer was now so manlike, her voice so deep, that it wasn't difficult to believe from what she was saying that she found Angie attractive.

"But what sort of a what's-its-name was she? What sort of a Night Warrior?"

Madeleine Springer stood behind Angie and took hold of her shoulders in both hands, directing her attention towards the black reflecting window.

"She was Effis; and so are you. Effis the light-skater. One of the very fastest of the Night Warriors, even faster than Xaxxa the slide-boxer. You can skate on light, wherever that light may happen to be. It may be the sun, dancing on the surface of the sea; it may be shining through a window. It may be a klieg light, pointing at the sky, or the flickering of pilgrim's candles. You need only the merest pinpoint, and you are away, fast as a flash."

"What if it's totally dark?" asked Stanley. "What happens then?"

Madeleine Springer turned to him and she was undeniably a young man now. A rather handsome young man, with a self-indulgent languor about him, but no less likable. His costume had altered, too. It was more of a leather jerkin than a basque; and although his thighs were still bare and he still wore thigh boots, he had developed smooth powerful muscles, and his boots were more like eighteenth-century riding boots, with turned-over tops.

Madeleine Springer said, "It's rarely dark in people's dreams—even in their nightmares—with the exception of some psychotic claustrophobics, who dream of being imprisoned in cellars or having their faces pushed into pillows. Effis can always find some light to skate on. She can dance on the flame of a single match. Besides, she almost always stays close to Kasyx the charge-keeper. He can usually give her sufficient light."

"Kasyx? Is that who Gordon's going to be?"

"No … you will have to wait to meet Kasyx. But first of all, let me show you what you will look like, Miss Dunning, when you enter the world of dreams."

Springer kept his hands on Angie's shoulders and closed his eyes for a moment. Gradually, in a sprinkling of tiny electrical pinpoints, her appearance shifted and flowed, and Stanley saw her not as Angie Dunning any more, the almost-punk from Herbert Gardens, London, but as Effis the light-skater, one of the swiftest and deadliest of the Night Warriors.

She wore a helmet that was constructed out of a lacework of fine silver wire, elaborately pierced and decorated, and twinkling with hundreds of minuscule white lights. The sides of the helmet were scalloped, like a clamshell, but the facepiece was shaped like a mask of Angie's face, a second skin of lights and flowers and pierced silverwork.

"This headpiece may *look* frail," Springer remarked, "but it is made of a combination of metals which was discovered by the Ecuadorian Indians thousands of years ago when they were trying to sinter platinum and gold. It feels like the softest lace, but it can withstand higher temperatures than platinum, over three thousand degrees; and it can also deflect a blow from any kind of battle-ax that you can imagine."

"What about battle-axes that we *can't* imagine?" asked Stanley.

Springer nodded and smiled at his perspicacity. "Battle-axes that you *can't* imagine have to be deflected by trial."

"No error?"

"If you make an error with an unimaginable battle-ax, you don't usually get a second chance."

Angie looked fantastically otherworldly in her mask-helmet; a butterfly-woman; a creature out of a carnival; but startlingly pretty. Her eyes were very wide and glistening and lambent, and Stanley saw an expression in them that he hadn't seen before. A greater alertness, a sharper intelligence, a *questioning* look. It was a look he had seen in the eyes of well-educated children who attended his master classes in violin. They were not necessarily prodigies. In fact, some of them were quite slow when it came to math and history and spelling. But they possessed a burning keenness to question; and to question again; and to find out. They consumed new knowledge like a brush fire burns oxygen, and still they raged for more.

Angie Dunning had never had that fire; but Effis did; and Stanley found it remarkable how much more self-possessed it made her, how much more magnetic. She still talked in her common South London accent, but she held her head straight, and every movement seemed to have more grace.

So much did Effis's body armor remind Stanley of the glitteringly ostentatious show costume of a star figure skater that he didn't realize at first that it *was* armor. It was a sheer leotard, halter-necked but cut so high on the thighs that her legs looked endless. Patterns of white light played and danced ceaselessly across the fabric, unfolding flower patterns, silently-exploding stars, diamonds, and ruffles. The halter neck was very high, and fastened tightly at her throat with a brilliantly-jeweled choker, four rows of dazzling diamonds, pressed into a thick band of solid platinum.

While it seemed so thin, and clung to her skin so tightly,

the body stocking lifted and separated Effis's breasts so that they looked even fuller and rounder and shaped her waist. She appeared to be taller, trimmer.

"What do you think?" Springer asked her. "The finest suit of dreamlight armor ever made."

Effis stared at herself in the window and said, "This ain't supposed to be *armor*, is it? It don't feel like armor."

Springer laid his hand appreciatively on her back. The dancing patterns of light sparkled along his fingers and around his fingertips. A few small sparks even showered from his lips as he spoke.

"This suit will protect you from every lightweight weapon that has ever been encountered by the Night Warriors in ten centuries of human dreams. The fabric's rather like the surface of a CD record ... it's programmed to alter its structure to deal with anything that happens to be fired at it. Darts, arrows, death-stars, stones, you name it; and a few things for which there *are* no names. For instance, what do you call a lance that's fashioned out of solid darkness, and nothing else?"

"You said it protects against lightweight weapons," Stanley put in. "What about heavyweight weapons?"

Springer shook his gradually-darkening hair. "Effis will be far too fast to have to worry about anything heavier. Once she's started skating on a strong light-source, she can pick up the momentum of the light itself, and travel faster than you and I or anybody else can even *think*."

"Right now, I don't know *what* to think," said Stanley.

Effis did a twirl in the window and then lifted both arms. She wore full-length gloves, as fine and as lacy as her helmet. But along the outside edge of each glove, all the way from the tips of her little fingers to her elbows, was a thin folded fan of shining silver metal.

"What are these for?" she wanted to know.

"Those are your razor-fans, your principal weapons," Springer told her. "You approach your target as fast as you can. You hold your arm straight out in front of you, hand flat. Then you flex the muscles in your arm and the razor-fan opens up."

Effis hesitated, but Springer lifted her right arm for her and showed her. "Now, *flex*."

Instantly, silently, the fan opened up into a series of five metal fins. The fin on the side of her hand was only two or three inches wide, but the fin on her wrist was a little wider, and the one halfway along her forearm a little wider still, until the fin at her elbow was over a foot wide.

Effis turned her arm this way and that, and reflections from the shining fins skipped and shivered around the room. "I don't see 'ow it works."

"Crouch down like a skater," Springer instructed her. "Imagine you're traveling at two hundred feet per second. That's not too fast, you can skate much faster than that. Hold both arms rigidly out in front of you, keeping your hands locked together, like a diver. There's a whole row of demons in front of you, all right? You flex your muscles, your razor-fans open up. You shout your battle cry, *Ashapola!* and you skate right through those demons on your ray of light, and you slice off everything that gets in your way."

Effis relaxed her arm muscles, and the razor-fan slowly closed. She looked uncertain. "I'm not too sure I like the sound of that."

Springer shrugged. "Effis the light-skater is one of the most feared of all the Night Warriors, believe me."

"That still don't mean I like the sound of cutting people to bits."

"Those who inspire the greatest fear in Ashapola's enemies have the greatest duty to perform," said Springer.

"But—"

"Before you say 'but,' take a look at your skates. They've changed a great deal from the days when Elisabeth Pardoe was Effis. In her day they were ash wood, with sharpened iron blades, and hand-ground lenses to take in the light. But so much of the Night Warriors' equipment has changed and developed. We would have been overwhelmed and routed centuries ago if we had allowed ourselves to remain complacent. Modern dreams require modern weaponry."

Effis looked down. Little by little, a pair of skating boots materialized around her ankles. They were gleaming silver metal, streamlined and wedge-shaped, with clusters of six or seven large white lenses around the ankles. The boots appeared to have no skates: Effis was standing flat on the floor.

"This is the greatest advance," said Springer, hunkering down beside Effis. "In the seventeenth century, the light was taken in through the lenses, focused, and directed along the cutting edge of the blade, so that it acted as a lubricant between the skate and the ground surface. With these skates, the light is taken in through the lenses, intensified over ten thousand times, and guided by fiber optics through to the sole of the boot, where it forms an actual skate blade made of pure light."

"But there's nothing there," Effis protested.

"There will be, when you're all charged up, believe me."

At last they approached Gordon, who had just woken up from a restless doze on the sofa. Springer knelt down beside him and gently laid his hand on his scarf-wrapped wrist. Gordon's face was colorless, and his eyes were widely dilated. When he spoke, his voice was slurred, as if he were recovering from anesthetic.

Stanley wondered if Springer had somehow "put him under" to ease the shock and the pain of what had happened to him. No matter how miraculous Springer's healing might have been, the loss of a hand must still have been hideously traumatic.

"Gordon ..." said Springer in a gentle voice. "How are you feeling?"

"Terrible," Gordon replied. "I feel as if a gerbil's been sleeping in my mouth. Do you think I could have a drink of water?"

"Of course. Stanley, would you mind? It's going to take you a week or two to get over the shock."

"What were those things ... those dog-things?"

"Guard dogs, if you like. Witches create them for their own amusement; and also to serve them and protect them. You've read fairy stories about witches stealing children ... Rapunzel, Hansel and Gretel ... they're based on truth. Witches used to steal babies and children and meld them supernaturally with the bodies of dogs, or cats, or goats. The children were always promised that—one day— they would be changed back into human shape, but in return they had to serve and obey their mistress without question. Those boy-dogs who attacked you at Tennyson were guarding the entrance to their mistress's memories … that rainy landscape, that barbaric world of pain and disease."

Stanley brought Gordon a glass of water, which Gordon drank thirstily and unsteadily, spilling some of it down the front of his coat.

"The boy-dogs were told to kill all intruders, whatever the cost," said Springer. "You were lucky to escape with your lives."

"I left my hand behind," said Gordon.

Springer slowly stood up and looked at Gordon with a mixture of compassion and acceptance. Stanley saw in his eyes the steadiness of somebody who knows that events must turn out as events must turn out; but somebody who can regret it, all the same. There are greater conflicts in the universe than the squabbles of men. There are far more monstrous planets turning than the planet earth; and far more agonizing losses than the loss of Gordon's hand.

All the same, the distance between the earth and Jupiter, at conjunction, was only 928 million kilometers; and the distance between Gordon and his lost hand was infinite.

Springer said, "Since you were born, Gordon, you were fated to lose that hand. You probably don't know it, but your great-great-grandfather lost the same hand, when he was called to the service of the Night Warriors. And three generations before that, *his* great-great-grandfather also lost his left hand."

"But *why*?" asked Gordon in a hoarse voice.

"It was a sacrifice, of a sort. A way of improving your ability to fight for Ashapola. Just as Amazon women removed one breast to make it easier for them to use a bow and arrow, your hand was given in the cause of the greatest battle of all."

"How the hell does losing my hand help me to fight better?" Gordon demanded.

"Let me show you. Are you strong enough to stand?"

Gordon nodded. "I think so. If I fall flat on my face, then you'll know that I'm not."

Springer helped him up and guided him over to the middle of the room. Gordon walked unsteadily and swayed a little as he stood facing the window, but Springer stood close beside him and held his arm.

"You are Keldak the fistfighter. Watch the window ... this is your armor."

Gordon said sarcastically. "*Fist*fighter? With only one fist?" but Springer said, "Wait, and watch."

Slowly, the outline of a heavy squarish helmet appeared around Gordon's head ... a helmet of softly-gleaming green metal, with the narrowest slit of a tinted visor. Attached to the left side of the helmet was a square illuminated grid, and less than an inch away from this grid, hovering in the air, was a holographic image of a globe, about four inches in diameter. Whichever way Keldak turned his head, the globe remained hovering at the same distance from the left side of his helmet, like an obedient planet.

"You use the globe to aim your weapon," Springer told him. "When the time comes for you to go into combat, it will swing around in front of your eyes, and you will be able to create a model of your adversary within it. Once your adversary has been targeted, and his image has been locked into the globe, he can never escape, even if it eludes you at that particular moment, and you don't come across it again until months or even years later."

Below his helmet, Keldak's chest and stomach were protected by green metallic body armor. A shaped triangular codpiece of the same green metal protected his genitals, and was fastened tightly between his buttocks with a thin leather strap. He wore green metallic boots with illuminated studs all the way down the sides, but otherwise he was naked.

"So where's my weapon?" he asked. He raised his bare right fist. "This isn't going to be very much use against demons. Come on, Springer, I couldn't punch my way out of a wet paper bag."

Springer smiled and said, "Hold up your left wrist."

Keldak did as he was told. Springer took hold of it and carefully unwrapped the scarf, baring the swollen skin of his stump. Although it was still reddened, it was miraculous how well it had healed. With conventional medicine, Keldak would probably have still been undergoing surgery.

Springer said, "The power that I am going to give you now is only a tiny proportion of the power that Kasyx the charge-keeper will give you. But it will be sufficient for a demonstration."

He closed his eyes for a moment, still gripping Keldak's left wrist. Keldak glanced uncertainly at Stanley, but all that Stanley could do was to shrug. He couldn't guess what was going to happen any more than Keldak could.

Angie whispered, "It's *unbelievable*, innit?"

So gradually that Stanley couldn't be sure at first that he was not simply imagining it, a pale luminous hand-shape appeared on the end of Keldak's left wrist. Springer kept his eyes tightly closed, and with each passing second the luminous hand grew brighter and brighter, until it shone almost as brightly as a halogen lamp.

Keldak turned his wrist this way and that, staring at the dazzling hand in amazement. It threw vast distorted shadows of all of them around the room. "I can *feel* it," he said. "I can actually *feel* it. I can wiggle my fingers."

"It's one hundred percent pure power," said Springer, opening his eyes. "When Kasyx has charged you up, it will be absolutely blinding. On the left side of your chest armor, you will find a gauntlet. Normally, your fist will remain covered; but when you are ready to fight, you will pull off the gauntlet, target your fist, and release it."

Keldak frowned. "*Release* it?"

"Do you want to try it?" asked Springer. "Why not target that vase?"

On the opposite side of the room, on the floor, stood a tall black glass vase, containing a stylized arrangement of silvery dried honesty.

"Are you sure?" asked Keldak.

"Go ahead, everything's replaceable."

Keldak hesitated for a moment, then raised his right hand and slid a small switch on the left of his breastplate. Immediately, silently, unerringly, the holographic globe quarter-circled around from the side of his helmet and floated right in front of his narrow visor.

"How did I know how to do that?" he asked in bewilderment.

"The skills of the Night Warriors are passed mystically

from generation to generation," said Springer. "With a little practice, you will become as adept as your forefathers. Now—target the vase."

Keldak pressed a series of small illuminated buttons on his breastplate, and a three-dimensional picture of the vase began to build up inside the sphere. It took no more than three or four seconds. Once it was done, Keldak pressed another button, and the glove returned to its "parked" position on the left side of his helmet.

"Raise your arm," Springer instructed him. Keldak did as he was told, looking quickly at Stanley and Angie for reassurance.

"All right, fire."

"Fire?"

"Go ahead. Don't you know how to do it?"

"I—" Keldak began, but without warning, his shining left fist shot from the end of his arm with a startling *sshhhhhheeeeeee-krakkkkkk!* and punched the vase from over ten feet away. The vase exploded in a fine spray of glittering black glass, and the sprigs of honesty were tossed across the floor.

Springer laughed. Keldak looked down at his stump. Another hand had already appeared, more pale and ghostly this time.

"That's amazing," he said. "That's absolutely amazing."

"Of course, your combat fist will be infinitely more powerful," Springer explained. "And each new fist will normally be just as powerful as the one before it. That's until you run short of charge. Then you'll have to go back to Kasyx for more."

Keldak's armor and helmet faded, leaving Gordon standing

tiredly in the middle of the room. "Come on," Springer urged him, "sit down. You've had enough for one night."

Gordon returned to the sofa. Stanley drained his vodka glass and went to the kitchen to help himself to a refill. Springer followed him and stood in the doorway watching him as he poured himself what British India-hands would have called a *burra-peg*, three fingers and a splash more.

"Well?" asked Springer. Somehow, he was beginning to change again, to become younger and more feminine. His hair seemed silkier and longer than it had just a moment ago, when he was showing Keldak his armor.

"Well, what?" asked Stanley. "Do you want me to say that I'm impressed? All right, I'm impressed. I can't say that I'm delighted, but I'm impressed."

"I hope you don't expect me to pretend that being a Night Warrior isn't anything but a burdensome and dangerous responsibility," said Springer in a tone that almost turned his words into a question. "But your forefathers made promises which bind you today; and which bind your children; and which will bind your children's children."

"The sins of the fathers visited on the sons," said Stanley caustically into his vodka glass.

Springer said, "You do understand, don't you, that for you personally, finding and destroying Isabel Gowdie isn't just a matter of controlling this epidemic of Night Plague? It's your only hope of saving your soul, Stanley."

"I'm not sure how much I *want* my soul to be saved."

"Well, you'll feel that way a lot of the time … that's one of the symptoms. You'll feel depressed and hopeless. You may even feel suicidal."

Stanley said nothing, but swallowed more vodka and shivered.

Springer came up to him. He was much smaller now, and his blond hair was almost touching his shoulders. He had become a young girl of eighteen or nineteen, very slim, almost breastless, with dreamy heavy-lidded eyes and a delicate mouth.

"I've seen the Carriers come and go," Springer told him. "I've even managed to follow them, two or three times. They've been searching for more Night Warriors to infect. But I still have no idea where Isabel Gowdie might be; not even a clue. You'll have to go into her dreams to find her."

"What are our chances if we do?"

"Better than your chances if you don't."

"So when do we start looking for her?" asked Stanley.

"Just as soon as Kasyx the charge-keeper and the fifth Night Warrior arrive."

"The fifth Night Warrior?"

"Zasta the knife-juggler. His forefather was killed, too, when Isabel Gowdie ignited the ratcatcher's brain. He has to have his revenge."

Stanley said, "How soon are they coming?"

"Within two or three days, no longer."

"And how are we supposed to know when they arrive?"

"You'll know. I promise you. You'll know for sure."

Stanley looked at Springer; pretty and youthful and gentle as a young animal; and for no reason that he could truly comprehend, the most appalling feeling of dread came over him.

Chapter Six

Rotten Rags

The telephone was ringing when Stanley and Angie arrived back at Stanley's flat at half past seven that morning. They had driven Gordon home first and then borrowed Gordon's car to get back to Langton Street. Stanley had been obliged to let Angie do the driving, even though she hadn't yet passed her test. He had never driven a car with a manual gearbox before—especially not a shuddering, rusty, rubbish-littered junker like Gordon's Montego.

The morning was gloomy and fogbound, and even though it wasn't raining, the deserted streets of Fulham and Chelsea were shining with wet. It was so bitterly cold that Stanley had kept his hands thrust deep in his pockets.

He first heard the phone as he slotted the key into the downstairs door. "What are you going to do?" he asked Angie. "Drive straight back to Herbert Gardens or stay for some breakfast?"

"Ain't you going to answer the phone?" Angie wanted to know.

"It's a wrong number, more than likely. I get dozens of

them. 'Is Stephanie in?' mostly. I think this flat used to be rented by the most industrious call girl in Fulham. Don't worry, if it's all that important, they'll call back later."

Angie looked at her wristwatch. "All right, I'll 'ave a cup of coffee. Don't s'pose Brenda and Sharon are awake yet, anyway. They usually 'ave a lie-in, Saturdays."

They went upstairs, and Stanley opened the door to his flat, The phone continued to ring, but he didn't answer it straightaway. He drew back the curtains and switched on the lights first, and stripped off his coat. Only then did he pick up the receiver and tuck it under his chin.

"Miss Thomson doesn't live here any more. I'm sorry to say," he answered. Then he paused and listened, and the expression on his face slowly melted from tired-flippant to tired-serious, "Eve? Eve, what's wrong?"

He placed his hand over the receiver and said to Angie, "It's my ex. She's calling from San Francisco."

Angie had dropped on to the big brown sofa and was sitting with her knees tucked up. There were violet smudges of exhaustion under her eyes. She didn't say anything, but untied the ribbon around her firework-style hair and shook it loose like a poodle.

Eve said, "What time is it? I tried to call you earlier, but there was no reply."

"It's seven thirty-five in the morning."

"Did I wake you?"

"I've been out. That's why you couldn't get me before."

"You've been out all night?"

"Eve, we're not married any more. I can do what I like."

"Stanley, my father's had a coronary. He's very, very sick."

"I'm sorry to hear that. Eve. Where is he?"

"He's still in Napa right now, but Dr. Fishman is talking about transferring him to the Polk Clinic in San Francisco when he's strong enough."

"Well, I'm sorry to hear that. Eve. Is he conscious?"

"He can understand what we say to him, but he can't speak just yet."

"Well, tell him how sorry I am—and if there's anything that I can do ..."

"As a matter of fact, Stanley, that's why I'm calling. There *is* something that you can do."

Stanley looked across at Angie and rolled his eyes up to show her that Eve was going on again, the way she always went on. Angie grinned at him.

"Stanley ...I'd like you to take care of Leon for a while."

"You'd like me to what?"

"Stanley, it isn't much to ask. Leon's so upset about his grandfather ... and he misses you so bad. I just think it would do him so much good if he could join you in London for a month. It would get him away from all of this trauma. And it would reestablish your relationship, too. Don't you think that's important? Father and son?"

"That's not what your lawyer told my lawyer, the last time they spoke on the subject of visitation rights. Your lawyer told my lawyer that you would rather have Leon spend weekends with the Wolfman than spend any time with me."

"I was upset, Stanley. Now I'm not upset. Well, not as upset as I was then."

"You mean this time you need me."

"All right, Stanley, I need you. Leon needs you. Maybe you need Leon, too, even if you don't need me."

"Eve, it's very early in the morning, I haven't slept all night, and this is getting too complicated. What exactly are you proposing to do?"

"I want to put Leon on the six twenty-five Pan Am Clipper tomorrow night. I want you to meet him at London airport. If you can have him in London for three weeks minimum, that'll be wonderful. If you can have him longer ... well, that would be even more wonderful."

Stanley was silent for a very long time. He didn't intend to play with the Kensington Chamber Orchestra for at least another month. That was if he ever played anything with anyone, ever again. The thought of opening up his violin case made him feel cold with anxiety. It might be teeming with worms. His violin might have collapsed into soft, silent dust. There might be something worse in there ... something infinitely vile.

Angie came over and stood beside him and looked directly into his eyes.

"What is it?" she asked him.

"My ex wants my son to come stay with me, here in London."

"Why not? I'll 'elp you. It might be a laugh."

Eve said, "Stanley? Stanley? Are you still there?"

"Yes, Eve, I'm still here."

"Well? Will you have him? He's your own flesh and blood, after all."

Stanley nodded wearily. "All right. Eve, pack his bag and send him over. What did you say? The six twenty-five Clipper from San Francisco?"

"PA 126 ... For goodness' sake, make sure you're there

waiting for him. And call me when he arrives. Don't wait to get home, call me from the airport."

"You've got it."

"Stanley—"

"Yes, Eve?"

"Nothing. I know this is short notice, Stanley, and I really do appreciate your having him, especially after everything that's happened."

"You made it happen, sugar, not me."

"Stanley, I—"

"It's too late, Eve. It's all too late. Just give my best to your old man, would you? And tell your old lady I take it all back, what I said about her black-bottom pie. And tell Leon I love him."

He put down the phone. For some odd reason, he suddenly thought of what Springer had said to him about the other two Night Warriors. *You'll know when they arrive.*

Angie said, "You don't look particularly chuffed about 'im coming."

"I don't know. I don't know what to think. Everything's so weird. That house last night … all that stuff about Night Warriors. I feel like I'm losing my marbles."

"Oh, cheer up," Angie insisted. She was standing very close to him, and when he tried to move away she caught hold of his shirt sleeve.

"I was going to perk some coffee," he told her.

She still didn't let go of his sleeve. "I don't think you're losing your marbles, you know," she told him. "It's true, all of it."

"You're very sure, all of a sudden."

"I've caught it, too, that's why," she said in a challenging voice.

"You've caught what?"

"That disease that Springer was talking about—that Night Plague. I've caught it, too, caught it from you. I know what it feels like because I can feel it inside of meself. I feel like shouting out loud, I feel like 'itting you, 'ard as I can. I feel like scratching your eyes out. I can't stand the sight of you. But I want to go to bed with you, too. I want to go to bed with you and do it and do it and do it in every single way you can think of and never stop."

Stanley slowly lifted her hand away from his sleeve. *Why not? She's a beautiful girl. And if she's really desperate for it, why not? Don't you remember what you said to Eve. "Eve, we're not married any more. I can do what I like." Prove it—prove you can do what you like. Take her to bed and do it.*

"You're overtired, that's all," he heard himself saying.

"Stanley, I'm not. I've caught it."

"How could you have caught it?"

"We 'ad it away, didn't we? We 'ad a dream that we 'ad it away. That's when I caught it."

Stanley laid his hands on her shoulders, almost fatherly. "Angie … you're overtired, that's all there is to it. I know what Springer said about passing on the Night Plague in dreams … but it's far more likely that you're exhausted, and that you're still suffering from shock. Let's face up to it, what happened last night was pretty damned extraordinary."

Angie stared at him for a long, tense second, her body taut, her back straight, her lower lip quivering.

"Stan," she said, "I've caught it."

He lowered his head, trying to be patient, "Listen, sweetheart—"

"*I've caught it, you stupid bastard! I've caught it!*"

She tore open the two top buttons of her clinging red woollen dress, then she wrenched the wool apart, exposing her scarlet nylon bra, filled to overflowing with her brimming white breasts. She wrenched the wool again, and again, and tore the dress completely off, so that she was standing in front of him in her scarlet bra and her scarlet panty hose and her high-heeled scarlet shoes, and that was all.

Stanley said, "Angie, this just isn't the time or the *(why not? why not? look at those breasts, look at the way those panty hose are tucked tight right between her legs)* impossible, not you and me, especially if Springer's right and we're *(you could lose your whole hand in those breasts, like plunging your fingers into soft bread dough)* can't do it, can't even *think* about doing it."

Angie paused. Her eyes seemed to be unfocused, as if she were high, or hypnotized. In exaggeratedly slow motion, she reached behind her and unfastened the clasp of her bra. Her breasts swung bare, with tiny tight sugar-pink nipples.

"Angie—" Stanley began; but the look in her eyes was enough to convince him to stay back. Her pupils were so widely dilated that he felt that if he looked into them with a flashlight, he would be able to see right down inside of her body, all the way down to the soles of her feet.

She kicked off her shoes, and then she tugged down her panty hose, stepping out of them and tossing them aside. Completely naked, she stood in front of him again. He hadn't realized how short she was, without her high heels. Her nipples were on the same level as his waist.

Look at her, look at that body, smell that perfume, smell that sex. She wants you so much that she has tears in her eyes.

"I want it," she mouthed.

He said nothing, couldn't think of anything to say.

"I want it," she repeated.

He turned away, toward the window. Outside, in the foggy air, he could see woodsmoke lying almost horizontal a few feet above the ground, motionless, unstirred by any wind; and a muddy rutted field, and a half-collapsed building that looked like a pig farm or an abattoir. He could see people walking through the fog huddled in gray blankets and tattered shawls; people who walked as if they had nowhere to go to, and no hope whatever.

I want it, said Angie inside of his mind.

Then—without any further warning—she took one step forward and raked her rough-bitten nails all the way down his left cheek, tearing the skin three layers deep.

The sting of nails was instant and excruciating. It hurt so much that for a split second he thought that she had thrown acid at him. But his reaction was so fast that he had slapped her across the face before he had even decided whether he was going to retaliate or not. She slapped him back, almost as quickly. He slapped her again.

"*You bastard!*" she screeched at him. Her face had turned into a contorted mask, terrifying in its hate and its intensity. "*You bastard!*"

He seized hold of her wrist and twisted her around, jamming her hand up between her shoulder blades in a hammerlock. She screamed and kicked and tried to struggle her way free *bastard bastard bastard bastard* but he managed to snatch her other wrist and catch both hands behind her back, gripping both of her wrists in his left hand.

He forced her forward in an awkward four-legged dance. She spat at him over her shoulder and swore at him filthily, a monotonous litany of blasphemy and hatred and dirt.

She staggered, and he pushed her against the door, which slammed shut. He pressed his weight against her, keeping her hands high up between her shoulder blades, and forcing them higher whenever she kicked back at him. *God you bastard you bastard I'm going to kill you for this you bastard.*

He grunted, pushed her harder. Her bare breasts were squashed against the panels of the door. With his free hand he tugged loose his belt buckle, wrenched at his buttons, tore open his zipper. His hardened penis rose from his shorts like a thick sculpture in dark red marble, the gleaming heart-shaped head, the corded shaft.

If she's crying out for it, the whore, she can have it. She can have it hard and she can have it till she screams at me to stop. And then she can have it some more. He opened her up with his fingers, stretched her lips apart. She shrieked and tried to break free, but he stretched her even wider. He was grunting, he could hear himself grunting. He sounded more like a beast than a human, a savage crouching primitive creature with a rearing erection.

He pushed himself into her, right up as far as he could go, forcing her even harder against the door. He pushed her again and again, and she wrestled and swore at him, but he kept on pushing even when she screamed, and his whole mind was filled up with shattering blackness, like the black glass vase that Keldak had shattered with his explosive fist of light.

He could feel his climax tightening between his legs. *Bastard*, she was screaming at him, *bastard bastard bastard thousand times bastard!*

He said, "Oh, God" but at that instant she roared at him, roared at him *Nooo!* and twisted herself around so violently that she broke his grip on her wrists. She dropped to her knees in front of him, seized his buttocks with fingers that dug into his flesh like claws, and pulled him forward into her open mouth, deeper than he could have believed possible, as deep as he could go. He gripped her hair, wound it around his fingers. He felt her teeth catching at his skin *God she's going to bite it off* then climaxed in terror and pain and incomprehensible ecstasy *ngugh nnngghh nghh* quaking and crying out as if all the doors of hell had slammed at once.

She said something, he couldn't understand what. She swallowed and swallowed again.

Then it was over and they lay side by side on the carpet staring at each other and saying nothing, their fingertips touching, that was all, and Stanley was sure and certain that Springer had been telling them the truth. They were in danger of losing not only their morals but their mortal souls, and there was only one way for them to save themselves.

They slept for most of the morning. Stanley woke at ten after eleven and lay staring at the ceiling for a while. He felt tired and nauseous, and his mouth was filled with sickly-tasting saliva. Without waking Angie, he eased himself out of bed and tippytoed through to the bathroom.

He switched on the fluorescent light over the bathroom

mirror. He stared at himself. His face appeared to be gray and bloated, like a man who has been found drowned in the Thames. His left cheek was scored with four scab-encrusted parallel lines where Angie had scratched it. There were reddened bite marks on his neck, too, and on his shoulders.

"Stanley," he told himself. "You look like you fought a monkey in a trash can and lost."

His stomach gurgled, and his mouth was filled with bile. He spat it out and reached for the water glass, but as he did so he suddenly coughed. He could feel something twisted and rubbery caught in his throat, and his stomach rebelled against it so violently that he let out a huge cackling retch and bent double over the washbasin.

His throat contracted again and again, and slowly, out of his stretched-open mouth, he forced out a tangled mass of brown squid's legs, glistening and suckered and still curling and uncurling as if they were alive, all stuck together with a wet gray mass that looked like hair and soap scum that had been cleared out of a blocked bathroom drain.

The thing completely choked him, so that he couldn't cry out. He retched and retched again, shuddering with pain and disgust, his eyes crowded with tears. Just when he thought it was going to suffocate him, it gave a last convulsive wriggle and dropped into the washbasin, where it lay writhing and twisting and unrolling, as if it, too, were suffering agonizing pain.

Stanley bent his head over the bath and turned on the cold faucet as far as it would go, and splashed handful after handful of water into his mouth. His stomach was still growling and protesting, and he couldn't stop himself from convulsing in horror.

At last, however, he sniffed, and stood up, and dragged a bath towel from the rail and momentarily buried his face in it. When he looked back at the washbasin, the tentacles were still wriggling, and he had to cover his mouth with his hand to prevent himself from puking yet again.

He heard Angie calling from the bedroom, "Stan? Stanley, are you all right?"

"I'm okay," he choked back. "I'm okay. Just don't come in here."

"Stan, what's the matter?"

"I'm fine … I've been sick, that's all. Just don't come in here."

The thing in the washbasin was trying slowly and painfully to slide up the sides of the slippery white ceramic. Stanley swallowed and shuddered. It was alive, damn it, it was really alive. It almost made him heave just to think that it must have been growing inside of his stomach. He picked up the lavatory brush and tried to poke it back down into the basin, but immediately its tentacles twisted themselves around the bristles and it started to climb out of the basin, dripping gray juice.

Stanley smacked the brush smartly against the side of the basin but the thing refused to release its grip. Whatever it was, it was tenacious and resilient and it was determined to get out of the basin. He smacked the brush again and again, but still the thing clung on.

"Stan-*lee*! What are you doing?" Angie demanded.

"Don't come in here, that's all!"

He dropped the lavatory brush, wrenched open the bathroom door, and hurried across the hallway to the living room. A half bottle of Wyborowa stood on the mantelpiece over the fire, beneath the strange painting of *Prince Baltasar Carlos with a Dwarf*. He picked up the bottle, and then crossed to the bureau in the corner and took a box of Swan matches out of the drawer.

By the time he returned to the bathroom, the tentacled thing had succeeded in struggling painfully up the head of the lavatory brush, and was beginning to entwine its suckers around the handle.

His hands shaking, Stanley emptied the vodka bottle all over it. The instant the spirit touched it, the thing suddenly writhed and wriggled, and Stanley breathed, "Shit!" and jumped smartly back, knocking his knee against the side of the bath. But he steadied himself for long enough to fumble a match out of the box and strike it. The match flared, but then its head dropped off on to the floor and sizzled out. Stanley scrabbled desperately in the box for another one. Already the dripping thing was halfway out of the washbasin, trying to overbalance itself on to the floor.

Stanley struck the match one—twice—then tossed it while it was still blazing into the middle of the creature's tentacles. There was a soft crackling *whoomph* and the thing was engulfed in a halo of blue flame.

Stanley kept his back pressed against the cold tiles on the opposite wall of the bathroom as the thing lashed and twisted and shuddered in agony. The lavatory brush caught alight, too, and the bathroom began to fill with thick looping curls of acrid smoke, and black feathers of burned plastic.

Gradually, the thing in the washbasin puckered and shriveled, its glistening tentacles drying out and curling up, its gray slime reduced to a fibrous ash. The flames guttered and burned out. Stanley cautiously approached the washbasin, picked up the handle of the half-burned brush, and prodded the thing to make sure that it was dead.

To his fascinated disgust, the brown mushroom-wrinkled skin in the middle of the thing peeled open, and he saw a single dead eye looking up at him. He prodded the creature, hesitated, then lifted it up with the brush and dropped it into the lavatory. He flushed it, and immediately it was swirled away.

He was still staring into the lavatory when the bathroom door opened and Angie came in, wrapped in a sheet.

"Gordon Bennett," she said. "What the 'ell's been going on in 'ere?"

Stanley ushered her out of the bathroom and back into the bedroom, closing the door behind him. He went quickly across to the window and tugged open the drapes. Outside, the landscape was the same as it had been last night. Dreary, rain-swept marshes, squalid buildings, and a girl pushing a handcart laden with joggling corpses.

"Can you see that?" he asked Angie, taking her by the arm.

She nodded, her face pale. "What is it? What does it mean?"

"I'm not sure. But don't you remember what Springer said—that it was raining inside Tennyson because Isabel Gowdie was dreaming it was raining, the way that it used to rain there, before the house was built? Well, the same thing must be happening here. If you ask me, this is Isabel Gowdie's memory of what this part of London looked like, before the Night Warriors finally got to her and locked her up.

"She can make her own dream world exist at the same time as our world. She can make all these fields and these buildings look as if they're really there. Maybe they *are* really there. Her dreams are so damned strong that they have as much reality as the real thing."

"But how can it be a dream if I'm not asleep?" asked Angie.

"It's a dream but it's not *your* dream ... that's why you can't work out whether you're asleep or awake. It doesn't matter whether you're asleep or awake because you're not dreaming it yourself. That's why you and I were able to have an identical dream about making love. It wasn't *our* dream at all. It was hers. It was Isabel Gowdie's."

"But how can we be in somebody else's dream?" asked Angie.

"I don't know. That's what Knitted Hood asked me. Who's *dreaming whom?* Maybe there's no real answer to that. Maybe—in a way—we're all dreaming each other. You know, Jung's idea about everybody sharing the same unconscious mind. When you come to think about it, it would account for a whole lot of things, wouldn't it? Psychic experiences, mind reading, premonitions."

It was plain that Angie didn't really follow what Stanley was trying to say, but she must have thought it *sounded* convincing, because she nodded as if she did.

Stanley said, "Maybe witches weren't really witches at all ... not flying around on broomsticks or anything ... but women who happened to understand the power of the human mind and can use it to their own advantage."

"Trouble is, 'ow can we get ourselves cured?" asked Angie. "I mean—Stan, I like you ever so much. But we can't go on doing what we did this morning. I mean, I just don't *love* you. I mean, not *that* much."

In his mind's eye, Stanley experienced a flickering Instamatic picture of Angie's eyes, wide open, as he climaxed, his fingers entangled in her hair. He said, "If Springer was telling us the truth, we have to find Isabel Gowdie, wherever she is, and kill her."

"But we can't do it until the rest of the what's-their-names get 'ere, can we? The rest of the Night Warriors?"

"I don't know," Stanley told her. "For you and me, it's urgent. Maybe we should try making a start today."

"What, actually go outside? Just as we are? Without any armor or nothing?"

Stanley went right up to the window and stared out at the gloomy, rain-glistening fields. The gray Thames clay looked like the clay of a freshly-dug communal grave. "I don't know … why not? The sooner we find her, the sooner we can get ourselves cured."

Angie stood with her sheet wound around her like a Roman toga. "I don't think we ought to," she said dubiously. "I don't think Springer would like it, would 'e, or *she*, or whatever 'e is? It's a bit like jumping the gun, ain't it?"

"Let's get dressed," Stanley suggested. "Then … if the fields are still there when we go outside, let's go looking for Isabel Gowdie. How about that?"

"What about all those dead people out there?"

"They're dead. What can they do?"

"Well, nothing. But what did they die of?"

"Bubonic plague, I expect, but don't let it worry you. These days, we have a cure for bubonic plague."

"Oh, thanks a lot."

They dressed. Angie was more modest this morning and turned her back on him. He couldn't help noticing the red bruises and the scratch marks on her shoulders and her bottom, however. It seemed extraordinary to think that he had practically raped her this morning. Now they were talking to each other in their actual, uninfected roles, as two affectionate acquaintances with nothing at all in common.

Stanley glanced toward the window; partly to make sure that Isabel Gowdie's dreadful dream landscape was still there; partly because he had felt something quiver in his consciousness, like a spider suddenly quivering on its web.

—swathe through the—

A few feet away from the broken-down fence of the pig farm stood Knitted Hood, motionless, the shoulders of his raincoat dark with rain. Had Langton Street been there, instead of this nightmare hallucination of the seventeenth century, he would have been standing exactly where he had stood on the morning that he attacked Stanley and infected him with the Night Plague, on the opposite corner, beside the postbox. Stanley shivered. He felt one reality overlapping with another; dream upon dream; until he couldn't be sure if he was really seeing Isabel Gowdie's dream, or if he was dreaming that he was, or if Knitted Hood was dreaming that he was.

He saw Langton Street as it was today. He saw it run backwards through a thousand changes, three hundred years skipping and dancing in front of his eyes like a speeded-up movie in reverse. Passersby blurred this way and that along the sidewalks, their lives no more than an evanescent flicker of light. Vehicles whirled around the street in a furious phantom carousel—bicycles, horse-drawn carriages, pushcarts, hansom cabs, horses. Trees flared up and shrank away again. Clouds raced threateningly overhead. Houses tumbled apart, cottages collapsed.

And then there was nothing outside his window but the rain and the mud and the silent, patient figure of Knitted Hood; more like a diseased hawk than a man; his perfect face nothing but a white smudge in the shadow of his hood.

Angie said, "Are you sure you want to do this, Stan?"

Stanley tugged on a thick maroon polo-neck sweater. "Couldn't be surer," he replied; although the only certainty he felt was a panic so rigid that he could almost feel it in his chest. "Let's go, hunh? There's a raincoat in the hall closet you can borrow."

They went downstairs. The house was gloomy and deserted. The only sound was the rustling of Angie's raincoat as she shrugged it on, and the noise of their feet on the thinly-carpeted stairs.

In the hall, before Stanley opened the door, Angie caught hold of his hand. "I 'ope you realize this is mad," she said.

Stanley gave her a humorless nod.

"I mean walking off into some old witch's dream. It's totally bonkers. I mean what 'appens if she wakes up, and we're right in the middle of a brick wall or something?"

"I don't know."

Angie looked away, hesitant. Then she said, "I'm scared."

"We have to do it, Angie. We don't have any choice."

"Supposing—" Angie began, but she couldn't find the words. Stanley lifted the collar of her raincoat and fastened up the top button for her, in a distinctively fatherly way. He kissed her on the forehead.

"You and me, we've both fallen foul of some kind of fight

between the probably-good guys and the very, very super-megaevil guys. The problem is, we *have* to get involved; otherwise this thing in our heads is going to make us wilder and weirder and if we don't end up killing each other we'll probably end up killing somebody else. *And* spreading this Night Plague around to God knows how many unsuspecting people, every time we dream."

Angie said, "You're just as scared as what I am, ain't you?"

"Yes," Stanley admitted. "I'm just as scared as what you are."

"One more thing," said Angie. "What was you burning in the bathroom?"

"You don't want to know."

"It must 'ave been something 'orrible. It *smelled* 'orrible."

"Listen—believe me—you really don't want to know."

"Was it something to do with you being ill?"

Stanley said, "Yes, it was. But just remember I've had this infection longer than you, and if we find Isabel Gowdie … well, we'll put an end to this plague before the same thing happens to you."

Angie said nothing, but it was clear from the expression on her face that Stanley had decided her. They had to go hunt for the witch, and they had to find her soon. What they had done this morning, the brutality of their sex together, was disturbing enough, but already Stanley had begun to have jagged splinters of fantasy about forcing Angie into even more sadistic and ferocious acts, and to encourage her to inflict pain on *him*, too. Chains, and locks, and straps, and blood.

His fantasies weren't only about Angie, either. He

continually glimpsed zoetropic images of greeting Leon at Heathrow Airport, shaking hands with him, and squeezing him so tightly that he crushed all the bones in his fingers. *Welcome to London, you little asswipe*, and then laughing a huge Vincent Price laugh while Leon screamed. He thought about catching the cat that caught all the mice and fledglings around Langton Street and shutting its head in a car door. *Crunch.* And how would the car's owner react when he came back to his vehicle and found a cat's body standing with the patience of rigor mortis beside his fender?

We shall cut a swathe, said Stanley inside his head. *We are the pestilence that was promised.*

He opened the front door. The fields were still there. Rain pattered on the churned-up clay, creating thousands and thousands of greasy gray puddles, wherever they looked. There was a strange smell in the air: wet and pungent, with a hint of sharpness in it. It was the smell of air that had never known the pollution of automobiles or factories, but which was cidertangy with horse manure and pigs' urine and sweet-laden with charcoal-burning and death.

Nobody could have prepared Stanley for the overwhelming smell of death.

"Cor, it don't 'alf stink," Angie complained. "Is this what it was really like, back in 'istory?"

Stanley took a cautious step into the mud. He sank up to his ankle, but after two or three inches, the clay seemed reasonably firm. He looked around, at the run-down cottages, at the scrubby trees and gorse bushes; at the neutral gray English sky which conceded nothing and promised nothing. *Plague that was.*

"What year do you think this is?" asked Stanley. His voice seemed oddly flat, as if he were speaking in a closed room.

"Search me," Angie replied, taking hold of his hand to steady herself. "This mud's going to ruin me shoes."

"I'll buy you another pair, okay?"

"Not like these. I got them from Footloose."

Stanley narrowed his eyes against the rain. He could see the pig farm only twenty or thirty yards away, its thatched roof dripping, its slatted walls black with wet-rot. Knitted Hood seemed to have disappeared, although he could easily have concealed himself behind the piggery, or a nearby copse of leprous-looking silver birches, or even beyond the horizon. Because the fields sloped so dramatically towards the Thames, the horizon was only a hundred yards away, and who could guess what lay beyond it?

We are the plague that was.

They trudged through the mud to the pig farm and looked around it. It was deserted, except for a starved and half-bald black cat that stared at them hysterically out of the darkness, a witch's familiar without a witch.

"'Ere, pussy, pussy, pussy," Angie coaxed it.

"I wouldn't encourage it if I were you," Stanley told her. "Most domestic animals in the seventeenth century must have had some kind of disease."

"Still—wish I'd brought a tin of Whiskas with me," said Angie.

They walked eastwards, trudging and stumbling through the ruts and the puddles. The rain continued to drum down on them, cold and casual and unrelenting. *Promised promised promised.* Stanley was surprised how hilly London was. It was so built up that he had always thought of it as reasonably flat, especially in comparison with his home city of San Francisco. But in spite of lying in the muddy basin of the Thames, the terrain undulated at least as much as New York's. They plodded up a long, low incline, and when they reached the top of it they were able to see the river off to their right, dull as unpolished pewter in the morning light. A few barges and triangular-sailed boats hung suspended in the haze. Off to their left, a line of gray forbidding hills overlooked London from the north, hills that would one day be Highgate and Hampstead and Harrow-on-the-Hill. Ravens wheeled slowly through the rain, silent and tattered and menacing.

Directly ahead of them, through a pall of rain and pungent woodsmoke, they could see the cluttered rooftops of the City of London. It was nothing like Stanley had expected. No steeples, no spires, no grandiose guild buildings, no palaces. Instead, it was a squalid huddle of narrow streets and low, dilapidated buildings, surrounded by woods and fields and a sprawling makeshift community of sheds and shanties.

He remembered from high school history that the Great Fire of London had raged for over four days, but he had never been taught that it had devastated thirteen thousand houses, St. Paul's Cathedral, ninety parish churches, the Guildhall, jails, markets, fifty-two halls, countless other public buildings, and that it had made nearly a quarter of a million people homeless.

It was the wretched dwellings of those homeless people that he was looking at now. *For, yea, we shall cut a swathe through the world*. And outside London, the Great Plague had still not subsided.

They were close enough now to be able to hear the dolorous tolling of a single bell, and the squalling of a hungry child, and dogs barking. There was another sound in the background, too, a low persistent moaning, like the wind blowing under a door, or hundreds of monks humming a dirge, or mourners at a Spanish funeral.

"Do you think it's safe?" asked Angie. Her hair was dripping wet now, and there was a smudge of mud on her cheek.

"I don't know. It's only a dream."

"It's not *our* dream, though, is it?"

"It's a dream, all the same."

"The rain's wet. The mud's muddy. It can't be that much of a dream."

Stanley wiped his face with his hand. "I guess that's a risk we're just going to have to take. We *have* to find Isabel Gowdie. We don't have any damn choice."

"Do you think you're going to find 'er 'ere?"

"Maybe. The idea is to look for my ancestors, the Eisner family. If anybody can tell me, they can."

"But if this is Isabel Gowdie's dream, she's not going to let you find 'er, is she?"

"I'm not too sure about that. I have a feeling she might. I think that's why Knitted Hood turned up at Kew Gardens ... he was encouraging me to follow him. It was only because Madeleine Springer intervened that I didn't."

"'E's 'ere now," said Angie, taking hold of Stanley's arm.

Stanley peered over to the far left, in the direction that Angie had indicated. She was right. Knitted Hood was standing gray and tall beside a half-collapsed lean-to. A damp fire was burning close by, and every now and then he disappeared from view behind the smoke; but there was no doubt that he was watching them, and waiting for them.

"It begins to make sense now," said Stanley. "Isabel Gowdie wants me for some reason ... and the only way to make sure that I absolutely *had* to come was to send Knitted Hood to give me the Night Plague."

"Why do you think she wants you so much?" asked Angie. It was miserably cold, here on the outskirts of the city, and she was shivering.

"I don't know. I guess we're just going to have to find her and ask her ourselves."

Knitted Hood vanished in the smoke. Stanley looked up at the sky and frowned. "It looks like it's beginning to get dark. We'd better get our asses in gear."

They plodded along a narrow track of poisonous black mud, churned up by cartwheels and horses and stinking of horse urine. As they approached the center of the city, huts and hovels and cottages began to crowd close to the sides of the track, and Stanley and Angie found themselves being suspiciously watched from almost every window and every door.

The denizens of Isabel Gowdie's dream-London were silent, mealy-faced, and surly. Almost all of them were misshapen or crippled or ugly. A boy with a huge encephalitic head watched them from an upstairs window. A woman with a raw cleft palate stood beside a fence, her front teeth and her nasal cavities exposed, whistling and dribbling. A large-nosed man with no arms or legs sat propped up on a filthy mud-caked cushion, his head protected from the rain by a huge drooping hat made out of whaleskin, watching them and singing to himself as they passed.

"Gut the pig and bite the toad,
Kill the cat that crossed the road."

Mangy and nasty-looking dogs roamed everywhere, and four or five of them began to follow Stanley and Angie as they penetrated deeper and deeper into this grotesque parody of seventeenth-century London. Stanley was amazed that Isabel Gowdie's dreaming imagination was so vivid and so detailed and so multilayered. But any woman who could work her influence across three and a half centuries must have an exceptional mind. And of course, she had the power of Satan on her side.

"We are going to be able to get back, aren't we?" asked Angie.

Stanley took hold of her hand and gave it a quick, reassuring squeeze. In truth, he had no idea whether they would ever be able to return to their own reality. They could be trapped here forever, like two ants underneath an overturned ashtray, walking around and around and never being able to find a way out. Maybe Isabel Gowdie would destroy them, the way that she had destroyed Stanley's ancestors.

His fear lay in the bottom of his stomach like cold soup. He had never been so frightened in his life, even when they were attacked by the boy-dogs at Tennyson. Here, in dream-London, he knew that they were entirely at the mercy of Isabel Gowdie's imagination; and that Isabel Gowdie, in her turn, was entirely at the mercy of the darkest and most terrible influence in the universe, the black thing that floated at the edge of human consciousness, the black thing that led people to kill, and torture, and rape, and in the end to deny their very humanity.

The street along which they were walking grew narrower and narrower, until the timbered houses overhung it on either side. The pavement was cobbled here, although it was greasy and slippery, and almost as hard to negotiate as the muddy tracks on the city's outskirts. After two or three hundred yards, Stanley found that his feet were bruised and that the backs of his calves ached. A gutter twisted down the middle of the street, but it was clogged with heaps of slippery entrails and horse manure and decaying cabbage leaves.

"Look," said Angie; but Stanley had already glimpsed the back of Knitted Hood's head, faintly distinguishable through the rain and the smoke. Knitted Hood was apparently guiding them onwards; because when they stopped, he stopped, too, although he didn't turn around. He waited until they started walking again and then led them further into the city.

Street after street was nothing but an acrid mountain range of wet black ashes and the skeletal remains of burned-down houses. Stanley saw weirdly-melted lumps of glass and lead, and an iron water pump that had turned by the heat into an extraordinary crucifix, with a melted-glass Jesus hanging from it.

They followed Knitted Hood's ever-receding back through a drowned and stinking market, where jostling crowds of hunchbacked people argued fiercely and viciously with each other about the price of damp-blackened turnips and slimy heaps of beige and purplish offal. At the opposite corner of the market, a handclapping circle had formed. A toothless man in a moth-eaten fur jacket and a bedraggled feather hat was playing a wild song on a hurdy-gurdy, and a cretinous-looking woman with a long blond pigtail had pulled down her rough brown dress to the waist, and was dancing an unbalanced hopping dance, her big white breasts bouncing up and down like two muslin bags full of cream cheese.

"Gut the pig and bite the toad,
Kill the cat that crossed the road."

Small hostile eyes followed them as they passed.

At last, they found themselves in a small dark courtyard, surrounded on all sides by houses with shuttered windows. Knitted Hood had disappeared, but Stanley had the feeling that they had arrived; that this was the place to which Knitted Hood had been guiding them. He walked slowly around the courtyard, with Angie watching him and shivering.

"Jacob Eisner was a ragpicker, that's what Madeleine Springer said. That means he probably had some kind of a shop, or a storehouse."

Angie said nothing, but shivered and waited. She looked exhausted after their walk through the rain all the way from Fulham.

Stanley tried knocking at two or three of the doors. There was no reply, not even an echo. He rattled one of the shutters. Still no response.

"They had a plague and a fire here," he remarked. "Maybe they all packed up and went to the country."

"Then why did Knitted Hood lead us 'ere?" asked Angie.

"Search me. That was only a guess."

"What do we now, if there's nobody 'ere?"

Stanley shook his head. "I don't know. We'll just have to go back and talk to Springer again."

"That's if we *can* get back."

They were just about to leave the courtyard when,

without warning, one of the doors opened, and a young man stepped out. There was no doubt that he was Jewish. He wore a black cloak and a skullcap and his sidelocks had been grown into the long *payess* of the Orthodox Jew. Stanley's great-grandfather had cut off his *payess* when he left Hamburg for America, and his great-great-grandfather had refused even to speak his name for the rest of his life.

The young man glanced at them briefly and incuriously and began to walk away. But Stanley called, "Eisner?"

The young man stopped and turned. He had a pale, oval face, and he was much slighter than Stanley, but Stanley could see a faint family resemblance. Something about the eyes and the shape of the head.

"I'm Eisner, yes," the young man said. "What do you want? I have business."

His accent was an almost incomprehensible mixture of Yiddish and seventeenth-century East End. It took Stanley a moment to understand that he was speaking English at all.

Stanley took a step forward and held out his hand. "I'm Eisner, too. Stanley Eisner."

The young man frowned at Stanley and then at Angie. "You are Eisner, too?"

"It isn't easy to explain … but I have to talk to you."

"I have business. I cannot stop to talk."

"Please," said Stanley. It was growing very dark now, and he could scarcely see the young man's face. The last faint light of the day shone on the raindrops on the shoulder of his black cloak. "It's about Jacob and Joshua."

"My father Jacob is dead. My brother Joshua is dead, too."

"I know that," said Stanley. "I also know how they died, and why."

The young man narrowed his eyes. "How is it you know that?"

"Because I'm a Night Warrior, too; the same as your father. The same as your brother."

"And this girl?" asked the young man suspiciously.

"Effis the light-skater."

The young man looked at Stanley for a long time in silence. The rain whispered all around them and gurgled down unseen gutters and hidden drains. Stanley had a feeling of this old, burned, sagging city, with rainwater glistening on its rooftops and finding its way by millions of secret and complicated conduits to the Fleet and the Walbrook and the City Ditch, and down to the filthy dun-colored Thames, and out to Greenwich and the Thames Estuary, and the sea.

Stanley said, "We need help. Otherwise, believe me, we wouldn't have come. If you believe in Ashapola, if you believe in things that are good and things that are evil— then you'll talk to us, at the very least."

The young man looked away, looked back again, then held out his hand. "Solomon Eisner. If you are truly Night Warriors, I greet you."

They shook hands. Then Solomon took out a jingling bunch of keys and said, "Come inside. My business was not important. Only the sale of some woollen shoddy. It can wait until later."

He unlocked the door. Stanley watched him in fascination. It was incredible to think that this man was an ancestor of his, that this man's children had given birth to succeeding generations of children, and that eventually one of his *ur-ay neklach*, his great-grandchildren, had given birth to Stanley himself.

Solomon led them into a small, low-ceilinged room, so dark that Stanley collided immediately with the heavy oak table in the middle of it and bruised his thigh.

"I'm sorry," Solomon told him. A small fire was still smoldering in the hearth, so Solomon took down a wax taper from the shelf beside it, poked it into the ashes to set it aflame, and used it to light a three-branched candelabrum. "I have struck that table many times myself. I should know where it is by now!"

Although it was so small, the room was warm and stuffy and comfortable. There were three or four leather-bound books on the shelf next to the fire, including the Old Testament and the *Teitsh Chumash* and a dictionary; and if Stanley knew anything about the seventeenth century, it was that anybody who owned as many as three books was impressively literate. There were two woodcuts, too, in plain wooden frames, one of Moses and one of Jerusalem.

"Can I offer you something to drink?" Solomon asked them. "I have water, or I have wine. I know a wine merchant who gives me sack in return for sacking. Not that I drink myself."

He set two roughly-molded green glasses on the table and poured them each a small measure of sack from a dark glass bottle. Stanley sipped his cautiously. Despite the fact that sack was *wyne seck*, or "dry wine," he found it almost excruciatingly sweet to a palate that was accustomed to Pouilly-Fumés and Sancerres.

Angie said, "You 'aven't got somewhere I could wash? I feel like I've been pulled through an 'edge backwards."

Solomon looked perplexed. "I have a bowl in the scullery," he told her.

"Oh, thanks," said Angie; and groped her way into the

shadows of the next room. Stanley heard her say, "Gordon Bennett," when she found the bowl. Then, "Bloody 'ell."

"You are strange people," said Solomon with unembarrassed frankness. "You are not like anybody I have ever met. Have you come very far?"

"I guess you could say that," Stanley replied. "Further than anybody else you ever met."

"But you are Night Warriors, and that makes you kin."

"I'm glad you think that way."

Solomon drew an invisible pattern on the bare tabletop with the end of his mittened finger, a Star of David, again and again. "I was the second son, so I was never chosen. But my father and Joshua were both ardent Night Warriors. They fought many, many battles; and then both would sit here in this room and tell me everything they had done in dreams. They would tell me about their fear, their danger, their moments of great excitement. Sometimes I felt jealous and wished that I could join them. But it was never to be. After what happened to both of them, I suppose that I should give thanks to God."

"Tell me about it," said Stanley softly.

"I knew that they had been searching for a long time for a witch-woman called Crowdie or Gowdie. She had given herself to the Devil, that is what my father told me, and the Devil had used her to turn the minds of hundreds of thousands of people against the Lord *Shaddai*."

Stanley, sipping his seventeenth-century sack, didn't fail to catch Solomon Eisner's use of the name *Shaddai* for God. It was a name which described God's satisfaction with the creation of the universe, rather than the essence of God Himself. Literally, it meant The One Who Has Said, Enough.

The Night Plague was the antithesis of God's satisfaction. The Night Plague was the sickness of the soul. The Night Plague was for those whose greed could never be satisfied—those for whom enough was *never* enough.

Solomon said, "They hunted her by day and they hunted her by night. They almost caught her one morning in the ribbon shop on London Bridge. There was a furious fight, and a chase, but she escaped. After that, she was careful to keep herself hidden, mostly in other people's dreams. But my father discovered that her favorite dreamer was a ratcatcher called Clark who lodged over a bakery in Pudding Lane. He had such fierce dreams, my father told me! Dreams of blood and teeth, and wading waist-deep through flooded cellars and stinking ditches."

Solomon paused, his eyes unfocused, as if he could remember his father speaking as clearly as if he were still in the room with them. Then he said, "Early last September, as we ate our supper, my father told me that he was determined to find the Crowdie woman that night and destroy her. He said that it would be dangerous beyond all imagination and that it was possible that he might be hurt."

He swallowed. His eyes were brimming with tears. "If he was killed in the ratcatcher's dream, he said, his soul would die and his sleeping body would never wake up. I was to leave him sleeping for two days, shaking him from time to time; but if he didn't wake up after that time, I was to understand that he was dead, even though he was still breathing, and that I was to bury him.

"That same night—" He swallowed, and smeared his eyes with his fingers. "That same night, my beloved brother came to me and said the same. 'I will appear to be alive,' that is what he said. 'But my soul will have died, and you must bless me and bury me.'"

Solomon looked Stanley directly in the eyes. "I begged them not to do it. I fell on my knees and took hold of my father's hand and I pleaded with him. But he said, 'I am a ragpicker, and that is an honorable trade; but I am also a Night Warrior, and that means that I have been called by Ashapola to risk my life for the greater good of the whole world; and *that*, my son, is not just honorable. It is divine.'"

Angie came back from the scullery, and as she opened the door, the three candles dipped and sputtered in the draft. Solomon said, "That night they lay in wait for the Crowdie woman and a dozen other witches in the ratcatcher's dream, but somebody had warned her, and she surprised them. She set alight to the ratcatcher's dream; and his brain caught fire, too; and all of the Night Warriors died before they were able to escape. The ratcatcher burned, and the bakery burned, and most of London burned, too. They had to blow up buildings with gunpowder so that the fire couldn't spread any further."

Angie stood behind Stanley's chair and listened in silence as Solomon continued. "Every hour for three days, I shook my father and my brother with tears in my eyes and begged them to wake up. They breathed, their hearts were beating, but they had no life in them.

"In the end, I had to take their bodies by night and bury them. They were both heroes; and yet they have to lie in graves without monuments or markers; and nobody will ever know what they sacrificed."

Stanley said, "I'm sorry, Solomon. You can't even guess how sorry."

"Well, it's past now," Solomon told him. "I carry on the business, that's the best I can do! Old clothes, that's what I know best. It's a calling, rather than a trade."

"What happened to the witch-woman?" asked Stanley.

Solomon shrugged. "I never knew."

"You know what happened to your father and your brother. So somebody must have talked to you, after they were killed."

"There was a man called Joseph Springer," Solomon admitted. "A strange man, more like a woman than a man. He came to see me about a week after I had buried my father and my brother, and he told me that other Night Warriors had succeeded in catching Isabel Crowdie. He said that they had not been able to destroy her, because her Satanic power was far too great. But he wanted me to know that they had imprisoned her in a secret place, from which she could never escape, and so my father and my brother had been avenged."

"Do you have any idea where?" asked Stanley.

Solomon shook his head. "Places of imprisonment are never divulged, in case a Night Warrior is captured and forced to reveal where a demon or a witch is buried. But Joseph Springer did give me the tokens of imprisonment."

"The what?" asked Angie.

"The tokens of imprisonment. My father had several. Every time the Night Warriors imprisoned a devil or a witch, they took tokens from the place where they had buried them. They were tokens of honor, like commemorative medals. When they buried the demon Abrahel, my father brought back a sliver of marble and a branch from a yew tree from the place where they had buried him."

"What were the tokens that Joseph Springer gave you after Isabel Gowdie was imprisoned?" asked Stanley.

"I have never opened them. They are supposed to remain sealed forever."

"Solomon, it's very important that we take a look at them."

"I do not know whether that would be right."

"Solomon—we think that Isabel Gowdie has somehow gotten herself free, or partly free. Her Carriers are out again, spreading the Night Plague. It's absolutely critical that we find her."

"She's free?" Solomon frowned. "Joseph Springer said that she had been buried in solid rock."

"Please, Solomon. If we allow her to get away, then your father and your brother will have died for nothing."

Solomon hesitated for a moment. Then he took out his jangling bunch of keys, went over to the corner of the room, and unlocked a small metal-bound chest. He came back to the table with a soft gray leather pouch, tightly bound with waxed string, and sealed.

"Joseph Springer said that I was not to open it," he said.

"He didn't say that somebody else couldn't open it, though, did he? Especially if that somebody else happens to be a Night Warrior."

"I am still not sure that I should do this."

"Solomon … there's one thing more that I haven't told you. Both Angie and I have been infected by the Night Plague. If we don't find Isabel Gowdie pretty damn soon, then we won't even *want* to find her any more."

Solomon said, "*You* have the Night Plague? Both of you?"

"That's why we're here."

Without demurring any further, Solomon took out a sharp clobberer's knife and cut the string around the neck of the pouch. Carefully, he shook out on to the table a small fragment of pure white limestone and a handful of tiny seashells. One side of the limestone had been cut flat, polished, and then engraved with the picture of a bearded man with what looked like a ruff around his neck.

Stanley picked up the shells one by one and examined them.

"They must 'ave buried 'er on the beach," Angie suggested.

"But Joseph Springer mentioned solid rock, didn't he?" Stanley asked Solomon.

"That is quite right. 'We have buried her in solid rock, so that in all eternity she will never escape.' Those were his very words to me."

"So ... they must have buried her in limestone, somewhere close to the sea."

"White cliffs of Dover," put in Angie promptly. "Or somewhere along the South Coast, anyway. It's all chalk."

Stanley nodded. "Dover, yes ... that makes a lot of sense. She could have been trying to get away from England. Or maybe it was that fishwife ancestor of yours, what was her name? Elisabeth Pardoe. She lived in Dover. She would have known of a place where Isabel Gowdie could be buried."

"We went to Dover on a school trip once," Angie added. "Those cliffs 'ave got thousands of 'oles in them—you know, what people dug during the war to make forts and that. They could 'ave buried 'er anywhere there."

"Hey, you're not just a pretty face, are you?" said Stanley.

"I got me O-level in geography, if you don't mind."

Stanley examined the piece of limestone. "I wonder whose

face this is supposed to be. They obviously engraved it on here for a purpose."

"Do you wish to borrow it?" asked Solomon.

"I don't know. I'm not too sure that I'll ever be able to find a way of giving it back to you."

Solomon smiled and nodded. "You are a Night Warrior, sir. You will find a way. Now, I must leave you, to do some work. If I do not work, my family do not eat. And you—you have your witch to find, Mistress Crowdie."

Stanley finished his wine, stood up, and clasped Solomon's hand. "I hope we don't fail you," he said.

"Do not think of failure," Solomon replied. "My father would never think of failure, not even in the smallest thing. A ragpicker learns that nothing need ever be wasted. Life is a dance that goes around and around, and what is failure to one man is success to another."

"Well, I guess you're right," said Stanley. He was beginning to feel irritable and tired, and his stomach was knotting up again. He dreaded that feeling of sickness—especially after this morning's experience in the bathroom. God knows what abominations he was going to vomit up next.

Solomon said, as he opened the front door for them, "You speak of failure? Everything has its place and its purpose. You see this black cloth cape? When it is worn out, it will be be patched and sewn by clobberers to make it look like new once again. Then, when it is very faded, it will be dyed by revivers, to restore its color. When it is both worn out and faded, the best pieces will be turned by translators into waistcoats, and smaller pieces will be sent to France and Russia and Poland, where the working people wear caps made out of black fabric. Any fragments will be ripped into shoddy, or mungo, which will be woven into new clothes. This can happen six or seven times to the same wool, until it is no longer fit for weaving. Then it is dug into the ground in hop fields, to fertilize the plants."

"Seems like even secondhand duds have their ecosystem," Stanley remarked.

Of course Solomon didn't understand what he meant, but he grasped his hand again, all the same, and said, "You will find the witch-woman, do not fear. When you do, promise me one thing, that you will speak my father's and my brother's names in her face before you destroy her. I would like her to know that she is being punished for taking them away from me."

"I won't forget," Stanley promised.

They were back outside in the dark, rainy courtyard. Although Stanley knew that this was only a dream, he was suddenly reluctant to see Solomon go. He yearned to be able to tell him who he really was, and to ask him about his family, and the way he made his living; and to explain to him what would happen to the Eisners in centuries to come.

It was impossible, of course. But he hugged Solomon in his arms and whispered *"Sholem aleichem, Solomon,"* and Solomon said, *"Aleichem sholem."* Then, without saying anything more, Solomon turned and walked off into the shadows, as black as his cloak, as black as his beard, as black as the thing that swam on the very edge of the human mind, the thing whose devouring hunger was never satisfied.

They stumbled their way back through Isabel Gowdie's dream-London in almost total darkness. Occasionally, a street corner would be fitfully illuminated by a tallow link, but most of London's twisting lanes and crowded courtyards remained unlit. It was easy to understand how cutpurses and murderers had thrived in a city like this.

Stanley tried to keep them headed westwards, but even in modern London, which was signposted and brightly lit, he frequently lost his way. By comparison, this illusion of seventeenth-century London was a wet, reeking, nightmarish maze. Several times they found themselves emerging from the streets on to the sagging wooden quays and piers that lined the Thames, and had to plunge back again into the inky-black alleys from which they had groped their way out, Idol Lane and Cloak Lane and Allhallows Lane.

They heard rats running through the fabric of the houses, and shutters opening and closing. They heard women screaming and men arguing, and the clatter of pewter tankards in a gin-house. They heard a man singing in a high, keening voice,

"*Gut the pig and bite the toad,*
Kill the cat that crossed the road.

"*All those men and all those masks,*
All those evil deeds and tasks,

"*All that blood so needless spent,*
All those angels came and went.

"*Gut the pig and bite the toad,*
Kill the cat that crossed the road."

Then they heard the plangent sound of a hurdy-gurdy, and the roar of lustful laughter. Stanley thought of the ugly, half-naked woman hopping in the rainy marketplace.

Stanley was exhausted and almost on the point of giving up when Angie gripped his hand more tightly and said, "Look! That's a torch, ain't it? Thai's somebody carrying a torch!"

At the very end of the lane along which they were walking, a tall hooded figure was standing in the shadows, waving a lighted link slowly from side to side. The flame made a soft flaring noise; and each time the link passed the figure's face, Stanley glimpsed the white chillingly-perfect features of Knitted Hood. *All those men and all those masks.*

"He's guiding us back to Fulham," said Stanley.

"Bleeding 'ell," Angie protested, hobbling on blistered feet. "If 'e wants to be so bleeding 'elpful, why didn't 'e just tell us where old Isabel Audi was in the first place, 'stead of making us walk all the way 'ere?"

"I don't think he *knows* where she is," Stanley replied. "And there was no way that Solomon would have told him, is there? Solomon was even more of a Night Warrior than me."

"I feel pukish," said Angie.

"The Night Plague," Stanley told her. "And, believe me, it gets a whole lot worse."

"It's all right," Angie said. "I'll manage. Let's just follow old Knitted 'Ood and get out of this stinking place."

It seemed to take them hours to walk out of the City of London and back through the muddy farmlands of Chelsea and Fulham. But the rain had died away, and although the wind was sharp, it had veered around the compass to the southwest, and it was far less cutting than it had been before. Knitted Hood stayed well ahead of them. Most of the time they could see nothing but his dipping, flickering link. But they followed because it was their destiny to follow, and because the only way that they would ever find Isabel Gowdie was to do what she wanted them to do.

Stanley thought: *She must know, too, that we want to kill her. She must be fearfully confident that we can't.*

Angie said, "Oh, God, Stan, I don't think I can walk any further." But at that moment, Stanley realized that they were passing the piggeries close to Langton Street; and the next thing he knew, Knitted Hood had stopped outside the front gate of his house, which rose like a mirage out of the marshy fields. Knitted Hood waved the link from side to side, as if he were beckoning them and challenging them, both at the same time.

Knitted Hood climbed the steps with an awkward, limping gait, and opened the front door. Before he went inside, he turned and tossed the blazing link as far as he could across the fields. It cartwheeled over and over, before landing in a shower of orange sparks in a nearby ditch.

"'E's in the 'ouse," whispered Angie. "What are we going to do?"

"We don't have any choice. We have to go inside. Otherwise we're going to be trapped in this dream forever; or for as long as it lasts. And God knows what will happen if we're still out here when Isabel Gowdie wakes up. You heard what happened to the Eisners."

"I don't 'alf feel sick," Angie told him.

"Come on, let's risk it," Stanley encouraged her. "Right now, Isabel Gowdie wants to find us just as much as we want to find her. That's my guess, anyway. Otherwise why would that gook have guided us all the way to Whitechapel and back?"

"I think I'm going to throw up," said Angie.

Without warning, she bent double in front of the garden gate and vomited. Out of her mouth poured hundreds of long white slippery strings which at first Stanley thought were spaghetti. Angie clung on to him and coughed and heaved and wept.

"Oh, Stanley, oh, God. Stanley I can't stand it. Oh, Stanley. Oh. God."

Stanley stood beside her until she finished. She retched again and again, and spat, and spat, until finally she stood up straight and clung to Stanley, quivering and sweating, her eyes filled with tears.

"Oh, God, Stanley, we've got to find 'er. I can't take any more of this."

Stanley looked down at the coiled heaps of white spaghetti that she had thrown up, and it was only then that he saw by the light from the open door that they were *moving*, they were alive. He closed his eyes and held her tight and almost vomited himself. It wasn't spaghetti at all. It was a tangle of blind, writhing tapeworms.

"Let's get inside," he said. His mouth felt as dry as cotton. He helped her up the steps and in through the front door, and closed the door firmly behind him. He didn't believe now that Knitted Hood intended to harm him any more. He *did* believe that if he closed the door, Isabel Gowdie's dream-London would be shut away, at least for now.

They climbed the stairs to Stanley's apartment. The door was ajar, and the lights were switched on, and all the drapes were closed. Stanley ushered Angie through to the living room and helped her to sit down. Her face was shiny and white; almost as if she, too, were wearing a Mardi Gras mask, like Knitted Hood. She couldn't stop shaking with disgust.

"I can still *taste* them, Stanley."

He poured her a large vodka, no ice, and handed it to her. She took a huge mouthful, furiously rinsed her mouth with it, and then spat it back into the glass. He poured another glass. "This one you can take straight down. Right now it won't do you any harm to be a little drunk."

She swallowed, with difficulty, and then let her head fall back on the dark brown cushions. All the time, Stanley kept his eyes out for Knitted Hood. He had entered the house, but where was he?

"Wait here," he told Angie. "I'm just going to take a quick look around."

"Believe me, mate," Angie told him, "the state I'm in. I'm not going anywhere."

Stanley went through to the kitchen and cautiously reached his hand round the door to switch on the light. It was empty, everything just as he had left it. He checked the bathroom. That was empty, too, although it still smelled of burned plastic and some other unidentifiable but deeply offensive odor, like scorched fish skin.

He was about to open the bedroom door when he saw Knitted Hood standing at the opposite end of the hallway, close to the front door. Knitted Hood looked unusually tall: his hood seemed almost to touch the ceiling. His face was concealed in shadow.

"*Do you know the place?*" he asked in his deathly whisper.

"What place?" Stanley retorted. "I don't know what the hell you're talking about."

"*Don't try to play games, Mr. Eisner, you know very well what place. The place where my mistress was imprisoned. The place where my mistress is* still *imprisoned.*"

"So what if I do know it?"

"*You will have to release her. Otherwise, the pestilence will surely take your soul.*"

"Why didn't you just *tell* me where she is, instead of going through all of this rigmarole?"

"*I do not know where she is; only that she awoke two years ago and that her awakening awoke me, too, and my fellow Carriers. She is still imprisoned; she is still unable to speak. All she can do is to dream.*"

"So you've been trying to find Night Warriors, to help you locate her, and to help you set her free?"

"*The choice is yours, my friend. Eternal damnation or eternal glory.*"

"Do you really think I'm going to tell you where she is?"

"*You will live in sickness and madness and agony for the rest of your life if you don't; and your soul will wander in despair for all eternity once you are dead. Those who have the Night Plague become the servants of Satan forever. The choice is yours.*"

"Not much of a choice, is it?" asked Stanley.

"*You disobeyed, you deserve no choice. I am the pestilence that was promised.*"

Stanley thought: *What now? If I tell Knitted Hood that Isabel Gowdie is probably in Dover, he may be able to find her; and if he finds her he may be able to set her free. On the other hand, he may not be able to. He may still need me, because I'm a Night Warrior, and the seals and bonds that keep her imprisoned were originally fastened by Night Warriors.*

"I must have time to think before I tell you where she is," Stanley replied.

"*You need no time to think. You must tell me now.*"

"And what if I decide not to?"

"*Then I will hurt the girl in ways that you cannot even think of.*"

"Supposing I don't mind if you hurt the girl in ways that I can't even think of? You gave me the Night Plague, after all. I'm beginning to get pretty interested in that kind of thing."

"*You are lying, my friend. I am a master of lies. I know when a man is lying.*"

"You lay one finger on that girl and I won't tell you anything."

Knitted Hood's white face gleamed in the lamplight. He still exuded that smell of cooking fat and sweat, and strong synthetic violets. "*Perhaps the girl herself will tell me what you have learned; if I hurt you instead.*"

He advanced on Stanley and Stanley, in spite of telling himself, *Stand up to him, stand up to him, don't let him see that you're afraid*, took two or three cautious steps back. As he approached, Knitted Hood seemed to defy perspective and grow surrealistically taller and taller.

"Don't you even *think* about it," Stanley began; but Knitted Hood gripped his shoulder with his gray-mittened hand and it was like being clamped in a metalworker's vise. He felt a surge of panic. He had managed to blot out of his mind the pain of being beaten and raped, but now the feeling came colliding back.

"*I could break your collarbone with one squeeze,*" Knitted Hood whispered harshly. "*Or perhaps you prefer the same kind of pleasure that I gave you before?*"

He lunged his hand between Stanley's legs and painfully squeezed his testicles through his trousers. Stanley gasped in terror and tried to struggle away.

"*Now will you tell me?*" he demanded.

But Stanley didn't even get the chance to answer. At that instant, the front doorbell rang; and was immediately followed by a loud hammering.

"Mr. Eisner? Mr. Eisner! This is the police! Detective Sergeant Morris, Mr. Eisner."

Stanley was about to call back, but Knitted Hood hissed, "*Silence! Do you want me to crush your shoulder?*"

"Mr. Eisner? One of our patrol officers saw somebody suspicious entering the downstairs door. Can you just confirm that everything's all right?"

Knitted Hood's breath rasped in and out of his saintly mask. "*One word,*" he warned.

The doorbell rang yet again. "Mr. Eisner? Can you hear me, Mr. Eisner?"

There was silence. For a long moment, Stanley thought that Detective Sergeant Morris had given up and gone. Knitted Hood's grip gradually relaxed, although he still didn't take his hand away completely.

"*Now speak,*" Knitted Hood insisted. But at that instant, the front door was kicked open with a shuddering bang, and Detective Sergeant Morris and two uniformed police officers came bursting into the hallway.

Chapter Seven

Golden Armor

K nitted Hood threw Stanley violently against the wall, so that Stanley overbalanced, stumbled, and hit his ear against the kitchen door frame. Although his vision was jumbled, Stanley saw him whirl around and thrust his gray-mittened hand directly into Detective Sergeant Morris's face.

The force of his grip must have been devastating. His first and second fingers plunged straight into Brian Morris's eyes. Blood and optic fluid jetted out over Knitted Hood's shoulder.

Brian Morris didn't even have time to cry out. Knitted Hood gripped the detective's upper arm to give himself leverage and support, and then, with his other hand, *tore the whole of his face off*, with a terrible crackle of fat and flesh and tearing skin.

For a moment, Brian Morris stood upright, his hands half lifted like a dog begging for a bone. His face had been stripped right down to the naked cheekbones, and it hung down from his chin, inside out, a wet and bloody beard. He staggered, his jawbone slowly dropping open because there was no longer any muscle to support it. A large bubble of blood formed between his teeth, then silently burst. Without a sound, without any kind of a cry, he collapsed on to the floor.

The two other police officers stopped where they were, staring at Knitted Hood in disbelief. One of them reached behind him and drew out his truncheon. The other adopted a crouching pose which suggested that he was a weekend karate enthusiast.

Stanley called, "Don't go near him, there's nothing you can do!"

The karate officer glanced quickly at Stanley and said, "You all right, mate?"

"Leave him, back off!" Stanley told him.

On the carpet, Detective Sergeant Morris began to shudder, as if an electric current were being passed through his body. The karate officer obviously didn't know what to do—whether to risk a rush attack on Knitted Hood, or to call on his lapel radio for reinforcements, or to take Stanley's advice and beat a hurried retreat.

His hesitation was fatal. Knitted Hood rushed at both officers, like a great gray berserk scarecrow, and even though the policeman with the truncheon managed to strike a clumsy blow at the side of his arm. Knitted Hood snatched both of them fiercely around the neck and smashed their heads together with such force that Stanley heard their skulls break.

They must have died instantly. But Knitted Hood grasped each of their faces in turn, the way he had grasped Detective Sergeant Morris's face, and ripped them free from their cheekbones. Then he twisted the two torn-off faces together, so it was impossible to tell whose lips were which, and whose nose belonged to whom. The final grisly insult: in death, he had robbed them of their human identity.

Knitted Hood turned to Stanley, and his gray gaberdine raincoat was sprayed with blood. A single crimson drop slid down the side of his white celluloid mask.

He said nothing. He had no need to. Stanley, swallowing back his nausea, raised both hands in surrender and said, "It's all right. I'll tell you where Isabel Gowdie is."

"*I thought that you would probably see reason.*"

"Reason?" said Stanley, almost hysterical. "For God's sake, I don't want to wind up without a face, that's the only reason I need to see!"

There was no sound from the living room where Angie was sitting. Stanley suspected that she was probably hiding behind the sofa or trembling behind the drapes. He didn't blame her, either. Given half a chance, he would have joined her.

Knitted Hood came closer. The reek of synthetic violets was even stronger. His eyes gleamed dull and impenetrable like the wing cases of black beetles, but Stanley could tell that he was calmer now; that he was satisfied.

"She's somewhere in Dover, on the South Coast," Stanley blurted. "Buried in the chalk, probably. We're not completely sure yet."

Knitted Hood slowly nodded. "*You did well. My mistress will be pleased with you, and so will my Master.*"

"What now?" asked Stanley.

"*What now? We have to go to Dover now, and find my mistress, and break the seals that have imprisoned her for so many years.*"

"We?" Stanley was still frightened, but he was also hugely relieved. If Knitted Hood needed him to come to Dover, too, then his guess had been correct: without a Night Warrior or even Night *Warriors* to help him, Knitted Hood was incapable of breaking the seals that held Isabel Gowdie.

"*You have no charge-keeper yet. You cannot become a Night Warrior until he joins you. But as soon as he does, we will go to Dover together.*"

"The charge-keeper is supposed to arrive tomorrow or the day after," said Stanley.

"*Very well. You will see me again when he is here.*"

Knitted Hood stepped long-legged over the police officers' bodies and made for the door.

"Wait!" Stanley called after him, in desperation. "You can't leave three dead policemen in my hallway. I'll be arrested; and then I'll never be able to become a Night Warrior."

"*You must go to the sanctuary of the one called Springer,*" said Knitted Hood. "*You shall hear from me again.*"

"But—"

"*Go now, and I will deal with these pitiful remains.*"

Stanley went into the living room. His knees would hardly support him. He found Angie standing by the window, rigid with fear, "Is 'e gone yet?" she asked him. "I tried to come and 'elp you, but when I 'eard those policemen shouting out, I just couldn't make me legs move."

"It's okay," Stanley reassured her, although he felt as if his own perception of what was happening had been cracked like a greenhouse window. "But we have to leave. He's— he's killed all of them, all three of them. They're dead. We can't stay here."

Angie said wildly, "What are we going to *do*?"

"We'll have to go to Madeleine Springer's place. We can take Gordon's car, pick him up later. Give me a couple of minutes: I just have to throw some clothes in a bag."

He went through to the bedroom, threw open his closet, and dragged down his battered Vuitton suitcase. He opened it up and heaved as many coats and shirts and pants into it as he could manage. Then he came back into the living room and took a last look around. He threw his Filofax into the suitcase, as well as two bottles of Wyborowa. "That'll do it," he said. "Could you bring along my violin case?"

With the suitcase bumping against the door frame, Stanley led Angie out into the hallway. "You don't want to look at this," he told her. "Keep to the left-hand side."

They edged past the dead policemen. Stanley hadn't realized at first how much blood Knitted Hood had splattered around. The hallway looked as if somebody had fired a .357 into an economy-sized jar of Old El Paso taco sauce. They had almost reached the doorway when one of the policemen's radios suddenly crackled and a woman's voice said, "Oscar Bravo to 625, Oscar Bravo to 625, where are you now, Ted?" and Angie shouted out *"Ah!"* in terror.

"We'd better hurry," said Stanley as they made their way down the stairs. "They're going to start missing those cops in a couple of minutes."

"Where's Knitted 'Ood?" Angie asked anxiously.

"Oh, he's here someplace. You can bet on it."

They went out of the front door and down the steps. Isabel Gowdie's dream had evaporated now, and they were back in Langton Street, harsh and real and commonplace. Two cars were parked alongside Gordon's Montego: a dented blue Sierra, which must have belonged to Detective Sergeant Morris, and a police Metro, with its blue light still circling.

Stanley unlocked Gordon's car and threw his suitcase into the trunk. He laid his violin case more carefully beside it, although for all he knew it contained nothing but dust and maggots. Angie said, "I can't drive, Stan. I just can't. You'll 'ave to do it."

"All right. I'll give it a shot," said Stanley, and eased himself in behind the wheel. Across the street, gray and tall, he could just make out the figure of Knitted Hood waiting on the pavement: a figure that made him shudder now more than ever before. A figure to which he had already promised his help, and to which he may even have promised his life.

He started the engine. It sounded weak and rough. Angie said, "Okay now, press in the clutch pedal with your left foot, all the way down to the floor. Then wiggle it into first gear. That's right. Then ease your left foot up really smoothlike; and at the same time gently press the accelerator with your right foot."

"God Almighty, this is more difficult than skiing," Stanley complained.

He revved the engine wildly, pulled his left foot up off the clutch, and the Montego bucked forward and stalled.

"Kangaroo petrol," Angie remarked.

"What?"

"That's what we call it, when somebody jumps along like that, Kangaroo petrol."

"Listen, this is my first time, okay, and it isn't easy."

He started the engine again. The car was still in gear, and it jumped forward again.

"Neutral, Stan, neutral!" Angie admonished him.

He was opening his mouth to answer her when they heard a deafening, ear-compressing explosion. All three front windows of his upstairs flat burst out into the street, millions of fragments of glass tumbling and glittering into the night. Stanley and Angie heard it clattering on to the roof of their car. Immediately afterwards, three massive fireballs roared out of the empty window frames, momentarily lighting up the entire block.

Stanley stared at Knitted Hood. "My God, he must have planted a bomb; Or *something*. Look at it!"

The whole second floor of the house was burning fiercely; as fiercely as if it had been doused in gasoline. Even from the street, Stanley and Angie could see the brown velvet drapes burning, and the lampshade crumpling up like a dahlia dropped on to a bonfire.

"Come on, we have to get out of here," said Stanley. He wrestled the gearstick back into neutral, started the Montego's engine again, and then slowly managed to bunny-hop away from the curb. After a few yards' progress, the engine began to whine in protest.

"You've got to change up!" Angie told him.

"What?"

"You've got to change 'er into second! Press down the clutch again, ease your foot off of the accelerator, wiggle it into second, then lift up the clutch and press down the accelerator again."

Stanley stared at her. "You mean you have to do this *every* time you want to change gear? Every single time?"

"Course you do, silly. That's what driving's all about."

"It's so damned primitive."

He effected a grinding gear change, and they began to drive a little faster. As they turned into the King's Road (which was mercifully almost deserted, and so he didn't have to stop and change down to first again), he gave Langton Street a last quick glance in his rearview mirror. A crowd had already begun to gather in the road outside his blazing building, and burning tatters of material were flying up into the night.

He knew with terrible certainty that Knitted Hood hadn't really planted a bomb; or even splashed gasoline around. He hadn't had time, and he certainly hadn't been lugging a jerry-can around with him. He was sure that Knitted Hood had invoked the power of Isabel Gowdie, the woman who had been able to stir up storms by slapping a rock with a wet rag. If she had been able to drown shipfuls of fishermen all around the coast, setting fire to three dead policemen shouldn't have caused her too much trouble.

Fire burn, and cauldron bubble, he thought. *No wonder Shakespeare wrote about witches. He was afflicted himself by one of the very worst.*

As they drove erratically westwards along the King's Road, they were passed by five fire engines speeding in the opposite direction, their sirens blaring. Two police cars followed.

"At least they ain't got time to worry about your driving," said Angie as Stanley catastrophically clashed the gears at the junction of Fulham Palace Road.

How he managed to drive Gordon's car all the way to Richmond, Stanley could never remember. They plodded over the Thames at Chiswick, then climbed at 20 mph with smoke pouring out of the exhaust pipe all the way up to the top of the hill where Madeleine Springer had first taken them. Stanley parked at an angle (no power steering) and climbed out of the car with his back drenched in sweat.

"Never again," he promised. "That was more difficult than playing Rimsky-Korsakov."

It was a still, black night. Below them, lights shimmered in the oil-black Thames. They crossed the slip road to Madeleine Springer's apartment building with the soles of their shoes scratching on the cobblestones. They rang the bell with the engraved card *Springer* beside it and waited shivering for her to reply. A TWA jet thundered overhead in the darkness, on its way to Heathrow. Stanley suddenly remembered that, tomorrow night, Leon would be crossing the Atlantic on his way here. *You'll know when they arrive, I promise you. You'll know for sure.*

Almost a minute passed before the intercom clicked, and a woman's voice said, "Who is it?"

"Madeleine? It's me, Stanley Eisner. And Angie, too."

"I've been expecting you."

The door lock buzzed, and they pushed their way in. Angie said, "'Ow come she was expecting us? We didn't telephone 'er or nothing."

"I don't know," said Stanley as they rose in the elevator to the top floor. "There's a whole lot more to Madeleine Springer than meets the eye. And I don't just mean changing her sex in the middle of a conversation. Even oysters can do that."

"Oysters can't talk, stupid."

"How do you know? Have you ever given an oyster the chance?"

Their banter was a brittle attempt to conceal their shock

and their nervousness. They were scared of Knitted Hood, but in another way they were equally scared of Madeleine Springer and everything that she represented. The armor, the weapons, the danger—and most of all the awesome responsibility of being the frontline troops in the battle against an evil which, up until now, they had believed to be nothing but allegorical.

Madeleine Springer was waiting for them in her open doorway when they stepped out of the elevator. She was wearing a black velvet skullcap embroidered with silver threads, and she had shaved off her eyebrows and covered her face in grayish foundation, with darker gray emphasis on her cheekbones. In spite of the nakedness and the severity of her makeup, her eyes were wide and luminous enough to give her face intense beauty and expression; and although her lipstick was gray, her mouth still looked sensual and desirable.

She wore a tight black velvet evening gown, with a deep V-shaped décolletage, and her shoulders had been covered in the same grayish foundation. She wore no shoes, and no jewelry.

"You're famous," she said as Stanley followed her into her sparsely-furnished flat. He looked around. Something had been changed: not the furniture, not the décor, but the shape of the room. The last time he was here, it was a long rectangle. Now it was almost exactly square. There was something else, too: a very fine-lined drawing on white handmade cartridge paper, of a shape that could have been a lily, or an ear of grass, or partly-opened lips.

Stanley sat down on the sofa. "You heard what happened?" he asked her.

Madeleine Springer closed her eyes momentarily to signify that she had. She walked across the room on her silent bare feet and closed the linen-slatted blinds. "There was a news flash on ITN. They think that it was Arab terrorists, blowing you up in revenge for Israeli shootings on the West Bank. After all, you are nearly the most famous Jew in London, give or take a Rothschild or a Seiff or a Barenboim or two."

Stanley said, "We went into the dream, Angie and me. We went right back into Isabel Gowdie's dream."

Madeleine Springer gave him a faint, knowing smile. "I thought you would. You're a lot more headstrong than you first appear. Underneath that mild-mannered musicianly exterior beats the heart of a true Night Warrior."

"Underneath this mild-mannered musicianly exterior beats the heart of somebody who's been infected with the Night Plague, and wants more than anything else to be cured."

Madeleine Springer went through to the kitchen, and Stanley heard her taking out glasses and pouring drinks. "Did you find what you were looking for?" she called.

"We found what Isabel Gowdie wanted us to find."

"We reckon she's in Dover, or somewhere like that," Angie put in. "Solomon Eisner give us this bit of chalk and all of these seashells."

"When the Night Warriors buried some demon called Abrahel, they brought back a piece of marble and a twig from a yew tree," Stanley added. "So it seemed to us that their tokens of imprisonment are always a piece of the rock in which the demon or witch was imprisoned, plus a small clue to the rock's location. In this case, we have the sea-shells, which tell us that Isabel Gowdie was imprisoned close to the ocean; and the limestone, which tells us that she was imprisoned in chalk. There's something else, too: Angie's ancestor Elisabeth Pardoe came from Dover, and she had probably suggested a place where the Night Warriors could bury Isabel Gowdie—even though Isabel Gowdie ended up killing her."

Madeleine Springer came back with a black lacquered Japanese tray and two large glasses of vodka and gin-and-orange.

"Are you hungry?" she asked them.

They both shook their heads. "We've been pretty damn sick," said Stanley. "The Night Plague's getting worse."

He looked at Madeleine Springer for a long time without saying anything. Then he added, "There's something else you have to know."

She remained silent, expressionless.

"Knitted Hood guided us through Isabel Gowdie's London. We couldn't have found our way if he hadn't. But he guided us back, too; and when we got there, he demanded to know where Isabel Gowdie Was imprisoned."

Madeleine Springer's face remained immobile, a face in polished gray wax.

Stanley went on, "He must have been seen by a passing police patrol. They called Detective Sergeant Morris. Even if he was at home, he lives just over the river in Wandsworth, so it couldn't have taken him more than five or ten minutes to get there, at that time of night."

He licked his lips, which were feeling dry and sore. "They knocked; then they broke down the door. Knitted Hood killed all three of them, right in front of my eyes."

"And that's when you told him where Isabel Gowdie was buried?" asked Madeleine Springer, her voice distinct and cool.

Stanley said, "Yes," so softly that Madeleine Springer obviously hadn't heard him at first. Then, "Yes."

"Well, I might have expected it," Madeleine Springer replied. "But it won't make your task any simpler. You will have to work out a way of keeping Knitted Hood and the rest of his Carriers well away from you, while you deal with Isabel Gowdie herself. You may not find that particularly easy. You will certainly find it very much more dangerous."

"I didn't consider that I had a choice," said Stanley, peeved that she hadn't appreciated how threatening Knitted Hood had been. "I've always preferred my head with a face on the front."

Madeleine Springer turned to Angie. "Have you had any symptoms yet?" she asked, completely changing the tack of the conversation.

Angie swallowed lumpily at the memory of the tapeworms. "I've been sick," she said.

"You know that it's going to get worse?"

"Yes," said Angie.

"Right …" Madeleine Springer told them. "You can stay here for the time being … in fact, you'll have to. I'm expecting Kasyx and Zasta to arrive the day after tomorrow. Then we can really start fighting back."

She turned to Angie. "And if you start feeling sick again or if you're feeling any other symptoms of the Night Plague, tell me at once. I can't cure it, but at least I can help you."

"Thanks," said Angie unenthusiastically. "Can't I go back to me flat?"

"I don't advise it. Supposing you have an attack of sickness? Supposing you dream about one of your flatmates? You'd really be better off here."

"I ain't got none of me clothes with me, that's the trouble."

"Oh, don't you worry about that." Madeleine Springer smiled. "I have closets and closets and closets full of clothes. You're welcome to borrow whatever you wish."

Angie smiled; the first smile that Stanley had seen from her since they had begun to make their way through Isabel Gowdie's dream. *Riboyne Shel Olem*, give a woman clothes and you'll have her eating out of your hand. But he didn't feel very enthusiastic about staying here himself. It might be safe; it might be comfortable; but it still felt very much like being conscripted into the armed forces.

He took his drink and walked over to the window and parted the linen slats in the blind. Outside he could see nothing but the prickling lights of a cold night in southwest London.

"You're worried that you haven't done very well?" Madeleine Springer asked him.

Stanley didn't answer. If only Detective Sergeant Morris hadn't come blundering in like John Wayne—maybe he and his officers would still be alive, and Stanley would have been able to win a little time, work out some kind of a deal which didn't involve telling Knitted Hood where Isabel Gowdie was, at least not immediately, the way he had been forced to by Knitted Hood's face-ripping tactics.

Madeleine Springer came and stood close beside him. He was sure he could detect the very faintest hint of lily-of-the-valley.

"The judgment was yours," she told him gently. "You and

your companions will have to deal with the consequences; but that is the way of wars. Sometimes a commander has to measure the cost of his mistakes in terms of other people's blood."

Stanley turned and looked at her. She really was exceptionally beautiful—elegant, overgroomed, strange; with eyes that were a journey in themselves.

"You will have your chance to vindicate yourself," she told him.

It was densely foggy at Heathrow Airport when flight PA 126 from San Francisco landed two and a half hours late. Stanley and Angie stood crushed against the barrier outside the customs hall, surrounded by Bangladeshis and Pakistanis and Tamils awaiting the arrival of their relatives from the east.

At last, Leon appeared, a skinny tousle-haired boy with dark circles under his eyes from trying to stay awake for most of the night. He wore a padded blue parka and jeans, and an extremely righteous pair of rainbow-colored sneakers.

Angie said, "That's 'im, ain't it? It must be! 'E looks just like you!"

She jumped up and down and shouted, "Leon! Leon" although there was far too much noise in the hall for Leon to be able to pick up anybody unfamiliar calling his name. Angie had done well out of Madeleine Springer's closet: today she was wearing a black square-shouldered fur jacket, with a matching fur hat, a yellow silk Jasper Conran blouse, and a black pencil skirt by Armani.

If only she could talk proper, she'd be stunning, thought Stanley.

Madeleine Springer had kept them apart for the last two nights. They had eyed each other with feelings of cruel lust over the breakfast table. They had dreamed about each other at night. Very early this morning, Stanley had looked quickly in Madeleine Springer's bedroom and seen that she was asleep. Then he had crossed silently to Angie's bedroom and eased the door open. She had been lying facedown on the white linen sheets, wearing nothing but a white silk slip. The slip had ridden up to expose her bare bottom.

Stanley had stood by the door staring at her for a long time; and had then taken a single step forward. He had been immediately confronted by Madeleine Springer, who must have been hiding behind the door. Although how? He had distinctly seen her sleeping in her own room, and there were no connecting doors.

"Not tonight," Madeleine Springer had cautioned him. "Tonight you must fight those feelings. Tomorrow night, you will become a Night Warrior, in all your glory. Like any knight, a vigil alone will help to purify you."

He had felt a snap of angry resentment against Madeleine Springer. For an instant, he could have slapped her. But even his infected soul cautioned him against angering the messenger of Ashapola. The Night Plague had made him devious as well as quick-tempered. He had managed a sour-twisted smile, and returned to his room, where he had sat on the end of his bed for over an hour and wrestled with demons.

—cut a cut a cut a cut a—

"Leon!" called Stanley. "Leon!"

But to Stanley's surprise, before Leon could see where he was, an elderly man walking beside Leon took hold of the boy's hand and bent down to say something in his ear. Leon nodded, and then turned to look for his father. By the time they reached the end of the fenced-off area outside the customs hall, the elderly man and Leon were walking together hand in hand as if they were grandfather and grandson.

Stanley stepped forward and held out his arms. "Hello, son," he said, and Leon came politely up to him and hugged him. "Hi, Pop," he said in a rather formal voice. The grandfatherly man waited patiently beside them while they greeted each other, but he showed no signs at all of going away.

"Did this gentleman help you off the airplane?" asked Stanley, stiffly rising to his feet.

Leon nodded. "He flew with me all the way from San Francisco. We talked and we talked."

"Didn't you get any sleep?"

"He got some sleep, don't worry." The grandfatherly man smiled. "Leaned his head against my arm all the way from Nova Scotia to Glasgow."

"Well, thanks very much, I appreciate it," said Stanley, holding out his hand. "It isn't everybody these days who cares about kids."

"Oh, Leon is no ordinary kid." The man smiled again.

"Sure, well, thanks. We'd better be going. This little guy looks like he could use some lying-down-type sleep."

"I'm not tired at all," Leon announced.

Stanley took hold of Leon's bag and together they began to walk out of Terminal 3 to the multistory parking lot. "Leon, this is Angie," said Stanley. "She's a real good friend of mine."

"Wotcha, Leon." Angie grinned. "I don't 'alf like your beetle-crushers."

Leon frowned up at his father. "She talks weird."

Angie laughed. "That ain't weird, that's proper English. Like, I called me skin and blister on the dog, and asked 'er to lend me a borrow of 'er jamjar."

"That's *weird*," said Leon.

"No, it ain't. Skin and blister is sister, get it? And dog is dog and bone, phone. And jamjar is car."

As they reached the door of the terminal, a voice right behind Stanley's right shoulder said, "Rhyming slang. The argot of the cockney thieving classes."

Stanley turned around and saw that the grandfatherly man was still close behind, listening to their conversation as if he had every right to. Stanley gave him a smile and a nod and said, "This is Leon's first time in Britain."

"Mine, too," the man told him.

"Well, I really hope you enjoy it," said Stanley. "It's kind of cold and damp this time of year, but there's a lot to see if you know where to look. Sussex is worth a visit."

The man smiled. "Oh, I won't have any time for that."

They continued to walk toward the multistory parking lot. They walked up the ramp to the second floor and made their way across to the other side where Gordon's car was parked.

"Is that your car?" Leon asked in amazement. "It's like a bumper car!"

"I borrowed it from a friend, okay?" replied Stanley testily.

"The steering wheel's on the wrong side!"

"It's a British car, Leon. In Britain they drive on the wrong side of the road."

"Don't they keep crashing into each other?"

While Angie got into the car, Stanley tossed Leon's bag into the Montego's rubbish-strewn trunk and was about to slam the lid when another bag was lowered into it. He looked around to see the grandfatherly man smiling at him.

"What's this?" he wanted to know.

"You mean you're not going to give me a ride?" the man asked him.

"Well, look, sir, I very much appreciate your talking to Leon on the way over, but I haven't seen my son in quite a while and we have a lot of private family matters to talk over. Besides, you don't even know where we're going."

"I assume that you're going to the same place that I am."

"Listen, I don't think so. I don't like to appear churlish, but—"

"Henry Watkins," the grandfatherly man announced, holding out his hand. "Your friend Springer might have mentioned me. Kasyx the charge-keeper."

Stanley stared at the grandfatherly man more closely. Sixty-six, maybe, sixty-seven. Maybe not as old as that. His hair was plumed with white, and it had been bleached by the California sun, but there were plenty of darker streaks over his ears. Stanley had seen an old-young face like that before: his own father, who had drunk a bottle and a half of Jack Daniel's every day for thirty years, and then stopped one Wednesday morning cold turkey because his doctor had told him he had only 120 more bottles to go before he would be discussing his bar bill with St. Peter.

Henry had a soft, withered neck, a very clean checkered sports shirt, and a good-quality green tweed jacket. He could have been any moderately-prosperous Californian geriatric making a cultural visit to Europe. But Stanley noticed something about his eyes. They had something of the same quality as Springer's. Clear, mystical, filled with evanescent light. They were the eyes of a man who had walked inside other men's minds; a man who had seen visions that no ordinary man could ever see.

"You'd better ... get in the car," Stanley suggested. "You don't mind riding in back? It's kind of messy. Just push that stuffed animal out of the way. I borrowed it from—"

"Keldak, yes, I know." Henry smiled and settled himself down in the back of Gordon's car with his Burberry folded neatly on his lap. "Springer told me that your transportation was a little rudimentary."

Angie, who was jabbing the keys at the ignition lock, suddenly stopped and twisted around in her seat. "Springer?" she asked Stanley. "'Ow does 'e know about Springer?"

"His daytime name is Henry Watkins," said Stanley. "But he has a nighttime name, too. Effis the light-skater, meet Kasyx the charge-keeper."

Angie was openmouthed. "*You're* Kasyx? I never would 'ave known! I didn't imagine nobody so—well, I thought you was going to be younger, know what I mean? You know, no offense meant, but it's not exactly a doddle, is it, being a—you know—"

Henry pursed his lips and flared his nostrils. "You make me sound as if I'm practically dead already. Well, maybe I am on the grave side of sixty. But you should see me when I transform. Eat your heart out, Arnold Schwartzenegger."

Stanley said, "That means that we're only one short now, Zasta. But we could still start without him, couldn't we? Four of us would be more than enough."

"No *way*," Leon protested.

"What's your problem, champ?" Stanley grinned, ruffling Leon's hair, and remembering (as soon as he had done it) that Leon loathed it. ("You make me feel like a Muppet.")

"I said no way is four of you enough."

Stanley laughed. "You don't even know what we're talking about."

"I do too know what you're talking about!"

"Leon, you've been in Britain ten minutes, and already you're starting to act like a brat!"

Henry laid a gentle hand on Stanley's arm and shook his head. "He's not behaving like a brat, Stanley. He's behaving like Zasta the knife-juggler."

Stanley was about to laugh again when he suddenly realized that Henry was totally serious. He stared at Henry and then he stared at Leon and then he stared back at Henry.

"*Him?* He's ten years old! *He's* Zasta the knife-juggler?"

"Does it surprise you? The Night Warriors are a hereditary line. The promises made by the forefathers have to be kept by their descendants."

"But Leon is just a kid!"

"Joshua was just a kid, too."

"But Joshua was—"

Henry looked grave. "Joshua was killed, along with his father, Jacob, yes. I have already told Leon about that. But Leon understands that all Night Warriors have to face unnatural dangers; and the choice is his."

"How can a ten-year-old kid have any choice? He doesn't even know what we're up against! These are creatures who tear people's faces off with their bare hands! You ever see anything like that? And you want the same thing to happen to my son? Well, you listen to me, Kasyx the charge-keeper, you've got another goddamn think coming right up next, after the break!"

Angie was driving them out of the airport now and eastwards along the M4 towards Brentford and Chiswick, over the ghostly sprawled-out encampment of the Great West Road and all its factories and warehouses, their lights gleaming dimly through the fog. She gave Stanley an occasional sideways flicker of her eyes, partly out of concern and partly out of conspiracy. She and Stanley shared something between them which Henry didn't share: they were both infected by the Night Plague. That gave their outlook on life an unpredictable perversity. They felt the same urgency to hunt down Isabel Gowdie as the rest of the Night Warriors, but their need was becoming disturbingly ambivalent. Did they want to find her to destroy her, or did they want to find her to set her free?

Henry said, "As he is now, I agree with you, Stanley. Leon is just an above-average grade-school kid. But in the form of Zasta the knife-juggler, believe me, you could never call him anything but a full-fledged Night Warrior. He's strong, he's fast, he's mature, he's quite capable of making his own decisions."

Stanley turned to Leon. "What did Henry tell you about being a Night Warrior?"

"I told him—" began Henry, but Stanley interrupted him. "Would you mind? I want to hear it from Leon."

Leon bit his lip. "He didn't just tell me, he *showed* me."

"What do you mean, he showed you?"

"On the plane, when it was dark, and nobody was

watching. He put his hand on my shoulder and he showed me my armor. It was all shining and it was golden."

Stanley looked back at Henry. "You did that to my kid without asking me first?"

"Since when have you been so interested in your kid?" Henry retorted. "Besides, there was no time to waste."

Leon said, "Pop, I know all about it. I know who I am. It's something I have to do."

"You don't *have* to do it, that's the whole point," Stanley replied. "I know it seems like it's exciting and grown-up and thrilling. But that's only the half of it. It's very dangerous, too, and very scary, and a lot of it is pretty damn disgusting."

"And boring," Angie put in.

"That's right," Stanley agreed. "And boring. A lot of it is very boring. You know, like being a cop can be boring. You know, paperwork, stakeouts, court appearances."

Leon was silent for a short while, but he obviously had something to say, and in the end Henry nudged him and said, "Go ahead, say your piece."

"Well," said Leon, "I know that I don't *have* to do it. But the fact is that I *want* to do it. Jacob Eisner was killed by Isabel Gowdie; and he was Mol Besa, the same way that *you're* Mol Besa now, so you're going to hunt her down, right, and get your revenge? Well, Joshua Eisner was Zasta, the same way that I'm Zasta; and I think I have the right to get *my* revenge, too, if I want to."

"Now, wait up," Stanley began, but Leon interrupted him.

"You left me. Pop. You walked out on me. You weren't interested *then* if I was scared or disgusted or bored or in danger or anything. So why are you so interested now?"

"Leon, that is crap! That is complete crap! I might just as well be listening to your mother, or your mother's goddamned attorney! Of course I was interested in you. But your mom didn't make it very easy. In fact, she made it very difficult. In fact, she made it impossible. Your mom is one of those people who don't believe in other people having a point of view. Well, they *can* have a point of view, but it has to be hers."

"Pop, you're just the same."

"Well, then, damn it, that makes two of us."

"But, Pop, I really want to do this. I want to do this so bad that it hurts."

"And I don't want you even to *think* about doing it. Listen, Leon, you have no idea of how dangerous it is. How can I take the responsibility of exposing you to all those kinds of things you find in dreams? Rats, dogs, diseases, fires—God knows what else."

"Don't forget arrows and explosions and killer robots and guns that suck the muscles out of your legs," Henry added in a warm voice as he watched the industrial scenery going by.

"Oh, Pop, you're such a spoilsport," Leon protested.

"Oh, yes?" Stanley demanded. "If protecting the life of my only son is being a spoilsport, then I have no qualms at all about being a spoilsport."

"I'm not frightened. Pop," said Leon. "I was frightened when you walked out on Mom and me, and left us. But I'm not frightened of anything now. You went, and that made me brave."

Henry smiled to himself. "That's one spunky kid you have there, Stanley. You can't deny it."

Stanley turned around and sat bad-temperedly watching the traffic as Angie drove underneath the concrete piers of the M4 around the busy Chiswick roundabout and turned towards Kew and Richmond. He thought of Tennyson as they drove past the junction with Kew Gardens Road, although it was too foggy for him to be able to see the house. He thought of the chilling rain, pouring through the ceilings, and the dogs with the heads of half-mad children. He didn't want to risk Leon ending up like that. *On the other hand, it might serve the little shit right, talking back to his father in front of strangers. How did Leon dare to compare him with Eve? That neurotic, carping, tunnel-visioned, money-grubbing harridan. She'd fought him so viciously for custody. She'd produced an endless succession of unctuous walleyed attorneys and conniving feminist child psychiatrists. "If his father has custody, he'll treat him worse than the family dog." He'd like to see her face if he sent Leon back with the eyes of a lunatic and the body of a bull terrier.*

They drove up Richmond Hill and parked. Angie collided with the curb and said, "Sorry!" Stanley hefted both bags out of the Montego's trunk and carried them across to Springer's front door, while Henry climbed stiffly out of the back seat. Before Stanley had reached the front steps, however, Henry called, "Stanley … just a word before we go in."

Stanley waited with closely-controlled impatience, without turning around. Henry came up close beside him and looked at him in a steady, fatherly way.

"Stanley, I know what kind of a battle you're fighting inside of yourself. I know it isn't at all easy for you. Springer isn't always sympathetic, either; because Springer's well ... Springer's Springer. Not so much of a person as a singing telegram from God Almighty. But I want you to know that *I* care about you, and about Angie, too, and I want to assure you that whatever you say to me, whatever conflicts we have between us, all of the power that I have at my disposal is yours, too."

He hesitated, and then he added, "When I was first called to be a Night Warrior, I was as soft as sponge cake and green as grass. But I've fought some real big battles since then, and I've lived through some strange times and some strange places that most human beings wouldn't even think possible. I have experience, and knowledge, and I can tell you this much: this Night Plague may be the very worst threat we've ever had to deal with, but we're going to do our level best to lick it, and lick it good, and we're not just going to lick it for the sake of the human race, we're going to lick it for you personally. And for Angie, too."

Stanley said, "Thanks. I appreciate it."

"And, listen," said Henry, "don't be sore about Leon. He has to face up to his birthright one day. It might just as well be sooner, rather than later. I'll take care of him if things start getting out of hand."

"Meaning that I'm not capable of taking care of him?"

"Meaning that you have yourself to take care of, my friend; and we all need all the taking care of that we can get. We're not talking about Pazuzu, or Abrahel, or any of those minor-league demons. This isn't Jack Nicholson making suburban women fly in the air. This isn't Linda Blair with a revolving head. This is His Satanic Majesty, Stanley. This is Old Scratch. This is It with a capital *I*."

"What are you trying to do, scare me into being nice to you?"

"I hope you're scared already, and I really don't care if you're nice to me or not. Just remember what Stendhal said. 'If you know men thoroughly, and judge events sanely, that's the first step toward happiness.'"

"You sound like a goddamned philosopher," said Stanley.

"You got it in one." Henry smiled. "Did you ever read my paper on Voltaire and Rousseau, 'Sand Against the Wind?' University of California, San Diego, 1967."

"That's one I must have missed," said Stanley as Angie pressed Springer's doorbell.

Springer was eccentric and evasive this morning. He appeared as a willowy, wan, androgynous youth, in a black linen suit and a fine white cambric shirt, with dozens of expensive accessories: a gold fob-watch, an alligator-skin cigarette case with the initials *MS* on it, and a gold-topped walking cane from Swaine, Adeney, Brigg & Son, of Piccadilly. His hair was cut short and brushed back with hairdressing wax, and he wore wire-rimmed spectacles with dark crimson lenses, like two circular pools of congealed blood.

"So this is Leon," he said, taking hold of Leon's hand with fingers as cool and thin as diluted milk. "Welcome to England, Leon. May the fog be with you."

He said nothing at all to Henry, but Henry continued to smile as if he were used to being treated this way. Springer showed them through to their rooms: a large eastwards-facing bedroom for Henry, with an antique stained-pine bureau and a desk with a typewriter and a bottle of Malvern water on it, and a bed with a handmade patchwork quilt; and a smaller dormer room for Leon, right next door to Stanley's.

Leon's room was decorated in Chinese blue and white, and looked out over the ghostly leafless oaks of Terrace Gardens and the fog-white invisible Thames. A white bookcase contained copies of Kipling's *Just-So Stories* and *The War of the Worlds* and *Beano Annual, 1968*.

"Well, what do you think of it?" asked Stanley, walking over to the window and looking out.

"It's really neat," said Leon, bouncing on the checkered blue and white bedspread. "It's going to be radical here."

"Sure, it's neat." Stanley watched a flight of ducks winging through the fog towards Twickenham. Then he said, "How much did Henry tell you about the Night Plague?"

"I guess he told me everything that *he* knew."

"So you know what it does to people, this disease?"

"For sure. It's like AIDS, only you don't get it in your body, you get it in your soul. If you catch it, you don't know what's right and what's wrong any more, and you can never get to heaven when you die. He told me about the way they spread it around, too. The Carriers, and the witches, and everything."

"He told you that it comes from the Devil?"

Leon nodded, his eyes widening.

"Did you believe him?"

"Not at first, but after he showed me my armor."

"I see."

"It was neat, Pop. It was dark on the airplane and everybody was watching the movie, and he laid his hand on my shoulder and it was like *zzzz-zzzz-zzzz*, I got this kind of electric shock and I lifted up my arm and it had armor on it, golden armor."

"So you believed him?"

"I sure did."

Stanley said, "Did he tell you anything else about the Night Plague?"

"Like what?"

"I don't know … what *kind* of people get infected, and how?"

"Well, I know they get infected by doing it."

"What do you know about 'doing it'?"

"I know everything about doing it. We're always talking about doing it at school."

"At Napa County Grade School you spend all your time talking about doing it?"

"For sure. What else is there to talk about?"

Stanley blew out his cheeks. "I don't know. There's art, there's history, there's politics. The meaning of life. The kind of things that adults discuss."

"Oh, yes," said Leon with enormous scorn. "Uncle Mikey took me to the Silverado Country Club and the men in the locker room were *definitely* talking about the meaning of life."

"Who's Uncle Mikey?"

Leon gave him a quick sideways look. "Mom's new friend, that's all."

"Mom's new boyfriend?"

"Well, she has to have somebody. You're not there. And who's this Angie, anyway? She looks like she knows you pretty good."

Stanley's right arm jerked up. *You little punk, don't you talk to me like that. I ought to smack you right across the face, and then I ought to shake you and shake you and teach you some goddamned respect.* But he caught himself just in time, and his right hand curved around to smooth down his hair, and he stood up straight, and shrugged, and gave Leon a sloping grin.

"We're just good friends, that's all, Angie and me."

"Are we going to get something to eat soon?" asked Leon, instantly losing interest in the topic of his father's "friends." "I'm totally revenooski."

"Sure," said Stanley. "How about a hamburger?"

He laid his arm around Leon's shoulders and gave him a squeeze. "Good to have you, champ," he told him. "Don't go forgetting that I love you."

"I love you, too, Pop. So does Mom. She doesn't say so, but she does."

"Let's leave Mom out of this, shall we? Wash up and change your clothes, and we'll go find some chow."

Springer took them to the Village Restaurant, just around the corner in Friar's Stile Road. They sat crowded together in two uncomfortable wooden booths, rather like a fourth-class Czechoslovakian railroad compartment, and ordered prawn cocktails and cheeseburgers.

Stanley could scarcely touch his cheeseburger. It was just another incarnation of that ubiquitous British "mince," with a half-melted Kraft cheese slice on top. But Leon was either too hungry to care or actually liked it. Stanley had always said that if you could eat a McDonald's you could eat anything.

Springer seemed unusually tense and fidgety. Henry on the other hand exuded tremendous calm, like a master craftsman brought in to finish a job at which he knows he excels. Stanley found it hard to believe that Henry had ever been as raw and as nervous as he was now. He seemed to have such power, such command.

Stanley was drinking too much, mainly because the Muscadet had been served at room temperature, and he hardly even noticed that it was going down. He was talking more loudly and more argumentatively than he ought to have been.

Springer took out a tightly-folded copy of the London *Daily Telegraph* and smoothed it out on the table. "There's no question at all that the Night Plague is spreading, and spreading very quickly. Look at this news item here: A lone gunman walked down the street of his home village in Lincolnshire yesterday and shot three innocent people dead and wounded seventeen others. When he was arrested he said that he simply didn't care about the people he had killed. 'They were nothing.' Then here's a case of a woman who set fire to her husband while he lay in bed because she suspected him of having an affair with another woman. 'He deserved to be hurt,' she told the judge, 'and if it was necessary I'd do it again.' And here: over a hundred and thirty drunken youths rampaged through the center of a market town in Hampshire, killing a police constable, disemboweling a police horse, and causing thousands of pounds' worth of injury and damage."

"But that sort of thing 'appens all the time," said Angie. "'Ow do you know it's the Night Plague?"

Springer folded the paper. "Incidents like these may be common in Britain today, my dear, but only two or three years ago, they were almost completely unknown. There were no Rambo-style gunmen; no revenge burnings; no 'lager-louts,' as the British call them. And all of these incidents have something interesting in common. None of the perpetrators showed even the slightest degree of remorse.

"There have been attacks in New York that have been manifestations of the Night Plague, too. The 'wilders' in Central Park, who rape and bludgeon innocent women and then express amazement that anybody should care. The increasing number of meaningless assaults on the subway. 'They were nothing,' that's all they ever have to say about their victims. 'They were nothing.'

"One of the most evil symptoms of the Night Plague is a total disregard for the lives of others; and, in the end, a total disregard for your own life, too."

Stanley said, "It's time we put a stop to it, then. Before—"

"Before it spreads all over Britain and Europe, and all across North America," Springer finished for him, "and before you and Angie start exhibiting the same symptoms."

It was then that Stanley realized that Leon was staring at him, a ketchup-dipped French fry forgotten in his fingers.

"Pop?" he whispered hoarsely. "Do you and Angie have the Night Plague?"

Stanley swallowed almost half a glass of warm white wine and then looked at Henry for moral support.

Henry shrugged. "He has to know, Stanley. It's for his own protection; especially when he's a Night Warrior. There may be a time when he has to make a life-or-death decision whether to trust you or not."

"Well, you've more or less told him now, haven't you?" Stanley retorted.

"Leon—" Henry began in a gentle voice, "the fact of the matter is that—"

"The fact of the matter is that we do," Stanley interrupted him. "Angie and I are both infected, and it's getting steadily worse. So if sometimes I start behaving like a different pop from the pop you knew—"

Leon said, "I never knew you, anyway, Pop. Not that much." But he was only being defensive.

"Well, thanks a lot. But what I was trying to tell you is that we're fighting against it, and fighting against it very hard; and when we find Isabel Gowdie we'll get rid of it forever."

Leon regarded his father with dark, unreadable eyes. "After that," he asked, "are we going to be happy ever after?"

Stanley didn't answer. Springer fished out his fob-watch and opened it. "It's time we were getting back. Gordon is coming to the flat at three o'clock, and I think we need to make a few plans before we go out tonight."

"We're going out *tonight*?" asked Henry, wiping his mouth with his paper napkin. "I haven't even had time to get myself acclimatized yet."

"There won't be time for that, I'm afraid," Springer told him. "Stanley and Angie will help you as much as they can."

They paid the check and walked back along Friar's Stile Road, past art galleries with sporting paintings in the window, and video-rental stores, and handsome Victorian houses where televisions flickered.

Unconsciously, Stanley and Leon held hands; and then Angie came and held Leon's other hand, and somehow to Leon they were more of a family than he and his mom and Uncle Mikey had ever been; Uncle Mikey with his hairy chest and his loud laugh and his six-packs of Coors Lite; and Leon smiled to himself in a way that Stanley couldn't remember having seen him smile before.

Henry, standing in the middle of the living room, said, "The way you can see yourselves now, by daylight, is only the faintest reflection of what you will look like in dreams. In dreams, you will become god-warriors, immensely powerful, immensely responsive, and with accumulated knowledge and experience of seven centuries of Night Warriors at your disposal."

He beckoned to Springer and then added, "Mol Besa, Effis, Keldak—you've already been given some idea of what your armor and your weaponry will look like. Now I'm going to show you mine—and Zasta's, too."

Springer rested his hand on Henry's shoulder, and gradually they became aware of a low vibration in the room, and the pungent smell of burned electricity. Tiny blue sparks began to crawl around Springer's fingers, and to form an outline all around Henry's head and shoulders.

There was a ballooning sensation in the room, as if the room itself were a spaceship, about to detach itself from the building and rise up slowly into the fog, dripping down sparks as it went.

Henry closed his eyes. The air around him began to darken, to form itself into shadows and shapes.

Gordon, who was sitting cross-legged in the opposite corner of the room, looked over at Stanley and raised his eyebrows. Stanley nodded and tried unsuccessfully to smile. He was struggling with one of his attacks of irritability again, and an imaginary ticker tape of ceaseless insults about Henry and his pomposity had been chattering through his mind ever since they had returned to the flat. He didn't even dare to think too much about Gordon. Gordon's wrist was almost completely healed now, and he had regained his strength and his color, not to mention his strutting BBC-radio-show sauciness, and Stanley found it almost impossible to tolerate having him here.

So you helped me in hospital, you faggot, just to make yourself feel more saintly. But I don't want around now, especially now that Leon's here. People like you are a plague on your own.

There was a low shuddering noise like somebody shaking a heavy antique closet. Then Henry turned around, and he was wearing the gleaming crimson armor of Kasyx the charge-keeper. Although Stanley didn't know it, Kasyx's armor had altered substantially since he had first become a Night Warrior. It was slabby and angular, as it had always been, but now every surface was covered with rows of radiatorlike fins, so that Kasyx could gather imaginary solar energy as he walked under the imaginary suns of other people's dreams. His helmet had been modified, too, to include a head-up visual display of the location of every Night Warrior within a particular dream.

Kasyx said, "You depend on me to replenish your weapons and your armor. As soon as you feel your power failing, you must return to me as soon as you can, for recharging.

I myself have no weapons … only the ultimate sanction of discharging all my energy at once, which can create a devastating power wave, but which then makes it impossible for us to escape from whichever dream we happen to be fighting in. We would then be trapped in the dreamer's subconscious until our physical bodies died of malnutrition."

Stanley asked, "What happens if the dreamer wakes up while we're still inside his dream? Or *her* dream?"

"That's the time to bail out," said Kasyx. "But you usually get plenty of warning. The landscape starts to dissolve, the images become unstable. You get a feel for it … you sense a change in pressure, not unlike slowly rising to the surface of a swimming pool. It's possible to remain inside the imagination of a waking person, but it's like a totally gray limbo, until they go back to sleep again and start dreaming. The problem with allowing *that* to happen is that your physical body remains at the mercy of whoever might happen to find it. Some Night Warriors have been killed during the day by demons who found their physical bodies sleeping."

Kasyx beckoned Leon forward and laid his hand on his shoulder. "Now let's see what this young gentleman looks like as Zasta the knife-juggler."

Leon stood with his hands at his sides and closed his eyes. Kasyx said, "Relax, Leon … everything's going to be fine." Then he closed his own eyes, and energy began to hum through his fingers and etch a fine glowing gold outline all around Leon's head and body.

In less than a minute, Leon had been transformed into Zasta the knife-juggler. He wore a brilliant golden helmet in the style of a Spanish *conquistador*, but with a plain gold visor which completely covered his eyes. His breastplate was made of thin curves of golden armor, similar to the flow fences on the wings of airplanes, and he wore shining golden boots, as pliable and as well fitted as the best riding boots, but made of malleable metal.

Stanley asked, "Is that visor solid? How does he see?"

Kasyx said, "Zasta is as sensitive as a knife-thrower in a circus, who throws knives blindfolded at a woman spinning on a wheel. He 'sees' by psychic power, and when the time comes to use his knives, he 'sees' nothing but his target. Normal vision would be a distraction." He added, "'Turn around, Zasta. Show them your weaponry."

Zasta did as he was told. On his back was an ingenious and complicated rack of dozens of knife scabbards; and each of these scabbards contained a differently-shaped blade. There were long thin throwing stilettos. There were massive saw-backed bowie knives. There were chivs and sticking knives and hook-bladed knives and gutting knives.

"How about a little demonstration?" Kasyx suggested.

"What can I use as a target?" asked Zasta. He spoke in Leon's voice, but with a new and quite formidable authority.

Springer looked around. "The lily picture, if you wish. I was tiring of it, anyway."

Zasta snapped his head sideways, sized up the lily drawing in less than two seconds, and then lifted his right hand. A gold-bladed throwing knife leapt out of its scabbard on its own and somersaulted over his shoulder into his hand. Without any hesitation, Zasta threw it at the picture, and it flashed across the room and hit the narrowest of pencil lines at the very top of the picture.

Before any of them had time to appreciate the accuracy of Zasta's throwing, however, another knife jumped over his shoulder like a goldfish skipping out of a pond, and he had thrown that, too, exactly an inch below the first knife and exactly on the pencil line. Without hesitation, a cascade of throwing knives followed, until the entire outline of the drawing had been embellished with golden blades.

"Looks like the right sort of chap to have on our side," said Gordon. "Bet he'd make a wonderful sushi chef."

The hum of psychic energy gradually died away, and Henry and Leon emerged from their armor. Now Springer came forward, fastidiously tugging at his white cambric French cuffs. He seemed distracted, and quite abrupt, but it occurred to Stanley that he was not so much irritated with them as worried about them. Ashapola cared for the least of His creatures, for all that He allowed them to choose their own destiny, and to believe in Him or not to believe in Him, whichever they wished. Ashapola was not an interfering God, but He cared about His creations.

"When you go to bed tonight, you will recite three times the sacred incantation of Ashapola," said Springer. "This will ensure that, when you fall asleep, your dreaming body will leave your physical body."

"What 'appens if I can't get off to sleep?" asked Angie.

"You will, once you have spoken the incantations and emptied your mind of all extraneous thoughts."

"What happens if somebody tries to wake me up while I'm away, so to speak?" said Gordon. "I mean, it's quite possible that Jeremy could come back, and fancy a cuddle."

"For God's sake," barked Stanley. "There's a ten-year-old boy here, in case you hadn't noticed."

"Hey, it's okay. Pop," said Leon. "I know all about gays. We had a gay awareness talk at school."

"There's a difference between being aware of them and having to listen to every sordid detail of their love lives," Stanley retorted. "And besides, what the hell is your mother doing, sending you to the kind of school where you talk about nothing but gays and doing it?"

"I think Gordon asked a perfectly reasonable question," put in Henry. "The answer is that once your dreaming personality has vacated it, your physical body cannot be woken. That is why it is advisable that you go to sleep in a place where you aren't likely to be disturbed. If you think your friend is going to try to wake you, Gordon, you should check in at a hotel tonight, or stay here, if you prefer it."

"I don't want him staying here," said Stanley. "Not so long as Leon's here, too."

"What the hell's got into you, all of a sudden?" Gordon demanded. "I practically saved your sanity, after you were attacked. I came and talked to you whenever you called me. I even lost my hand because of you!"

Stanley said nothing, but turned away. The bilious hostility which the Night Plague had aroused in him had begun to subside, and he felt ashamed of himself for what he had said. At the same time, he still wasn't prepared to apologize. He caught Angie looking at him with an expression of sympathy. *She* understood the struggle that was going on inside him, even if nobody else did.

Springer said, quite quietly, "We had better be aware that two of our number have been infected by the Night Plague. Both of them are essential to our task, but there may be times when their judgment and their motivation are not always what they ought to be."

He walked across to Stanley and Angie, and added, "Whenever you feel yourselves weakening, remember this: your mortal souls are at stake. You are as close as any human beings can ever be to true damnation."

"It depends what you mean by damnation," said Angie cockily.

Springer looked at her seriously. "You've seen those boy-dogs. You've seen a Carrier for yourself. You've seen the inside of Isabel Gowdie's dreams. Imagine living like that, forever and ever, without any hope of escaping it."

He turned back to the rest of the Night Warriors. "Our first task is to find where Isabel Gowdie is. Once we have done that, Stanley can be rid of his Night Plague, and we can hunt down her Carriers, and destroy them, too."

"What about Angie, and everybody else who's already been infected?" asked Gordon. "There must be thousands already."

Springer said, "To grow, and to take over an individual's whole personality, the Night Plague virus must be constantly fed by Satan's psychic energy. Satan created the virus, after all, and like any parent he must feed his children.

"He does this through the chain of infection and secondary infection. *He* feeds Isabel Gowdie, Isabel Gowdie feeds her Carriers, the Carriers feed their primary victims—like *you*, Stanley—and the primary victims pass on the psychic energy to the secondary victims—like *you*, Angie.

Springer paused, and then he said, "All we have to do is break the chain of infection. Destroy Isabel Gowdie, and that will starve the viruses of the energy they need to develop.

They will eventually shrivel from sheer malnutrition, and die a natural death."

"And that's going to put an end to all of this violence we've been seeing lately?" asked Stanley. "All these riots and random shootings and rapes?"

"Not altogether. Even when somebody has been cured of the Night Plague, his morality remains scarred, just as your face remains scarred after smallpox. But, yes, there should be some noticeable improvements. And it shouldn't spread any further."

"So where do we start?" asked Stanley.

"We start in Isabel Gowdie's own dream. We have to. She's been bound in such a way by the Night Warriors who imprisoned her that she cannot escape from her own dreams into anybody else's dream. Obviously it will be much more dangerous, to fight a witch in her own dream, and she will have her Carriers to help her. But there is no alternative. In her own dream is where you will find her; and in her own dream is where you will have to destroy her."

Gordon, rather sulkily, agreed to take a room at the Petersham Hotel, only a hundred yards away from Springer's apartment building, down a steeply-descending road called Nightingale Lane. Springer refused to involve himself in the conflict between Stanley and Gordon. When Gordon appealed to him to make Stanley see sense, he simply turned away and shrugged. He was nothing but a singing telegram from God Almighty, after all.

There was an atmosphere of high tension in the apartment that day. The Night Warriors scarcely spoke to each other, and at about four o'clock in the afternoon, as it was growing dark, Springer retired to his room and closed the door. Leon sprawled on the living room floor, drawing a large sprawling picture of Napa Airport with colored pencils, while Angie lay beside him and watched him.

"Here's Jonesy's famous hamburger restaurant," Leon explained, "and here's me coming out of it. Here's Bridgeford Flying Services ... and here's me, getting into a plane for a flight to the Golden Gate ... and here's me being airsick. Look, you can see all the half-chewed hamburger."

"Oh, that's nice," said Angie. She was wearing a very short black designer dress with buttons down the front, and black panty hose, and little black pixie boots, all borrowed from Springer's wardrobe. Although she was watching Leon draw, she kept glancing up at Stanley, who was sitting on the Chinese-French sofa, playing drafts with Henry. Stanley was aware that she kept looking at him, but he pretended not to notice. His blood was inflamed enough as it was, burning its way through his arteries as if it were alight. He didn't know whether he felt hot or cold, although his forehead was crowned with beads of perspiration.

He had seen Angie's breasts, pressed against the polished floor. He had seen the curve of her bottom, where she had lifted one leg. He was playing drafts with Henry to calm himself down, to keep his mind orderly, to stop himself from raging around the apartment in an explosion of frustrated lust and ungovernable hatred.

He had once wondered (in what now seemed like a life that he had never even lived) how muggers could approach total strangers and hit them or stab them without any hesitation and without any apparent qualms. He knew now.

He was boiling with such utter contempt for everybody around him, such furious selfishness, that when Henry managed to crown his first draft, he had to clasp his hands tightly together to prevent himself from hurling the board across the room and hitting Henry in the face.

Henry glanced at him quickly. "If I win, you won't kill me, will you?"

"Are you psychic, too?"

Henry shook his head. "Just observant. Ever since I dried out, I started taking notice of the world around me. I couldn't believe how much of it I'd missed, in forty years of boozing." He crowned another draft. "I guess you could say that, these days, I see things the way that a small child sees them."

"What made you stop drinking?" asked Stanley.

"This did, being a Night Warrior. Understanding for the first time that other people relied on me. Drinking is a way of copping out; of failing to live up to your responsibilities. Being a Night Warrior is just about the direct opposite of that."

Stanley put down his glass of vodka.

"Oh, don't mind me." Henry smiled. "I'm just one of those guys who never knew when to stop."

"Maybe I should, too," said Stanley.

Henry said, "A little Dutch courage won't do you any harm, not tonight."

Later, Springer emerged from her room wearing a tight white woollen dress, her blond hair cropped in a shining crew cut. Without a word she went into the kitchen on very high-heeled white shoes and started to prepare them a meal. She didn't call any of them or even look at them, and they gathered that she wanted to be left alone.

"Never seen her so tense," Henry remarked, looking up from his newspaper.

Stanley said, "Do you think she has any cause to be?"

Henry shrugged. "We've never sailed quite so close to the wind before. Never come quite so near to Old Scratch himself. I should think that Springer's pretty worried about what kind of catastrophic wrath we're going to be stirring up, filling a contract on Satan's favorite domestic. Imagine what God would feel like if a couple of demons took out St. Ursula."

"Are you kidding me?" Stanley asked him.

"Only partly," said Henry. "This is pretty damned dangerous stuff, what we're expected to do tonight."

Stanley was silent for a moment. Then he said, "Henry ... I want you to promise me something."

"Say the word."

"I want you to promise me that if I start doing something crazy ... something that jeopardizes everybody else—well, I want you to promise that you'll deal with me. Do you understand what I mean?"

Henry stared back at him for a long time. "Yes, Stanley, I understand. I already made that promise to Springer."

Springer had made them a sparse and elegant Japanese meal, served in black lacquered *bento*, or lunch boxes, each with an open top shelf and two drawers underneath. On the top layer she had arranged a dried chrysanthemum leaf with a sliced clam on top and a skewer of ginkgo nuts and a bundle of spinach. In the second layer, there were two fish balls separated by a chrysanthemum leaf, glazed beans, one rice ball, and a knot of *wakame* seaweed. The bottom layer contained a cube of pickled pork, three flower-shaped slices of carrot, three shrimps alternated with slices of lemon, and a tiny mound of finely-shredded radish.

For Leon, she had prepared shrimp and sesame toast, which happened to be his favorite oriental food. She had invited Gordon to come from the hotel to join them, but in Angie's words Gordon had "got the 'ump," and said he would order something from room service, thank you very much.

Stanley appreciated the sparsity of Springer's meal. It felt more like a last supper than a warrior's breakfast. They spoke very little, except to compliment Springer with exaggerated politeness on her cooking. When it was over, and Leon had helped Springer to clear away, they sat around the living room for a quarter of an hour, until Henry stood up and cleared his throat and said, "This is my bedtime, folks."

He went around to each of them and shook their hands. "I'm not going to make any speeches," he said. "But I want you to know that what you're about to do is something brave and noble; and that however it comes out, it will never be forgotten, not ever, not as long as there are Night Warriors to tell the tale. Now, all I can say is—see you in the morning, I hope."

Chapter Eight

Chalk Face

Stanley climbed into bed feeling as if his brain had been laid bare and lashed by armfuls of stinging nettles. He lay back in the darkness, staring up at the patterns of light on the ceiling, and took four or five slow, deep breaths to relax himself. But deep breathing did no good at all. It only made him feel hyperventilated and giddy, and his brain still throbbed with half-formed anxieties and misshapen terrors.

He licked his lips and haltingly recited the sacred incantation of Ashapola.

"Now when the face of the world is hidden in darkness, let us be conveyed to the place of our meeting, armed and armored; and let us be nourished by the power that is dedicated to the cleaving of darkness, the settling of all black matters, and the dissipation of evil, so be it."

He said it three times, as Springer had instructed them, but by the time he had finished he was no more sleepy than he was when he had first climbed into bed. A panicky thought came over him: supposing all the other Night Warriors fell asleep, and he didn't? Supposing they went in search of Isabel Gowdie and left him behind?

Knitted Hood wouldn't be very pleased with him then. *(Because there had to be a compromise, after all, a way of persuading Isabel Gowdie to cure him of the Night Plague, without actually having to destroy her, surely? And only he was capable of reaching such a compromise.)* He couldn't even imagine what revenge Knitted Hood would exact if things went wrong.

He switched on his bedside light. Ten after eleven. He never went to bed this early—or, even if he did, he never went to *sleep* this early. He picked up the book he had borrowed from Springer. *My Life*, by the artist and naturalist Thomas Bewick: "On setting out, I always waded through the first pool I met with and had sometimes the river to wade at the for end. I never changed my cloaths, however they might be soaked with wet and though they might be stiffened with frost on my returned home at night."

Stanley read five or six pages, then replaced the book on the bedside table and switched off the light. In spite of himself, he started to slip in and out of sleep, and had extraordinary dreams of Thomas Bewick crossing rivers on stilts, and of a hanged naval officer that Bewick had once come across, rotating on the end of his rope, while his dog sat below him and watched him spin.

He thought that he could hear voices, although he couldn't decide where they were coming from, whether they were near or far away. He sat up and listened. They seemed to be coming from the living room, and it occurred to him that everybody else must have fallen asleep and that they had already become Night Warriors.

He rose from his bed and moved silently across the room. As he did so, however, he realized that he was *gliding*, rather than walking. In fact, he didn't even have to move his legs. He raised one hand in front of his face and saw that it was transparent. He could see the outlines of the door right through his fingers.

In fear and fascination, he turned around and looked back towards his bed. He was still lying there, his eyes closed, his mouth slightly open, one arm resting outside the covers. He had left his body. He was nothing more than a dream self, a sleeping memory of what he was really like.

He passed through the wall of his bedroom into the living room. The molecules of the wall made a *ssshhh*ing noise against his ears as he penetrated it. He was right. All of the others had already left their sleeping bodies— including Gordon, who must have floated over through the night from the Petersham Hotel—and they were gathered in a circle waiting for him. Springer was standing a little way away from the Night Warriors. She wore a floor-length robe of pure white silk, rather like a priestess, and her hair was gathered in a silver-threaded snood.

"Your time has now come," she told them as Stanley joined them, standing right behind Leon. "You are Night Warriors now. You are members of that great and glorious host who captured and chained all nine hundred and ninety-nine manifestations of the Devil, and who earned for all time the gratitude of Ashapola and the Council of Messengers. You have dedicated your dream selves to the extinction of evil, and in particular to the pursuit and capture of Isabel Gowdie, the witch-woman, Satan's most favored servant, and all of her Carriers."

She raised both arms, closed her eyes, and lifted her face upwards. Around her slender wrists, five bangles of golden light materialized. She whispered, "Ashapola, lend your power to these your servants," and slowly and silently the bangles rose over her hands and floated across the room, so that each of the five Night Warriors was crowned by a golden halo.

Almost immediately, the haloes dissolved and disappeared; but as they did so, Stanley felt a huge surge of energy in every muscle. Around his head, his glass helmet appeared, with its contra-rotating metal circlets; his body was clad in dull bronze armor. He looked down at his chest and checked the mathematical calculators that winked and flashed on his instrument panel. To his surprise, he could read and interpret them easily, as easily as reading a music score or the page of a book.

In a fraction of a second, he calculated the temperature and air pressure in the room, the precise constituents of the air, the exact time, the phase of the moon, the velocity of the earth, and the angle and speed at which they would fly away from the earth's surface if the planet happened abruptly to stop rotating.

The other four Night Warriors were also fully dressed in their battle gear. Keldak in his green metallic armor; Effis in her masklike lacework helmet and endlessly-changing leotard of lights; Zasta in his golden armor, with his racks of shining knives; and Kasyx in his slabby metallic suit of darkly-gleaming crimson.

Kasyx was fully charged with energy—almost *over*charged, because dazzling blue lightning was crackling and snaking around his shoulders and along his arms, and every time he brought his hands close together, a zig-zag electrical discharge would leap from one to the other, like a Van de Graaff generator.

"Here, Mol Besa," he said, and Stanley stepped forward. Kasyx laid his hand on a special chrome-polished triangular plate on Stanley's left shoulder, and instantly Stanley felt a juddering surge of enormous power. Every nerve in his body fizzed and tingled, and he felt as if he were strong enough to fight anything and anyone. Knitted Hood included. He had *become* Mol Besa. He was no longer transparent. He appeared as solid as he did in reality. Although who was to say, now, what was reality and what was a dream? *Am I dreaming you or are you dreaming me?*

One by one, the Night Warriors stepped up to Kasyx and were charged up with power. Now they glittered and glowed, their lights and their dials and their instruments filling the living room with a firework display of celestial energy. White fire sparkled from Effis's body armor, and gradually her light-skates materialized from the soles of her boots—two blindingly-bright blades that were curved at the front and trailed behind her for almost a foot. From Keldak's left wrist, a dazzling hand appeared; a hand which he flexed, formed into a fist, and then proudly covered with a thin green metallic glove.

Zasta's knives shimmered; and the visor of his helmet gleamed. Mol Besa grasped his shoulder and said, "You look terrific. I'm proud of you. You're still sure you want to do this?"

Zasta nodded. "More than ever."

"All right, then," Mol Besa told him. "I can't say that I blame you. I don't know what your mother would say."

Springer said, "Listen to me, we have very little time to lose. Kasyx will tell you that, usually, when we wish to enter somebody's dream, we have to locate the dreamer, and to approach him as close as possible. Very few people have dreams that radiate very far beyond their immediate surroundings. This case, however, is completely different. We have no precise idea of where Isabel Gowdie is ... but her dreams are so strong that they can manifest themselves miles and miles away from her physical location.

"We will have to go to the house called Tennyson and enter Isabel Gowdie's dream there. Once we are inside the dream, we can hunt her down."

Mol Besa put in, "You realize that Knitted Hood will be following us."

"Yes," said Springer. "But how you deal with Knitted Hood, Mol Besa, is up to you. That is a difficulty that you have created for yourself."

Mol Besa resented Springer's censorious remark, but said nothing. *My time will come*, he thought to himself. *Then you'll see who's the master around here*. He caught Effis looking at him through the fire and flower patterns of her face mask; and he knew that she knew what he was thinking.

Springer said, "I will take you as far as Tennyson. After that, you must find Isabel Gowdie on your own."

"Very well, then," said Kasyx. "Let's do it. Mol Besa? Shall we go?"

One by one, the Night Warriors rose through the ceiling of Springer's living room, through the attic where the water tanks gurgled, through the tiles of the roof, and out into the frosty night. They flew silently, like kites, absorbed by the air, crystallized by the frost, invisible except for the faintest of glitters and the slightest distortion of the sky.

They circled over a cold and sleeping London; a London

through which the Thames lazily curved; a London of orange streetlights and silent formal squares. From high above Richmond, looking towards the east, Mol Besa could see the wan moonlike face of Big Ben and the secretive Gothic spires of the Palace of Westminster. It was too foggy for him to be able to see Nelson's Column or the dome of St. Paul's; but he was strangely reassured by knowing that they were there, as they always would be.

This was the London over which Peter Pan and Wendy had flown; and there was still something childishly magical in the way that the Night Warriors wheeled over Kew Gardens and descended towards Tennyson.

Mol Besa noticed that, as Springer flew through the night, she left behind her a trail of absolute darkness. No stars, no lights, nothing. A darkness of such intensity that nothing could penetrate it. He wondered if absolute darkness and absolute light were one and the same, perpetual, yin and yang; if Ashapola was Satan and Satan was Ashapola; and if, therefore, the Night Warriors were being asked to risk their lives for nothing more than the spinning of the same two-sided coin.

He could feel that same two-sidedness within his own personality. On one side, the calling to be selflessly heroic, to burst through the realms of darkness with a sword of righteous light. On the other side, the lust to damage and destroy.

—to cut a swathe through the—

The Night Warriors circled over Kew Gardens Road. Springer said, inside of their minds. *I must leave you now. This task is yours. May Ashapola keep you and bless you and may you all return safely from the realm of dreams.*

"I'll second that," said Mol Besa under his breath.

Kasyx led the way. In a diving, corkscrew motion, he descended through Tennyson's roof, through the ceiling, and into the upstairs bedroom. The rest of the Night Warriors followed him in quick succession.

"It's raining in here!" Kasyx exclaimed in astonishment.

The storm was dramatically worse than the first time that Stanley and Angie and Gordon had ventured into the house. The whole room shook with thunder, and the rain lashed down so hard that Mol Besa, in his glass helmet, was almost blinded.

"This is her dream!" Mol Besa shouted to Kasyx. "Her Carriers use this house as a way of escaping from the real world!"

"I'm soaking!" Effis complained.

Kasyx looked around the room. Then he nodded. "We should be able to enter this dream as easily as any other. The dream's pretty hostile, and the dreamer's a long ways off. But—why not? Let's give it a try. The quicker we get ourselves in, the quicker we'll be able to get ourselves out."

"I'm all for that," said Mol Besa.

"All right, then, stand close together," Kasyx ordered. The five Night Warriors stood back-to-back in a circle, their hands clasped together. Zasta looked up at Mol Besa, his blind visor giving nothing away; but Mol Besa sensed his question in the angle he was holding his head.

"Everything's going to be fine," he told him. "We'll have this witch licked before you even know it."

"Pop—"Zasta began; but Mol Besa shook his head.

"I know, son. Believe me, I feel the same way." *In spite of everything, I love you.*

Kasyx lifted one hand and described an octagon in the air above their heads, in pure blue energy. The octagon hummed and trembled for a moment. Then slowly it began to widen and sink, until it shimmered on the floor all around them, as if they had been lassoed by vibrant blue light.

"Before, we were looking at the dream and experiencing it secondhand," Kasyx explained. "The moment we step out of this octagon, we will be *inside* the dream, living it."

"Just like it's real?" asked Effis.

Kasyx slowly shook his heavy-helmeted head. "It won't be *like* real. It will *be* real."

They stepped out of the octagon and found that they were stepping off sodden carpet on to muddy ground. The walls of the bedroom had vanished, and all they could see was a rainswept landscape of low horizons and huddled huts. Mol Besa took two or three steps forward and then stopped, listening to the rain pattering on his helmet. In the distance, sheet lightning flickered fitfully behind the piggeries. He was back in Isabel Gowdie's seventeenth-century London; the London of rutted roads and mud and plague.

Gut the pig and bite the toad.

Kasyx came trudging up to him through the mire. "I hope you know the way to Dover," he complained, "because I sure as hell don't."

Mol Besa punched a series of small silver buttons on his holographic astrolabe. Immediately, a three-dimensional image of the southeast of England appeared on his instrument panel, with hills and forests and villages. A gold-glowing ribbon indicated the route they should take to Dover.

Keldak came up and peered over Mol Besa's shoulder.

"That's over sixty miles away," he complained. "I couldn't walk sixty miles in a week, let alone a single night. Let *alone* arrive in a fit condition to do battle with a witch."

"Don't worry about that," said Kasyx. "Mol Besa can formulate a way for us to get there."

Mol Besa tapped two different programs into his instrument panel. The first program proposed converting the psychic tension they had created simply by trespassing in Isabel Gowdie's dream into kinetic energy. This energy would be more than enough to enable them to fly to Dover in the same way that they had flown over London. But Mol Besa was worried that depleting this tension might seriously reduce the validity of their physical presence in the dream, so that they would be wavering right on the very edge of dream and reality. Isabel Gowdie would then find it comparatively easy to expel them from her dream, if she wanted to.

The second program suggested time-compression: speeding up a twelve-hour walk to twelve seconds. The snag was that this program would use up most of their backup energy: they would be able to fight with the energy they had already, but there wouldn't be anything left in reserve.

"It's a hell of a risk," said Kasyx. "We could easily find ourselves in the position of having to choose between destroying Isabel Gowdie or escaping from out of the dream. In other words, this could be a kamikaze mission. Once our energy's gone, there's no way of getting back; not unless another charge-keeper comes in to rescue us."

"Isn't there any other way of getting to Dover?" asked Keldak. It was raining hard now, and his green helmet was beaded with drops of water.

Mol Besa shook his head. "We could levitate in low-level orbit, and allow the world to pass under us; but that would take all of the energy in Kasyx's reserves."

"What's it to be, then?" asked Kasyx.

Mol Besa said, "Time-compression, that's my personal choice. We can get to Dover in twelve seconds flat, which will make it much more difficult for Knitted Hood to follow us, and if we're fast enough, we might be able to locate Isabel Gowdie before he realizes where we are."

"We can find her," put in Zasta. "We can find her easy."

"Oh, yes?" asked Mol Besa. "And how're we going to do that?"

"Springer gave me this," said Zasta, and held out the talisman that Mol Besa had found in the drawer in Springer's kitchen, the rusted Celtic cross tied with rotten linen. "Springer said that it was torn from Isabel Gowdie's throat when she was condemned to be burned by the Scottish court. It's supposed to bring people back to life. But it would never work for anybody else, only Isabel Gowdie. When it gets close to Isabel Gowdie, it's supposed to sing. The judges in the Scottish court blindfolded it, because they thought it could see."

Mol Besa held out his hand, and hesitantly Zasta wound up the talisman's string and passed it over. Mol Besa pressed the talisman tightly against the palm of his hand. It was dead cold; and it was silent. "She's not here, she's nowhere near here. But if this really works—"

"Springer said she was sure that it works," Zasta insisted.

"Why did she give it to you, instead of directly to me?"

"She said you might not believe her."

"And what else?"

"She said that you might have argued against taking it into the dream. She said that half of you wants to find Isabel Gowdie and the other half doesn't."

"I see," said Mol Besa. "If that's the way she feels, then you'd better keep it, in case I accidentally on purpose lose it, or pretend that I can't hear it singing."

"It's all right," said Zasta. "*You* keep it. Springer said you should. It's kind of an act of faith. Something to help you to focus your belief."

It was extraordinary for Mol Besa to hear his ten-year-old son talking like this. But Kasyx had been right. As a Night Warrior, Zasta was far more mature, far more assured. As well as the education of a good modern grade school, he had the wisdom of the centuries and the inherited experience of scores of previous lives.

"Okay," said Mol Besa, and lowered Isabel Gowdie's talisman around his helmet. "Let's go witch-hunting."

The Night Warriors stood close together, their armor trickling with rain. Mol Besa punched into his instrument panel the full formula for time-compression, which was a fascinating reworking of Einstein's theory of relativity, formulated laterally rather than progressively.

As he completed the formula, Mol Besa saw a dark triangular shadow emerge from behind the piggeries. It remained motionless for a long while; then it moved slightly and he could see the pale oval of Knitted Hood's face. As he had promised, Knitted Hood was watching him, following him. Mol Besa smiled grimly to himself. He hoped for Knitted Hood's sake that he was capable of traveling at eighteen thousand miles an hour, because that was how fast the Night Warriors would be traveling on their way to Dover. He took a shining cartridge out of his ammunition belt and slotted it into the side of the instrument panel. There was a brief, high-pitched gabbling noise as the program was loaded into the cartridge. Then Mol Besa took the cartridge out, drew back the sliding chamber of his equation gun, and loaded it.

Knitted Hood watched him without moving. Acrid brown smoke drifted through the rain, carrying the smell of wet timber smoldering, and hessian, and human flesh. Isabel Gowdie's dream was a charnel house, a crematorium of the human spirit.

Mol Besa said, "Ready?" and prepared to fire. As he did so, however, the girl with the cart appeared, only fifty or sixty yards away, trundling another load of nodding white bodies along the rutted track. She turned her head to stare at them as she passed them by; and again Mol Besa had the nagging sensation that he knew her, that he had seen her somewhere before. Yet he couldn't place her; and before he could look at her more closely, she had turned her head away and continued along the track.

A dead arm swung from the side of her handcart, beckoning, beckoning. A child's body slipped sideways as she negotiated a particularly-deep rut; and stared at Mol Besa with bruised unseeing eyes.

"Some dream," Keldak remarked. "This is more like a nightmare."

"Life *was* a nightmare in those days," Kasyx commented. "Just think about it: we've only had antibiotics since World War II. If you caught anything serious in the seventeenth century ... if you caught the *flu* in the seventeenth century, you'd be lucky to survive it."

"Come on, let's get it over with," urged Effis. "I 'ate this place. The sooner we're out of it, the better."

Mol Besa lifted his equation pistol and squeezed the double trigger. There was a sharp crackling noise, and a thin beam of red laserlike light came whipping out of the muzzle, curving around them. It spun faster and faster, around and around, until it had enclosed them in a basket of interlaced red light.

They could hear nothing but the laser's deafening crackle, like having an untuned radio pressed against each ear. Then there was a taut, deeply-pressurized implosion. Zasta shouted out loud. The world rushed in on them from all sides, like an avalanche, and they were buried in solid silence. They couldn't move, couldn't speak, couldn't see. All they had was the helpless understanding that they were compressing twelve hours of their lives into twelve seconds; that for each of those seconds they were hurtling towards Dover at an unimaginable velocity, disobeying the laws of time and space and gravity.

Twelve seconds seemed to last forever. But then Mol Besa heard rain prickling against his helmet again, and opened his eyes. The Night Warriors were standing together on the gray battlements of Dover Castle, overlooking the battleship-gray waves of the English channel.

The strange thing was that this was present-day Dover, with its customs sheds and warehouses and cross-Channel ferry terminals. Through the rain and the mist, Mol Besa could see a Sealink ferry disembarking trucks and cars, and a hovercraft leaving on its way to Boulogne.

"This isn't the seventeenth century," said Keldak. "We seem to have traveled in *time*, as well as space."

But Kasyx said, "No, no. We're in a dream, and dreams don't have any kind of logic like that. You can walk from one room to another in a dream, and jump three hundred years without even blinking."

Mol Besa clasped the talisman in his hand and looked around. "She's here somewhere. She must be. She knows present-day Dover because she's close; she can feel it. She may even be able to see it. But London looks like seventeenth-century London because that's the only London she ever knew."

"Then she can't be very far away."

Mol Besa held up the talisman in the flat of his hand. "If it sings, then we'll know she's here for sure.

"*Sing*," he pleaded under his breath. "Come on, you have to *sing*." He turned the talisman one way, and then the other way.

"It's not singing yet," said Effis dubiously.

"It will," Zasta retorted.

"Well, it might and it might not..." said Kasyx. "There's no harm in giving it a try."

Mol Besa walked along the wet granite-gray stones of the castle battlements, lifting the talisman this way and that, and calling on Ashapola to help him. Kasyx would have been surprised if he hadn't. Entering a dream for the very first time was wildly unbalancing and infuriatingly disconcerting; and it was only after eight or nine dreams that Kasyx had eventually acquired his "dream legs"—his ability to keep his balance and his sanity, no matter how much the ground cracked open beneath his feet, no matter what imaginary monsters he had to face.

Mol Besa stood facing the rain-laden wind, looking around him. The hovercraft had long disappeared towards France in a fuming cloud of spray; the ferry stood empty, waiting for refueling. Dover looked wet and dismal, all the way from Cowgate Cemetery to East Cliff. Through the rain, Mol Besa could see the tower of the Pharos, the lighthouse that the Romans had built to guide them towards Dover, and St. Mary's Church. The Channel looked so realistic, with its mud-streaked waters, that it was difficult to believe that this was somebody else's dream.

Effis slid up to Mol Besa on her shimmering skates. "P'raps we ought to take a look at the cliffs ... she might be 'idden in one of the tunnels."

Mol Besa lowered the talisman and nodded. "Maybe you're light. I just hope that Dover was the right guess. She could have been buried anywhere from here to Brighton. It could take us *years* to find her."

Keldak came up, too. "No luck, my love?" he asked.

Mol Besa shook his head.

"I'm sure she's here," said Keldak. "I can *smell* her, do you know what I mean? And I'm sure Kasyx is right ... if she *weren't* here, she wouldn't know what present-day Dover looked like, would she?"

He nodded toward the talisman. "No joy with that?"

"Nothing."

"It's just an idea ... but perhaps you should try taking off the strip of linen. I mean, if the Scottish court put it on because they thought the cross could *see* ..."

"Maybe you've got something there." Mol Besa lifted the talisman, and Effis unpicked the tight linen knot with her fingernails. Soon the corroded Celtic cross was unbound, the way it had been when Isabel Gowdie wore it herself. Mol Besa held it up again and said, "Ashapola ... guide us. Ashapola ... help us to find the witch-woman."

There was a long moment when they heard nothing but the wind from the Channel buffeting in their ears, and the occasional clanging from the docks. The rain sprinkled against their helmets and dripped from their fins and their weapon racks and their power hookups. Then—very softly, very thinly—they heard a keening sound. It was like the squeal of wheels of a distant freight train, in a marshaling yard, squealing on and on and on.

Mol Besa lifted the talisman higher, and the keening grew sharper and louder. There was no question about it—it was Isabel Gowdie's talisman, calling to its mistress. *Mistress, I'm here! Mistress, I've found you at last!*

Mol Besa turned around in a circle. There was no question that the talisman keened more loudly when he held it towards the southwest.

"What's in that direction?" he asked Effis.

"Folkestone," said Effis. "The next port along."

"Anything else?"

"I dunno. I'm not a blinking geography expert, am I?"

"Tunnels! You mentioned tunnels!" Keldak said, his voice almost falsetto with excitement.

"That's right," said Effis. "They was always digging tunnels in these cliffs."

"But they've started digging another tunnel, much more recently! A tunnel that the Night Warriors in the seventeenth century couldn't possibly have imagined would ever be dug!"

Kasyx frowned behind his visor. "What are you getting at?"

"The Channel Tunnel, of course! They've started digging

the Channel Tunnel just southwest of here! They're doing it from a place called Shakespeare Cliff!"

Shakespeare Cliff. The Bard's Disease. Suddenly, the reappearance of the Night Plague began to make an awful kind of sense. Mol Besa punched in the map inquiries to locate the English end of the Channel Tunnel working, and then overlaid the coordinates with the directional signal from Isabel Gowdie's talisman.

A three-dimensional image of Shakespeare Cliff and the tunnel that had been bored beneath it was created in scintillating light and color on his instrument panel. A hill, a cliff, an approach road. Even tiny moving images of the contractor's vehicles, crawling in and out of the tunnel entrance.

Across this image, a penetratingly thin green line passed from one side to the other—representing the exact direction in which the talisman keened the most loudly. The thin green line passed precisely through the eastern wall of the tunnel, 175 yards in.

"That's it," breathed Kasyx. "We've found her. She's there."

They left the castle and descended into the town. Although it was a sharp representation of modern-day Dover, almost unreal in its clarity and detail, the people who filled the streets were the same distorted cripples and plague victims who had populated Isabel Gowdie's dream-London. Suspicious eyes watched them from shops and cafés and garages. As they passed the offices of the National Union of Seamen, they saw blue-tinted lobsterlike faces pressed against the glass.

Some of the passersby were blurred and only half formed, as if they had been painted in oils and then smeared while the paint was still wet.

It took them nearly a half hour to reach the Channel Tunnel workings. A wide cutting had been hewn through the chalky downs, and earth-moving trucks toiled in and out of it, their wheels thick with whitish mud. The Night Warriors stood above the tunnel entrance for a while, the five of them silhouetted against the rainy sky, listening to the noise of drilling and blasting and the blaring of heavy vehicles.

"All right, then," said Kasyx at last, "let's take a look at this lady."

They descended the wet chalky slope. Mol Besa noticed that Zasta stayed close to him, and thought to himself: *He might be a Night Warrior, but he's still my son.* He turned around and saw that Effis was close behind him, too. Maybe he could still give people strength; maybe he could still give them guidance. The Night Plague hadn't yet overwhelmed him altogether.

They had almost reached the tunnel entrance when a heavily-built misshapen man appeared. He wore a builder's donkey jacket and chalk-filthy overalls, and he walked with a swiveling limp. He stood in front of them, leaning to one side, barring their way. His eyes were small and colorless and piggish, and the waxy skin of his face seemed to ripple and shift.

"'Ere, you're trespassing," he told them. His voice was a treble-noted blare. "Don't you know it's dangerous?"

"We're inspectors," said Kasyx ambiguously.

"You can't come down 'ere," the misshapen man repeated.

"We have to," said Kasyx.

"You're not allowed to," the misshapen man insisted, taking a threatening step towards them.

Keldak started to peel off his left-hand glove; but Kasyx

leaned towards Mol Besa and Keldak and whispered, "Remember—he's a figment of Isabel Gowdie's dream. She's checking us out, protecting herself."

He was right. The misshapen man circled around them, eyeing them up and down. His face constantly altered as he looked at them: his chin bulging, his cheeks sinking, his forehead sloping. But after he had completed a full circle, he said, in a peculiarly feminine voice, "All right. You can take a look around if you want to."

He stood aside, and one by one they walked past him and into the massive vestibule of the tunnel. There were lights and generators and trucks everywhere, and miles of snaking cable; and vast yellow-painted earth-boring machines bellowed past them on their way to the tunnel face.

The noise inside the tunnel was shattering. Mol Besa could hardly hear himself think. What Isabel Gowdie must have suffered when the Channel Tunnel company came boring into Shakespeare Cliff, he couldn't even imagine.

The five of them walked along the tunnel until Mol Besa's instrument panel told them that they had reached the precise point where the talisman's signal intersected with the holographic map of the Channel Tunnel. Mol Besa lifted his hand and shouted, "This is it! We're here! We've made it!"

The rest of the Night Warriors stopped and looked around. The tunnel walls were chalk-white and glossy with wet; white and glossy as Knitted Hood's mask. There were lights everywhere; working-lamps and halogen inspection lamps; so bright that Kasyx had darkened the glass of his visor; but no sign anywhere of Isabel Gowdie.

"You're sure this is the right place?" Kasyx bellowed at Mol Besa.

Mol Besa lifted the talisman up to the side of his helmet and he could hear it singing: a high-pitched screaming that tore through his ears like the blade of a tile-cutting saw.

"The cross seems to think that it is!" he shouted back. "And my instruments are absolutely sure of it!"

"Then where is she?" Kasyx demanded. "I don't see her anywhere!"

They prowled up and down, running their hands over the walls, kicking at the floor, staring up at the thirty-foot ceiling. All the time, compressors roared, drills hammered, and workmen shouted to each other.

"She's not here!" Keldak called out. "If you ask me, dear, she's been leading you all round the bushes!"

"She's here!" Mol Besa insisted, jabbing at his instrument panel. "Look at this image … this is the tunnel, and this is where the Celtic cross is creating the maximum signal. It's audiovisual mathematics, plain and simple. She's *here*!"

"All right, then, if she's here, where is she?" Keldak demanded. "If you're so incredibly clever, *where*?"

It was then that Zasta tugged at Mol Besa's arm. Mol Besa looked down at him and saw that Zasta was pointing halfway up the drilted-chalk tunnel wall. "What?" he said. "What is it?" But Zasta said simply, "Look."

Mol Besa peered up at the wall. At first he couldn't see anything at all. But gradually he realized what he was looking at. There were four small protrusions on the surface of the chalk, no larger than fingertips. And that is what they were, fingertips. The Channel Tunnel drilling machines had missed Isabel Gowdie's imprisoned body by less than twelve inches, although they had broken away just enough of the solid chalk to expose her fingertips.

Mol Besa stood for almost half a minute, staring at those fingertips. They belonged to a woman who had been incarcerated for over three centuries in solid white limestone: a woman whose evil had been so fearful that the Night Warriors had found it necessary to seal her and bind her and keep her imprisoned in the deepest cliff they could find. Only the unforeseeable progress of civil engineering had released Isabel Gowdie from her eternal bondage; only a circumstance which would have seemed beyond imagination in 1666—even to those who were used to running through the wildest imaginings of dreaming men and women.

Kasyx shouted, "She's still trapped! But all she needed was the smallest access to the outside world—that would have been more than enough for her to wake up her Carriers!"

"What do you suggest we do?" asked Mol Besa.

"We have to dig her out of there, first of all. Then you and she have to do the business ... otherwise you're going to be stuck with that Night Plague for all eternity. Then we have to zap her."

"Easy, no problem," said Mol Besa with undisguised sarcasm.

"It won't be, believe me!" Kasyx yelled back. "Keldak! Effis! Zasta! Keep guard! I'm going to chisel this lady out of the rock!"

"But this is only a dream!" Mol Besa shouted.

"That's right! She was imprisoned in a dream, we can dig her out in a dream!"

"But if it's only a dream, how come she was freed by the *real* digging of the *real* Channel Tunnel?"

"Because, my friend, her body was buried in the waking

world, while her soul was buried in the dream world. You can't bury a soul in the waking world, it will never rest ... as anyone who has ever had a dream about a dead husband or a dead wife or a dead friend will tell you. By the same token, you can't bury somebody's fleshly body in the dream world, either. That's why people find it so important to *physically* bury their dead. The Night Warriors buried Isabel Gowdie in both waking and dreaming states ... just to make absolutely sure that she could never escape, never again."

"And now we're going to dig her out?" asked Mol Besa, looking up at the wet chalk wall with awe.

Kasyx nodded. "That's right, Mol Besa. Now we're going to dig her out."

Mol Besa looked at him narrowly. "Supposing I told you that I didn't want to do this? That I'd rather leave her where she is? I mean, surely we can cover up her fingers, and that'll seal her off again."

"Mol Besa, you have the Night Plague," Kasyx shouted back. "Thousands of British kids have the Night Plague, too. This woman is feeding it; this woman is Satan's soup kitchen. You have to get rid of your own infection; and then make sure that everybody else gets rid of it, too. You have to!"

Mol Besa nodded. He felt as if his head were bursting apart. Kasyx beckoned to Keldak and shouted in his ear, "Target your fist to knock away the wall ... a cuboid, okay? About that size. I don't want her injured. It looks like she's probably caught up in some kind of struggling posture ... you see what I mean? One hand out in front of her, and the other one behind, like she's running through solid chalk."

Keldak looked quickly at Kasyx and then said, "Okay ... I'll do what I can."

The Night Warriors stood away from the limestone wall; all except Keldak, who approached it slowly, sizing it up with foxy, perceptive, calculating eyes. As he did so, he peeled off his left glove, and the well-lit tunnel workings were even more brightly lit by the beams of solid energy that radiated from his fist. His fist was so dazzling, in fact, that Mol Besa had to shield his eyes with his hand; and then, his eyes swimming with dozens of afterimages of Keldak's fingers, Mol Besa had to turn away as well.

The holographic satellite that floated in the air on the left side of Keldak's helmet orbited silently through ninety degrees until it was hovering in front of his facepiece. Keldak programmed it deftly and competently ... creating within its target parameters a six-foot cuboid in the limestone wall in front of them ... a block of chalk which would contain Isabel Gowdie, entire and unhurt.

"I hope this works," he told Kasyx nervously. "I've never done anything like this before."

Kasyx smiled. "Sure you've done it before. You've probably done it hundreds of times before. Keldak was mentioned in one of the earliest Night Warriors chronicles that I've ever seen ... way back in the thirteenth century. Just because you've forgotten that you've done this before, that doesn't mean you can't remember how to do it."

"If you say so," Keldak replied without much conviction.

His holographic globe swung smoothly back to its "parked" position on the left side of his helmet. He slowly lifted his left arm, with its blindingly-bright fist, and for two or three seconds he closed his eyes tight, concentrating.

"Come on, Keldak, now's the time," Kasyx encouraged him.

Keldak arched his back, stiffened his arm, and shouted out, *"Ashapola!"*

His fist flew from his wrist with an ear-splitting rush like a subway train. It struck the curved chalk wall and hammered right into it, hosing a spray of pulverized limestone behind it. It disappeared completely into the rock, although flickering shafts of blinding white light played through the dust as it furiously chiseled out the cuboid that Keldak had programmed it to cut for him.

There was already so much noise in the tunnel that the hammering of Keldak's fist went unnoticed. But Effis and Zasta still kept watch on the tunnel entrance, where trucks and workmen came and went, and sheets of rain still poured steadily down from a gray and doleful sky.

More chalk dust spurted out of the groove that Keldak's fist had cut. Then, for a while, the light subsided, as the fist cut out the back of the cuboid, which would detach the block from the tunnel wall. Keldak raised his left arm, and already a second fist was forming on the stump of his wrist, to replace the one which was exhuming Isabel Gowdie.

"You ever deal with a witch before?" Mol Besa shouted.

Kasyx shook his head. "One or two demons. Never a witch."

"I'm scared," said Mol Besa.

"What of? Yourself or the witch?"

"Myself, mostly. I don't know what I might do."

"Just hang in there," Kasyx replied. "If you think you're going to need help, just don't hesitate to ask for it. Night Warriors work together, remember. We're a team."

Mol Besa nodded. But all the same, he was beginning to feel the stirrings of some extraordinary blackness inside him, like a stick stirring molasses. His blood jangled through his veins, and he was breathing in short, stressful gasps. *I've found her*, he thought. *I've found her at last. Now she can change the world in the way that she was always meant to change the world. Now she can spread the Night Plague from pole to pole.*

He swallowed dryly and glanced quickly at Keldak to make sure that Keldak hadn't picked up any psychic echoes. In dreams, you never knew what powers other people might have; what inspirations. Keldak, however, was much too busy watching his dazzling fist hammer out the last of the limestone block. His green armor was covered by a fine film of chalk dust, and he had raised his visor so that he could see better.

Mol Besa looked towards Effis. Behind her lacework mask, Effis's eyes appeared unusually dark, and when she realized that Mol Besa was watching her, she bared her teeth in the briefest of suggestive grins. It was a grin that said *I'll do things to you that you never imagined possible. I'll love you and I'll hurt you, you bastard. I'll love you till you bleed.* So she was being affected, too. The Night Plague had infected them both with the lust and cruelty and faithlessness of Satan; and here they were, only feet away from Satan's favorite servant. Their stomachs churned with nausea; their arteries were burning. The baleful influence of Isabel Gowdie grew stronger and stronger with every hammer of Keldak's fist.

There was a clattering tumble of rocks and heavy lurching noise. Keldak's fist had now smashed its way all around the limestone block. All that remained now was for the block to be forced out of the tunnel wall. Keldak swung his holographic globe around again and retargeted it. His second fist flashed from his wrist, *zwafffff*! blinding them all with its magnesium-bright flare. It vanished into the groove around the block in a brilliant interplay of dust and light. There was a second's pause, and then it detonated all of its energy at once, forcing the block to shudder two feet out of the rock face.

When the dust had settled, Kasyx stepped forward and laid his hand on the block. "Mol Besa, you and I can lift this out between us. If you can just give us a little mathematical assistance ..."

Mol Besa punched three different equations into his instrument panel. The first postulated freezing the air just below the lower edge of the block, to form a ramp of ice down which they could slide the block with the minimum of effort. The second suggested sending this whole section of the tunnel wall far into the future, to a time when Shakespeare Cliff would have been worn away by natural erosion. The third was simply to create a localized vacuum just in front of the block, so that it would be forced out of the tunnel wall by the surrounding air pressure.

He checked the comparative energy levels which these differing solutions would require. The vacuum pull would be the noisiest and the most untidy, but by far the least extravagant. They needed to be thrifty with their power: especially if Knitted Hood caught up with them before they managed to destroy Isabel Gowdie.

"All right, let's stand clear," he said. "I'm going to evacuate a cuboid of air exactly equivalent to the size of the block, so the block will be pushed right out of the tunnel wall to fill it. Once it's out, it's going to drop two feet, and that's probably going to damage it. So watch out for flying debris."

"And watch out for Isabel Gowdie, too," warned Kasyx. "She's one powerful witch, and she's been imprisoned in this cliff for three hundred years, so she's going to be seriously pissed."

Mol Besa loaded his vacuum equation into a cartridge and then slotted the cartridge into his gun. "Are you ready?" he asked Kasyx.

Kasyx nodded. "Let's do it. Ms. Gowdie wants out, and out is what site's going to get. But let's just remember one thing, huh? This is *her* dream, she controls it, and we're just here under sufferance. If things look for a moment like they're going wrong, that's the moment we pull the plug and exit. We can always get her another day."

"Says you," put in Effis.

Kasyx didn't quite know how to take that comment, but lifted his hand and said, "All right, Mol Besa. Let's get this block out of the wall, shall we?" All the same, he kept his eyes on Effis. Behind the mask of a Night Warrior, he could detect the voice of somebody who was already half suborned to Satan.

As Kasyx turned away, something in Mol Besa's head whispered *SATAN*. He looked around, his hair prickling. He didn't realize that Isabel Gowdie had picked up the name of her Master from Kasyx's thoughts, and amplified them through solid limestone in a desperate *cri de coeur*.

SATAN, the voice echoed and reechoed, like the voice of somebody falling and falling down an endless nightmare well. *SATAN is the pestilence that was—*

"Promised," said Effis. The other Night Warriors stared

at her: all except Mol Besa, who knew exactly what she meant. Without any further hesitation, he pulled the double triggers of his equation gun, and the cartridge flashed into the air and exploded right in front of the limestone block.

Mol Besa knew that he was converting mathematical formulae into pure energy, but he hadn't seen an equation cartridge explode before. Glittering numbers burst through the air like a napalmed bowl of alphabet soup, actual numbers and letters, $1/\sqrt{(1 - v2/ c2)}$ m $mo/\sqrt{(1 - v2/c2)}$. They tumbled and whirled, and then assembled themselves into thin sparkling lines of tingling incandescent energy.

"God Almighty," said Effis; and then the huge limestone block was wrenched out of the tunnel wall with a thunderous rush, and collapsed on to the tunnel floor, falling over on to its side and splitting from one corner to the other.

The Celtic cross around Mol Besa's neck shrieked so piercingly that it made his teeth ache. He tugged it away from him, breaking the string, and thrust it into one of the wallets around his waist.

There was a moment's pause, while the chalk dust gradually settled, and large pieces of limestone dropped off the sides of the block and fell cloaking on to the tunnel floor. Mol Besa quickly looked around, but none of the workers in the tunnel appeared to be taking any notice of what they were doing ... presumably because Isabel Gowdie didn't want them to. They were creations of *her* imagination; they would do whatever she wished.

Suddenly, a startling white light shone from the center of the broken block. It streamed out in all directions, like the sun rising over the Arctic, like a blinding welding torch, *white white totally white death white bone white eye-blinding white*. It was so brilliant that, by comparison, Keldak's fist looked like a dull light bulb.

Large rugged triangular lumps of chalk began to fall away. The block was disintegrating in front of their eyes. The dazzle from inside it was so intense that all of them darkened their visors or shielded their eyes. The energy was pure white but there was no question at all about its origins. It was the power of *total absolute* evil. It was Satan's power: relentlessly destructive, like unshielded radiation. The kind of power that could pass right through your body and phosphorize your bones and curse your family's genes for generation after generation, one distorted chromosome after another.

All the children down all the centuries to come, who would suffer pain because of this single blast of blinding power. *And we shall cut a swathe through the world.*

Mol Besa stepped back, tugging Zasta back at the same time. He had imagined Isabel Gowdie in dozens of different manifestations. A hag, a harpie, a blank-eyed siren. A seductive young woman with a bagful of spells. But he had never imagined that she would look like this; or that when she appeared, he would be so overawed.

The last fragments of chalk dropped aside, and Isabel Gowdie was free. She lay on her back on a bier of crumbled limestone, one hand still defiantly raised. It was that gesture of defiance that had led to her fingertips being exposed by the tunnel diggers; and to the Carriers waking up, after three hundred years, and to the renewed spreading of the Night Plague. Out of those four fingertips had passed the Satanic energy that had cursed England for the past two years with sickness and violence and tragedy—air disasters, rail crashes, prison riots, shootings, maimings, mindless murders, rapes, burnings—a sickness that would eventually spread dream by dream all over the world, if the Night Warriors didn't destroy Isabel Gowdie tonight and spread her ashes so widely that they could never be gathered together again.

Isabel Gowdie was tall and slender, emaciated by centuries of entombment. Her skin was white, her cheeks hollow, her jawline sharp. Her long white tangled hair rose into the air in a coruscating fan, giving off boundless energy and light. A white linen blindfold had been tied around her eyes, and her temples were studded with a coronet of seventeenth-century screws, which in those days had simply been twisted nails. The screws had been driven right into her skull, and Mol Besa intuitively knew that they were part of the Night Warriors' ritual of sealing a witch's mind, the Crown of Screws.

She was completely naked, with protuberant ribs and hook-like hipbones. Her breasts were small and slanted, and on each nipple the Night Warriors had placed their seal of black wax, imprinted with the double cross of Ashapola. More black-wax seals had been placed on her shoulders, on her knees, on her ankles, and on her wrists. It was only because the seal on her right wrist had cracked and split apart that she had been able to raise her hand while she was being buried in the limestone; a momentary gesture which, after more than three centuries, had at last assured her release.

Between the hairless lips of her sex, the shaft of a huge tarnished silver cross had been inserted; a last sacred gesture to ensure that—even if she were found—no demon or devil would be able to have intercourse with her, to reproduce their kind, and that even if Satan had made her pregnant before she was imprisoned, his offspring would never be able to leave her body.

Mol Besa slowly approached her. His emotions were churning wildly; his blood surged through his arteries; his brain boiled. She remained motionless and blindfolded, her one arm raised, with white light streaming in all directions. He felt her power. It was like standing in a hurricane-force wind, or opening a blast furnace, or falling a thousand feet into an icy Arctic lake. He felt wildly exhilarated, bursting with power. *This is what I've been searching for, all these years. This power, this influence. This, this, this! Now I'll be able to play the violin again, and play not like Stanley Eisner, but like God Almighty! Now they'll fall in front of me, now they'll weep!*

But there was something else, too. He was terrified of her. She was sightless and naked and fastened with holy seals, but he was terrified of her.

"What am I supposed to do?" he asked, turning to Kasyx. His mouth felt as if it were stuffed with dry cotton wadding.

"You have to withdraw the cross; then you have to have sex with her," Kasyx told him. "At the instant you ejaculate, the Night Plague virus will rush back into her body."

"Why should it do that?" Mol Besa asked.

"Simple," Kasyx explained. "The virus is always voraciously hungry. It's always trying to get back to its Maker, the one who created it, the one from whom it derives its nourishment. I mean, why should it put up with irregular supplies of thinly-strained baby food, when it can suckle directly from Satan's favorite servant? Or even, if it's lucky; from Satan himself?"

"What then?" asked Mol Besa numbly.

"That, my friend, is when we take her apart. That precise instant. Effis will cut off her head, Zasta will cut her to pieces, and Keldak will pulverize those pieces into dust, and then yours truly will incinerate that dust into ash. Then all five of us will scatter that ash as far apart as any ashes were ever scattered, in the definite hope that Mistress Gowdie is lost and gone forever."

"*Riboyne Shel Olem*," Mol Besa whispered.

"Absolutely," Kasyx agreed. "Now you know why I gave up drinking. The kick you get out of this makes Smirnoff seem stupid."

Mol Besa stood as close to Isabel Gowdie as he dared. He knew that she couldn't move; he knew that she was powerless, except to direct her Carriers. All the same, he felt overwhelmingly intimidated; and having sex with her seemed impossible.

Kasyx came up and stood beside him. "Mol Besa," he said, "it's the only way. It's either this or damnation; and I've seen a glimpse of damnation, and I'd rather have sex with Isabel Gowdie every morning before breakfast for the rest of my life, believe me, than be sent to hell. It's hell in hell. Take my word for it."

"You've *seen* hell?" Mol Besa asked him. Anything to delay the moment when he would have to climb up on that bier of shattered chalk and—

Kasyx took hold of his elbow. "I've dealt with all kinds of demons. Mol Besa … and when you look a demon right in the eye, that's when you see hell. Believe me."

He was calm and reassuring and steadfast, but Mol Besa still felt rigid with panic. *He could have everything;*

everything he had ever craved. He could be wealthy, famous, Eve could be killed in an automobile accident. All he had to do was break those seals and take out that tarnished cross and—

Kasyx said, "Come on, Mol Besa. We don't have too much time."

"I don't know," Mol Besa replied. "Maybe we should give her a chance."

"A *chance*? Look at her! Look at the power that's pouring out of her! That's devilry, Mol Besa. She gave up everything for that. Her humanity, her morality, her mortal soul. She was screwed by Satan, Mol Besa! Not just a nightmare! Not just a figment of anybody's imagination! That monster that floats around inside of our minds; that black thing inside of our joint imagination; that is what physically and actually had intercourse with this woman, Mol Besa, and what he passed on to her she passed on to *you*!"

"I know that," Mol Besa protested. "I know. It's just that—"

Kasyx looked away, making it obvious that he wasn't prepared even to listen.

Mol Besa hesitated, and then he said, "Okay. You win. If that's what I have to do. But do you mind if the others look the other way?"

As it happened, the other Night Warriors were already facing the other way. Not only was the light that Isabel Gowdie radiated too bright for anybody to look at for very long, but they were watching the tunnel workings, and the entrance to the tunnel, for any sign of trouble.

Mol Besa unlatched his belt and his instrument panel and handed them to Kasyx. Then he unclipped his bronze armored leggings, until he was wearing nothing but his helmet, his breastplate, and his boots.

It was damp and chilly in the tunnel. Mol Besa's breath steamed inside his helmet, partially fogging it up, so he took that off, too. The very last thing he felt like doing was having sex. He probably wouldn't be able to manage it, anyway. He was too cold and too frightened and Isabel Gowdie's fleshless body was shining at him as if it had been sculpted out of a winter moon.

Keldak turned around and gave Mol Besa a long, appreciative stare, until Mol Besa grimaced and glared back at him. "Go on, lovey." challenged Keldak. "Do your worst. We're running out of time."

Effis looked at Mol Besa appealingly, eyes wide, although he didn't know whether she was appealing to hint to finish off Isabel Gowdie, to give her back the filthy disease that had infected both of them, and then to chop her to bits and burn her; or whether she was appealing to him to forgive her and to let her go. Zasta didn't even turn around, but vigilantly watched the entrance to the tunnel. Perhaps Zasta didn't want to see the Night Warrior who was his father having sex with any other woman apart from his mother. Mol Besa didn't entirely blame him.

"Come on, Mol Besa," urged Kasyx. He was growing noticeably anxious now. "You have to."

With a sinking sensation of dread, Mol Besa climbed up the crumbling sides of the limestone bier on which Isabel Gowdie was lying. Chalk slid beneath his boot heels. Then, cautiously, he knelt astride her knees. It was so cold that his penis had shrunk to the size of a nine-year-old boy's, but he tried not to think about it, the way that he tried not to think about it when he had been unable to get it on with Eve. *Don't think about it, it'll come up when it wants to.* And sometimes it had.

Isabel Gowdie flared just as brightly. Her hair rose and fell as if she were floating in the sea, except that millions of tiny sparks flowed from the ends of her hair and sparkled out over the tunnel. Mol Besa laid one hand gently on her right thigh. It felt utterly chilled. He hadn't felt anything as cold as that since *(February, Chicago, when he and Eve had been walking together past Marshall Field, and Eve had pressed the palm of her hand against the window and her hand had frozen to the glass.)* He took hold of the tarnished silver cross and slowly withdrew it. There was the faintest tugging sensation as it came out, her pale vaginal lips peeled apart. It was an English altar cross, solid silver. It was untarnished where it had been buried inside her.

Mol Besa handed the cross to Kasyx, who laid it carefully on the ground. Then he shifted himself higher up on Isabel Gowdie's thighs, and took hold of his penis in his hand, and pressed it against her vulva. *This is ridiculous. I can't to it. It's cold and I'm half dressed in armor, and Kasyx and Keldak are watching me, and I'm supposed to be making love to a blindingly white witch with frozen-cold skin who scares me so much that all I want to do is vomit.*

At that moment, Zasta called, "There's somebody coming! Look, over there!"

Mol Besa frowned in the direction that Zasta was pointing. Zasta was right. There were four hooded figures marching down the wet chalk slopes that led to the tunnel entrance. They were difficult to distinguish through the rain, but they had a diseased and raggedy look that reminded Mol Besa of Knitted Hood. They were walking very fast, their coats flapping around their ankles. They were accompanied by six or seven huge dogs, who trotted close beside them, their spines protruding through their brindled rain-slicked skin, saliva swinging from their tongues.

"Carriers," warned Kasyx. "Somebody must have told them that we were here."

Mol Besa said, "What the hell do I do now?"

"Get on with it," Kasyx snapped at him. "The sooner you do it, the sooner we can finish her off."

"Kasyx, I can't!"

"What the hell's the matter with you? Think of something erotic! I don't know—Brigitte Bardot!"

"Brigitte Bardot's about a hundred!"

"Do it!" Kasyx yelled at him. "Whatever turns you on!"

Zasta and Keldak and Effis spread themselves defensively across the tunnel. The Carriers continued to hurry towards them at the same fast walking speed, their coattails flapping in the rain and the wind, their dogs trotting evilly beside them. They looked like the merciless villains in a spaghetti western—faceless, relentless, fast. Their coats were spattered with white mud and their masks were as pale as death.

Mol Besa looked down at Isabel Gowdie. She hadn't moved. Her right arm was still raised, clawing for freedom the way it had clawed for freedom three hundred years ago. He jiggled his penis, but he knew that it wasn't going to rise. He was far too frightened; far too stressful; far too cold. *Perhaps if you take off her blindfold.*

He hesitated. He reached forward with a careful hand. He touched the soft old linen of her blindfold. *Perhaps if you take off her blindfold.*

Kasyx said, "The dogs! Look out for the dogs!"

As the dogs came nearer, closely followed by their bustling masters, the Night Warriors could see that they weren't ordinary dogs. Their faces were pale, their eyes were wide. They were Dobermans and German shepherds and half-breed weimaraners, but they had the heads of men. Men with staring, grotesque expressions, and lips stretched back across their gums. Men with bristling hair and madness in their eyes, but men all the same. As intelligent as men. As cruel as men. But quick, and vicious, and fearless as dogs.

Zasta tried a long shot, to give Mol Besa more time. He lifted his hand for a heavyweight long-distance throwing knife, and it cartwheeled, shining, over his shoulder. He caught it deftly. Then he aimed, reached back, and whipped the knife at dazzling speed straight towards the leading Carrier.

The knife hit the Carrier straight in the face. He clutched the knife handle with both hands, spun around, staggered, and then pulled the knife violently out of his hood. Along with it, he brought his white celluloid mask.

"Again!" said Kasyx, and Zasta tossed two more heavyweight knives. But the Carriers were still fifty yards away, and now that they were ready for them, they dodged the knives easily. They continued to hurry towards the Night Warriors with all the fussy haste of determined killers. They were afraid of nothing; not even death. Hadn't their mistress promised them life everlasting?

Mol Besa found the tightened knot of Isabel Gowdie's blindfold. He picked at it, failing to loosen it at first; but then he managed to pull out one end of it, taking all the tension from it. He hesitated, breathing hard. He glanced at Kasyx but Kasyx was too busy with the Carriers and the men-dogs. What he did now was up to him. What he did now was his decision; and his alone.

"*Hurry*," Kasyx urged.

Mol Besa tugged at Isabel Gowdie's blindfold. The fabric was rotten and began to tear; and through the separated well he caught the pale glittering glimpse of an eye. He tugged harder and dragged the blindfold right off, setting off a shower of white sparks from her hair. And there she was staring at him, the witch-woman, the woman who had touched her foot with one hand and her head with the other, and promised everything in between to Satan.

Her eyes were the palest green, with whites that had the sticky consistency of scarcely-boiled eggs. They were pale, but they had an electrifying effect on him. He felt as if he had been abruptly gripped by the spine and jolted upright; as if every ganglion in his nervous system had been illuminated with cold white light.

The seals, she told him. He didn't know whether she had spoken out loud or not; but he had heard her distinctly. *You must break the seals, Mol Besa.*

Kasyx shouted at him, "Mol Besa? What's wrong?" But the Carriers were hustling even closer now, and the man-dogs had broken into a threatening lope. Kasyx was too busy directing Effis and Zasta and Keldak to be able to worry about Mol Besa.

Effis crouched low over her light-skates, her armor twinkling. The lenses on her skating boots revolved to catch the maximum brightness from the halogen lights in the tunnel; and almost at once her skate blades intensified to brilliant gold. She hesitated for a second, but then Kasyx shouted, "*Go!*" and she flashed across the floor of the tunnel at almost a hundred miles an hour.

She skimmed diagonally across the ground like the most elegant speed-skater there had ever been, building up velocity with easy flourishes of her skates. The man-dogs saw her coming and scattered, but she had targeted a heavy black and ginger German shepherd with a bristling head like Vincent van Gogh. Along the sides of her forearms, her razor-fans opened.

"*Ash-a-pol-aaaaaahhh!*" she screamed. She flashed past the German shepherd as it tried to twist towards her and snatch at her arm. Her razor-fan sliced the side of his face right through to the bone, and all along the side of his body, cutting through fur, muscle, ribs, and internal organs. The man-dog collapsed sideways in a cascading splatter of blood. His tongue fell out of his cheek; his prune-black liver slipped on to the floor. Then, in a thrashing convulsion, stomach and intestines slithered in a heap out of his abdomen, leaving his body as empty as a fur sack.

A whirl of hot, pungent body steam was twisted away by the speed of Effis's passing.

One of the Carriers tried to catch Effis as she skated close by, but she turned a triple somersault in the air, skated around him in a quick, powerful circle, and then turned on him. She flurried her fists in the air like a boxer pummeling at a punching bag, and her razor-fans tore relentlessly into his coat in a whirlwind of sharpened steel. Shreds of fabric flew everywhere. Then the Carrier screamed, a chilling, whistling, high-pitched scream. Lumps of flesh began to burst through the air, then bone. Then his mask was sliced in half, revealing his face.

It was then that Effis stopped pummeling and quickly twisted away, pirouetting as she did so. The Carrier had been revealed for what he was, and as he stood on his feet dying, the other Carriers paused, although they didn't look at him. They kept their eyes on the Night Warriors; and on Isabel Gowdie.

Underneath the mask, the Carrier was exposed as a leper. He was in the last stages of lepromatous leprosy, and his nose and upper lip and most of his jaw had already been ulcerated. His blistered scalp had only a few diseased-looking tufts of hair, and his ears had long gone, leaving him with nothing but dark, encrusted holes.

The leper uttered a strange keening noise, *hoooo-eee-oop*, which was all that he could manage with his collapsed palate and eroded nasal cavity. It was both plaintive and disgusting. Then he dropped to his knees and fell forward. Chunks of gray fibrous flesh fell out of his coat and scattered across the chalky tunnel floor.

The other Carriers had already started to advance on the Night Warriors again; a little more cautiously than before, but still walking at a steady pace. The man-dogs began to fan out, with the obvious intention of circling around them.

Mol Besa meanwhile had done nothing to consummate the act of intercourse with Isabel Gowdie. He sat astride her still, his back rigidly upright, his teeth clenched, with sweat trickling coldly down his back. He was conscious, but he was powerless to move. He understood now why the Night Warriors had blindfolded the witch-woman before they entombed her. She had the Satanic power of hypnotism. The strength of her will streamed from her eyes like the exhaust from twin jet engines, rendering Mol Besa deafened and numb.

Break the seals, she commanded him.

He tried to shake his head. She had persuaded him to remove her blindfold and to lay himself open to a psychokinetic hammerlock, but he was still capable of willful thought; and he knew that if he broke her seals, that was the finish. The Night Warriors would have lost the war, and the Night Plague would sweep across the world in a massive tide of darkness.

Imagine a world without morals or pity. Imagine a world of drugs and cruelty and urban collapse.

Break the seals, Mol Besa, she repeated. Her green eyes widened slightly. *Use your mathematicks; and break the seals.*

Keldak was firing one dazzling first after another. He hit a man-Doberman straight in the face, and the creature's nose-bone cracked and was punched right into his brain. For an instant, the magnesium-bright light from Keldak's fist flashed out of the man-dog's eyes, so that he looked like a hound straight out of hell.

Keldak hit another Carrier, too; a blindingly-bright punch which was swallowed up in the folds of the Carrier's coat. There was a noise like chair legs breaking; and then the Carrier fell to the ground in a flicker of light and a burst of powdery dust.

Zasta threw knives with laconic accuracy. He sent three whirling at one of the man-dogs as it tried to outflank them. The first hit the man-dog in the neck and pinned it against the tunnel wall. The second struck it in the spine; the third caught its back legs. It remained shuddering and shouting, half paralyzed and unable to move, until Zasta threw a heavy execution knife which hit it directly in the heart.

Mol Besa ... you must break the seals ... if you refuse to break them, you will surely die. My Lord and Master will see to that, no matter what happens to me.

Mol Besa squeezed his eyes tightly shut and tried to shake his head. It was then that he felt a cold clawed hand on his naked leg. He opened his eyes again and saw that Isabel Gowdie had managed to move her free right arm, and that her fingers were gradually inching their way up his thigh.

Break the seals, my darling Mol Besa.

"I can't—do that," he gasped. "I came here to—"

One sharp fingernail probed the division between his testicles; one sharp thumbnail scratched at his pubic hair.

I have been taken by the Lord and Master of the Whole World ... surely you didn't think that you could satisfy me?

Slowly, her long chilled fingers began to massage his penis; slowly and erotically, an extraordinary mixture of fear and pleasure, irritation and arousal. As his penis swelled, she began to tug down harder on its outer skin and to dig her nails harder into his flesh.

Break the seals. Mol Besa ... then perhaps I will let you take me.

"I can't," he replied, although it sounded more like a prayer than a denial.

She rubbed the swollen head of his penis up and down between the smooth cold lips of her sex, up an down, up and down, parting it but never quite penetrating it. *Don't you want me, Mol Besa? Don't you want me? Break the seals, Mol Besa, and you can have me!*

She continued to massage him, harder and harder, until

he began to feel that tight knotting between his legs that told him a climax was imminent. If he could only force his way inside her. If he could only warn Kasyx. But Isabel Gowdie's grip on his mind was as uncompromising as the grip on his penis, and the tunnel all around them flashed and flickered with the light of battle, as Kasyx and the rest of the Night Warriors fought to keep the man-dogs and the Carriers at bay.

"*Kasyx!*" shouted Mol Besa.

Kasyx turned around, but at that instant a huge black shaggy wolflike man-dog sprang up on to his back and buried its teeth in his accumulator connections. The man-dog's teeth crackled with blue sparks. Electrical fireworks crawled across his eye brows and poured out of his nose. The tunnel was filled with the reek of burned fur and frying human lips. The man-dog was being electrocuted but wouldn't or couldn't let go. Kasyx swung his shoulders, trying to shake the heavy man-dog loose but it wouldn't relinquish its grip. All the time, pure energy was streaming out of Kasyx's accumulators, discharging itself in a frenzy of blue sparks from the bristling tips of the man-dog's fur.

God, thought Mol Besa, *we're down to the last of our energy in any case ... we daren't lose any more.*

He tried to get up, to help Kasyx dislodge the man-dog. But Isabel Gowdie gripped his penis and his brain even tighter, and hissed at him ferociously, *Break the seals, Mol Besa, if you want to escape me. Break the seals, Mol Besa, if you want to be anything more than a eunuch, trapped forever in a witch-woman's dream.*

She gave his penis three harsh, triumphant rubs, and he ejaculated, pearl-white semen on pearl-white skin. He coughed, saw blackness, saw stars. But even as he softened, Isabel Gowdie still wouldn't let him go. *Break my seals, Mot Besa, you miserable wretch! Break my seals.*

Kasyx was roaring in desperation as his precious energy poured away through the burning, swinging body of the man-dog. Zasta, with only four knives left in his armory, began to edge backwards. Keldak needed more power: his fists were fading, and even though he was still hitting the man-dogs, there was so little force in his blows that the man-dogs did little more than flinch. All around them, fast as a flash, Effis was still skating and circling and slicing, but the Carriers were swinging balks of tunneling timber at her now, making it increasingly difficult for her to come close.

"Mol Besa!" Kasyx shouted. "Mol Besa, get this damn dog off me!"

Isabel Gowdie kept her grip. *Seals first, Mai Besa.*

He had no choice. He knew that he had no choice. "You witch," he mouthed at her. Then, without any further hesitation, he punched out a program which would liquidize the wax in the seals; and which would convert the religious energy with which the seals were invested into the briefest crackle of tame lightning.

Isabel Gowdie watched him with thinly-disguised greed as he loaded the program into a cartridge and slotted the cartridge into his equation pistol. He fired it, aiming upwards, and the cartridge ricocheted from one wax seal to the other—wrists, ankles, breasts, knees.

Each black seal sizzled for a split second and then vanished in a small puff of evaporated wax.

For a moment, Mol Besa and Isabel Gowdie were surrounded by curtains of white lightning. Then the lightning died, and the smoke cleared away, and the pale naked form of Isabel Gowdie was free. *You have done well*, she growled at him. Her voice was quite different now. Thicker, coarser.

"Then let me go, for God's sake," Mol Besa insisted. "It was part of the deal."

Deal? Do you think I make deals?

"Mol Besa! For God's sake!" Kasyx was clamoring. Two more man-dogs came running up to him. They had recognized now that he held all of the power. The Carriers, on the other hand, were keeping their distance, their faces expressionless, their faces perfect, probing and parrying, just to keep the Night Warriors occupied while Kasyx's energy slowly bled away.

—and we shall cut a swathe—

Isabel Gowdie rose from her bed of limestone. *I killed you before, Mol Besa. I'll kill you again.*

"But you promised—"

Do you really believe that a witch's word is worth anything? You're new, aren't you? Green as grass, soft as a baby's cheek. Come here, Mol Besa, let me show you what a witch's mouth is for; and it's not for making promises.

The witch-woman rose naked from her bed of limestone, with her eyes as green as soft-boiled death. Her hair floated white and sparkling all around her, her forehead still crowned with corroded screws. One by one, the screws unwound, until they dropped tinkling on to the chalk. Isabel Gowdie's temples were punctuated with rusty, oozing holes; but she was free of the mental bondage that the Night Warriors had once imposed on her, in the hope that she would never be able to think Satanic thoughts again.

Slowly, with a terrible stretching sound, her scalp parted,

and her flying hair sank down to her shoulders. White skin peeled away from the top of her head layer by layer, fat was rolled back, hair roots dragged away.

When her scalp had completely opened up. Mol Besa saw to his horror that Isabel Gowdie had another face on top of her head, a cold white perfect face that exactly resembled the Mardi Gras masks of her Carriers. She was a woman inside another woman; and there could even have been more women concealed inside, layer by layer, sheath by sheath, a thousand evil personalities in one outwards manifestation.

The face on top of her head opened its glutinous eyes, as pale and as green as the first eyes that Mol Besa had encountered. It stared at him, and her other face stared at him, too, and both of them gave him the same mocking smile. Then she bent her head forward, and the face on top of her head whispered, with a string of glutinous liquid still clinging like a spiderweb from one lip to the other, *Kiss me.*

"*Mol Besa!*" screamed Kasyx.

No choice. Mol Besa closed his eyes and leaned forward slightly and kissed her. The lips of the face on top of her head.

Instantly, her arm snaked around and grasped the back of his head and pressed his face against hers. A long cold fish-tasting tongue pushed its way up between his teeth and probed every crevice of his mouth. *A tongue that came out of the top of her head.*

Mol Besa gagged. His stomach convulsed. But still Isabel Gowdie licked his tongue, licked his teeth, thrust that long thick trout of a tongue all the way down his throat. *You're mine, you bugger. You set me free and I love you. You and I will always be one now, always be lovers, always be twined.*

Mol Besa! yelled Kasyx inside of his mind.

But Isabel Gowdie hadn't quite finished with him yet. While the face on top of her head watched him with sly satisfaction, licking her lips after their fishy kiss, her other face bent forward and took his penis between her tongue and the roof of her mouth. She sucked it slowly, quite hard, but very methodically, and then let it slip back out again.

He stared at her. At both of her faces. The tunnel was filled with smoke, light, barking, and screams; and the endless grind of tunneling machinery: drills, cutters, trucks.

I have swallowed your seed, Mol Besa. Now I shall have your baby.

"What the hell are you talking about? You can't have a baby by doing that!"

Oh, yes, I can! And hell is exactly what I'm talking about! There are no rules in hell, are there, my fine gentleman? No one to say not, sir! No one to say, impossible! If you want to have a baby by sucking seed, then you can have a baby by sucking seed! It will grow in my stomach, along with my porridge, along with my chops, and I shall give birth to it by sucking it up! Then I shall suckle it and fatten it, but I won't baptize it—because when it's fine and fat I shall kill it, and boil it for fat—unbaptized fat!—and I shall mix that fat with monkshood and henbane, deadly nightshade and mandrake; and smear my body with it, and fly from one side of England to the other, in the twinkling of an eye! Just imagine it! A witch giving birth to a Night Warrior's baby! And making such a flying ointment!

Mol Besa had never encountered the real madness of Satan before. Those New York muggers had been nothing, compared with this. This was a world without any kind of order. This was a world without any kind of moral structure whatsoever. If you wanted to fly, what did you do? You killed unbaptized babies, boiled them, mixed up their fat with witch's herbs, then smeared it on your body and flew.

This was a world where dogs were men and men were living corpses and women had secret faces under their hair.

Shaking, shocked, right on the brink of hysteria. Mol Besa slid, half tumbled, down the chalky slope.

Kasyx reached out for him, with the man-dog still spitting and crackling and burning on his back. "*Mol Besa!* Get this thing off of me! We've got to get out of here fast!"

Mol Besa tried to grasp the fuming, spark-spitting body of the man-dog, but he was given a jolt that made his teeth fizz in their sockets.

He stumbled back and hurriedly punched out an equation that would convert the man-dog into sound, rather than physical energy. He loaded the equation as quickly as he could, aware that with every second, the Night Warriors' chances of returning to the real world were rapidly diminishing. As the cartridge loaded, he looked around and saw Isabel Gowdie standing on top of her bier of limestone, her hair flying with fire, naked and white, her arms crossed over her scrawny breasts. He had never seen a face so transfigured. Her eyes stared wide, her lips were drawn back over her teeth. She was evil incarnate; hatred incarnate; the Devil's domestic. It was scarcely possible to imagine that three hundred years ago, she had been born to some lowly mother as an ordinary child.

Now the Carriers and the man-dogs were closing in. Effis

circled behind them, trying to dodge between them to rejoin the Night Warriors; but one of the Carriers had picked up a length of scaffolding and was swinging it over his head in a figure-eight pattern to keep her away.

Mol Besa's cartridge clicked. It was ready for firing. With fingers that would scarcely obey him, he loaded his equation pistol, then swung around to face Kasyx and the man-dog who smoldered on his back, and he fired.

There was a moment when he couldn't believe that his equation had worked. Then he heard an echoing sound like a terrible shout down a subway tunnel, and the man-dog vanished. Kasyx swayed for a moment, then dropped to his knees, weakened and shocked, his accumulator connections still discharging random bursts of energy.

Mol Besa knelt beside him. "We zapped the dog. Are you okay?"

"Get back," Kasyx insisted. "We have to get back."

"But I still have the Night Plague!" Mol Besa insisted.

Kasyx looked up at him. "If we don't get the Godfrey Daniels out of here now, then believe me, Night Plague will be the last of our worries."

With Mol Besa's help, he heaved himself up on to his feet. "Effis!" he called. "Keldak! Zasta! Come back here! Fast as you like!"

Effis dodged left, then right, then slalomed her way through the motley company of Carriers, scattering three or four snarling man-dogs, and pirouetted into position close beside Mol Besa, as if she had just successfully completed a winning round in an international ice-dancing contest. Keldak came back more slowly, followed by Zasta, who had only one knife remaining, a heavy throwing knife which he had been saving for his last defense. To cut his own throat, if necessary.

Mol Besa said, "It's not quite Alamo time yet, old buddy. Leastways, I hope not."

The dream was beginning to change. Having been released from her limestone tomb, Isabel Gowdie was waking up. The tunnel walls began to darken, the halogen lights began to fade. The cacophony of drilling began to take on a deep, rhythmic throbbing. As they came nearer, the man-dogs' flesh dwindled on their bones, until they were stalking across the floor of the tunnel as wolfish skeletons.

The Carriers, too, started to lose their substance, until they were scarcely more than stained gray sheets from a plague hospital, billowing in the wind.

Kasyx raised his hands above his head, and with the last of his power reserves, created the flickering blue octagon which was their portal back to the real world. He guided it slowly downwards, all around them, and the upstairs bedroom at Tennyson reappeared. The last they saw of Isabel Gowdie's Channel Tunnel was the slimy tunnel floor, which had now flushed a deep crimson color, a dream metaphor for Isabel Gowdie's sex.

Then the dream vanished, and they were back.

Wearily, they looked around. The room was the same as before, except that it had now stopped raining. The drapes were still sodden, and water dripped everywhere, but there was no wind, no storm, no feeling that Tennyson was two different locations at once.

"She's woken up, she's alive," said Kasyx.

"I thought if I took off the blindfold—" Mol Besa began. But then he admitted, "I don't know what I thought. She had me wrapped around her little finger."

"She takes her power directly from Satan," said Kasyx. "We didn't stand more than a one-in-ten chance of destroying her, anyway."

"Who said that?" asked Effis.

"Springer," Kasyx told her. "I know that she didn't tell you, but then she didn't want to knock your confidence, first time out."

"God Almighty, knock our confidence," Mol Besa retorted. He smeared sweat from his forehead with the back of his hand. "We were an inch away from being massacred."

"What do we do now?" asked Zasta.

Kasyx said, "We have to report back to Springer and recharge our energy. Then we have to go searching for Isabel Gowdie again."

"But if she's escaped from the tunnel, how are we ever going to find her?" Keldak wanted to know.

"Oh, we'll find her," said Kasyx. "Whether we'll have the power to destroy her when we do ... well, that's something else altogether."

One by one, the Night Warriors rose into the air, their molecules absorbed through Tennyson's ceiling, and out through the roof. Outside, it was already morning. A sullen red sun shone through the freezing fog, and West London lay spread out beneath them like a deserted Macedonian battlefield after the Visigoths had stormed their way through.

They followed the curve of the Thames until they reached

Richmond Hill, where they sank at last through the fog, and back through the roof of Springer's top-floor apartment. Mol Besa grasped Zasta's hand for one brief moment, and then they sank back into their sleeping bodies, as softly and silently as leaves falling on to the surface of a trout pool.

Chapter Nine

Frightening Child

Stanley was woken up by a violent spasm in his stomach. His whole abdomen was distended, churning in the throes of peristalsis. He tried to cry out, but his throat was dry and tightly constricted, and he could hardly draw breath.

God, I'm choking, he thought. *God help me, I'm choking*.

He pushed back his bedclothes and fell sideways out of bed on to the floor. His stomach heaved again, and the dryness in his mouth was suddenly awash with acid bile. He pressed his hand against his stomach and he could feel it heaving and twisting, almost as if there were some kind of living creature inside it, trying to struggle its way out. The last time he had felt anything remotely like it was when Eve had been expecting Leon, and Leon had kicked her as if he had an exercise cycle inside of her.

Stanley managed to drag in one long, thin, whining breath. He climbed up on to his knees and then heaved himself upright by hanging on to the side of the bed. He felt something in the back of his throat, something whiplike, and he retched explosively. Step by step, he staggered across to the door, opened it, and crossed the corridor to the bathroom.

He scarcely made it. He didn't have time to reach the toilet, so he dropped on to his knees next to the bathtub, and hung over the edge of it. The full force of the Night Plague stirred his stomach and convulsed his throat, and then he felt a thick greasy bulk forcing its way upwards, right up into the back of his throat, something that stank sweetly of decaying garbage.

He couldn't speak, couldn't cry out. He arched over the bathtub, and inch by inch, convulsion by convulsion, out it came. A huge tangled mass of rats, some of them fully grown, their eyes staring and their fur slick with stomach juices; some of them half grown; some of them embryonic, with pink mutated bodies and eyes like blood clots.

Stanley vomited and vomited, until the last tails and legs writhed out between his lips, and a three-foot mass of rats lay gray and shuddering in the bathtub. Stanley was too weak and disgusted to do anything but kneel by the tub with his forehead pressed against the cold metal, spitting and spitting in an attempt to rid his mouth of the foul taste of twenty or thirty rotting and partially-digested rats.

He could see that the rats' tails had become inextricably intertwined, which occasionally happens in an overcrowded nest. The more they try to pull away from each other, the tighter the knot becomes, until they form a ratking, from which they can never escape.

At last, Stanley was able to climb to his feet. He went to the basin and poured himself a large glass of water and swilled out his mouth. Then he squeezed toothpaste on to his tongue and sucked at it until his tongue and his cheeks burned with peppermint. He looked at himself in the mirror over the basin. His face was gray and waxy and he looked exhausted. *How long*, he thought, *before this Night Plague kills me? How long before I end up in hell, unredeemed, unredeemable, an outcast for all eternity? Poppa, Momma, was I born for this?*

He found a large gray dustbin bag in the kitchen, returned to the bathroom, and queasily swung the mass of rats out of the tub. He listened, but it didn't sound as if anybody else were awake yet. He dragged the bag into his bedroom and dressed. Then he quietly left the apartment with it.

The morning was very cold and ghostly. With the bag on his back, he walked down the hill and crossed the road to the banks of the Thames. The water was dull, like breathed-on steel. It even *smelled* cold. Through the fog, he could see the trees of Eel Pie Island and the outlines of moored boats.

He dropped the bag of rats into the water, and it swirled and bubbled and sank. *I'm going to beat you. Isabel Gowdie*, he swore to himself under his breath. *You can take anything you want from me; but not my soul. My soul is my own.*

He began to trudge slowly back up the hill. An invisible airliner thundered through the fog, somewhere above him, and it sounded as if the sky were splitting. He looked up toward the railings above the Terrace Gardens, and he could see Knitted Hood standing beside them, watching him, his face as white as candlewax.

For the first time, Stanley felt determined, rather than afraid. He carried on walking up the hill and passed within ten yards of Knitted Hood, on the opposite side of the road. Knitted Hood didn't turn as he passed; nor give any indication that he knew he was there. But Stanley wanted to show him that he didn't care, that he wasn't afraid, and that he was grimly confident that the Night Warriors would return Isabel Gowdie and all of her Carriers back to the earth to which his ancestors had once consigned them.

He went back up to Springer's apartment and rang the doorbell. Springer answered, a blond-haired woman of about twenty-five years old, wearing a white tubelike minidress and dozens of jingling silver bracelets.

"You've been sick," she remarked as Stanley stepped inside. The rest of the Night Warriors were up now—Leon in his Star Trek pajamas, Henry in a brown beach robe that had obviously seen more debonair times, and Angie in a Marks & Spencer nightshirt with a picture of Betty Boop on the front.

"Yes," Stanley replied, "I've been sick."

"Was it very bad?"

"It's not an experience I'm keen to repeat."

"Angie's been sick, too. Meat fat, heaps of it. With the Night Plague, you're always sick with the things that disgust you the most. It's intended to reduce your self-esteem to the lowest possible level."

Angie gave Stanley an unsteady smile, although there was nothing for either of them to smile about.

"There's something else, too," said Springer, walking through to the kitchen. "Angie had a dream of her own this morning, after you arrived back from Isabel Gowdie's dream, and before she woke up."

"I couldn't 'elp it," said Angie. "I tried not to 'ave it, but I couldn't stop myself."

Springer was making espresso coffee in a French *cafetiere*.

"She dreamed that she was having sex with her boyfriend Paul, and with Paul's best friend—"

"Mack," put in Angie. "'Is real name's Kenneth, but 'e comes from Glasgow."

Springer said patiently, "Paul and Mack, yes. That means that both of them are now victims of a secondary infection of Night Plague. And only Ashapola knows how many girls they know between them, and how quickly the Night Plague will spread once *they* start dreaming."

Stanley stood close to Springer, watching her make the coffee. Although he had been so violently ill this morning, and his stomach still ached from all the muscular convulsions he had suffered, he found that she aroused him. Maybe she intended to arouse him. Maybe she was testing his licentiousness. Maybe she was seeing just how far his morals had decayed.

Her breasts swayed under the thin white wool of her dress; the curve of her bottom was clearly defined. But as he moved closer, she picked up two cups of coffee and deftly moved away.

"Remember," she said, arching one eyebrow. "I am nothing more than Ashapola's messenger."

He followed her into the sparsely-furnished living room. While they had been talking in the kitchen. Gordon had arrived from his hotel, wearing baggy green corduroy trousers and a floppy yellow sweater with stains on the front.

Springer said, "None of us are overjoyed at what happened last night. But you are Warriors, fighting a sacred war; and in this war like all others you will have to face up to serious setbacks."

"What do we do now?" asked Gordon. "If Isabel Gowdie can escape into other people's dreams, she could be anywhere."

"You can find her," Springer assured them. "The first thing to do is for you to travel to Dover and inspect the real workings for the Channel Tunnel. You will probably discover that when you dug Isabel Gowdie out of the chalk in her dream, there was a natural collapse of rock which released her body in reality, too. When you left her, she was waking up; and she will have left the tunnel as a real woman as well as a dream woman.

"Real people can be followed. Real people can be traced. She has no clothes, no money, and very little knowledge of modern Britain. If you can find where she went in reality, then you will have a much better chance of picking up the resonance of her dreams, too."

"So we're off to Dover again, are we?" asked Gordon.

"You can borrow my car." Springer smiled.

While Stanley was brushing his hair, Angie came into his room, still wearing her Betty Boop nightshirt. She stood beside him watching him for a while. Then she said, "Do you think we'll ever find 'er?"

Stanley put down his hairbrushes. "Oh, we'll find her all right. We have to. Otherwise you and I are going to wind up dead and damned."

She said nothing for a while. Stanley tugged a rust-colored sweater over his shirt and put on his Rolex, the one that the San Francisco Baroque Ensemble had given him after their performance of Frescobaldi's *Fiori Musicali* at Carnegie Hall, in New York. The New York *Times* music critic had described Stanley's playing as "sublime ... the description 'baroque' may have been etymologically derived from the words for 'rough pearl,' but Eisner is the most polished pearl in an ensemble ... that is a crown of polished pearls."

Angie said, "That dream I 'ad this morning ... about Paul and Mack."

"What about it? It was only a dream."

"Yes, I know. But it was the same sort of dream I 'ad about you. I was all ... well, I was all wet afterwards."

"What do you want me to say? That's I'm jealous? How can I be jealous of a dream?"

Angie came up close to him. "I shouldn't 'ave done it, though, should I? It gave Paul the Night Plague, too, and Mack."

"That's the nature of the Night Plague, sweetheart. That's how it spreads itself. It wasn't your fault."

"But I should be punished, shouldn't I?"

"Punished?"

She tugged up the front of her nightshirt, twisting it around in her hands. "You should beat me or something, for 'aving a dream like that, don't you think so?"

Stanley looked her up and down. He was about to say. *Beat you, of course not*, but then a small dark feeling uncurled itself inside of his mind, like a curled-up centipede. He came up to her and cupped his hand without any hesitation between her legs, and roughly kissed her forehead. "Maybe you're right, Maybe I should beat you."

She closed her eyes and offered her mouth. He kissed her lips and then clenched her tongue tightly and painfully between his teeth. He tasted blood. She winced and tried to cry out, but it was almost ten seconds before he let her go.

"When we get back from Dover," he told her, "I'm going to give you just what you deserve."

The fog cleared as they drove through Kent, and by midmorning the day was cold and golden. They stopped for lunch at the Bell, in a picturesque village called Smarden. Stanley was enchanted by the Bell. It had been built in the fifteenth century, with stone floors and open fireplaces. They sat together at an oak table, close to the fire, and ate huge steak-and-kidney pies and drank pints of Theakston's bitter. The winter sun shone through the woodsmoke; and for a while Stanley could understand how easy it was in England to pass in a dream from one century to another. Here, in Smarden, the centuries were layered one on top of the other like the pastry layers on top of his pie.

They drove on, until they were crossing the chalky Downs just above Dover, with the landscape already beginning to grow grainy and dark. None of them had spoken much during their drive. They were too anxious about how they were going to find Isabel Gowdie and what they could possibly do to deal with her when they did. Springer's old Humber was automatic, so Stanley had been able to do most of the driving. Henry had declined. He didn't like to drive, especially in a country where nobody else on the road knew their left from their right, and where they all drove so damned fast.

As they descended Jubilee Road, the curving ramp that led them down toward the docks, the streetlights flickered on. The English Channel was congealing in the gloom like cold gray wallpaper paste. Gordon said, "I can't see how

Ms. Gowdie could have gone very far. Not without any clothes. Not without money."

"Don't ever underestimate the servants of Satan," said Henry. "She managed to survive a death sentence from the Scottish court. She managed to survive three centuries buried in solid limestone. She managed to get away from five of the most powerful of all the Night Warriors. Finding herself some clothes isn't going to present much of a problem to a lady of that kind of determination."

They drove westwards from Dover until they reached the Channel Tunnel workings. In Isabel Gowdie's dream, they had been able to gain direct admission to the tunnel. In reality, they were stopped at the high wire perimeter fence by a security officer with a beefy face and a blue paramilitary sweater. He slid open the window of his prefabricated office, letting out a strong smell of paraffin heaters.

"Can't let you in without proper authority," he announced.

"Actually, we're looking for somebody," put in Gordon, winding down his window and sticking his head out.

"Who's that, then?" asked the security officer.

"A woman. Rather pale. We wondered if you might have seen her."

"She belong to the company, then?"

"Well, not exactly. But we're certain she was here."

"What was her name, then?"

"Erm, Smith."

The security man slowly shook his head. He was obviously beginning to think that he was dealing with a carload of fruitcakes. "Nobody like that around here, mate. Lost is she, or what?"

"Sort of lost, yes," said Gordon.

"Police station's your best bet, then. She wouldn't be wandering around here. We've had to clear the site in any case."

"You had to clear the site, why?" asked Stanley.

"Didn't you hear it on the news? Had a bit of an accident last night, down in the tunnel. Whole load of Semtex went off. Side of the tunnel collapsed, two blokes killed, six injured. So there wasn't much chance of any woman wandering around."

"All right, Officer, thank you," Stanley told him.

They turned the car around and drove slowly back towards Dover. Stanley said, "So that was how she got out of the tunnel net in real life. Once her dreaming self was released, she was able to arrange a little accident to release her real self. This is one magical woman."

"You sound almost *admiring*," Gordon remarked. "As far as I'm concerned, she's a total and absolute bitch."

"Whatever we think of her," said Henry, "the question is how do we find out where she's gone? She could still be in Dover; she could have gone anywhere."

"Maybe that security guard had the right idea," said Stanley. "Maybe we should try asking at the police station. If somebody's seen a naked woman walking around the streets of Dover, then they've probably reported it. Likewise, if Isabel Gowdie's stolen any money or any clothes."

It was dark by the time they found the Dover police station. The duty officer behind the counter was patient but unhelpful. No, he couldn't tell them if any thefts of women's clothing had been reported during the day. No, he couldn't tell them if a pale-faced woman had been seen stealing money. No, he couldn't possibly divulge if any naked women had been observed near the Channel Tunnel excavations. And why did they want to know?

They left Dover feeling despondent and drove back towards London on the main road. After they passed the first roundabout outside Dover, however, they came to a lengthy lay-by, where six or seven large trucks were parked, and tea and hamburgers were being sold from a small white-painted caravan with an awning in front of it.

Two girls in jeans and duffle coats were standing at the end of the lay-by, with rucksacks on their backs, thumbing for a ride.

Stanley pulled the Humber into the lay-by and switched off the engine.

"What are you doing?" asked Henry.

"Just trying something," said Stanley. He climbed out of the car and walked across to the tea caravan, smacking his hands together to warm them up. Two truck drivers were standing beside the caravan drinking huge mugs of tea and eating bacon sandwiches, and smoking at the same time.

Behind the counter, a fat woman in a pink gingham overall was wiping the work surfaces with a grayish cloth. Stanley momentarily prayed that the next time he was sick, he wouldn't puke up that cloth.

"Cuppa tea, dear?" she asked him.

"No—no thanks. I was just wondering if you'd seen a woman today, hitchhiking."

"We get loads of them, dear. Students, mainly."

"I don't think you could have missed this particular woman," Stanley told her. "She's real thin, with green eyes, and white, white hair. I don't know what she was wearing, but that's the way she looks."

The woman blasted steam out of her tea urn. "Oh, yes. She was here a little bit earlier on, as a matter of fact. She asked me for a cup of hot water, and when I gave it to her, she drank it straight off, even though it was practically boiling. I said, you'll scald your insides, doing that, but all she did was smile."

Stanley felt a burst of excitement. *Found you, you witch-woman!* he thought. *Tracked you down! Now we'll see who can manipulate whom!*

"Did you see which way she went?" he asked the tea lady.

"She got a lift," the tea lady sniffed.

"Gissa 'nother cuppa, Doris," said one of the truck drivers, banging his mug on the counter. "Oh, an' a packet of cheese-'n'-onion, too, would you?"

"Did you see who gave her the ride?" Stanley persisted. "Was it a truck or a car?"

"It was a lorry, I think," the tea lady told him. "One of them big foreign ones, Dutch or something. Blue and white, with a kind of a blue and white flag on the back."

"What time was this?"

"Oh, not all that long ago. About an hour, hour and a half, not much more."

"You're an angel," Stanley told her. Thinking: *Shit, we must have practically driven past her.*

One of the truck drivers gave a forced, hollow laugh. "If she's an angel, mate, then I think I'd rather go to hell."

Stanley gave him a tight smile. "Believe me, friend, you wouldn't. Not at any damned price."

He returned to the car and immediately started the engine. "She was there, only about an hour ago. She was given a ride in a blue and white truck. It was a big truck, so I guess the chances are that it's going to stay on the motorways. God, I wish I had a half-decent car, instead of this junker!"

They drove steadily through the darkness, mile after mile, checking out every single truck they passed. They flagged down one Danish truck, loaded with garden furniture, but the driver hadn't picked up any hitchers today. They gave him a pack of Benson & Hedges for his trouble, and drove on.

"This is like looking for a needle in a needle factory," Gordon complained. "They could have turned off anywhere."

"We'll find her, believe me," Stanley insisted. "I just have this feeling about it."

Sixty miles further on, however, when they crossed the Kent border on the M25 motorway and started to head westwards through Surrey, even Stanley was beginning to despair. There were no blue and white trucks anywhere, Dutch or Danish or domestic, and soon they would have to turn off toward Richmond and back to Springer.

They crossed the multilevel cloverleaf where the M25 intersected with the southbound M23, and it was then, toiling up the long slow hill ahead of them, that Stanley saw a blue and yellow truck, with a blue and yellow flag painted on the back of it, along with the words *Zwart-Wit Lithos, Mercurius Wormerveer, Leiden*.

"That's it, that has to be it!" said Stanley excitedly. He shifted the Humber down into second, and the old car's transmission whined and juddered in protest as it pursued the blue and yellow truck up the hill.

Gordon leaned out of the passenger window and waved his arm up and down to signal the truck to pull over on to the hard shoulder, which it eventually did, with an immense sighing and shuddering of air brakes. The denim-jacketed driver climbed down immediately and looked all around his truck, obviously thinking that they must have been warning him about an open rear door, a fuel leakage, or a punctured tire.

Stanley approached him as he came around the rear of his truck, a burned-down cigarette filter pinched between his tips.

"Pardon me, sir, I'm real sorry to stop you like this. But we're looking for a girl. A hitchhiker, very pale face, green eyes, white hair."

The truck driver nodded. "Yes," he said in a glottal Dutch accent.

"Have you seen her?" asked Gordon.

"Yes."

"Is she on board your rig now?"

"No."

"Do you happen to know where she went?"

"I let her off back there, on the motorway. She wanted to go to the sea."

"To Brighton?" asked Angie.

"Well, it was somewhere that sounded like Brighton, but, you know, not quite the same."

"Brighthelmstone?" suggested Gordon, as a sudden inspiration.

"That's right, that's the place," the truck driver agreed.

"Where's Brighthelmstone?" Stanley asked Gordon.

"It's the old eighteenth-century name for Brighton, before the Prince Regent discovered it and made it fashionable ... back in the days when it was nothing but a fishing village. Isabel Gowdie would have called it that."

"That's great, what are we waiting for?"

They sped as fast as they could to the next exit, drove around the roundabout, and back toward the M23 and Brighton.

Although it was dark, Stanley was conscious of the shape and smell of the countryside through which they passed. In some ways, it reminded him of driving through Connecticut—less densely forested, less rural, but indescribably *older*. In Connecticut, there were plenty of ramshackle coaching inns down scarcely-used side roads, and some sad and abandoned country mansions. But here the coaching inns were lit up, ready for business, and lights shone across the fields from grand and distant houses.

"Why does this put me in mind of Transylvania?" he asked Angie. "I feel if we stop at one of these pubs, we're going to find everybody wearing garlic round their necks, and turning their backs on us when we ask for a pint of beer."

They inspected the passengers of every car and truck they overtook, but by the time they reached the South Downs they still hadn't caught sight of anybody who remotely resembled Isabel Gowdie.

"I don't think we have much chance of finding her this evening," said Henry. "But at least we're close. The best thing we can do is find ourselves someplace to stay for the night and go searching for her as Night Warriors."

"I'll second that," said Stanley. "I could use a drink."

The South Downs were vast and humped and shrouded in mist, a huge slumbering dinosaur sprawled across the landscape. Gordon guided them up a winding back road to Devil's Dyke, on the summit of the Downs. To the south, just below them, they could see the lights of Brighton glimmering across the horizon, and beyond Brighton the foggy darkness of the sea.

"This is a shortcut," Gordon told them. "We may even arrive in Brighton before Isabel Gowdie."

Brighton, to Stanley, looked like San Francisco's aged aunt. It was precipitously hilly, it was on the sea, and it was crammed with antique shops and fashion boutiques and shops selling 501s and studded motorcycle jackets. What impressed Stanley, however, was how much older it was than even the oldest quarters of San Francisco. As they passed a roundabout called Seven Dials, they passed the sweeping curve of a white-painted eighteenth-century terrace, and then they plunged downhill between rows and rows of small Regency houses towards the seafront.

Gordon guided them along the front until they reached the Palace Pier, a cast-iron Victorian pier strung with lights, with a funfair right at the very end of it, a half mile out to sea. Then he directed them further east, towards Kemp Town.

"I have a friend here, an artist. His house is absolutely vast. Provided we cross his palm with silver, he'll put us up for the night."

Stanley parked the Humber in the private slip road in front of a huge flat-fronted Regency house. They climbed out stiffly, and Gordon went to ring at the doorbell. A foggy, briny wind blew off the sea, and Stanley could hear the ceaseless seething of the tide.

They waited for two or three minutes before the black-painted front door was opened, and a tall thin elderly man in a fez and a smoking jacket stood before them. Mounting the stone steps, Stanley could see that he was wearing dangling diamond earrings and purple eye shadow, and that his wrinkles were thickly powdered.

"Gordon, my dear boy! What on earth are you doing here? Who are all these people?"

"Hello, James, these are some friends of mine, over from America. I decided on the spur of the moment to show them the sights of Brighton."

James pursed his lips. "I didn't know that *I* was one of the sights of Brighton!" he replied in a tart Noël Cowardish voice.

"Well, actually, you're not," Gordon replied. "But we could do with somewhere to stay for the night."

"What's wrong with the Grand?"

"Somewhere quiet and private," said Gordon.

"You're not thinking of having an orgy, are you?" James demanded. He pronounced "orgy" with a hard *g*.

"James ... we simply need somewhere to stay. Somewhere completely undisturbed."

James peered at them disapprovingly. "Well, I don't know, Gordon. It's scandalously short notice. And then there's—what—five of you, and that's five beds, unless you're all thinking of sleeping in the same bed, mind you. And that's five complete sets of bed linen that have to go to the laundry. Not to mention the general *disturbance*, and the use of electricity, and hot water, and wear and tear on the carpets, they're all original Tabriz carpets, you know, the *knotting* is superb!"

Henry stepped forward and opened up his billfold. "Would two hundred pounds cover it?"

James stared at him. "I think so, thank you," he said, obviously offended by Henry's abruptness, and turned and left them on the doorstep to make their own way in.

Gordon had been right: James's house was enormous. It was richly but fussily decorated with exquisite hand-printed wallpapers and gilded mirrors, and the walls were hung with hundreds of watercolors and oil paintings of the Sussex countryside. All of the furniture was antique, all of the drapes were velvet, with swags and ties and silk bows. In the main living room, a huge log fire was burning in an Adam fireplace, while two bulbous-eyed Boston terriers basked in front of it on a huge Chinese cushion.

"This stuff must be worth a fortune," breathed Henry.

"James inherited it all from his mother. Lady Hurstpierpoint," Gordon remarked. "God knows what's going to happen to it all when James passes on."

"Looks more like a museum than someone's 'ouse," Angie remarked.

Leon said, "I think it's neat. It's just like one of those old movies."

"You could only be American," James said to him, sweeping in from the opposite doorway. "Only an American child could be impressed by great art because it reminds him of a film. I suppose *I* remind you of Laurence Olivier."

"No, Roddy McDowall."

"Who?"

"You know, he was in *Planet of the Apes*."

James fixed Leon with a purple stare. "I think I'd better show you *folks* to your rooms, before you poison the air even further with your crassness."

The bedrooms were all furnished in the style of an English country house, with pale Regency stripes and mahogany four-poster beds. Angie took hold of Stanley's hand and squeezed it and said, "It's brilliant, isn't it? Only a pooftah could decorate a house like this."

It was well past eight o'clock, so they decided to go for dinner. There was a strange new camaraderie between them, partly because Stanley had been less cantankerous today. He still felt nauseous and headachy and irritable. He was still troubled by the blackest of momentary thoughts. Pain. Violence. Sadistic acts. But he felt more positive today. They were tracking down Isabel Gowdie, they were hunting down the very source of the Night Plague; and if they managed to find her and destroy her tonight, their achievement—although it would never be known, never be recognized—would affect the course of human history for centuries to come.

They would be saviors greater than any waking mind could ever imagine.

Henry had an appetite for Dover sole, so they went to Wheeler's in Market Street, a small crowded Victorian fish restaurant on three rickety floors, and ordered Colchester oysters and grilled sole, with a bottle of chilled white wine. They walked back to James's house feeling warm and well filled, and as relaxed as they possibly could be. Leon yawned and said, "I'm so tired, I could sleep for a week."

Leon went to bed while the rest of the Night Warriors sat in front of the dying fire with James, and shared a bottle of Fleurie.

James said, "I sense something peculiar about you, Gordon. You seemed to have changed a great deal since the last time you were here. You seem to have gone slightly mad, if you don't mind my saying so."

Gordon held up his left arm and tugged down his sleeve. "Not just mad, James."

James stared at his empty sleeve. "Is that a trick? Where's your hand?"

"Lost it," said Gordon. "Dog bit it off."

James was shocked. "A dog bit your hand off? I can scarcely believe it! Didn't it *hurt*?"

"Of course it hurt, you idiot."

"But don't you *mind*?"

"Too bad if I do, it won't grow back again. I didn't particularly want to be a professional juggler, in any case."

"My dear boy," said James, still shocked, but increasingly enthralled. "Do have another drink."

It was well past twelve o'clock before they went to bed. Not many hours of the night left for fighting. Stanley checked that Leon was asleep and then tiptoed along the board-creaking corridor to his own room.

In the large four-poster bed, Angie was waiting for him. She was lying back on the plumped-up pillow, the silk-covered eiderdown drawn up to her waist, bare-breasted, her eyes misted with the kind of desires that most girls could only guess at.

"We have to sleep," Stanley told her, unbuttoning his shirt.

"You promised to punish me."

"If you go to sleep now, I'll punish you twice as hard tomorrow."

"You promised." Her voice was congested with passion.

Stanley said nothing, but finished undressing. When he

was naked, he walked over to the bureau and picked up a silver-backed hairbrush. Then he crossed over to the bed and dragged back the eiderdown. Angie held out her arms for him.

"Oh, no. You wanted punishment. Punishment is what you're going to get."

He seized Angie's wrist and tried to turn her over. But Angie kicked and fought back, her breasts bouncing, her teeth clenched. Stanley grabbed hold of her hair, twisted his fingers into it, and forced her to turn over on to her stomach. She screamed and wrestled, but he pulled her hair even harder.

"You bastard, that hurts, let go of me! You bastard, you bastard, you bastard!"

He pulled her over his knee, still keeping his grip on her hair, and smacked her hard on the bottom with the hairbrush, bristle side down. Her white bottom flushed red. He smacked her again, and then again, while she screamed and panted and swore at him, and the scarlet flush spread wider and wider across her cheeks.

He noticed, though, that she wasn't struggling any more; not really struggling. He spanked her again, and again, and as he did so he released his grip on her hair. Her panting grew harsher and deeper, and she parted her legs wider and wider, breathing, "Bastard, you bastard, you bastard!"

Her eyes tight shut, she raised herself up on her arms, her back arched, her buttocks clenched, and then she gave a deep suppressed shudder. Stanley couldn't tell how much self-control it had taken for her to bury her orgasm so deeply, but when she rolled off his knees and on to her back, her eyes were completely unfocused, like the eyes of somebody concussed.

"You bastard," she whispered.

Stanley kissed her open lips. "We have to get to sleep now."

"Can't I sleep here?"

"No ... just in case something goes wrong."

"You're not married any more."

"All the same, I have to think about Leon; and I have to think about my mother, too."

"You're too good to be evil."

"I'm fighting it, believe me."

Angie touched his bare shoulder, traced the line of his collarbone with her fingernails. "Do you think we're going to die tonight?"

He didn't smile. "Everybody has to die sometime."

She turned her head sideways and sank her teeth into the muscle of his forearm, so hard that she drew blood. Stanley winced and wrenched his arm away.

"Now you'll have to punish me again tomorrow," she whispered.

He half turned away, then he slapped her face with his open hand, once, and then again. Her cheeks flared scarlet.

"Get to bed, you bitch!" he snapped at her. "We're going after this goddamned witch."

Stanley lay back in bed with his mind a kaleidoscope of ideas, memories, voices; but there was scarcely any traffic passing through Brighton at this time of night, and the shushing of the breakers on the shingle beach was so repetitive and soothing that he soon began to feel calmer. He repeated the sacred incantation of the Night Warriors, but he was so dozy that he was scarcely able to finish it.

"Now when the face of the world is hidden in darkness, let us be conveyed to the place of our meeting, armed and armored; and let us be nourished by the power that is dedicated to the cleaving of darkness, the settling of all black matters, and the dissipation of evil, so be it."

After less than ten minutes, he was asleep. His consciousness sank deeper and deeper, like a jolly boat full of drowned sailors sinking and bumping down an ocean shelf, before plunging silently into the fathomless depths of sleep.

He rose from his sleeping body, and he could still hear the sea and the persistent rattling of his sash window. He moved across the carpet and was absorbed through the bedroom wall.

The Night Warriors had agreed to gather in James's living room. Kasyx was already there when Mol Besa arrived; Keldak and Effis arrived a few minutes afterwards. It was almost ten minutes later when Zasta appeared, rubbing his eyes. Mol Besa put his arm around his shoulders and said, "You're sure you want to come with us tonight? You don't have to if you don't want to."

"I have to come," Zasta told him.

"He has a right to," said Kasyx. "He may be your son, Mol Besa; but his vow to the Night Warriors comes first."

One by one, they stood next to Kasyx and were charged up with crackling, burned-smelling power. On their cushion beside the fire, James's Boston terriers awoke, and stared at the Night Warriors in alarm. One of them jumped down from the cushion and hid behind the sofa.

When all five of the Night Warriors were fully charged up, and clad in their armor, Kasyx said, "Let's go out on patrol. If Isabel Gowdie is anywhere in Brighton, we ought to be able to locate her."

They rose up through the several floors of James's house, through the attic, and out into the chilly, windy night. As they wheeled silently over the rooftops of Kemp Town, they could see the sea foaming in the darkness, and the spectral white cliffs of Rottingdean and Peacehaven. They turned over the town center, over the Steine, and glided over the extraordinary oriental domes and spires of the Brighton Pavilion. To Stanley, the Pavilion looked as if it had arrived by magic carpet straight out of the Arabian Nights; but inside of his mind, Keldak said, *Exterior by John Nash, early nineteenth century. Quaint, isn't it?*

Circling around the Pavilion, they crossed the Lanes, an enclave of eighteenth-century shops and houses built on a higgledy-piggledy medieval street pattern.

Kasyx said, "Let's circle again, I'm picking something up."

Silently, invisibly, like ink stains absorbed by darker paper, they turned over the Lanes for a second time. But Kasyx said, "It's still not too clear. Her body may be sleeping here—there are scores of pubs and hotels and boardinghouses—but her dreaming personality is somewhere else. Not too far away, though. I can sense it."

They widened the circle of their search. At last, Kasyx said, "It's stronger in this direction, on the seafront."

They began to sink lower. Mol Besa kept close to Zasta

as they approached the shingled beach. But Kasyx was sure of his target now; the magnificent white-fronted Victorian façade of the Grand Hotel. "She's here … in one of the suites … that's where she's hiding tonight."

As they drifted towards the Grand, Zasta suddenly said, "Look! Look down there!"

They turned and looked downwards, and glimpsed a tall figure striding along King's Road, before turning suddenly into Ship Street, towards the Lanes, and disappearing. Knitted Hood, his gray gaberdine coat flying in the salty wind. Now they knew for certain that Isabel Gowdie was here in Brighton.

"What I want to know is, why did she come *here*, of all places?" Mol Besa asked.

"I don't know," Kasyx replied. "But I expect we'll find out. Satan never does anything without a very deliberate reason."

They sank through the roof of the Grand Hotel and into the suite where Kasyx's sensitivities had guided them. It was a large, lavishly-decorated suite, one of the most expensive. A cooler with two empty bottles of Moët champagne stood on the table in the living room, along with vases of roses and ashtrays crammed with burned-down cigar stubs. Evening clothes were strewn around the sofa. A lacy garter belt lay tangled beside the bedroom door.

In the bedroom, on a king-sized bed, a man and a woman lay heavily sleeping. The room smelled of stale alcohol and cigar smoke and sex. The man was in his early fifties, bulkily built, with a florid face and greased-back hair. The girl beside him couldn't have been older than twenty-five. She was a bubbly-permed blonde, with false eyelashes, one of which had partially come adrift.

The Night Warriors surrounded the bed. "Who's dreaming the dream that Isabel Gowdie's hiding herself in?" Mol Besa wanted to know.

Kasyx slid open an instrument panel on his wrist; a psychic DNA analyzer. Its principal purpose was the quick identification of friendly or hostile forces, but it had a data bank capable of identifying almost anyone.

"Isabel Gowdie's hiding herself in the girl's dream," said Kasyx. "She's a high-class prostitute. This man brought her down to Brighton from London, for a few illicit days together."

"But why would Isabel Gowdie want to hide inside somebody like 'er?" Effis asked.

Kasyx punched out some more data on his wrist. "I think I'm beginning to get the picture. He's a politician. A member of the Cabinet. The girl knows plenty more of them; and *sleeps* with plenty more of them. Isabel Gowdie's probably having sex with her, inside of her dream, to infect her with the Night Plague. Think of what could happen if half of Her Majesty's Government lost their souls to Satan."

"If you ask me, half of them have already," put in Keldak.

"This isn't a joke, Keldak," Kasyx told him, the dim light glinting on his crimson helmet. "We're talking about a whole nation here, ruled by men without any principles at all, except the principles of cruelty and mayhem and massacre. You've seen what the Night Plague's done to your country already. You've got riots in your country townships, looting and mugging in your urban ghettoes. The London subways used to be safe: now they're as dangerous as New York's. Now you're going to have *official* chaos. *Official* insurrection. You're going to go back to the Middle Ages, my friend, when nobody was safe."

Keldak said, "Let's just get after her, shall we?"

"You bet," Kasyx told him. "Now, stand close."

The Night Warriors stood shoulder-to-shoulder. Kasyx lifted his arms, and the brilliant blue octagon materialized above their heads. Slowly, it sank downwards to the floor, encircling them, reflecting from their visors and their armor plate.

Instantly, they were flooded with sunlight. They found themselves standing on the Brighton seafront on a warm midsummer day. The sky was bright blue, with tiny puffy clouds; the sea danced brightly on the shingle. Sea gulls swooped around them, catching the wind in their wings, crying like children.

The promenade was crowded. Not with the usual Brighton day-trippers, but with hundreds of the young prostitute's acquaintances. Spivvy-looking Maltese men in white suits with wide lapels; a harassed teacher in a green tweed sports coat; crowds of jeering and shuffling boys; a frowning social worker. A nun, in a wide white wimple, gliding past as calmly as a ship.

Open-topped double-decker buses trundled up and down King's Road, each of them crammed with silver-haired men in three-piece suits and brassy women with scarlet lipstick and clinging gold-lamé dresses. Rolls-Royces with ministerial badges on them drove bumper-to-bumper with chugging 1960s American cars with rebel flags and British number plates. Somewhere, a maddening calliope was playing a screaming, discordant version of "I Do Like to Be Beside the Seaside."

The Night Warriors pushed their way along the jostling promenade, heading towards the Palace Pier. Kasyx said,

"I can sense something ... Isabel Gowdie's here someplace. And it wouldn't surprise me if some of her Carriers were, too."

"Knitted Hood's still awake," said Mol Besa.

Kasyx nodded. "He was probably going to the lodging where Isabel Gowdie's hiding herself, just to make sure that nobody disturbs her while she's asleep."

They passed fish-and-chip restaurants *(rock salmon & chips, bread & butter & cup of tea, 7/6d)*; they passed sweetshops crammed with candy walking canes and luridly pink Brighton rock and sugar false teeth. Zasta picked up a stick of rock and said, "Can you eat candy in a dream?"

Mol Besa smiled. "I don't know. Maybe you can in your own dream."

Zasta said, "Look," and handed Mol Besa the stick of rock. All the way through it ran the pink lettering *I am the pestilence that was promised*.

"Maybe you'd better not eat it," Mol Besa suggested, looking around. The influence of Isabel Gowdie was closer than he had first imagined.

They crossed the shingle, towards the pier. The people on the beach were even stranger than the people on the promenade. Most of them were naked or dressed in their underwear. A large-breasted girl in nothing but a lilac nylon G-string and lilac stockings was trying to paddle through the foaming shallows in stiletto shoes. Not far away, a middle-aged man in voluminous undershorts was watching her intently. He was still wearing his bowler hat and had a tightly-furled umbrella and a copy of the *Financial Times* under his arm.

Further along the beach, a ginger-headed man in a crumpled gray suit kept falling sideways into the surf, while his wife tried to snatch him upright. He fell again and again and again, like an endlessly-repeated newsreel. He was watched impassively by bulky blue-black lobsters, slow-moving, as big as sheep, and pale waiflike children with seaside buckets and spades.

The Night Warriors reached the entrance to the Palace Pier. Pierced cast-iron railings ran along each side of it, painted pale green, and below their feet was a boarded deck through which they could see the barnacle-encrusted pilings of the pier, and the crisscross support, from which hanks of seaweed waved like the hair of magical hags.

"She's here, she's real close," said Kasyx.

Their feet drummed on the boarded walkways as they advanced swiftly along the pier. Halfway along, three gray figures materialized in front of them out of the hot summer air. Carriers—probably the last three Carriers surviving, apart from Knitted Hood, although Isabel Gowdie would be able to infect many more, now that she had been freed from her imprisonment.

This time, the Carriers had only three man-dogs with them. They were all on leashes, but they were huge black shaggy beasts whose claws scratched and skidded on the deck boards, and flecks of rabid saliva flew from their stretched-open jaws. The Carriers wielded weapons, too, complicated pikestaffs with gleaming blades.

"Careful," warned Kasyx. "I've seen weapons like that, before. Spirit spears."

Mol Besa said, "Spirit spears? What are spirit spears?"

"Each time one of those spears kills somebody, his spirit is trapped inside it. So the next time the owner wants to use the spear, he promises the spirit inside it that he can have the body of whoever he happens to hit, and live again ... while the spirit of whoever he kills has to take his place inside the spear."

"Bloody 'ell," said Effis bluntly.

Kasyx nodded. "Believe me, the spirits inside of those spears make absolutely certain that they hit their targets. Wouldn't you?"

Mol Besa said, "In that case, time to do a little mathematical conversion."

But there was no time to waste. The Carriers let slip the leashes of the man-dogs, and the huge beasts came bounding along the pier towards them, screeching and snarling and roaring in rage.

Keldak fired a fist at the leading dog. It exploded through the man-dog's teeth and vanished with a hollow whistling noise down his throat. The man-dog stopped short, shuddered, his mouth a smashed-apart ruin. Then he blew up, and ribbons of intestine and grisly fur sprayed in all directions, and the fortune-telling booth close beside him was instantly painted red.

Zasta reached his hand up, and a shining golden knife jumped over his shoulder, followed by another, and another. As each knife leapt into his hand, he turned it around, so that the blades were interwoven together, and he was left with a three-bladed throwing star made out of razor-sharp knives. He flung it with a curving spin, the knife-thrower's equivalent of a jughandle-pitch in baseball. The improvised throwing star flashed in the sunlight for one split second, then sliced off each of the man-dog's legs in turn, and the man-dog rolled screaming and limbless on to the boards.

It was left to Effis to deal with the third man-dog. She hopped up on to the cast-iron railing, balancing for a moment on her dazzling light-skates. Then she flashed away into the air, high away from the pier, skating through the sky with an easy, speedy style. She turned over the sea, against the sun, so that Mol Besa could only see her by darkening his visor. For a while he lost sight of her altogether. Then he heard a soft rushing sound, and Effis reappeared, her light-leotard sparkling, crouching low, her skates leaving behind her a long twin trail of iridescence.

She didn't attempt to use her razor-fans. Instead, she reached down and snatched the dog's chain collar as she flashed past him, heaving him high up into the air.

The man-dog roared in anger as Effis swept him out to sea, hundreds of feet over the ocean. Then she let him drop, and he turned over and over in the air before he hit the water with a faint, faraway splash.

As the other Night Warriors fought off the man-dogs, Mol Besa had been furiously busy with his keyboards. Using four-dimensional physics, he had formulated an equation for converting the spirits in the spirit spears into solid crystalline matter—an accurate and highly-stylized adaptation of the way in which mediums and psychics made spirits appear as ectoplasm. He loaded his equation pistol and aimed it at the three Carriers.

But before he could fire, one of the Carriers leaned back and launched his spirit spear. They could all see it coming. It flew through the sunshine with a faint sighing sound, more regretful than hostile. Kasyx shouted, "Look out!" and discharged a blast of pure energy from the ends of his fingertips, but there was nothing that any of them could do.

The spirit spear struck Keldak's helmet and penetrated right through to the back of his head. Blood sprayed all over the deck boards.

For an instant, Mol Besa was stunned. Somehow, he had found it impossible to believe that any of them could be casualties. This was only a dream, wasn't it? This wasn't even real! But Keldak's left leg was kicking against the railings as he went through the last throes of brain death, and Mol Besa knew for certain that he was never going to wake up, never again.

"*Back!*" Mol Besa roared to the other Night Warriors, his voice strained with fury and grief. Then he fired his equation cartridge.

The cartridge had been programmed to seek out each spirit spear in turn, and it ricocheted from one side of the pier to the other, and then back to the spear that was embedded in Keldak's head.

Isabel Gowdie's dreams were different. With the influence of Satan behind her, she could dream dreams that obeyed no natural laws. But in this young prostitute's dream, the laws of matter still applied, even if they were distorted beyond recognition. One of the laws of matter was that no two objects could occupy the same space at the same time.

The first Carrier's spear exploded in a shattering blast of subnuclear fission. The Carrier was blown apart in a blizzard of ash and mold and tattered fabric. A second later, the second Carrier exploded. His substance vanished across the sea like smoke. Then Keldak exploded, an instant cremation that left the shell of his green armor bunting fiercely on the side of the pier, and destroyed the spirit who had been promised his body, too.

One Carrier was left. Unarmed, with no man-dogs to protect him, he began to edge away. But Zasta stepped quickly forward and singled out one enormous gold-bladed knife. He threw it diagonally across the pier, and it hit the Carrier with such force that the Carrier was nailed to the side of the amusement arcade. He hung there, twitching, while pieces of dry decayed flesh dropped from his empty sleeves, and dust sifted from his empty trousers. Eventually, the wind caught his perfect white mask and tossed it away; and as the Night Warriors passed him by, they saw nothing inside his hood but a blindly-staring skull, with turkey-leg skin stretched across it.

Mol Besa glanced back briefly at the smoldering remains of Keldak's armor. The calliope continued to pump out *"I Do Like to Be Beside the Seaside."* Mol Besa looked back at Kasyx and asked, "She's still here? Isabel Gowdie? You're still picking her up? I want her now, Kasyx. I want her real bad."

Effis was tearful. "Is 'e really dead?" she kept asking. "I mean, what's going to 'appen to 'is real body?"

"He won't wake up, that's all," Kasyx explained grimly. "We'll have to find some way of disposing of him."

The four of them spread out across the pier and made their way towards the funfair at the very end of it. The pier seemed like an isolated world of its own, out here, a half mile away from the shore. Looking back, they could see Brighton and the Downs and the sparkling shoreline. In front of them towered an old-fashioned Victorian helter-skelter, painted red and white, with a notice saying that you could see France from the top of it, on a bright day.

No sign of Isabel Gowdie. No sign of anybody. The dodgem

cars stood abandoned; the candy-floss stall was empty. At the very end of the pier, however, stood a Hall of Mirrors.

"There," said Kasyx.

Without hesitation, the Night Warriors advanced on the Hall of Mirrors and went inside. The calliope played, *I do like to stroll along the prom, prom, prom ... with the brass band playing tiddly-om-pom-pom ...*

Mol Besa stopped for a moment and watched himself in one of the tarnished mirrors as—in readiness for meeting Isabel Gowdie—he punched out a program that would convert a human being into a Möbius strip of harshly-colliding atomic particles. In other words, he had decided to convert Isabel Gowdie into an endless loop of agony ... to give her pain everlasting, amen.

It was sadistic, he knew that. But it was the Night Plague that had made him sadistic. Isabel Gowdie would receive a punishment which, without the infection that she had given him, he would have been incapable of carrying out. He relished the irony of that.

He shuffled further into the Hall of Mirrors. He saw Effis passing in front of him, but obviously she couldn't see him. He saw Zasta, turning this way and that, hurrying through the mirror-maze in the frantic way that children always do. He looked to his left and saw Kasyx, feeling his way with every step.

The Hall of Mirrors was hot and stuffy and smelled as if it hadn't been swept out for fifty years. Mol Besa kept going, deeper and deeper, watching six of himself advancing towards the end of a corridor, until he discovered that the corridor had no end, but was a sharp left turning instead.

He turned again and shouted, *"Ah!"*

In the mirror facing him stood Isabel Gowdie, her face white, her eyes milky-green, with white fire streaming from out of her hair. She was wearing a garment like a white kaftan, embroidered with white, although one breast was exposed, baring a nipple like a small curled-up mollusc.

You dare to pursue me, Mol Besa! she hissed in his head, in a voice like a frying pan full of snakes. *I killed you once, I will kill you again!*

"Not this time, Ms. Gowdie," Mol Besa told her, and stepped cautiously forward lifting his equation pistol. "This time, the Night Warriors get their revenge."

Isabel Gowdie's eyes brightened. *You threaten me with pain? You threaten me with punishment? I am the Queen of Pain! I am the Queen of Punishment!*

"Then, believe me," said Mol Besa, preparing to squeeze the equation pistol's double trigger, "this one you're really going to enjoy!"

You'd punish your children, too? Isabel Gowdie shrilled at him. *You'd sentence your children to eternal pain?*

Mol Besa hesitated. At that moment, he was joined by Kasyx, who said, "Mol Besa—whatever you do, don't fire yet."

"What's happened?" Mol Besa demanded. "What are you talking about? What children?"

Isabel Gowdie laughed shrilly. Then she dragged up her kaftan to expose her naked body. Her white stomach was hugely swollen and marbled with veins, as if she were seven or eight months' pregnant.

She grinned. *This is one of your children! You gave him to me only yesterday, don't you remember? Swallow him down, sick him up!*

"How can you have a baby in a day?" Mol Besa retorted.

You poor foolish Night Warrior! In a dream, you can have a baby in an hour! In a dream, you can have a baby in a minute!

Mol Besa tightened his finger on the trigger. "That's no baby; that's just a ploy."

Oh, it's a baby, all right. Our baby. The first unnatural union between a Night Warrior and a servant of Satan, and what a baby that will be! Brave, noble, powerful, and utterly corrupt! My Lord and Master will be delighted! And somebody will have to rule this world, when the Night Plague has cut such a swathe through all of you!

"That's it," Mol Besa told her. "I've heard enough."

You'd condemn your children? Isabel Gowdie grinned again.

"That child inside of you is no child of mine."

But what about this one? asked Isabel Gowdie. She reached out beside her, and to Mol Besa's horror she dragged Zasta into view. His knives had all been stripped from his back, and he was tightly bound with white-sparkling brambles.

"Let him go, you bitch!" Mol Besa bellowed at her. "Let him go!"

Why should I? He and his brother About-to-Be-Born will make good companions. Besides, he needs to learn a thing or two, does Zasta. Like the dangers of looking for witches in mirrors. Witches understand mirrors. Mirrors understand witches.

Zasta cried out, "Mol Besa! Kill her! Don't worry about me!"

For a chipped-off fraction of a second, Mol Besa was tempted to fire. But he could feel that it was the Night Plague tugging at his judgment. The black nudge of Satan.

He slowly shook his head, backed away, and said, "No, Zasta. No way."

The mathematicks, ordered Isabel Gowdie. *Unload the mathematicks.*

Mol Besa slid back the breech of his equation pistol and removed the cartridge. "All right; are you satisfied now? Will you let Zasta go?"

Let him go? Are you mad? Never, as long as you come following me, Mol Besa! Never, never, never! He can be the best of my boy-dogs, the snappiest of all my slaves! You thought of it yourself. Mol Besa! You thought of it yourself!

In a fury. Mol Besa swung his armored fist at Isabel Gowdie's mirror image. It burst apart with a shattering crack, and thousands of laughing images of the witch-woman flew everywhere. Then, all around them, the Hall of Mirrors began to explode. Glass fountained up into the air and then showered down on their shoulders. Huge triangular shards of glass fell ringing to the floor.

Mol Besa smashed his way to the front of the Hall of Mirrors. The pier was deserted now; the sea was gray. The sky was beginning to cloud over, and lightning stilt-walked over the Downs.

"She's taken Zasta," Mol Besa told Kasyx with a dry mouth. "Kasyx, she's taken my son."

Effis said, "She won't kill 'im, will she? Or turn 'im into one of them dogs?"

"Wait," said Kasyx. "She hasn't gone far. It's almost morning now, she won't have wanted to travel too far away from her sleeping body."

Mol Besa looked frantically around, but the seafront was

empty. A crumpled fish-and-chip wrapper was tossed over and over by the rising wind.

"Is she still in this dream?" asked Mol Besa.

Kasyx checked his wrist instruments. He waited for the holographic data to bleep back at him, then he shook his head. "She's left it. But she's still in a dream state, and she isn't far away."

"Then—?"

"The man in bed with her, the Cabinet Minister. She's gone into hiding in *his* dream now!"

They returned at a steady jog to the Grand Hotel. They were watched from the windows of cafés and pubs by creatures with faces like huge rodents. It began to rain, and the raindrops trembled on Mol Besa's visor. They pushed their way through the hotel's revolving door and took the stairs three at a time.

As soon as they were back in the dream location of the Cabinet Minister's bedroom, they gathered around his bed, and Kasyx held out his hands in front of him. With a soft sparkling sound, a thin blue line appeared, bisecting the air between his upraised thumbs. He plunged his fingers into the line as if it were the join between two curtains and stretched it apart. He was opening up the fabric of the prostitute's dream and letting them through to the Cabinet Minister's dream, like stepping from one room into the next. He passed through the opening he had created, and Effis and Mol Besa followed him.

They were swamped immediately in raging noise. They were inside the House of Commons, making their way along one of the back benches. The oak-paneled Gothic chamber was swarming with thousands of screeching and screaming creatures, all of them dressed as men, in black tailcoats and starched white collars, but all with the heads of diseased and misshapen beasts.

A creature like a vast cockroach sat in the speaker's chair, while the floor in front of him glistened with thousands of black beetles. A huge looming animal like a man-horse was standing on its hind legs, overshadowing every one of the animals around it, whinnying and screaming and pawing the air with its hoofs. Other creatures crawled and dropped from bench to bench and writhed down the gangways. Mol Besa saw massive slugs and huge translucent grubs and things like praying mantises that shivered and whined.

"A politician's nightmare!" Kasyx yelled, over the screaming and screeching and roaring. Wincing in concentration, he checked his instruments. "She's gone that way. See that open door!"

The three of them hurried out of the Chamber, Kasyx and Mol Besa at a steady trot, Effis sliding effortlessly behind them on shining light-skates. Mol Besa's boots crunched beetles underfoot. Outside the door, they found themselves back in the pouring rain, back in Isabel Gowdie's miserable and plague-ridden London of the 1660s.

Isabel Gowdie hadn't walked far. She probably hadn't expected Mol Besa to be foolhardy enough to follow her. They could see her sixty or seventy yards away, on the far side of the boggy straw-strewn tract that would one day be Parliament Square. Her white hair glittered in the rain, her kaftan flew and flapped. Beside her, with a fast obedient limp, walked Knitted Hood, and Knitted Hood was dragging along the reluctant but thorn-bound Zasta.

"What the hell are we going to do?" Mol Besa asked

Kasyx. "If we try anything too threatening, she's going to kill him."

Kasyx looked serious. "That's the risk we all have to take. Zasta knew the dangers of what he was doing, just the same as you."

"Kasyx, he may be Zasta but he's still my son. And this time history isn't going to repeat itself."

Effis said, "You 'ave to give it a go, though, Mol Besa. You don't want 'im turned into one of them 'orrible dogs. 'E'd never forgive you for that."

Mol Besa closed his eyes. God, Ashapola, whoever you are, give me courage. With his eyes closed, he was conscious of that dark stingray that glides silently over the shoals of the human consciousness, Satan, with his smile and his dead expressionless eyes, and he thought to himself, with a nerve that only the Night Plague could have given him, *You can help me, too, my Lord and Master, Your Satanic Majesty, you unmitigated son of a bitch.*

He opened his eyes. Then he glanced at Kasyx and Effis and said, "Okay. Let's do it."

They marched steadily through the rain and the mud, following Isabel Gowdie and Knitted Hood with dogged determination. They hadn't gone far, however, when they heard the creaking of a handcart. Prom behind the low wall of a dripping ramshackle farmhouse, a girl appeared, the same girl that Mol Besa had seen so many times before, pushing a load of joggling, lifeless bodies.

She stopped when she saw them, and stared at them. Mol Besa stopped, too, and stared back at her. He had suddenly recognized her for who she was.

"*Eve,*" he breathed in disbelief. "How can you be here?"

She was a younger Eve, a much younger Eve, the Eve when they had married. He was amazed that he hadn't recognized her before. The mud, and the poverty, and the strangeness of Isabel Gowdie's dream surroundings—they had all conspired to make her appear different. And there was something else, too. Over the past few months, his own rejection of her had changed his perception of what she really looked like. Litigation had made him remember her as ugly.

She tilted the handcart so that its shafts rested on the muddy ground. "We all have our different vows to attend to," she told him simply.

"Are you a Night Warrior, too?"

She smiled, shook her head. "My vows are much more important than that."

Kasyx touched Mol Besa's arm. "Look—they've stopped. They've seen us."

He was right. Through the driving rain, through the darkness, Mol Besa could see that Isabel Gowdie and Knitted Hood were standing quite still, waiting for them.

Kasyx said, "Time for a showdown, I believe."

They walked past the handcart and through the puddles and the clinging mud. Isabel Gowdie was soaked, her kaftan clinging to her pregnant belly. She stared at Mol Besa with a maddened smile on her face, the smile of Satan. Beside her, Knitted Hood remained silent, his exquisite white face watching the Night Warriors without expression.

So you decided to risk everything and follow me? Isabel Gowdie challenged them.

Mol Besa took two or three steps forward. "I want you to let my son go. If you like, you can take me instead.

You've already infected my soul; there isn't any future for me, anyway. But his life is just beginning. His soul—well, *his* soul is young and pure, and I simply don't want you to have it."

Isabel Gowdie arched her head back and looked at Mol Besa under dripping eyelashes. She said nothing for a long time, then she slowly, slowly shook her head. *You can follow me through a million dreams, Mol Besa; from pole to pole; from Africa to South America. I will never give you back your son.*

Knitted Hood uttered a hollow, dry whistling laugh. *Hoooo-eeeee, oop.* Then he lifted Zasta up by one wrist, so that his feet were clear of the mud, and let him spin around. Zasta screamed in terror.

Mol Besa shouted, "Let him go! Haven't you had enough? Haven't you spread enough of your goddamned misery around?"

Oh, no, Mol Besa. Isabel Gowdie grinned. *Not by a long chalk.*

Kasyx stepped forward and laid his hand on Mol Besa's shoulder. "Mol Besa," he said, "come on. Leave it for tonight. This is one of those times when discretion is the better part of valor."

Mol Besa knew that he was right. He hesitated, with tears in his eyes, then he turned away. "If she so much as *touches* that boy ..."

As he turned away, however, he was astonished to see Eve walking towards them, her arms by her sides, her face oddly illuminated. She passed between the Night Warriors and walked right up to Knitted Hood. She stood in front of him, the rain staining her linen bonnet and the plain brown shoulders of her dress. Then she said, quietly but clearly, "Let him go."

Isabel Gowdie glared at her in amazement and fury. *Let him go, you ugly sow? How dare you tell my Carrier to let him go?*

Eve turned to Isabel Gowdie and said, "Because I am Eve. Because I will always be Eve. Because ever since Eve, every mother has always had to undertake to love and protect her sons, no matter what the cost, forever. Sometimes we have had to weep for our sons. Sometimes we have had to bury them. But I shall not weep for my son; neither shall I bury him. You will let him go."

Knitted Hood stared at Eve, and then grasped Zasta around the neck and squeezed him. Zasta kicked and thrashed and cried out; but Eve unhesitatingly stepped forward and pointed one finger directly at Knitted Hood's face. *Let him go.*

There was a moment of total silence, except for the pattering rain. Then Knitted Hood's fingers gradually opened, and Zasta dropped down to the ground.

A split second later, the knitted hood that had given him his name burst silently apart. His head softly detonated, and his half-putrescent brains streamed upwards, into the sky, in a thick and poisonous rope. Right in front of their eyes, the contents of his body poured vertically out of his neck, hurtling faster and faster, lungs and spleen and bladder, a sudden liquid rush of intestines, until the gray gaberdine raincoat collapsed empty in front of them, and Knitted Hood vanished into the stormy sky.

Eve took Zasta's hand and stepped away from Isabel Gowdie. "Now," she said, "you will do what you have to do, to release my husband from the Night Plague, and all those you have infected through him."

You sanctimonious bitch! You daughter of a dog! And what if I won't?

"I can't harm you. I haven't the power. But I do have the power to protect the baby that has grown inside you."

What are you talking about, bitch? flared Isabel Gowdie.

"Your baby is my son's brother; and I am pledged to protect brothers down all the centuries of all mankind; as all mothers are; to atone for the crime of Cain, who killed his brother Abel."

I will boil this baby, you bitch!

"No. You cannot. If you so much as touch one hair of that baby's head, *then* I will have the power to punish you, beyond any punishment that you can imagine possible. You would be better advised to do what you have to do, to release my husband from the Night Plague, and to surrender your baby to whatever destiny lies in wait for it."

Isabel Gowdie's eyes narrowed. *You're lying.*

But Eve stepped forward, pointed her finger directly at Isabel Gowdie's forehead, and touched it, the lightest touch. Instantly, blood spurted from the screw wounds around Isabel Gowdie's temples. The witch let out a piercing shriek.

You're lying!

"You want more?" demanded Eve. "You want your brains to spew up into the sky, like those of your Carrier?"

Isabel Gowdie trembled. Sparks flew from her hair in all directions, her eyes blazed white. *I shall be revenged for this. Eve, daughter of a dog, wife of Adam.*

"Do what you have to do," Eve insisted.

The sparks in her hair subsided. Isabel Gowdie rubbed

her left arm, and for a moment Mol Besa could see in her the thin unconventional Scottish girl she must have been so many centuries ago, before she had given herself to Satan.

We'd better be doing it, then, Mol Besa, she said. Staring at him proudly and defiantly, she lifted her kaftan up around her waist and knelt on the ground, with her forehead pressed deep into the mud. The rain fell on her bare white buttocks.

Mol Besa glanced at Kasyx, and Kasyx nodded his assent. Slowly, Mol Besa climbed down on to his knees behind Isabel Gowdie and opened his armor. Eve turned away, although Effis watched, her face curiously sad.

He was only just stiff enough to penetrate her. She was cold, but hot inside. He thrust at her in unsteady, jerky movements. His mouth was dry and it was hard to stop himself from shaking.

What was worse, as he coupled with her, the parting of her hair began to widen, and her scalp peeled apart, layer by layer, until the face on top of her head reappeared. One face, pressed against the ground, groaned in ecstasy. The other face, lifted to the rain, screamed in pain. Mol Besa felt Isabel Gowdie's thin rib cage convulse and convulse and tighten in spasm. Something pale slipped out of the mouth on top of her head, something which she caught in her upraised hands. At the same time, painfully, unpleasantly, Mol Besa ejaculated.

He stood up, rebuckling his armor. Isabel Gowdie lay where she was for a moment, while her hair closed over the face on top of her head.

She said softly, *It's done now. The plague is returned to me. You may have heaven, whatever heaven is worth.*

She stood up, muddied and wet, her white hair bedraggled

but still twinkling with sparks. She was cupping something in the palms of her hands.

And this, she said, *this is what a servant of Satan and a Night Warrior can produce together, when good and evil reconcile their differences.*

She went from one to the other and showed them a tiny perfect baby, no longer than six or seven inches, a little boy, shining and naked. She kissed it, and then she lifted it up, and it floated out of her hand as if it were sparkling thistledown, as if it weighed nothing at all, and swirled around once, and vanished into the night.

That was when Mol Besa pulled the trigger of his equation pistol and turned the rest of Isabel Gowdie's infinity into an endless scream.

Stanley was leaning on the railing of the Embarcadero watching the docking of an Argentinian training ship, with all of its hands aloft in the rigging, when a slender young man in a white Armani suit came and stood close beside him.

San Francisco being San Francisco, Stanley edged a few inches away. It was only when the young man said, "How's life, Stanley?" that he looked up and realized that it was Springer.

"Life's fine," said Stanley guardedly. "You haven't come to offer me any more work have you?"

Springer smiled and shook his head. "Just came to see how you were. Warm today, isn't it?"

Stanley nodded, said nothing.

"How's Leon?" asked Springer.

"Leon's fine."

"And Eve?'

"We seem to be rubbing along okay. Time will tell."

"Henry sends his best," Springer told him. "Angie married that Paul of hers."

"Angie," Stanley repeated. It sounded like a name from another life.

"There's one more thing," said Springer. He fumbled in his pocket and produced a soft red velvet bag. "I kept this by me. Some people don't always have time to say goodbye."

He opened the drawstring and showed Stanley what was in it.

Stanley frowned. "Bones?'

"The bones of Gordon's left hand, to be precise," Springer explained.

He opened the bag wider, lifted it up, and without ceremony shook the bones into the harbor. They fell with a light pattering splash.

Stanley looked down at them, watched them sink. "Goodbye, Gordon," he said. "It was pretty good to know you."

It may have been nothing more than a swirl in the water, a glint of the sun; but he was sure that he saw a hand rise out of the harbor for a moment and give him one last regretful wave.

If you ever hear the most elegant Baroque violin music on your stereo, then it will probably have been played by Stanley Eisner.

On the other hand, if you ever hear inexplicable screaming in the night, screaming that seems to come from nowhere at all, and goes on and on and on, then you will know that Isabel Gowdie has passed you by.

And if you ever hear a baby crying, plaintive, and small, you will know that it is the Night Child, son of a witch and a Night Warrior, spurned by Satan, unloved by God, who can never, ever find his way home.

About the Author

GRAHAM MASTERTON is best known as a writer of horror and thrillers, but his career as an author spans many genres, including historical epics and sex advice books. His first horror novel, *The Manitou*, became a bestseller and was made into a film starring Tony Curtis. In 2019, Graham was given a Lifetime Achievement Award by the Horror Writers Association. He is also the author of the Katie Maguire series of crime thrillers, which have sold more than 1.5 million copies worldwide.

Visit www.grahammasterton.co.uk.